# Love through Time

Barbara Woster


ISBN—13: 9781733660235
eBook IBSN—9781732843370

# DEDICATION

For my family, without whose love and support
this book would never have been written.

# ONE

## Present Day

"I thought I'd find you here with your nose stuck in a book!" Tyeshia exclaimed and, without waiting for an invitation, plopped into the chair opposite Savannah.

"Keep your voice down, Ty!" Savannah whispered the command. The whip-like delivery would have startled anyone—except Tyeshia. "We *are* in a library, you know."

"You aremak *always* in a library!" Tyeshia complained deliberately loud and provoking.

"Hush!" She did not know why she even bothered trying to get Tyeshia to conform to the rules. She knew she would not, for Tyeshia was a nonconformist. Still, she felt she owed it to the others around them. Those poor people did not know Tyeshia as she did, so could not know that her behavior was deliberate. She tried a different tact, "Even if you don't respect the institutional edicts, you really should consider others around you that are trying to study in a *quiet* environment. If they wanted to read without concern for noise, they'd do so at a rock concert, which is about the same decibel output as your voice right now."

She had not realized her own voice had risen an octave until a few people nearby shushed *her*. She blushed then, and quietly apologized before turning back to speak to Tyeshia.

"You're drawing attention to yourself, which is, as a consequence, drawing attention to me!"

"I draw attention wherever I go. I have a certain impact on people." Tyeshia pulled out a mirror and a tube of fuchsia-colored lip gloss from a makeup pouch she always carried in her satchel.

"Yeah! Your behavior impacts everyone," Savannah retorted then stuck her nose back in her book.

"Well, well, someone woke up on the wrong side of the bed this morning," Tyeshia provoked, snapping her compact closed and sliding it back in her satchel, "You do realize that a good man could help with those sleepless nights, and then you'd wake up rested and less cranky."

"I am *not* cranky. I'm busy," Savannah retorted, trying to concentrate on the words in front of her while conversing. "Some of us are more concerned about our education than about men, you know?"

A young librarian, newly hired, started to move from behind the counter as the two women's conversation gained momentum and volume, but an elderly woman standing nearby stopped her, shaking her head in bemusement.

"This happens at least once a week," the head librarian whispered. "Give it another few minutes and the young woman will leave with the same flair in which she arrived. I've discovered that it doesn't do any good to interfere. It's annoying to the other patrons, to be sure, but that young woman seems determined to save her friend's soul from the world of knowledge that she's trapped in. It can get quite amusing."

A third librarian, sorting books, snickered softly at the comment and shot the head librarian a look of long-suffering, then went back to her duties, occasionally glancing at the two young ladies still engaged in heated argument at the nearby table.

Savannah and Tyeshia garnered the same bemused exasperation wherever they went, and yet most people were awed by the rapport and friendship that bonded the two women together; yet kept them at each other's throats, almost like an old married couple. More amazing was how that friendship maintained despite their dramatically different personalities. For most, it was as bewildering as the thought of the President becoming fast friends with a dictator of a Communist country.

Although they differed in character, both transcended beauty—though even that they carried dissimilarly. Tyeshia was statuesque, an athletically built black beauty with a model's grace, but her manners tended to dull that exquisite façade when acting boorish—which she did more often than not. She exuded a confidence that approached conceit. To her, the way to succeed in the world was through a good man that would provide a comfortable living for her, not through academia. In fact, the thought of acquiring knowledge on any level bored her. She much preferred to spend time on the latest beautification techniques; taking great pains with her appearance. She refused to be caught dead in public unless perfectly coiffed and made up to perfection.

Savannah, contrarily, was a bookworm and a diligent student who took her loveliness in stride. She often pulled her honey-blond tresses into a quick, no-nonsense ponytail and when she chose to wear makeup, she applied it lightly to the point of appearing nonexistent. She was shorter than Tyeshia's five-foot-ten stature by three inches, but carried herself with a graceful confidence that made her as lovely as Tyeshia without all the accouterments.

Although Savannah could probably attract the attention of just as many men as Tyeshia did daily, she had no desire to do so. Her academics were of more concern to her than snaring the captain of the football team.

These differences were the cause of constant contention between the two of them. Tyeshia was determined to show Savannah the error of her beauty ways and Savannah was intent on proving to Tyeshia that men were not the only thing in life worth aspiring to. It was as if both women had determined to take on the other as an extra credit project. Still, through all the squabbling, their unusual friendship sustained. A friendship that most people found difficult to comprehend yet would be hard-pressed to come between. A friendship forged through trial and concession.

When the two teenagers met two and a half years earlier, both were late for college registration and the registrar informed them that only a single dorm room remained available. Tyeshia eyed Savannah critically and Savannah perused Tyeshia unfavorably.

"Ain't happening," Tyeshia snapped.

"Isn't there anything else? A broom closet perhaps?" Savannah added.

"I'm sorry girls, but unless you two wish to rent a room off campus, you are going to have to share. Perhaps if you'd arrived sooner, you'd have had you pick of the litter, so to speak. Since you did not...well, you'll just have to make do, won't you?"

Reluctantly, they agreed to give it a go, but after their first day, both wished fervently that they had talked their parents into money for room and board off campus.

World War III erupted every morning, noon, and night for nearly the entire first year of their college lives as Tyeshia partied long into the night, refused to study, and continually ragged Savannah about her appearance.

Savannah's problem, according to Tyeshia, was that she did not bother enhancing her natural beauty, so she became Tyeshia's mission in life. Savannah, on the other hand, regularly scolded her roommate for her excessive partying and nearly nonexistent study habits.

When the first year of college was over, those that knew the young women thought the two combatants would seek other quarters but they had not. In fact, Tyeshia approached Savannah with an offer to be her roommate for the remainder of their time there.

"Who else is going to put up with me?" She said shrugging her shoulders.

"Don't you mean that you haven't transformed me into a work of art yet, like you?" Savannah teased in return.

"Yeah, that too."

Two and half years later, they were still roommates and still trying, albeit half-heartedly, to correct the other's obvious flaws. This is what had brought Tyeshia to the library again. Savannah was the only reason that Tyeshia would step foot in a library and that was simply because she felt the need to save Savannah from her academic self—at least once a week.

"You know the party is in just a few hours," Tyeshia said.

Savannah glanced at her watch and snorted, "Try five-and-a-half hours.

Besides, Ty, I really don't want to go. I have an exam next week that I need to study for, and you should be studying too, for that matter."

"What subject?"

"American History."

"Oh, right! Well, that's always been your favorite subject, not mine."

"You don't have a favorite subject!"

"Sure, I do."

"Right. What might that be—lunchtime?"

"Bingo!"

"You know Ty; you're not going to make it through college if you don't study more often. What does favoritism have to do with studying anyway? You don't have to like a subject necessarily to study and pass it, you know."

"La de da de da," Tyeshia said in her favored singsong voice.

"You really should take your academics more seriously."

"What about you? Don't you think you should take your appearance more seriously? I mean, look at you!" Tyeshia gave a less-than-flattering once-over to Savannah's T-shirt and jeans. "How are you ever going to find a man looking like you do?"

"I don't intend to 'find a man', as you so eloquently put it, until I can take care of myself."

"Not this girl!" Tyeshia said, checking her appearance again in her compact. "I intend to marry the smartest geek in this school and live high off the hog for the rest of my life."

"What happens in twenty years when he decides to leave you for a younger woman?"

"Then I'll wipe him out in the divorce and live happily ever after anyway."

"You are too much, Tyeshia!" Savannah shook her head slowly, but could not help grinning at her friend's plans for the future, which seemed to change as often as Tyeshia's hairdos.

"Well, you just ain't enough!" Tyeshia countered. "Why don't you let me fix you up for tonight's gala event and when the men start flocking around you, which they will once I get finished with you, you'll forget those books. Especially once you see how delightful all that male attention is. Maybe you'll find a rich Mister Right, too. What do you say?"

"Very well, Ty. I'll let you *help* fix me up if for no other reason than to get you off my case," Savannah conceded, but quickly lifted her hand to silence her friend when it looked like Tyeshia's enthusiasm was going to get away from her. "However, I will not leave the room looking like a street hooker. Is that clearly understood?"

"Clear enough." Tyeshia busied herself in her handbag waiting for the explosion she knew was about to occur. It did not matter though; she usually won the battles in the end.

"Hey, wait a minute! What just happened here?"

"Shush." Several people at the next table put their fingers to their lips in unison and sent Tyeshia and Savannah another round of scathing looks.

"Yeah, shush," Tyeshia teased, "and what do you mean, "what just happened here"?" Tyeshia appeared intent on scrutinizing her reflection in the compact she again removed from her satchel, but Savannah could see by the twinkle in Tyeshia's eyes that she knew exactly about what she was talking.

"I just said that I wasn't interested in attending your party and yet you somehow managed to rope me into it and into letting you fix me up. How in heaven's name do you manage to trap me like that?" Savannah asked, trying hard to keep her volume only slightly above a whisper, when what she really wanted to do was to scream loudly enough to bring the rafters down.

"I'm just simply smarter than you. Books are not the end-all to intelligence."

"Cute, but it isn't going to work this time. I'm not going and that's final." The twinkle in Tyeshia's eyes remained however, despite Savannah protests. "Besides, I need a little more time to study. A lot more time, in fact."

"Your reading material is very undesirable, you know that?" Tyeshia crinkled her nose at all the reference material littering the tabletop. "Are encyclopedias the only thing you know how to read?"

"No. I read Biographies and Classic Literature also."

"I'm serious. Don't you ever relax even a little?"

"I don't have time to relax, Ty. I'm attempting to get a degree, remember?"

"In history?" Tyeshia scoffed. "What are you supposed to do with a history degree?"

"Maybe I'll become a history professor at this college someday," Savannah defended, trying without much success not to let Tyeshia ruffle her feathers.

"Oh! Now that's *really* exciting!" Tyeshia rolled her eyes. "And shush yourself," she snapped at the people behind them.

"Lower your voice and perhaps they won't get so irate with you. This is a library, you know. You're supposed to keep your voice at a *whisper*."

"All right," Tyeshia reluctantly acquiesced, and then turned to address the people at the next table again, "I'll try to keep it down. Okay?"

"So, what happened to your plans of being discovered by a modeling agency and becoming a world-class model, anyway? That was your goal last week, now this week it's marriage?" Savannah asked in an attempt to steer the conversation away from herself and the party she was determined not to attend.

"That's before I found out how much work modeling entailed," Tyeshia cringed, and Savannah giggled. "Forget that."

"Finding a rich husband would just be easier, right?"

"Right."

"What do your parents think about your aspirations? Surely they don't approve of your ambitions, or lack thereof. I mean, aren't they spending an awful lot of money to pay for your college education?"

"Sure, and I'm passing enough to keep them satisfied. I've managed to make it through three years without flunking out, haven't I? So, I must be doing something right."

"I don't know how you do it. I don't think I've ever seen you pick up a book. One that wasn't a romance, anyway."

"Hey, don't knock my romances. After all, my books are the only things that keep me sane in this misery that we call college."

"That and men, right?"

"Now, you're learning. Hey! How about we make a deal?"

"Oh, no! The last deal I made with you was a disaster, and I've already determined I'm not going tonight." Savannah waved a dismissive hand hoping to dissuade her friend from continuing, but Tyeshia only laughed.

"My deals aren't *that* bad and neither are my parties."

"They never are—for you."

"Well, this deal is harmless, okay? I promise you." Tyeshia smiled and pulled her handbag onto the table, rummaging through its contents. Savannah watched in wonder, marveling at how she ever found anything in the mammoth-sized shoulder bag.

"Aha!" She exclaimed a moment later and flung something on top of the papers strewn in front of Savannah.

"What's this?" Savannah asked truly perplexed, which made Tyeshia giggle.

"A romance novel, dummy."

"I know that, but why are you flinging it in my direction?" Savannah looked at the book as if it had a contagious disease.

"I want you to read it," Tyeshia said in exasperation as if the intent had been clear.

Savannah laughed loudly, then threw a hand over her mouth when she realized she was doing the same thing she'd accused Tyeshia of doing. She cast a sheepish glance at the angry people around her, the blush in her cheeks as red as her T-shirt.

"Sorry," she murmured for the umpteenth time, then turned back to address Tyeshia. "You can't be serious?" Savannah giggled at the picture of the scantily clad couple clinging to each other seductively on the cover of the book. "Why should I read this trash?"

"It isn't trash," Tyeshia defended. "It's the best source of history I've ever read."

"History? You must be joking?"

"Sure. Look." Tyeshia closed Savannah's reference book and pointed to the cover. "See. *A Guide to the Native Americans of the Central and Northwestern United States.*"

"And?" Savannah prompted when no more information was forthcoming.

"And," Tyeshia picked up her romance novel and placed it beside the reference book, "this is about Indians too. See?"

"Ty," Savannah shook her head wearily, "sometimes you are just too much. The guy on the front of this book isn't even a Native American, for goodness sake. He's just some buffed up sexy model they got to sell the book. You know if they put a real Native on the cover..."

"You know, you really aren't giving this a chance," Tyeshia interrupted petulantly.

"Giving what a chance? What kind of deal could possibly involve a romance novel?"

"Okay, here it is." Tyeshia leaned forward her arms lying across the table. "I won't drag you to any parties for the next month, except tonight because Bobby Ramirez is going to be there and he really wants to meet you."

"Who?" Savannah's question went unanswered as Tyeshia continued talking, ignoring her sudden outburst.

"That is, should you agree to take time out of your busy study schedule to read this book."

"I don't understand," Savannah said truly perplexed. "Why should I do this other than to get out of a few parties that I don't really have to attend anyway if I don't want to?"

"Yes, you do," Tyeshia grinned wickedly. "When was the last time you ever got out of a party that I was determined to get you to?"

"Point taken, but why a romance novel?"

"Because you can't go through life with an encyclopedia in one hand and a slide rule in the other. You have to learn to live a little."

"You're forgetting the Thesaurus I carry around in my mouth," Savannah fired back mischievously. "Besides, the fact that you do manage to drag me to your parties constitutes living-it-up a little, doesn't it?"

"Are you kidding?" Tyeshia crinkled her nose again. "You are like the invisible woman at those parties. You stand against the wall hidden in the shadows and vanish before I even know you're gone. I don't know why I even bother trying to introduce you to the many eligible men on campus!"

"I keep trying to tell you I'm hopeless." Savannah could not help smiling at her friend's accurate description.

"Well, this way I can add a little spice to your life and you won't even have to leave our room. As fast as you read, it won't even take a week of your time."

"I don't know." Savannah stared in disgust at the book before her.

"Just say yes. You will anyway, inevitably."

"Oh, all right. I'll read your blasted book! If only to have a reprieve from your utterly dull get-togethers."

"Great!" Tyeshia stood and threw her purse over her shoulder. "I've got to head back now and start getting ready for the party, and if you're not there in an hour to start getting ready too, I'm sending out the hounds."

"Two hours, Ty. I promise."

"That's cutting it awful close, but we'll manage, I suppose. I'll go through my closet and find a dress for you. I think I still have a few things hanging around from my fatter days," Tyeshia teased.

"Ha! Ha! I'm laughing so hard my sides hurt," Savannah called after Tyeshia's retreating form. "Hey, Ty?"

"What?"

"Who is Bobby Ramirez anyway?"

"You'll see, and my parties are not dull," Tyeshia said, then bounded down the stairs.

"Hush." The irritated request came from the next table again.

"Oh, hush yourselves!" Savannah shouted. She picked the romance novel up by the corner, careful only to touch it with her fingertips. Crinkling her nose in loathing, she dropped it into her satchel then looked at her watch again. One thirty-five. She still had a lot of reading left to do if she was going to be back to the room by three-thirty. She shook her head in wonder, turning the reference book back to the page she was on before her whirlwind of a friend had blown in.

The party was at seven tonight. Did she really need three-and-a-half hours to get ready? Oh well, she'd worry about that later. Right now, she had an exam for which to study.

"Chapter Twelve," she read quietly to herself. "Custer's Last Stand."

# TWO

Savannah's head ached. She rubbed her hands up and down along her arms, her heavy-lidded eyes inspecting them for the bruises that had not yet developed, although she had not a doubt that they would be too numerous to count come morning.

She still could not get over how she spent the entire evening batting away Bobby Ramirez's aggressively mauling hands. Dancing with the arrogant buffoon was like wrestling with an octopus. No matter how much she pressed her hands against his chest to provide distance to breathe, he refused to take the hint, even when she stamped down on his toe. He merely said it was okay if she 'couldn't dance that good', then yanking her closer still. It was the most horribly claustrophobic night in her entire life.

After the dance ended, she sought to escape, but he latched onto her arm with vice-like determination, and drew her toward a private veranda. She dug her high heels against the floor, leaving huge black scrape marks, which she knew would not be a welcome sight to the owner of the house.

Despite her protestations, no one came to her aid and she simply was not strong enough to pull away. She slapped and pulled at his fingers ineffectually, but he merely grinned at her over his shoulder.

"Don't be shy, gorgeous. A few kisses from me will loosen you up and you'll be begging me to escort you home. If you catch my drift."

The veranda loomed nearer and Savannah panicked. "Would someone please pull this great ape away from me?" She yelled, but no one heard her over the din of music and loud conversation. A couple, close-by, glanced her way, but judging by their glazed expressions, they would not be of any assistance.

Bobby gave Savannah a final tug that literally lifted her off her feet and straight into his embrace. He pinioned her in a corner, against the railing, and without waiting for an invitation, latched his lips onto hers.

For the first time, Savannah realized that Bobby had been drinking. She had not known until then, but the taste of beer and something she could not quite distinguish invaded her mouth and nose. The smell was so overpowering that she wondered how she missed it before. The alcohol went a long way toward explaining his thickheaded acuity, but it in no way excused it.

Savannah stopped struggling. Not because she wanted his overeager affection, but because she knew that alcohol and determination were formidable forces, against which she could not combat; a fight she was losing to begin with. To win this fight she was going to have to use her brains against his brawn. Waiting for an opportune moment however, was not going to be easy. At five-foot-seven, she stood shoulder-to-shoulder with most men, but Bobby dwarfed her with his six-foot-six football-player physique.

Just when she felt as if she would collapse from lack of oxygen intake, his lips detached from her mouth and immediately latched onto her neck. The suckling sound from his mouth was loud and disgusting and Savannah winced. His lips were going to leave a large mark come morning. She pressed her head down in an attempt to dislodge his mouth but it did not work. The hickey she would have on her neck unnerved her; the thought of carrying Bobby Ramirez's mark around campus for the next week horrified her, and spurred her into making another attempt at freedom.

She jammed her head sideways again with as much force as she could muster, but he remained fastened to her rapidly increasing sensitive skin.

*Geez,* she thought, *even octopi don't have a stronger latching power than Bobby's lips.* What had her friend been thinking setting her up with such an arrogant idiot? After all this time, she was certain that Tyeshia would understand her tastes better than this. *Or not,* Savannah silently admitted. After all, she had not really met anyone worth getting to know better since coming to college, so Tyeshia would not be familiar with her likes and dislikes.

Bobby shifted his weight to his other foot; his lips remaining firmly in place on her neck, but the movement provided a gap between them, wide enough for her to strike. With a mighty tug that jammed her elbow backwards into the railing and sent a pain shooting through her arm, she freed her hand from his grip, and pulled on his hair until she felt his lips break free.

He lifted his head and looked down at her quizzically, but before he could utter a protest, she reddened his face with a slap that resounded through the night air. Her leg quickly followed her first assault and drove into his groin. Any other man would have buckled under the driving force, but Bobby merely gripped his privates and moaned, bending slightly at the waist.

Still, it was all Savannah needed. She sidled past him, eyeing him like a hiker passing a rattler, before bolting into the main salon. Without bothering to find Tyeshia to say she was leaving, she quickly retrieved her handbag and took off. She did not slow her pace until she reached the darkened parking lot. Her breathing was coming in great gasps as she spun around, desperately looking for her car. After what seemed an eternal search, she found her gray Honda Accord, and breathed a great sigh of relief.

She fumbled through her purse, found her keys, dropped them, and had to start the search again. By the time she finally had a decent grip; her hands were shaking so badly from humiliation and anger that she scratched the paint around the keyhole long before she managed to insert the key. A noise from behind startled her and she spun on the dreaded three-inched spiked heels that Tyeshia insisted she wear, nearly twisting her ankle.

"Get away from me before I spray mace in your face and damage you where you'll never produce offspring," Savannah said. Her rage had never been so intense, and he following her to the car showed audacity that startled her.

"Hey, listen! I just wanted to find out what went wrong in there. See if we could start over," Bobby said. He held his hands up in surrender; his demeanor wary of the keys she held like a knife pointed in his direction.

"Start over?" Her voice rose shrilly and she breathed in, trying to control the pitch and slow the rhythm of her frantically beating heart. "Why would I want to start over? You can't even take the hint when a girl is trying to tell you no."

"Why didn't you just say it then? I thought you were playing hard to get is all." If he had not looked so blasted innocent, Savannah would have laughed hysterically in his face. Instead, she could do no more than stare at him in disbelief, wondering if he could really be as dense as he sounded. She decided that he could, so she turned her back on him, finished turning the key in the lock, pulled the door open, and started to get in.

A crushing grip prevented the latter and she almost sprained her ankle a second time as Bobby yanked her back around to face him.

"Where are you going? We haven't finished talking yet."

With strength, she did not know she possessed, she brought her knee up in perfect contact between his broadened stance, and delivered another blow to his groin area. This blow, combined with the earlier one, doubled him over. He collapsed onto the asphalt, gripping his privates and groaning pitifully. It made her wonder whether her threat to prevent him from producing offspring might prove a reality. She hoped so. She could not imagine any more Bobby Ramirez's roaming around freely on the planet.

Savannah dove in her car and nearly ran him over in her haste to get away.

Now, as one hand groped for the light switch in her dorm room, the other hand unwilling to leave her temple, which was throbbing severely, Savannah vowed she would never allow her friend to talk her into such foolishness again. A serious talk with Tyeshia was definitely on her to-do list. Right now, however, she was more concerned with finding an aspirin and calling it a night, if she could relieve her mind of enough stress to relax and fall asleep.

She plopped heavily on the bed and reached for her satchel that was lying nearby. Lackadaisically, she dumped the contents beside her, more concerned with finding her aspirin bottle expediently than for the mess she made. She struggled for a moment with the childproof lid on the aspirin bottle, and then popped two of the white pills in her mouth, struggling to swallow the uncoated tablets.

Her gaze fell on the book that Tyeshia had given her at the library earlier that day. She picked it up and read the cover again, an incredulous grin on her face.

"How can people read this stuff? I mean the stories are all the same," Savannah said. Flipping the book over in her hand, she scanned the story summary then improvised the contents, "Boy meets girl, boy likes girl, boy and girl have conflict, boy and girl have sex, boy and girl falls in love and lives happily ever after". Why should I even consider reading this? I mean, I've already decided I'm not going to attend any more of Ty's stupid parties anyway, right? Right," she debated with herself.

"Still, if I don't read this, she'll hound me," she concluded quickly. "She's right. I always end up saying yes, anyway. If I read this, then I'll at least have a month's reprieve. Besides," she decided with finality, "I need some mindless drivel to help take my mind off tonight as well as my pending exam."

Savannah finally stood and cleaned the junk from her bed. She took a soothing shower, made a cup of Apple Cinnamon Herbal Tea, and settled under her blankets. She picked up the book from the nightstand and held it for a moment, fighting a battle with her intellect over whether she should actually insult her mind and open it. Her intellect lost and she opened the cover and began reading.

"Chapter one," she said, "and this had better be good."

# THREE

"Well, I'll be jiggered!" Tyeshia exclaimed, borrowing from Savannah's own unique, expressive vocabulary. Savannah dropped the book in her hand and stifled a scream as her friend sauntered into the room and pushed the door closed behind her with her foot. "It's two o'clock in the morning and I come home and find you are still awake and totally absorbed in my trashy novel? A good thing it's an extremely long weekend or you probably could not get up for class tomorrow."

Savannah glanced over at the clock on her nightstand and blushed. "I wasn't tired is all. I was hoping I could read myself into oblivion and simultaneously finish our agreement—preferably tonight."

"The book too good to put down, huh?"

"Want a medal, Tyeshia?"

"No, just want to hear you admit that my books aren't all trashy."

"Well, your taste in books may hold merit, but your taste in men leaves a lot to be desired."

"So, I don't need to ask what you thought about Bobby?" Ty asked quietly, knowing the answer the minute Savannah slung her book aside, leapt from the bed and began pacing animatedly back and forth in front of her.

"If I never run across that overbearing son of a burro again, it will be too soon. Do you have any idea of what I endured at the hands of that octopus?"

"Well, if the hickey on your neck is any indication..." Tyeshia started then stopped when Savannah squealed and ran into the bathroom.

"It's showing already? Oh, dear Lord in Heaven! How am I supposed to hide this monstrous thing?"

"Wear a scarf for the next week," Tyeshia yelled from the bedroom.

"You are not funny, Tyeshia!" Savannah said, coming back from the bathroom and flopping onto her bed. "That thing is horrible. How can women think that a hickey is attractive?"

"Well, usually the girl is a willing participant, so it's not such a bothersome outcome."

"Cute," Savannah snapped. "If you could have been there tonight and seen what that brute was attempting to do, ooh, it makes my blood boil just knowing I'm going to have to relive it every day when I look in the mirror and see that giant bruise on my neck."

"From what he's telling everybody, he had to pry *you* off him."

"What?"

"Yeah. He's saying that you're like some raging nymphomaniac. That you were just too much to handle so he told you to get lost and came back to rejoin the party."

"So, how did he explain the red palm print across his egotistical face and the new limp in his stride?"

"That you liked getting rough with guys, but that just wasn't his scene," Tyeshia said and broke into a fit of the giggles.

"Exactly what is so funny, may I ask?" Savannah stood with her fists pressed against her hips, her stance wide, and her gaze blazing.

"The picture he's painting..." Tyeshia's giggles quickly turned into gales of laughter.

"Well?"

"Anybody who's ever met you would know that 'ice princess' describes you better than 'raging nymph' any day."

"Ice princess, is it?"

"Hey! I only calls 'em like I sees 'em, unlike Bobby-boy. Can you imagine the beating his ego must have taken for him to spread such vicious baloney?"

Savannah suddenly felt drained and she sank onto her bed, pulling her knees cross-legged and laying her chin in the tent of her palms. She sighed heavily and looked to where Tyeshia was sitting, her laughter slowly fading.

"Hey! You aren't gonna let one guy get you down, are you, Savannah?"

"Of course not, Ty. He's not worth getting down about."

"Just riled over?"

"Not even that. That's why I calmed down." There was a trace of a smile on her lips now. "He's not worth my wrath. Didn't you know what he was like before you took me to the party, Ty? I mean, he wasn't at all the kind of man I find attractive."

"I didn't have a clue. He was just a cute face in a gorgeous bod. Sorry about that."

"It's history. Not worth mentioning again."

"Consider it forgotten."

"Do you really think I'm an ice princess, Ty?" Savannah wondered why it mattered so much what her roommate thought about her. She'd never given a fig what anyone thought and should not now, but somehow what Ty thought *did* matter to her. She was the closest friend that Savannah ever had. Although she had the most volatile emotional makeup she'd ever encountered in an individual, and though they were as different as they could possibly get, Savannah realized that Tyeshia's opinion was more important than ten Bobbies put together.

"Not really. I just see you as an intelligent bookworm who cares a heck of a lot more about her future than I do. Still, you looked hot enough tonight to melt half the icebergs in Iceland."

"I think icebergs are near Greenland, but thanks just the same."

"So, where are you in the book?" Tyeshia asked, deftly changing the subject from Octopus Ramirez.

"About three-quarters finished."

"Really?"

"Yeah, really."

"So?"

"It's interesting enough and does seem to have a good story line. Although if I were the heroine I would have shot the guy long before now."

"Why?" Tyeshia asked while she shed her party clothes in favor of her more comfortable lounging wear.

"He whines like a banshee," Savannah explained. "I mean she's a lot stronger than he is, and he's supposed to be this brawny Native American who is not afraid of anything, except commitment of course."

"Of course. Any other reason you want to do away with him?" Tyeshia grinned, sitting cross-legged on her own bed.

"He's just annoying is all. I mean, all he's done is try to run from the woman he obviously loves, nearly the *entire* book, because he thinks that she will mean his eventual death. How imbecilic. Of course, come to think of it, she's not much better."

"I thought you said she was a woman of strength."

"She is, but a woman today would never sit around and wait for a guy to get over his complexes. Get real! On top of that, it does not help that she's pregnant and he doesn't seem to care."

"It's just a story, Savannah, made up from someone's imagination, and designed to take us hardworking women away from the stresses of reality."

"I know, but where do women come up with stuff like this. The sex scenes are enough to make a prostitute blush, and the man? Guys like this just don't exist, Native American or otherwise."

"Maybe, but you have to admit that running across a guy like that in real life would be delightful."

"Without the whining, no doubt. Still, like you said, it's imagination, remember? If men were this drop-dead sexy and perfect—except for the whining—women wouldn't need books like this to keep them entertained."

"Don't I know it? I've dated enough, and not even one comes close."

"So why put yourself through it?" Savannah argued in her typically logical way. "I mean, think about it. If no man you are ever going to meet can possibly measure up to these fictitious hunks, how is anyone ever supposed to find satisfaction with what they eventually end up with?"

"You are just too much," Tyeshia groaned. "Nobody is ever going to meet the perfect guy. That's why they invented these." Ty pointed to the cover of the book lying in Savannah's lap. "To give us women something to dream about at night, and dreams you will have—a whiny banshee or not."

Savannah wanted to argue that she did not give a fig about the character in the novel, but she'd never been good at being dishonest, and had not a doubt that her friend was right. Black Hawk would definitely haunt her dreams tonight.

"No problem. Want a drink or something, or would you rather keep reading and see what happens to Black Hawk and Lady Catherine?"

"I think I'll finish up the book. After all, I've got less than a hundred pages to go."

"Piece of cake for you. Let me know what you think of the ending in the morning."

"What are you going to do?"

"I'm going to sleep! It's freakin' two-thirty in the morning. You got to be crazy to be up at this hour," Ty teased, then rolled over and turned out her night light. She was asleep within minutes.

Savannah smiled at her sleeping friend, and then picked up the book where she'd dropped it when Ty had barged into the room.

"Chapter Fifty," she began, stifling a yawn. "The sun was peeking over the horizon when Black Hawk rode into town on his pinto mare..."

# FOUR

"Morning sleepy head. Sleep tight?" Savannah grinned as Tyeshia lumbered drowsily into the kitchen a few hours after sunrise and plopped heavily into the chair beside the table. With a grunt, she laid her head lethargically onto her leaden arms.

"Uh," Ty muttered.

"Think a cup of coffee will revive you, or do you need some—tomato juice and raw eggs, is it?"

Tyeshia raised her head just long enough to send her friend a scathing look then lowered it again. "I do not have a hangover, smarty."

"Then a cup of coffee is all you need to get your motor running."

"Uh huh."

Savannah turned and measured coffee into two cups, trying hard to suppress the laughter that welled inside her. The two of them differed in nearly all aspects of their appearance and living. Tyeshia's penchant for late nights, parties, and sullen mornings were the antithesis of Savannah's studious, solitary, cheery morning personality. It did not matter what time Savannah bedded down for the night, she always woke in a positive frame of mind.

Even this morning.

She had a hard time falling asleep because reminders of Bobby and thoughts of Black Hawk inundated her brain, swamping it with both sensual and hostile feelings that tumbled around in her mind, combating each other, vying for her attention. At five a.m., the battle finally played out with Black Hawk the victor, and she spent a few hours restful sleep in the arms of the imaginary character from Tyeshia's book. That pleasant dream in conjunction with the knowledge that she would not be attending any more of Tyeshia's parties for the next month elevated her spirits considerably, making it hard for last night's fiasco to intrude, even when she thought about the marks lining her arms and the meteor-sized hickey on her neck.

Of course it helped that she avoided the mirror this morning, had a silk scarf picked out to wear today along with a long-sleeved, rose-colored silk shirt, instead of her normal T-shirt. She only hoped it was cool in Montana or she'd sweat to death.

She hummed a tune while she waited for the kettle to boil; trying to decide the best way to approach Tyeshia about an idea that had formed earlier this morning, when she realized it was going to be an extended weekend. Normally those extended days off from classes saw Tyeshia shopping and partying, while Savannah generally chose to make a short trip home to visit her family in Montana, followed by a few days with the Blackfoot tribe, visiting her friend, Black Calf, to gather research for her History term paper.

She always flew to Montana, and then made the long drive to the reservation alone. However, this was her last trip before her term paper was due, so it would be her last trip until summer break. She'd broached the subject of Tyeshia coming with her more than once, always using research as an incentive. Of course, research was an unknown word to Tyeshia, so she always shot the idea down, and then she was gone shopping long before Savannah could turn on her powers of persuasion.

Today however, she had an ace up her sleeve and she intended to use it. After all, had she not gone along with every idea that Tyeshia had thrown at her in the last three years? Therefore, she reasoned, Tyeshia should accept one of her proposals. At least her idea would be beneficial to her friend, not result in bodily harm. She decided that if Tyeshia did not buckle down in the next year and really concentrate on her education, instead of focusing on which man she would be entertaining for the evening, then she would not graduate. As beautiful as she was, beauty did not guarantee a marriage that would support her the way she wanted. *Did it?* She wondered for a fraction of a second then quickly dismissed the silly notion.

She eyed her friend while she stirred the coffee creamer into the coffee cups and wondered whether she could convince Tyeshia to go along with her. As far as she could see, Tyeshia owed her a huge debt for setting her up with Octopus Ramirez. Besides, she reasoned, it would be good for Tyeshia, and for once, she'd appreciate the company on her trip. Now she merely needed to convince Tyeshia of all of that—*if* Tyeshia woke up long enough to have a conversation, which appeared doubtful.

She placed the cup in front of her friend's inert form and sat down across from her, sipping her coffee and trying to figure the best way to broach her idea. She glanced at her watch and sighed. No matter how she approached it, it would have to be soon, or it would be too late.

A loud slurp drew Savannah from her musings, and she giggled at the sight before her. At least she knew Tyeshia still had a little life left in her. So did her hair. In fact, her hair seemed to have sprouted a life of its own. Huge clumps reached out in opposing directions, each section attempting to set a record for extending furthest from the scalp. Added to that ridiculous sight were the black globs of mascara that had dislodged from its previous location during the night and smeared beneath her currently baggy eyes.

If Savannah were an adolescent, she would have squealed in mock terror at the sight and run from the room screaming. Of course, Tyeshia would not have found the reaction amusing, so she remained seated, trying desperately to control the laughter that threatened to overwhelm her. She knew better than to laugh at her friend's appearance for it was not conducive to remaining in good health. To mention her mien anytime other than when she dressed to kill could result in Tyeshia killing her. Of course, failing to mention her appearance when she decked out in her finest was equally hazardous.

The slurping continued from Tyeshia's semi-lowered head. It looked to Savannah as if she was trying desperately to suck coffee from her cup without actually having to raise the cup—or her head. A giggle escaped before she could stop it.

"What are you laughing at?" Tyeshia sent her friend yet another scorching glare, when she realized Savannah was aiming the giggling in her direction.

"Want a straw?" Savannah giggled softly. "Sorry," she apologized when Tyeshia continued glaring at her. "Really, though...well, you are a sight, you know. Why, in heaven's name do you put yourself through this?" Savannah asked, not really expecting an answer and not receiving one. "Look at you. You have an exam Tuesday in American History to study for, for which you are not prepared. A term paper due at the end of the semester a few weeks away, for that same class, which I'll bet you haven't even come close to starting. Yet you can't get your head off the table to start the day."

"And a roommate nagging me at the start of the day is not going to help me lift my head or my spirits any faster, so why don't you do me a favor and hush."

"This is serious, Ty," Savannah continued, undeterred. "What happens when you fail History, hmm?"

"I'll sleep with the professor," Tyeshia moaned. "Now, go away."

"The professor is a woman, Ty," Savannah sighed, "and I know you aren't *that* desperate for an 'A'."

"Crud," Tyeshia said beneath her breath. "I'll worry about it when I worry about it, so will you shut up now."

"No, Tyeshia, I won't." Savannah persisted. "We've been friends too many years for me to watch you throw your education out the window."

"Why don't *you* go jump out the window and put me out of my misery?" Tyeshia slurped another bit of coffee that dribbled messily down her chin.

Savannah handed her friend a napkin then stood to prepare a tomato sandwich for breakfast. "Want one?" She asked over her shoulder.

"Not on your life."

"You're welcome."

"Smart butt. Why are you so gosh-darned cheery this morning?"

"I'm always perky in the morning. You know that."

"Not *this* perky. You've been one heck of a perky-jerky since I got in here this morning, not to mention a chatty-Kathy, and I'd like nothing better than for you to shut up. However since I can see by the gleam in your eye that it's not likely to happen, just spit out whatever it is that's gnawing at you so that I can go back to moaning in peace."

"I want you to fly to Montana with me this morning," Savannah blurted out, returning to her seat at the kitchen table.

"Haven't we discussed this before?" Tyeshia said.

"Yes, but today is different, because you are going to agree."

"I am?"

"Yes, and I've already called the airline and they have a seat available, which I took the liberty of booking for you. I've also called my parents and they are expecting you. They are looking forward to meeting you, I might add..."

"Just hold it right there!" Ty interrupted, still staring at her friend incredulously. "What in heaven's name is this all about, and why would I give up my party weekend—and it's a four-day weekend, I might add—just to go traipsing off to that barren landscape with you? Especially when you know that I'm going to say no already; and where do you get off planning and booking my day without consulting me first?"

"I want to help you. Besides which, you owe me one."

"Exactly how do you figure that I'm in your debt, and why ever would you need to help me?"

"I'm going to Montana for a reason, not just to visit my parents..."

"You haven't answered my questions, Savannah, which you'd better do quickly because I'm getting ready to hop in the shower, hop in my car, and go mall-hopping this morning, which means you will have to get a refund for that airline ticket and make my excuses to your parents."

"Okay, here it is."

"Finally," Ty muttered under her breath taking another sip from her rapidly cooling coffee.

"Whenever we have an extended weekend, I go to Montana to see my parents..."

"I already know this. Would you mind *not* building me a clock just to tell me the time?"

"And would you mind *not* interrupting me with your droll sarcasm every time I open my mouth to explain?" Savannah countered.

"Deal. Just talk faster, will you? Precious shopping time is ticking away."

"Fine. Anyway, you also know that while I'm in Montana I take the opportunity to visit a local tribe to do research for my term paper, which, may I remind you yet again, is due in just a few weeks."

"So noted, but what's that to do with me owing you and you helping me?"

"Well, I figured that we could fly out there together so that I could help you study for your exam, which is..."

"Tuesday. So you've said."

"Maybe you can interview some tribal elders yourself for your own term paper, which I can also help you with this weekend."

"That's cool of you, but next you're going to tell me why I can't just turn you down, walk out of this room, shower, change, and go shopping, right?"

"Bobby Ramirez could very well have raped me last night and I wouldn't have been in that situation if I hadn't agreed to your hair-brained bargain in the first place. I told you your deal would end with me getting screwed. Well, not literally." Savannah pulled up the sleeves on her terry-cloth robe and Tyeshia winced. "All these bruises lining my arm, and the enormously large hickey on my neck," Savannah tilted her head so that Tyeshia could see that as well, "are the result of Bobby's over eager attempts last night."

"Gosh, Savannah. I hadn't realized...gee, I'm really sorry."

"Sorry enough to go to Montana with me? I really would like the company, and besides I upheld our bargain and finished your trashy romance novel early this morning, which, I'll readily admit had an interesting ending, to say the least. Not that I'm ready to trade in my encyclopedias for them, so I figure it's time you accepted a bargain from me."

"The Bobby point is punching below the belt, but it is a valid point. All of it is valid which is why I'm going to go shower and pack for Montana."

"Oh, Ty! That's great!" Savannah leapt from the chair, and overturned it in her haste. She hugged her friend close. "I'm sorry I fought dirty."

"Well, if it wasn't true, I'd have never gone along with your suggestion." Tyeshia moved to the kitchen door then stopped, turning to face her friend again. "I forgot to eat breakfast."

"Are you sure you don't want a tomato sandwich?"

"Heck, no! I'll just grab a Big Mac on the way to the airport. What time's the flight anyway?"

"In three hours." Savannah hoped her friend would not hear her whispered response, but she did.

"Three hours!" Tyeshia yelled. "How am I supposed to pack and get ready to leave in three hours?"

"Well, actually, Ty," Savannah winced, "you've only got an hour. We have to be there..."

"Oh, just shut up and make me a tomato sandwich—to go!" Tyeshia shouted as she stormed from the room.

# FIVE

They arrived in Montana early in the afternoon. Savannah's parents were waiting at the airport, as they always were when Savannah came home.

"Welcome, Tyeshia," Abigail Warren said, embracing Tyeshia as if Tyeshia was her long-lost child. If not for her dark skin, Tyeshia's blush would have been very noticeable.

"Yes, it's good to have you visit," Thomas Warren added. "Savannah has told us quite a bit about you."

"I can just imagine," Tyeshia said glancing at Savannah.

"So, ladies, where would you like to lunch today?" Abigail asked. "The Country Club?"

"Wherever you want, Mom," Savannah said, taking her friend by the arm and leading her to the waiting limousine.

"How long before you have to head out this time, Savannah?" Thomas asked.

"We really should be on the road in about an hour, Dad?"

"Okay," Thomas said, flipping open his cell phone, "I'll just have George get the Mustang checked and gassed."

"Thanks, Dad."

Tyeshia watched the exchange in wonder. Obviously, Savannah was extremely close to her parents and that they held great affection for their daughter. However, what had not been apparent, from Savannah's dress and behavior at college, was how wealthy she obviously was. It was a little disconcerting.

Now as two girls sped down the highway toward their destination, Tyeshia was a little more than curious what drove her friend. With her wealth, she certainly did not need an education to live well for the remainder of her life.

"So why do you make this trek, anyway?" Tyeshia shouted above the roaring wind in her ears as the ruby-red Ford Mustang convertible whipped down Highway 2.

"You mean to the reservation?" Savannah pushed the button to raise the top, allowing them to talk without having to yell at the top of their lungs.

"Of course I mean to the reservation! What else would I mean?" Tyeshia shouted even louder so that Savannah could hear her over the wind and the whirring of the top as it slowly descended over their heads and clicked into place. "Oh, that's much better; now I won't have to worry about getting laryngitis."

"Funny, Ty."

"So, why didn't you tell me you were stinking rich?"

"You're stinking rich too," Savannah said with a laugh.

"Yes, but I *act* stinking rich," Tyeshia pointed out. "You, on the other hand, behave as if you are attending school on the good graces of the government."

"Truly?"

"Yes, so why go? Your family obviously has more money than my parent's do, so you could easily relax and travel until your bones turn to dust."

"Well, why do you go? Your family is rich."

"Yes, but not as rich as yours. Besides, Mom says a good place to meet a husband is at college, so she sent me."

"Really? That's the only reason you're there? You weren't joking about that?"

"Of course I'm joking," Tyeshia laughed. "My mother has a Master's Degree. She met my father at college all right, because the college invited them both to give a speech to the students on the same day. It's kind of been a family joke that they met 'at college'".

"Oh. I don't get it."

"You wouldn't. So, are you going to explain why you feel the need for an education, when it's obvious you don't really need one?"

"Only if you explain why you feel the need to throw your education away."

"Point taken. So, how about explaining why you have to drive out to the middle of nowhere to do research? Why can't you simply conduct your research the old-fashioned way? On the Internet, like everyone else? I know you can afford a computer."

Savannah burst into distracting laughter and had to swerve to avoid running into a ditch. "Oh, Ty! You really are something else. You know that?" Savannah continued laughing, trying to maintain control of the car and her mirth.

"Well, I'd like to remain a *live* something, if you don't mind," Tyeshia squealed, holding tight to the arm of the door, her ebony face ashen.

"I'll try to be more attentive of my driving, if you promise not to make any more absurd comments. Internet! Good Lord!"

"Well, it's a lot safer to surf the net than it is for you to be behind the wheel of a car, that's for sure!" Tyeshia's knuckles were nearly white where she gripped the door handle.

"You're perfectly safe, I assure you."

"A little late for assurances, but I'll take that as a future promise."

"Well, to answer your question as to doing research on the Internet—I do, somewhat. However, surfing the net doesn't put you in touch with the heart and soul of your research. It's not real. It's just a bunch of words on a page. You can't see your subject, feel it, touch it and therefore, how can you possibly comprehend its meaning, its history, and its beauty? Also, the Internet can only give you so much information, and since flawed humans generally write the information, it's prone to error. Understand?"

"I don't research topics in any form, shape, or fashion, so I could not possibly understand. All I know is that you've somehow managed to talk me into driving out to some Godforsaken wilderness..."

"Wrong, Tyeshia. The hand of God touches this wildness. The reservation we're heading to belong to the Blackfoot Indians, namely the Pikuni Tribe. It borders Canada on one side and Glacier National Park on the other and is the most awe-inspiring land to which you'll ever bear witness. It makes you wonder why man would destroy such beauty in favor of concrete and mortar."

"Well, right now all I see are few trees and even less beauty, so you aren't exactly preaching to an attentive congregation here, sister."

"It'll change. Believe you me, it will change."

"So why did you choose to do your research on this tribe? This Pikinu Tribe? Isn't there a tribe closer to the college?"

Savannah laughed again, but this time was careful to watch her driving. "That's Pikuni, Ty. Pikuni."

"Whatever."

"I'm from Montana."

"So? I'm from Georgia, but that doesn't mean I need to fly down there every time I want to know something about Cherokee Indians."

"I'm amazed you even know what Indians live in that region," Savannah said, genuinely surprised.

"My brother-in-law is half Cherokee."

"Well, that explains it."

"What *is* your interest, Savannah?" Ty prodded, bringing their conversation back on track.

"There are many tribes in Montana. The Crow, Cree, Nes Perce, Flathead..."

"Now there's a good name for a tribe," Tyeshia said, sarcastically.

"Anyway, the Blackfoot always fascinated me more than any of the others did. The Blackfoot tribes extend from upper Montana into Canada."

"Uh oh! Here comes one of your lectures!" Tyeshia rolled her eyes heavenward and groaned loudly.

Savannah sighed. "I thought that was the idea. To come with me and learn, so that you can be jump-started into doing your own research in the hopes that you might actually pass American History."

"La de da de da. Actually, I came because you made me feel guilty about Bobby Ramirez."

"Guilty you should feel. Now, are you going to listen and learn, Ty, or is this going to be a wasted trip? You know, you might consider listening, since it might be good to know a little about the people you are visiting. That way, the culture doesn't seem so foreign to you when you arrive."

"All right, all right! I give! I give! Know-it-all! Consider me your attentive pupil for the next—how long until we arrive?"

"We left Havre about forty-five minutes ago, so we have about two hours drive time left."

"Two hours!" Tyeshia squealed. "Where exactly is this place?"

"About forty-five miles north of Kiowa, near the Canadian border. If we get there early enough, we can spend a good deal of time at my friend's house and then head back to Browning to spend the night."

"Well, I'm likely to fall asleep long before then so if you want to give me some background you'd better start doing some fast talking, Miss Academia."

"And I'm not a know-it-all, Ty," Savannah sighed impatiently. "If I were, I wouldn't have to study so hard just to have learned what little I do know."

"I'm sorry Savannah. I guess being out of civilization makes me a little cranky. Forgiven?"

"Forgiven, as always. Now, back to my lecture on the Blackfoot."

"I thought you said Pikini?"

"It's Pikuni, and I did," Savannah sighed in exasperation. "The Pikuni is a branch of the Blackfoot."

"Oh, well, start talking before I start snoring."

"Actually, my research is not so much on the Blackfoot, as a single incident that occurred involving the Pikuni that took place back in eighteen-seventy. Have you ever heard of a man named Malcolm Clark? No, I don't guess you would have."

"No. Is he new to the college?"

"Not unless they've started admitting ghosts. He's not a well-known historical figure, but I did find a very small reference to him when I was researching the massacre at Marias River in January of eighteen-seventy[1].

1 The Marias River Massacre is an actual historical event, however, events denoted in this book are mostly fictitious. Further information may be found at the Legends of America website @ http://www.legendsofamerica.com/na-mariasmassacre.html

That's what my term paper is going to be on. Anyway, while I was reading about the incident at Marias River, they mentioned Malcolm Clark's name briefly.

"When I went to find additional information about the man however, I could only find one paragraph referencing a Malcolm Clark. Piegan warriors killed Clark in retaliation for his killing of a Blackfoot Indian. All it says about his death is that the Blackfoot killed Clark on his ranch in Helena in October of eighteen-sixty-nine. Nothing else exists about him. At least nothing that I've been able to find."

"So, why the interest?"

"Well, it would appear that the attack at Marias River was a direct result of Malcolm Clark's murder the previous fall."

"Why did the Blackfoot kill Clark?"

"From what I gather, Clark killed a Blackfoot so the Blackfoot killed Clark. Retribution killing was commonplace back then. What's so strange is the army's involvement. What was so special about Malcolm Clark—just one man—that would cause the army to send a detachment of soldiers to retaliate against the Blackfoot at Marias River?"

"Okay, maybe Malcolm Clark wasn't important enough to make the history books."

"See, that's the thing. If Malcolm Clark was a nobody, why send an entire army unit to seek justice for his death? Yet, if he was such an important figure, why did I find only a small reference to him when I was surfing the web?"

"So you think he had to be someone important? Important enough to warrant military involvement?"

"Right. The sad thing is though; the army unit sent to seek retribution purportedly attacked the wrong tribe. A man named Mountain Chief led the tribe responsible for Clark's death. The tribe that they attacked belonged to a man named Heavy Runner; the tribe that lived on the Marias River. I found some written speculation when I was doing my research that the attack against Heavy Runner's people was not an accident."

"I'm not sure I follow," Tyeshia replied, confusion clearly etched on her ebony face.

"Listen my children and you shall hear of an undocumented massacre..."

"All right already. Enough with the melodrama and just tell me what happened."

Savannah giggled and then grew somber. "The date was January 23, 1870. A band of Piegan warriors was living peacefully along the banks of the Marias River. A man, by the name of Heavy Runner, led this band of Indians," Savannah recounted, as if reading the text directly from the encyclopedia. "In camp this cold Saturday morning was about two hundred women, children, sick, and elderly."

"Where were the men?"

"Not anticipating any trouble, the young men of the tribe had gone hunting."

"Hunting?" Tyeshia said truly perplexed. Then realization dawned. "Oh, that's right; they didn't have grocery stores back then."

"Oh, Ty! You really are too much."

"What? Just because I'm not an expert on the history of our country, doesn't mean that I don't know some things." Savannah glanced over at her high-strung friend.

"Okay. Let's not start World War III over it! Now where was I?"

"The morning that the men had gone hunting," Tyeshia offered, but continued to sulk.

"Oh, yes. An army unit commanded by a man named Colonel Baker had come up from Fort Ellis. That morning they were watching Heavy Runner's camp from the surrounding hillside. When Heavy Runner saw the soldiers, he came out from his lodge carrying a safe-conduct paper—the equivalent of a white flag of truce."

"You mean they *knew* they were a peaceful tribe and *still* attacked them?" Tyeshia's horror was growing with each word her friend spoke. Somewhere deep inside, Tyeshia knew the history of her country wasn't necessarily a pretty one, but she never imagined that unprovoked attacks had been part of it.

"Something like that. From what information I've been able to gather in my research, Colonel Baker was drunk and could not care less whom he was attacking. He ignored a scout who told him that they had the wrong camp. When one of his other scouts opened fire, dropping Heavy Runner where he stood, all hell broke loose. By the time the dust settled, a lot of Pikuni lay dead and they took the rest prisoner. Now, bear in mind that some of the research is bound to be biased depending upon the source. The information I've been able to glean so far has been from the Internet so I can't depend on its accuracy much."

"You mean that women, children, and elderly fought Army personnel and then they took the survivors into custody for defending their home against an unprovoked attack. Wow! I can't get over the fact that the army took women and children as prisoners."

"Well, that's what the author of the article I read claimed. Although it wouldn't be the first time in our history that women and children were victims of war. Still it gets worse, if you can believe it." Savannah warmed to her subject.

"It can't possibly get worse."

"Oh, but it does. When word of the massacre reached bigwigs in the

East, there was a big stink created. General Sherman did his best to quell the anger by sending orders to Baker's army to release the prisoners; that's probably also why no additional massacres took place at that time."

"That's good, isn't it?" She asked the question, but knew by her friend's expression that what was coming next would crush her hopeful query.

"In a way, I guess it was. They *did* release the prisoners. However, they did so in the middle of winter with inadequate clothing and food supplies. They were also more than ninety miles from the nearest fort and on foot. Most of them died making the trek back to their home."

"No way!"

"Way."

"All this because a tiff between one white man and some Indians."

"Yeah. I guess I want to know why all of this happened and then see if I can't put it into words that will please my History professor."

"It sounds like all you have to do is tell it like you've just told me." Tyeshia's honesty brought a blush to Savannah's alabaster cheeks. "So, if you know everything that you already know, why do you need to do more research? I mean, why come to see this character...what's his name?"

"His name is Black Calf, and I'm coming to see him because I'm hoping he can fill in some gaps. Maybe he can tell me more about Malcolm Clark and his involvement with the Blackfoot."

"He's really old enough to be able to supply you with that kind of information?"

"Come on Ty! Do your math! No one lives to more than a hundred thirty nowadays."

"Then how can he help?"

"Black Calf? I really don't know if he can to be honest. I guess I'm counting on stories that they have passed down from generation to generation. That sort of stuff. It's got to be more accurate than the Internet, anyway."

"What if his people didn't pass down stories about this Clark, what then?"

"I can always try the Hall of Records in Helena or something like that. Of course, that's another two or three hundred miles south of here, so I'd like to avoid that option if I can. Especially since this is my last trip out here this school year. If Black Calf can't fill in the gaps, we'll have to make a special trip to Helena tomorrow and pray I find some additional information. If I can't, my term paper is kaput, or I'll have to reassemble my previous information and simply do a biography on the Blackfoot which seems kind of boring now that I've discovered this new information."

"You'll think of something. You're smart enough. So why didn't you have Black Calf fill in the gaps on your last three trips out here?"

"Because I've just discovered the Marias River incident this past week. Initially, it was my intent to do a documentary on the Pikuni, but when I was surfing the net and found the information on the Marias River incident, it sparked my interest. I only hope it isn't a dead-end. What about you? Do you think this trip will help you come up with something short notice for a decent term paper?"

"I've already learned a great deal," Tyeshia admitted. "I never knew there were so many interesting things that I could glean from history."

"It might surprise you to know that you can discover interesting things about your own history, if you look far enough back."

"I don't doubt," Tyeshia laughed.

"You know, there's another thing that I forgot to mention about Black Calf," Savannah said in a mysterious tone that made Tyeshia nervous.

"What's that? You're not going to tell me he's some kind of fruitcake, are you?"

"Not a complete fruitcake, no," Savannah grinned. "I mean he's not exactly ready for a strait jacket or to be locked away in an institution or anything like that. He's just a strange old coot. Sweet, but strange."

"Oh, great!" Tyeshia rolled her eyes heavenward and sighed heavily. "You're dragging me to meet Mr. Not-quite-yet-certifiable-but-close. Is that what you're telling me?"

"Yeah, I suppose, but it's not as bad as all that. He's just been having these dreams lately."

"What sort of dreams?" When Savannah didn't answer immediately, Tyeshia's temper snapped. Especially since she knew that Savannah was baiting her, and she was allowing it. "If you don't spit it out this instant, this car is going to be minus a driver!"

"I'm sorry, Ty," Savannah laughed. "It's just too easy to tease you. Okay, here it is." Savannah took a deep breath and then blurted it out. "I don't know."

"What?"

"Really!" Savannah tried to maintain control of the car and ward off Tyeshia's slapping hands simultaneously. "I'm sorry I teased you so, but would you mind letting me concentrate on my driving, since we both want to arrive in one piece!" After a final slap, Tyeshia pulled back to her side of the car and crossed her arms over her chest, a big pout on her full lips. "All I know is that the last few times I've come to visit, Black Calf has told me that he dreams of me, but the dreams are never complete."

"Either that or they're just so scary that he doesn't want to upset you," Ty snapped nastily.

"That's possible," Savannah said her brow knitted thoughtfully. "If that's the case, I don't particularly want to know the outcome." Savannah fell silent and concentrated on her driving, trying to keep her mind off Black Calf and their upcoming visit. She had been very honest with Tyeshia about the dreams, but her friend had come closer to knowing her fears than she'd realized. Savannah too felt that the dreams foretold of something unpleasant, and that Black Calf knew much more than he was letting on. She also had a feeling she'd be learning more than just about Clark on this last visit to the Blackfoot tribe.

# SIX

"Welcome, my child. I am always happy to see you," Black Calf smiled as Savannah approached. "There is much you wish to know, is there not?"

"It's good to see you again, Black Calf." Savannah returned Black Calf's smile and hugged the elderly Shaman like a long lost friend. Tyeshia had driven the last thirty miles, then dropped Savannah off near the tribe's dwellings and offered to find a place to park, promising to join her friend quickly. "And yes, I have a thousand questions as usual."

"Good. I like a learning mind. We will go and sit in my house..." Black Calf stopped talking and halted in mid-turn, his face suddenly ashen. He gripped the shirt near his heart in a tight fist and his breathing grew shallow.

"Black Calf, are you okay?" Savannah clutched Black Calf's arm, ready to offer any assistance. When she moved into his line of sight however, he pulled her aside with a surprisingly strong grip.

*At least I can rule out a heart attack,* she thought, and then turned around trying to find what it was that had upset the elderly man so much. After only a second of searching, she found what had drawn Black Calf's attention, and found herself speechless as well. He was staring intently at Tyeshia, who was making her way toward them.

"Tyeshia, may I introduce Black Calf?" When Tyeshia finally reached their side, Savannah's voice was shaky; just a hair above a whisper. Tyeshia looked at Black Calf, then at her friend. The way they stared at her made her want to turn and flee.

"Now I understand." With that mysterious pronouncement, Black Calf shook himself from his self-imposed trance and smiled pleasantly. "It is an honor to meet the friend of my friend. We will all go to my house now. There is much that you must know."

Black Calf turned and hobbled away, leaving Tyeshia and Savannah gawking after his retreating form. After a moment, Tyeshia turned her gaze, blazing with anger toward her friend's perplexed visage.

"What in Hades was that all about?" Her voice was a mere whisper, but the demanding tone snapped Savannah out of her own stupor. She turned to face Tyeshia and saw the fear in her friend's eyes.

"I wish I knew."

"He was staring at me like he could see straight into my soul, dagnabbit!"

"I know! I don't understand, but he seemed frightened when he saw you coming. It was almost as if he *could* see into your soul."

"Are you telling me I have a scary psyche?"

"I'm not telling you anything. Maybe we should just find out what all of that was about." Savannah turned and started toward Black Calf's home, but stopped when she realized that Tyeshia was not following. Reluctantly, she returned to her friend's side.

"Coming?"

"Preferably not."

"He's not going to bite."

"I have my doubts about that."

Savannah looked back toward the house. Black Calf had long vanished inside. She wondered whether he had an inkling of the impact his words had on the two of them. Her normally logical mind became active and she envisioned the old man sitting comfortably in his living room giggling at their discomfort this very minute. Her heartbeat increased as her temper flared. She took deep steadying breaths to calm herself.

"You're going to hyperventilate if you keep breathing like that," Tyeshia remarked offhandedly, her own arms wrapped tightly around her waist. "Why don't we head on back to the car and find the nearest bar?"

Savannah swung an incredulous gaze toward Tyeshia, "Neither of us drinks."

"Not yet, we don't."

"Cute. You mean you can walk away from a build-up like that and not find out what caused it?"

"Heck, yeah! No offense to your friend in there, Savannah, but I can do without the melodrama. Especially from an old eccentric who thinks I have a scary psyche."

"And you aren't the least bit curious *why* he looked at you so strange?"

"Would you want to know?"

"I think I would," Savannah said but then amended her answer quickly. "I know I would."

"You're full of it!"

"No, what I am full of is curiosity."

Tyeshia turned to leave, but Savannah placed a restraining hand on her arm. "Remember I already told you that Black Calf has been having strange dreams?"

"Yes."

"Maybe it has something to do with the dreams. Besides, I still have a term paper and thesis that I'm researching, so would you humor me and come inside? Please? I'm certain that the worse that will happen is that we will have a creepy sensation running up and down our spine. I mean, get real, what else could possibly happen?"

"I don't know and I don't want to know, but if anything does happen I'm using you as a human shield."

The two walked hesitantly toward the house clasping each other's hand firmly.

"This kind of feels like it does when I walk into a classroom unprepared for a major exam," Tyeshia muttered.

"I wouldn't know. I'm always prepared for my exams."

Without bothering to knock, Savannah pushed open the worn screen door. They moved inside hesitantly, and stood in the entrance for a moment, allowing their eyes to adjust to the dim interior.

"Creepier and creepier." Tyeshia moved to stand behind Savannah.

"I was wondering if you two were planning to join me today," Black Calf called from the living room. "Please, come in and have a seat."

Both inched their way into the living room and sat close together on the faded couch.

"No disrespect intended, Black Calf," Savannah began, "but would you mind explaining that little episode?"

Black Calf let his gaze drift over the two young women, lingering on Tyeshia. "It makes me happy that you decided to stay. I'm sorry if I upset you outside. Your appearance simply took me by surprise."

"Yeah, sure. No problem."

"Now that you are both here the pieces of my dreams have fallen into place and I can tell you everything. Before I talk to you of that, tell me what it is you came to ask me about on this trip, Savannah?"

Black Calf surprised Savannah. She was disappointed that he was not going to answer her question immediately. Still, she wanted to complete her research so she would allow him time before explaining.

"I wanted to know if you had ever heard of a man by the name..."

"Malcolm Clark," Black Calf finished. Savannah's jaw slackened in surprise and she could only nod dumbly.

"Creepier and creepier," Tyeshia muttered from the corner of her mouth. "I told you."

"How did you know that?" Savannah asked quietly.

"My dreams revealed all to me. I will tell you a little of what I know, but what you need to know you can only learn firsthand."

"What do you mean?" Tyeshia asked.

"You will see. I also must tell you of another. Someone, of whom you must beware," Black Calf said somberly shifting to look into Tyeshia's widened gaze, "but first I will tell you of Malcolm Clark. You made a discovery during research that there was a massacre at Marias River in January of eighteen-seventy, correct Savannah?" Savannah nodded again and Black Calf continued speaking. "The massacre was against Heavy Runner's people. It was in retaliation for the Pikuni killing of Malcolm Clark, that previous year."

"I thought the attack against Heavy Runner's people was a mistake. Are you now telling me that it *was* one of Heavy Runner's people that killed Clark, and not someone from Mountain Chief's people like history claims?" Savannah asked, her shock and disappointment passing as the academic in her came surging to the surface.

"No, not exactly. Yes, the Pikuni killed Clark, but, no, it wasn't one of Heavy Runner's people. It *was* someone from Mountain Chief's tribe. Did you know that the army killed many of Heavy Runner's people that day, and they took those that survived prisoners? Did you know that?"

"I ran across it in my research. The men of the village had gone hunting, right?"

"That's right. One of those men was my Great-great-great-great-grandfather, Yellow Beaver. It is because of stories passed down to his descendants that I know what I know. You were counting on that, weren't you?"

"Yes, I was."

Black Calf smiled, then took a deep breath and continued. "Deciding what to tell you first is difficult, so I guess I will just start at the beginning."

"Can I ask how this relates to your dreams, and how you knew I would be asking about that particular incident today?"

"I dreamed it. As far as the Marias River incident, I do not think it was an accident that you found a small piece of information relating to that, although my people have not spoken of it in all this time. I think you were supposed to find that information, because you will need it."

"I will? Black Calf, no offense, but you are simply confusing me rather than clarifying anything," Savannah sighed.

"Let me see if I can help fill in some information about the incident and then I will tell you why it was important that you know that information, okay?"

"Very well, and then perhaps you can explain how Tyeshia is involved as well."

"I will do what I can."

"Thank you."

"You are very welcome," Black Calf said, and then took a deep breath, and began. "A good number of young Pikuni warriors were getting into trouble because they were angry over the number of whites settling onto their lands; killing their buffalo. They were angry at the white man's broken promises. Yet the Pikuni's mischievousness never strayed outside the boundaries of the law, so the army would not touch them. Still, that same

Army kept a sharp eye on those young men, waiting for a day when they would cross the line and they could punish them. They were always looking for a reason to punish the Blackfoot. What they really wanted to do, of course, was to destroy us.

"In October of eighteen-sixty-nine, Piegan warriors killed Clark. This of course was retaliation for Clark's killing of one of their own. The Army needed no other excuse. The army went in and butchered the tribe at Marias River."

"Still, why that particular tribe?" Savannah asked.

"I cannot say, but rumors were that the Colonel was drunk and simply attacked the wrong tribe; maybe the army came across that particular tribe first."

"That's what I read."

"Anyway, that Colonel probably would have done much worse had the news not reached the East so quickly, causing Sherman to stop it fast."

"Whom did Clark kill that would cause the Pikuni to murder him? Or did it matter who it was?"

"It would not have mattered. No one raises a hand against a member of the Pikuni tribe without the whole of the society coming down on his head."

"Nevertheless, there was more to it, wasn't there?" Savannah sensed there was, and wished she had a pen to take notes. Fortunately, her memory was superb.

"Yes, much more. Clark was more than just a white man that killed a red skin. Clark was an honorary member of the Pikuni tribe. He was a member of Mountain Chief's tribe through marriage. The fact that Clark murdered Mountain Chief's brother..."

"Brother?"

"That's right. The Pikuni that Clark murdered was Mountain Chief's banished brother. So you see it *was* Mountain Chief's tribe that hunted down Clark and killed him. The army was searching for Mountain Chief's tribe; nevertheless, they found Heavy Runner's tribe instead and so occurred one of the saddest times in our history—the Marias River incident."

"Still, why would Clark kill Mountain Chief's brother, and why was Mountain Chief's brother banished from the tribe? What was his name anyway?"

"See, it is a twisted tale; hard to untangle. Still, I will tell you more and see if we can't make sense of it all, but first we must eat. My wife will not be pleased if I delay us and her dinner gets cold."

Savannah started to argue but Tyeshia placed a restraining hand on her arm.

"We haven't eaten since breakfast, Savannah, and it won't do any good to press for more information when he's determined to have his meal."

Despite the disappointment at not continuing with the conversation, Savannah smiled politely and followed Tyeshia and Black Calf into the adjacent dining room. His wife, Little Feet, was already there waiting for them. She smiled at Savannah and Tyeshia and motioned to a chair. Black Calf said a blessing then they began to eat.

They discussed the girl's trip out west, what they were studying in college, even young men, but no one dared mention the subject of Marias River. That, Black Calf had informed them was a discussion for *after* their meal. This left Savannah with the impression that what was coming would leave them feeling none too good.

# SEVEN

Savannah and Tyeshia again settled onto the faded couch in the living room. Twilight had come, and the one lamp in the room cast an eerie shadow across the room's meager furnishings. Black Calf sat across from Tyeshia and Savannah on his leather lounger, with its mismatched patches. Leaning forward with his elbows on his knees, he looked first at Savannah and then at Tyeshia. He gazed at them for so long, that Tyeshia wanted to shout at him to take a picture, it would last longer. She refrained from the infantile outburst however, not wanting to show disrespect to Savannah's friend—even if he was loony, in her opinion.

She sat quietly beside Savannah and waited until Black Calf was ready to reveal what he knew. One glance at Savannah told her that she was thinking the same thing.

"Now, where were we? Oh, yes. Malcolm Clark and Mountain Chief's brother, Many Feathers. That's his name, by the way. A little background on Clark might help you understand him better and probably why he killed Many Feathers the way he did." Black Calf settled in and Tyeshia rolled her eyes, looking at Savannah helplessly. Savannah grinned knowing that Tyeshia knew another dreaded lecture was coming on.

"Malcolm Clark was a young man with big dreams, high ideals—and a hot temper. He came to Blackfoot land in search of wealth and freedom, as did many young men long ago. Anyway, I learned from my grandfather that they kicked Clark out of West Point at the age of nineteen because of his temper. You know of West Point?"

"Yes."

"That temper drove him after Many Feathers, even after Mountain Chief warned him to stay away. Nevertheless, I'm veering off track a little," Black Calf said. He paused to collect his thoughts and then continued. "Clark had been out here for a few years when he met White Dove. She was a member of Mountain Chief's tribe. He fell in love with her and married into the tribe, something that happens rarely. This didn't sit well with Many Feathers because he felt that she had disgraced herself by falling in love with a white man."

"Didn't Mountain Chief oppose the union?"

"I do not know if he was pleased with the union, but he did not oppose it. He was seeking to bring harmony with the whites and felt that this was another step toward peace. Because of the times that the Pikuni had to go to war, and because of their reputation as fierce warriors, people often do not realize that they were mainly peace loving. They much preferred to talk than to fight. They only went to war when needed. At least most did, anyway."

"Not Many Feathers though, right?"

Black Calf smiled indulgently, "That is right, child. Many Feathers was not a well man, but let me finish with what I know. Did you come by Many Feathers name in any of your research, Savannah?"

"No. At least I can't remember whether I saw it." Savannah edged closer to the front of her seat.

"I'm not at all surprised. It is a name that the Pikuni spent years trying to forget; a name that spawned terror in whites and shame in our own people. Still, I could not erase him from my mind." Savannah wanted to ask what he meant, but she could tell by his posture that he was trying to organize his thoughts again, and knew that to keep interrupting him would not be wise.

"Many Feathers was a warrior bent on vengeance," Black Calf continued in a near whisper. "He was an angry young man; would kill without a second thought for the slightest insult, real or perceived. White man or Indian, young or old, man, woman, or child—it did not matter to him. Many Feathers fabricated many reasons for why he killed, so in his own mind he felt justified. Of course, you cannot justify evil." Black Calf stood, running arthritic fingers through long graying hair. He began hobbling back and forth, his aging body unable to keep pace with his racing mind. "Many in the tribe felt that Many Feathers had allowed the evil one possession of his soul and sought to have him banished; however, they could not."

"Why?"

"He was Mountain Chief's brother." Black Calf stopped pacing and faced the two young women sitting stiffly on his old worn couch. His gaze searched Savannah's as understanding dawned. "That's right, Savannah, it isn't anything more complicated than that. His brother's position in the tribe saved him from exile more than once."

"I can understand that, but you still haven't told me why Clark would murder him. Clark was now a member of the tribe through marriage, so you'd think he'd go out of his way to get along with everyone—evil or not."

"I'm getting there." Black Calf lowered himself back into his leather lounger. "There is so much to tell you and so little time, I fear."

"We'll be here until you tell us everything, Black Calf, so take your time."

"That is the problem, child. You may not be." Black Calf stood again, his agitation apparent but before Savannah could question him further, Black Calf returned to his pacing and his story, "Anyway, after a time, most people in the tribe accepted Clark's presence because of how well he cared for White Dove."

"Not Many Feathers?"

"Not Many Feathers. He warred with whoever angered him at the time. This time it was White Dove with her treasonous marriage to Clark. Therefore, while Clark was out hunting one day, Many Feathers took advantage of his absence and killed a pregnant White Dove in broad daylight and with many witnesses. It took her death, the death of one of their own, for Mountain Chief to banish Many Feathers."

"He didn't have him killed?"

"No. Mountain Chief felt that the evil one had possessed his brother and that was what controlled his actions. He decided it best just to banish him from their presence. Mountain Chief permitted no one to speak of him, or to him, ever again."

"Of course, this didn't sit well with Many Feathers or Malcolm Clark?"

"It did not," Black Calf confirmed. "Clark had purchased a ranch near Helena and had planned to move his wife and newborn in that next spring, when their child was old enough to travel and the winter snows had melted. After White Dove's death, Mountain Chief could see the anger welling inside Clark and felt compelled to warn him. Mountain Chief would not allow him to retaliate against Many Feathers for his wife's death. If he sought vengeance then the Pikuni would come after him. It did not matter how far he went; they would find him.

"Shortly after, Clark packed his meager belongings and moved to the ranch alone. He did not remain there, however. Disregarding Mountain Chief's dire warning, he set off in the late summer—July, I think it was—to find and kill Many Feathers.

"Sometime in August, Clark found Many Feathers camped beside the Muscle Shell River—surprisingly alone and asleep. Without even thinking twice, he charged into camp with his knife drawn and stabbed Many Feathers to death—while he slept. Clark quietly returned home, justice served."

"The Pikuni retaliated," Savannah supplied, bringing the story full circle. "October of eighteen-sixty-nine, they found Clark at home on his ranch and killed him."

"Yes. My people believe Clark's death was the reason the Army finally began to attack our people. Because of the death of a white man, the army massacred many of Heavy Runner's people. It was the excuse they needed, to do what they had always wanted—wipe the Native people off the face of the earth." Black Calf stopped speaking and sat suddenly.

"Yet how did they know that Clark is the one that killed Many Feathers? It could have been anyone," Tyeshia, who had been sitting quietly during the entire time, finally spoke up.

"I do not know it was Clark that killed Many Feathers, but that is how the Pikuni pass down the story. They held Clark accountable for killing Many Feathers because he swore vengeance for his wife's death. Clark was a prior military man, so we also assume that when they discovered his death, which a hundred years ago could have taken many months, the army decided it was time to teach the Pikuni a lesson. Anyway, what's done is done. I have been impolite. Would you like something to drink?" Black Calf sprang from his lounger like a wound spring.

Savannah and Tyeshia stared at Black Calf as if he'd suddenly sprouted another arm. They shook their heads simultaneously. They did not want anything to drink. Black Calf smiled sheepishly realizing that he must be behaving strangely, and lowered himself back down onto his aged recliner.

"I apologize for my unusual behavior but this subject of Many Feathers makes me nervous. It is as if speaking his name will cause disastrous events and so much has already happened because of him."

"So much heartache and pain," Savannah sighed.

"Yes, so much, and I wish that it were over, but it's not."

"What do you mean?" Tyeshia whispered. "What happened did so over a hundred-fifty years ago. How could it not be over?"

"Because Many Feathers' spirit still seeks justice." Black Calf's shoulders bowed as if carrying a heavy weight. "I fear that he will not rest, always haunting my dreams, and upsetting the forces around him, until he finds that justice."

"Why would he seek justice when the Pikuni killing of Clark served justice?" Savannah was truly confused now. "They killed Clark. They avenged his death."

"Many Feathers did not have the chance to defend himself," Black Calf explained patiently. "Clark killed him in his sleep. A coward's death. If he had died fighting, it would have been an honorable death and he could have gone on in peace. Malcolm Clark however, although a major player in all of this is not your worry—Many Feathers is."

"You mean Many Feathers *was* a major player," Savannah corrected but felt a strange sensation creeping along her spine.

"No, I mean *is*. Now I have the unpleasant task of telling you something more; something that I have only just begun to understand myself." His gaze focused on Savannah. "I have told you since you began visiting me that I have been dreaming of you, Savannah." Savannah nodded. "It is not so much a dream now as a revelation and it is because of you," he said meeting Tyeshia's gaze head-on, "that the unclear becomes clear and the missing pieces are found."

Savannah looked at Tyeshia's ashen features. She gripped Tyeshia's hand tightly in her own, knowing it was the only reassurance that she could offer her friend then. If Black Calf had looked at her in the way he was looking at

Tyeshia, she'd need support too.

"How does the death of two men more than a hundred fifty years ago relate to us?" Tyeshia asked hoarsely. "I mean, no offense intended, but when I arrived you looked at me kind of funny. Are you telling me it relates to all of this?"

"Until you arrived today, dear girls," Black Calf started piercing Tyeshia with his opaque gaze, "I did not understand the dreams that have haunted me. When Savannah began visiting me with questions regarding our people, they began and increased steadily in intensity and clarity until you came here today, Tyeshia. The dreams are of the warrior Many Feathers, Malcolm Clark—and you both," Black Calf paused to see the reaction his statement had on them. He could tell he stupefied them.

"You mean you've seen me in your dreams with this nutcase, and you said nothing?" The tone in Savannah's voice was one of accusation, but Black Calf did nothing to defend himself against it, merely explained things the best he could.

"I did not really understand that it was you that I saw, child. Not until I saw you two together did the vision reveal itself fully to me and now I will reveal what I can to you. Nevertheless, you must be strong and control your temper." He directed his gaze at Tyeshia as if he understood she was the one likely to explode. "Many things I will say to you will probably make you angry because of your lack of understanding."

"We'll try to remain calm and understanding, won't we, Ty?" Savannah squeezed Tyeshia's hand reassuringly, but felt anything but.

"Sure." Tyeshia smiled weakly at Savannah but her smile quickly faded and her promise to maintain calm vanished with Black Calf's next words.

"I have seen in my dreams that you are Many Feathers' woman." Black Calf stared at Tyeshia, his gaze unknowingly accusatory.

"What are you talking about, old man?" Tyeshia jumped from the couch, forgetting courtesy and respect. For her, with an opening statement like that—all bets were off.

Savannah stood and placed a restraining hand on her friend's arm, whispering something in her ear that Black Calf could not hear. It must have worked because Tyeshia settled reluctantly back down onto the couch.

"Has Many Feathers visited you in your dreams?" He tried to keep his voice even and the accusatory tone to a minimum.

"This is a joke, right?" Tyeshia looked to Savannah for support.

"Just try to think, Ty. Do you remember dreaming about this man?"

"I don't even know what in Hades the guy looks like, so how am I supposed to recall if I've dreamed of him!"

"Perhaps I asked the question incorrectly. I will rephrase it. Have you dreamed of an Indian male recurrently? One that stands out in your dreams more than another does?" Black Calf amended, prodding as gently as time allowed.

"I suppose I have, but I can't remember that much about him or the dreams."

"Good." Black Calf slapped his hands on his thighs. "Then there is still time."

"Time for what?" Tyeshia hissed. "What is going on?"

"I have watched you; have seen in your eyes and your mannerisms that your vanity equals his, which makes you his perfect mate. That is why he has chosen you." Black Calf was unmindful of the deadly gaze that Tyeshia was aiming at him. "Because you do not remember much about him when you awaken means that he has not fully reached your subconscious. Although I'm certain he tries and will continue to try until you remember him asleep or awake. Then he will own you and you will do for him whatever he wishes."

"That's the most absurd..." Tyeshia began, but Black Calf signaled her to be silent.

"You were there in your dreams when he died. You *will* be there when he dies," Black Calf corrected and continued hurriedly. "Only by awakening him when Clark attacks, and allowing him to fight to an honorable death, will you send his soul to rest in peace. By that, assuring that your life here will belong to you again."

"You're telling me," Tyeshia said sarcastically, "that I'm supposed to fall asleep tonight, force myself to dream of a time of which I have almost no knowledge, try to wake a man from sleeping while *I* am asleep, and watch him fight to the death? Well, guess what, mister," she said as she barged toward the living room door, "you're a lunatic and I'm outta here!"

Savannah sadly watched her friend storm from the room. Her heart dictated that she should go after her, for she had not a doubt that Tyeshia would need her, but she could not move. She had to know everything that Black Calf had to say. There was more, of that she had no doubt either.

"Well, that went good." Savannah turned again to face Black Calf's drawn countenance. "You probably could have handled that with a little more tact."

"You do not go with her?"

"You know I can't," Savannah grinned wryly. "Especially when you haven't explained how I'm involved in all of this. So spit it out."

"Very well, Savannah." Black Calf rubbed his tired eyes with the palm of his hands, "I will explain, but I fear you are not going to like what I have to say."

"Try me."

"Very well. You brought him to her and you must stay with her through this and keep her safe." His explanation was enigmatic at best and Savannah felt like throttling him.

"You need to explain better than that, Black Calf, or I'm going to get up and walk out of here too."

"You are free to leave any time, child." Black Calf waved his hand toward the door. "But it would be unwise to do so before you are fully armed with the knowledge that I have."

"Does that mean you'll dispense with all of the dramatics?"

"Of course."

"Then I'll stay."

"First, let me ask you this. Why do you think there is so little information documented about what happened back in eighteen-sixty-nine and eighteen-seventy that pertains to the incidents we discussed?"

"I was wondering that myself, but I'm not going to wonder long because you are going to tell me, aren't you?"

Black Calf nodded. "Many Feathers's spirit roams about unable to channel his anger. He cannot do this because he has no one through whom he can use to channel it. Do you understand so far?"

"Sort of."

"Good. The Pikuni does not speak about Many Feathers, and have not since he was outcast. We know his evil is strong and I believe that if Tyeshia provides an outlet, he will return to wreak havoc on whoever crosses his path. We do not speak of or write about him to prevent Many Feathers from finding a doorway and allowing him access back into our world. Somehow, someone managed to write and release information about the incident. It should never have happened, but with technology today, curtailing the eagerness of a few individuals who are determined to write what they want is hard. Is it becoming clearer now?"

"Getting there."

"Your inquiries into the Army's massacre of Heavy Runner's people at Marias River drew Many Feathers to you. It was his door to reenter our world. He probably tried to use you, but could not. Still through you, he found your friend, Tyeshia. He knew she would be more accepting of his influence than you would. She has a vain soul, but a romantic heart, does she not?"

"I can't say. I know she likes to read romance novels a lot, but I don't know if that would characterize her as a romantic. Although I can see how you would think she would qualify for his attentions whereas I would not."

"You are more levelheaded than your friend is. That is what kept Many Feathers away from you; it is what will keep you both safe on your journey."

"What do you mean 'keep us safe on our journey'? Where exactly are we supposed to be going?"

Black Calf paused before answering, knowing that his response would not be well received. "Your steadiness will keep Tyeshia from doing something foolish; help her remember why she is with Many Feathers, and return her home safely. Without you, she will falter and remain under the spell of Many Feathers' evil influences. Without you—she could very well die."

"Black Calf, you're scaring me." Savannah rubbed her arms vigorously, trying desperately to ward off an invisible chill that had settled over the room. "How can I possibly keep her safe from her own dreams?"

"Not from her dreams, my child," Black Calf said, his tone a menacing whisper, "but from Many Feathers, himself—in the year eighteen-sixty-nine."

# EIGHT

Savannah sat on Black Calf's worn couch long after he retired for the evening.

"Please make sure you lock the door on your way out, Savannah," He murmured at the foot of the stairs as if he had not just lowered a bombshell in her lap.

She stood experimentally after a while, testing the steadiness of her legs then slowly retreated from the ramshackle house. Her mind was still racing. Nevertheless, her legs moved her slowly along as if they'd developed their own will, and that will had decided it best not to run or they would collapse.

When she reached the car, the only thing her mind could think of was retiring to her motel room, taking a hot shower, and sleeping on all that she'd discovered, but it was not to be. The moment she crawled into the car, Tyeshia declared her desire to return to Havre posthaste, having no desire to stay around the reservation a second longer.

"Tyeshia, I know you are upset," Savannah tried to reason, "but the hotel is closer and I'm a little more than tired. There's no reason to make the trek home at this hour and we won't make it back to my parent's house until nearly midnight even if we leave this very second."

Tyeshia met her pleading however, with stone-cold silence, so Savannah acquiesced. Tired as she was, she understood all too well the emotions tumbling around inside her friend. What she learned unnerved her and she had not been the direct recipient of the worst of Black Calf's revelations.

Still, as she sped down the interstate, she wished that Tyeshia would say something to her; anything to break the monotony of the two-lane highway and the darkened landscape. Her eyes started to droop and she reached instinctively for the thermos of coffee, realizing only after she unscrewed the lid that she forgot to refill the container before leaving the reservation. With her coffee mug empty and her friend still sitting silently, staring out of the car toward the horizon, Savannah wished she were more adamant about staying in a hotel. Browning was now out of the question, but perhaps they could find vacancy along the way. If not, she would definitely need to find an all-night truck stop and refill her thermos. Savannah groaned at the reminder that she was out of the delicious, eye-opening brew.

"What are you groaning about? I'm the one with the screwed-up psyche," Tyeshia snapped softly without turning her gaze from the window.

"I'm out of coffee and without it I may not survive the drive back to Havre."

Savannah was joking of course, but her friend did not rise to the bait as she normally would have. "Come on, Ty," Savannah coaxed, "at least tell me that my driving will kill us long before my lack of coffee will. Anything!"

"I shouldn't have come," Tyeshia murmured in a voice so low that Savannah almost missed what she said.

"I think you're wrong," Savannah sighed, forgetting her attempts at levity. Tyeshia just wasn't up to it. She needed reassurance that her life would go on as before, not jokes about coffee fixations. Of course, telling Tyeshia that she was wrong about her decision to come did not help either. She could not see her friend's face in the darkened interior when she turned, and was relieved. Somehow, she knew that if she *could* see Tyeshia's face, her burning gaze would turn her to ashes.

"That was the scariest experience of my life! How could it possibly have been good for me to be here?" Tyeshia's voice was a mere whisper, but the anger behind her words reverberated like thunder in the compact car.

"Think logically for a moment, Ty. If you hadn't come, then you would not have known about Many Feathers."

"Many Feathers is a dead man!" Tyeshia's voice steadily increased in volume. "He died over a hundred fifty years ago! He doesn't exist, and your friend is absolutely insane trying to convince us otherwise!"

"What if Black Calf is genuinely sane?"

"I don't play 'what if' games. Are you telling me you believe in ghosts now, Savannah? You, who are normally so practical?"

"I'm just trying to figure this out. I mean, why Black Calf would go to all the trouble of telling us this just to scare us makes no sense. Why would *you* be so scared if what he said meant so little to you? You could have just brushed him off and gone about your way, but you haven't. You're still mulling over every word, aren't you?"

"Wouldn't you be?"

"Of course," Savannah agreed. "Unless I felt that what he said held no merit."

"So you think that all that boloney is for real?"

"I believe that *he* thinks it's real. You have to remember that some Native Americans take dreams very seriously and you admitting to dreaming about a Native only added fuel to the fire."

"So you're saying that I should have lied?"

"I don't know what I'm saying, Ty," Savannah sighed. "Neither of us was thinking clearly enough to have lied. You know what they say about hindsight being twenty-twenty. Well, I think that's the case now," Savannah explained. "It's easy to sit here and think of what the most logical course of action *would* have been, and explain away all that happened rationally when we're no longer under his sphere of influence."

"So you're saying we should just go back to Virginia and forget all about what happened here today?"

"If we make it that far," Savannah said with a wry grin on her face.

"Just what is *that* supposed to mean?" Tyeshia was still in no mood for her friend's jesting.

"Sorry, Ty, I'm trying to lighten the mood, and I'm also thinking about something that Black Calf said after you left."

"The last thing that will lighten my mood is talking about that loony or about anything that happened in the last few hours."

"Gees, Ty, he really got to you didn't he?"

"Yeah, I guess he did."

"Yeah, well, I have to admit that Black Calf rather shook me up as well, especially..."

"I said I don't want to discuss it further, Savannah, and I'm not joking."

"I know, Ty. It's just that I think you need to know this one last detail, then maybe we can let sleeping ghosts..." Savannah started to explain, then stopped. "I don't recall passing any major cities along this route, do you?"

Tyeshia looked into the distance at the myriad of lights spanning the horizon. The lights looked like thousands upon thousands of male lightning bugs fighting over a single mate. The twinkles of the dim yellow lights seem to go from horizon to horizon, leaving little room for the darkness to penetrate.

As the car topped a ridge and moved into a valley, the lights disappeared, but when they topped the next ridge, the lights were still there.

"Maybe we're closer to Havre than we thought," Tyeshia interjected in the growing silence.

Savannah stole a glance at her odometer, "Not unless they moved the city since we left. We just passed Shelby a short while back and shouldn't be anywhere near another city until we reach Chester. Not that it matters, since I've never seen city lights that twinkle like that or that twinkle that brightly."

"Perhaps there's a fair or something going on that's lit up the sky with unnatural brilliance?" Tyeshia offered helpfully.

"You had to use the word 'unnatural', didn't you?"

"Sorry, but it was the only word that fit, and it's the only reasonable explanation that fits."

"Yeah, but you are forgetting that detail about there not being any cities between Shelby and Chester, and no, I'm certain that there isn't one that I forgot with lights bright enough to rival the stars. Unless they built one while we were at the reservation today."

"Maybe Chester is having a big to-do about something."

"First, the lights are practically smack dab in the middle of the road, Ty, which makes it unlikely that it would be a city. Even if a city did just happen to appear here since my last visit and was hosting a special fair—have you ever seen a fair that lit up the horizon like that before?"

"Well, you don't have to get so snappish about it. I was only trying to figure this thing out. How fast are you going, anyway?" Tyeshia whispered, their brewing argument temporarily forgotten.

Savannah stole another glance at her panel reading the digital speed display aloud, "Seventy-five miles per hour. I have it on speed control, so that hasn't fluctuated since we left the reservation. Why?"

"Take another look at those lights."

"Yeah...holy mother..."

"My words exactly," Tyeshia croaked, "those lights are getting larger and closer by the millimile."

"Millimile couldn't possibly be a real word," Savannah corrected instinctively.

"Like I'd know, but it seems for every fraction of a second we move closer it moves a thousand times closer to us. Maybe you should stop and turn around."

"Why? We can probably drive right through it, don't you think?"

"Those lights are not some mutant firefly swarm that's going to fly right by us without a second glance. I can feel there's something wrong here."

"What are you thinking, Ty?"

"I'm not *thinking* anything, but my gut tells me that those lights aren't what they seem and it would be best to hightail it outta here, so could you please turn this dadblasted car around?"

"I don't think it would matter, Ty."

"Why not?"

"Because I think you are right, and those lights are moving faster than we are," Savannah said, an obvious tremor in her voice, "which means it will overtake us whether we turn around or not. I'd have to drive at the speed of light, literally, to get away from *those* particular lights."

"Heck, no! I ain't buying that. Turn this car around right now, Savannah, and floor it. We're getting the heck out of dodge *now*."

The Ford Mustang's tires squealed loudly in protest as Savannah slammed on the brakes. The car fishtailed across the two lanes and Savannah was thankful for the lack of oncoming traffic. She gained control of the car and completed the U-turn, hitting the accelerator the moment the car straightened.

Tyeshia twisted in her seat, staring out of the rear window, her gaze widening in disbelief. Savannah glanced in the rearview mirror and let out a string of curses.

"Can't this bucket of bolts go any faster?"

"I'm already going over one-hundred-twenty miles per hour now, Ty."

"Oh my God in heaven, we're really not going to outrun it, are we?" Tyeshia moaned, her head flopping onto the headrest. "Why are we slowing?" She snapped her head up and stared at the speedometer...one-hundred-five, one-hundred, ninety-five.

"It's pointless, Ty," Savannah whispered, glancing again in the rearview mirror, "we simply can't outrun whatever it is, and if we keep driving like lunatics we're going to end up dead."

"If we stop then we'll be sitting ducks, and whatever that thing is will kill us anyway."

Savannah pulled to a stop along the grassy knoll of the small highway, laid her head on the steering wheel, and took several calming breaths. "Aren't we overreacting just a little bit?"

Tyeshia looked at the rapidly approaching lights, "No."

"Perhaps it's just what you said—a swarm of mutated fireflies, which would be nothing to get alarmed about. So why not just sit here and let it bypass us? Then we'll turn around and head for Havre," Savannah laughed nervously. "You know, I think we just got worked up over our little conversation with Black Calf and now we're seeing boogie men around every corner."

"No offense, Savannah, but I think your logic circuits are on a lunch break. I mean, really, when have you ever seen anything like this? Yet you just want to sit here and let it overtake us? Which by the way, could be any minute now."

Savannah glanced in the rearview mirror again and her grip tightened on the steering wheel. "I am being logical—unfortunately. You wouldn't happen to be as scared as I am, would you?" Savannah murmured as she watched the lights move closer still. They were close enough now that she could tell that they were not mutant fireflies or car lights or anything she'd ever seen. The lights looked more like billions of stars that had fallen from the sky and were moving along trying to pick up enough speed to slingshot themselves back into the vastness of space.

"I'm so scared I can't even wet myself," Ty whispered. Savannah looked at her friend's face and smiled grimly.

"I can see the lights twinkling off your skin now," she murmured irrationally.

Tyeshia lifted a hand instinctively to her face as if she could discern a difference in her skin. "You, too," she whispered, running a finger down the bridge of Savannah's nose.

"You are my best friend in the whole wide world, Ty. I just want you to know that."

"Think we'll still know each other in the afterlife?" Tyeshia whispered as the car began filling with the brilliance of light.

"I don't think we're heading to the afterlife." Savannah sat looking at the light that began to surround them, a sudden awareness gripping her like a warm embrace. "Actually, I'm certain Heaven isn't going to be a part of this at all. If what Black Calf said is true then..." Savannah wanted to finish, but just then the brilliance of the light flared, washing over them, blinding them with its iridescence.

Tyeshia screamed. She squeezed her eyes tightly closed, but Savannah dared to keep her eyes open. She watched in marvelous wonder the myriad of colors swirling around her. Her doubts fled as Black Calf's words settled over her and realization dawned. She closed her eyes then, gave Tyeshia's hand a reassuring squeeze, and waited for their journey to be over. A journey that was most certain to find them in the year eighteen-sixty-nine.

# NINE

## 1869

"Watch out!" Savannah heard a split second before the stranger slammed her and Tyeshia onto the hard dirt ground. Savannah glanced up in time to see a stagecoach go barreling down the narrow dirt lane, then lowered her weary head again, relieved to be alive. She felt a heavy weight lift from her body and glanced up again to see the silhouette of a man dusting the dirt off his clothing.

"What were you two thinking, walking out in front of a team of horses like that? You could have gotten yourselves killed." The man was yelling at them and attracting a crowd, his hand brushing angrily at his pant legs.

Savannah glanced up again at the silhouette. He stopped attempting to remove the dirt covering his clothes, and was now standing with his hands splayed angrily on his hips.

Savannah raised a hand, shakily, to block the sunlight from her eyes, but could not make out any features. She lowered her aching head and her gaze found Tyeshia laying inert a few feet away. Forgetting her own aches and pains, she scooted along the ground, lifted Tyeshia's head, and gently laid it on her lap.

"Is your maid going to be all right, lady? Should I fetch Doc Mitchell?" Another voice broke through the haze in her mind, and she shook her head with a thankful yes.

"Ty, wake up. You don't know how important it is for you to hear me right now," Savannah whispered and tapped Tyeshia's face lightly. She smiled as Tyeshia emitted a loud moan. Tyeshia's face scrunched up against the insistent patting, and she swatted blindly at the hand. Savannah hugged her friend close, grateful that the trip had not hurt either of them. Of course, if it had not been for the timely intervention of the man standing over them, their arrival might have signaled certain death.

"I never saw someone so happy to see her maid alive," a voice murmured nearby.

"And look at their clothes," an older voice huffed. "Why, it's unseemly."

Savannah did not need to be a rocket scientist to realize that she and Tyeshia had traveled through space and time; otherwise, their clothing would not draw undue attention. She also did not need a master's degree to grasp the inappropriate attire they were wearing for the era they were in. Holy cow! Blue jeans! How was she supposed to explain the fact that she was wearing blue jeans to a bunch of crones and uneducated hicks from the nineteenth century?

Okay, maybe she was being a little harsh on the folks in this town. Perhaps they all attended Harvard. Still, there would be no way of satisfactorily explaining their attire unless she was suddenly possessed of a quick wit and lying tongue. Perhaps Tyeshia should handle this, she thought irrationally, then felt guilty. Yes, Tyeshia could outsmart and outtalk the brightest Professor; nevertheless, that did not mean she was possessed of a deceitful mind and could talk them out of their present situation. Nor could she ask her to try—or could she?

She glanced at her friend and decided she'd better take the lead, especially since Tyeshia looked as if she were about to have a serious nervous breakdown. Savannah listened with half-an-ear to the chatter going on around her. Her mind was busily searching for an explanation as to their sudden appearance and their state of dress. She glanced again at Tyeshia who was also listening to the conversation, her eyes getting wider as she gave herself the once-over.

She looked at Savannah, whispering from the side of her mouth. "What is going on here, and where exactly are we?"

"I'll explain later," Savannah whispered back, "right now just follow my lead—when I have a lead to follow."

"I'm Lieutenant Mitchell, ma'am," the person who'd knocked them out the way of the oncoming horses introduced himself, reaching down to offer Savannah a hand up. It was only then that Savannah could make out the military uniforms that all of the men were wearing. "Mind telling me just what you were doing strolling down the middle of the street? And could you possibly explain where in blue blazes you came from and why you are dressed like boys?" His statement brought attention back to her blue jeans and all gazes darted in that direction. Savannah had never felt so uncomfortable in all her life and she suddenly wished that she'd not tucked her blouse in her pants.

She shot a desperate look in Tyeshia's direction, but Tyeshia merely shrugged her shoulder and gave her an 'I'm trying to melt into the ground' look. Savannah brought her gaze back to the Lieutenant and smiled nervously. When he did not return her smile, she figured she'd just blurt out the whole story and throw herself on the mercy of whatever justice there was in eighteen-sixty-nine. Or maybe not.

She abstractedly brushed at the dust on her clothing, racking her brain for a plausible excuse, when the proverbial lightbulb shined bright in the recesses of her brain. She shot her friend a conspiratorial wink and looked back at the Lieutenant. He was not looking at her any longer however, but at the hands that were still absentmindedly brushing off the rear of her jeans. She blushed disconcertingly when she realized that all gazes had reverted in that direction.

She rolled her eyes in exasperation, *It would appear that men in all centuries have a one-track mind*, she thought then cleared her throat loudly and brought her chin up a notch. The action had its wanted effect as the Lieutenant and the other surrounding soldiers blushed as pink as any virgin on her wedding night.

Savannah felt a small triumph over her situation and cleared her throat again. The idea that had sprung to her mind was a long shot and she would not exactly bet any money on it in Vegas, but it was the only thing she could think of that might see them through this; the only plausible explanation.

"Renegades attacked us," she blurted, and was thankful to hear a few 'oh mys' and 'Lord have mercy's' from the crowd. Even Tyeshia added a 'what?!'. Fortunately, no one heard Tyeshia's outburst, or Savannah would have had to explain her 'maids' memory lapse.

"When did this happen?" One man asked from the back of the crowd.

"A couple of days ago."

"I knew it was only a matter of time..."

"Thank you, Sergeant Harvey," the Lieutenant interrupted.

"Odd that this is the first we're hearing of it? You'd think that if something like that happened, we'd have heard. Word spreads like wild fire on the prairie around these parts," another man spoke up.

"Thank you too, Private James."

"Well, we are the only ones that survived the attack," Savannah countered, and heard the intakes of breath. She suddenly wondered how she was going to prove this lie if someone challenged her further. Instead, she tried to end the story without weaving the web of lies any more intricately.

"We heard a noise when we were down by the river, saw the Indians riding our way," she continued, winging it, "then we hid in some bushes until the attack was over."

"That's plum awful."

"Yes, it is," the Lieutenant agreed. "Still, it doesn't explain how you became dressed as you are and how you ended here at the fort."

"Yes, well, um, we didn't have a choice. I decided that it would be, um...too dangerous to try to traverse across hostile land in women's clothes. I figured it would be easier if we dressed like men. That way if someone spotted us, we, um, wouldn't draw undue attention to ourselves. That's why we decided to dress like this. It may not be the appropriate attire, but could you really see us trekking across miles of hostile territory in hoops and skirts?"

To her ears, by Tyeshia's incredulous look, and by the Lieutenant's arched brow, her story rang false. She waited anxiously for someone to call her a liar and string them both up for whatever reasons they strung people up for back then. She did not know if her tales warranted such drastic measures, but she knew that if she were in their shoes, she'd punch that lame story full of holes and burn them as witches. Okay, maybe nothing as dramatic, but she'd eye them with a lot more suspicion.

"Them there clothes attract a might bit more attention than they should, little ladies," another Sergeant commented appreciatively, his gaze scanning the snug fitting jeans.

"Yeah! Who'd you take 'em from—young boys? They sure are snug-fittin'," another soldier shouted, laughing when he heard snickers from his male companions.

Savannah blushed again, and was ready to tell these crass boars that their behavior was not that of a soldier, but the Lieutenant was already speaking again. "Okay, okay, everybody settle down. I'm sure this lady has been through enough without our adding to it. We need to be thinking about those poor people left behind. If there was an attack, then it's important to find the remains of those poor people; maybe see about getting word to the families so that they can have a proper burial."

Savannah moaned inwardly, realizing that her deception was definitely causing a tangled weave from which she probably could not free herself.

"What's going on here?" The crowd parted and an elderly soldier came through with a matronly woman clinging possessively to his arm.

"Sir!" The Lieutenant snapped to attention, presenting a sharp salute that the elderly soldier returned. This must be the commander of the fort, Savannah thought. "A wagon went by, sir, nearly running down the lady and her maid."

"At ease, Soldier," the commanding officer said simply.

"Sir, yes sir!" The Lieutenant snapped. His stance spread apart slightly and he clasped his hands tightly behind his back. Savannah glanced quickly around her and noticed that the other soldiers were standing similarly.

"I'm Colonel Baker. In charge of the garrison, here. Are you all right, my dear?" The Colonel spoke with a gentleness that surprised Savannah.

"Yes, sir," Savannah answered automatically.

"I'm glad for it. I'm sorry to hear about what happened to you, though you appeared to have escaped unscathed. Mind telling me what you and your maid were doing in the middle of the street and where it is that you came from exactly?"

When Savannah did not answer right away, the Lieutenant stepped forward and spoke for her. "Sir, the lady only just arrived. It would seem renegades attacked the party she was traveling with, sir."

"Tarnation!" The Colonel muttered. Savannah noticed the slight squeeze that the Colonel's wife applied to his arm. He shot a glance at Savannah, flushing slightly. "My apologies for the language, my dear. We just haven't had any difficulties with the native people lately, and I'm almost certain that we'd have had some indication of discord before an attack. Have you heard anything at all, Lieutenant?"

"Nothing, sir. We were quite shocked to hear of the lady's plight as well, sir."

"Yes, well. Even so, we'll have to look into this and see to the dead."

"Already taken care of, sir," the Lieutenant responded. "I've ordered that men go out and search for the remains. All we need now is an approximate location from the lady, sir."

All eyes turned toward Savannah, including Tyeshia's. Tyeshia had been sitting quietly watching with ever-growing dread while they lost themselves further and further in the labyrinth of lies that Savannah had been spinning. She stood shakily and moved closer to Savannah, wondering just how her friend was going to get the two of them out of this mess. Fortunately, just then, it appeared that she was the invisible woman.

"I'm not sure I can help too much with that, sir. My sense of direction isn't great. It's just pure luck that we stumbled around, until we came to the fort or we may have been wandering about aimlessly for quite a long time."

"I see," the Colonel muttered. "Well, what about your maid? Think she might remember anything that might be of assistance?" Savannah's swung her gaze toward Tyeshia's, which was increasing by the second. Her head began moving rapidly from side-to-side, which everyone interpreted as her not knowing anything, but Savannah knew she was really telling her, 'Don't you be dragging me any further into the middle of this nightmare'.

"Well, that does present a quandary," The Colonel said, his brows knitted in concentration as he thought about what to do. "Well, Lieutenant, simply do the best you can do."

"Yes, sir. Will do, sir." The Lieutenant snapped to attention again, presented a sharp salute, and then turned to issue orders to a nearby Sergeant.

The Colonel's gaze was still focused on Savannah however, making her a little more than uneasy. "Is there anyone that we can notify as to your well-being, my dear?"

"I have no family left, sir," Savannah whispered, and for the first time since arriving in this period, spoke the truth.

"Colonel," the woman by his side spoke for the first time, "I really need to take the young lady and see her suitably clothed, and I'm more than sure that she could use some rest."

"What? Oh!" The Colonel started as if only realizing his wife was still standing next to him. "You're right, of course, my dear. Just another question and then I'll leave her to you." His gaze swung back to Savannah and narrowed slightly, causing a shiver to run down her spine. "I just need to know exactly *how* you managed to get past the soldier at the gate."

Savannah's gaze swung to the front of the fort down at the end of the street and sighed with relief when she saw the gates wide open. It would have been extremely awkward had they been closed and she'd been forced to improvise *that* particular detail. What would she say—that they could scale extremely high, non-scalable walls with no effort? Of course, if she said that they simply strolled through the gate, then she was more than certain that the soldier responsible for sentry duty at that post would be in a heck of a lot of trouble. She felt bad for the person, but what other way could her explanation of their sudden appearance be acceptable?

"The soldier at the front was looking intently at something in the opposite direction when we walked up, so we thought that coming in would be okay. After all, we're not exactly dangerous," Savannah laughed nervously.

"Very well, my dear," the Colonel sighed, casting a quick glance at the gate. "You go with my wife and she'll see to your comfort, and I don't want you to worry about a thing, now. You're safe here at the fort and I'll see to it that you're taken care of."

"Yes, sir," Savannah repeated, too nervous to say much more.

The Colonel's wife placed a protective arm around Savannah's shoulder and maneuvered her through the reluctantly dispersing crowd.

"I'm Mrs. Colonel Baker," the woman declared by way of introduction. "My husband is in charge here," she announced, obvious pride in her voice.

"So I gathered," Savannah muttered under her breath.

"What was that, my dear?"

"Nothing. I was just saying a quick prayer of thanks that we got through that ordeal okay."

"It had to have been awful," the Mrs. Colonel murmured, "watching your family killed like that."

It took Savannah a second to realize that they were not talking about the same thing. Especially since the only real ordeal she and Tyeshia had suffered through was the inquisition that had just taken place. Of course, as far as the Mrs. Colonel was concerned, the fictitious attack by the renegades was a far more disturbing occurrence. "Fortunately, Tyeshia and I hid well, so we did not see anything happen," Savannah lied gracefully and winced.

*I had better learn to be a very quiet, demure female in this time or I'm going to say something to trip up my own lies. Then Tyeshia and I will be in a world of hurt,* she thought, and then became suddenly aware of the fact that Tyeshia was not with them. Savannah glanced over her shoulder anxiously, but did not see any signs of her friend.

She stopped walking and turned completely around. She looked up and down the street, trying to see over all the bodies walking back and forth. Nevertheless, no tall dark-haired, dark-skinned females stood out, which she was certain Tyeshia would have. "Where is Tyeshia, by the way?"

"Who? Oh, you must mean your maid. The other women have taken her to see my laundress, Mirabel," she said solicitously, continuing to tug insistently on Savannah's arm; all too eager to get her in doors in all haste. "She is a sight bit shorter and plumper than your maid, but I'm sure they'll come up with something a bit more suitable than the men's attire she was wearing. Now, don't you go and worry about a thing," the Mrs. Colonel said, noticing Savannah's continued distraction, "she'll be well tended to, I assure you."

"Ma'am, Tyeshia isn't my maid, she's my friend. We were attending college together back east. When I decided to make a trip out here, I invited Tyeshia to come along." A look of astonishment came over the woman's features and then she smiled slightly.

"Well, I guess since the war, things are a might bit different in the east; more so than they used to be, obviously. People apparently are less discriminating about whom they select as their friends. Still, while you're here, you'll need to choose your friends with a little more care."

"Tyeshia is a smart, educated, funny..."

"Negro," the Mrs. Colonel finished callously. "Now I know you've been through a harrowing experience, but you have an appearance to maintain. If not for yourself, then for me and the Colonel. We're responsible for your well-being now, child, and we can't allow you to embarrass us with inappropriate acquaintances."

Savannah wanted to berate the woman's narrow mindedness, but until she had a bath and managed to get a clean set of clothes, she was not about to alienate the only person within miles willing to help her. She was also the only person within perhaps a hundred miles that could make her stay in this century pleasant or a chapter straight out of Dante's *Inferno*.[2]

---

2 Inferno – "hell" in Italian – is Chapter one of three in the work, "Divine Comedy", by 14th-Century poet Dante Alighieri. Chapters two and three are entitled *Purgatorio* and *Paradiso, respectively.*

# TEN

**Present Day**

"Mr. and Mrs. Warren?" A voice asked quietly from behind the couple who were standing solemnly beside their daughter's gravesite. Thomas and Abigail Warren turned slowly to face the man that addressed them. "My name is Tyrez Morgan, and this is my wife, Patrice," the tall, black man continued quietly, but Thomas and Abigail kept staring numbly at the couple, uncommunicative in their grief.

"Our baby girl, Tyeshia, was with your daughter, Savannah, on her trip, when their car crashed."

Understanding dawned in Thomas Warren's eyes, followed quickly by apologetic sympathy. "How is your daughter, Mr. Morgan?" He asked in a quiet whisper.

"In a coma," Tyrez replied, the pain in his voice sharply evident. "The doctors give her a sixty percent chance of recovery. Good odds, especially since our Ty is a fighter. If anybody can pull out of this trauma, our baby girl can."

Thomas Warren nodded, understanding, but could not force any words past the lump that had reformed in his throat. He was happy for them but could not help selfishly wishing that it were Savannah lying in a hospital bed—not the other way around.

"We wanted to stop by on our way to the hospital to...well, to say just how sorry we are for your loss. I know how Tyeshia will sorely miss her," Tyrez said. "We also wanted you to know that we don't blame Savannah for what happened. Not one bit."

"Thank you." Abigail fought back renewed tears. "Maybe we can stop by the hospital in a couple of days to check on Tyeshia, if that's okay."

"I'm sure that would be just fine," Tyrez said.

Patrice placed a comforting hand on Abigail's shoulder.

"Well, we best be getting on," Tyrez murmured solemnly. "We want to be there, just in case..."

"Thank you again for coming to the funeral. I'm sure Savannah would have been pleased..." Abigail began, but could not finish. She put her hand to her mouth to try to prevent the agonizing sob that threatened to escape, but did not succeed. She turned into her husband's arms, and quickly forgot the couple beside them.

"Maybe in a couple of days we'll stop by," Thomas murmured, then turned his wife toward their car.

"You didn't tell them," Patrice said and watched the retreating couple sadly.

"I guess I figured this wasn't the time, or the place," Tyrez replied quietly, also watching the couple leave. "A funeral is hardly the place to tell a person that their daughter should have walked away from the crash."

"I don't think any time is going to be appropriate to tell a mother and father that there is no way their daughter could have died in that accident. Nor should Tyeshia be comatose," Patrice continued, agitated.

"They'll find out soon enough through the proper authorities," Tyrez said, hoping that he would not have to be the bearer of that bad news.

"Would you want to find out through the proper authorities, or would you prefer to hear it from someone who understands the loss?" His wife berated, knowing her husband well enough to know the answer.

"We need to get back to the hospital." Tyrez tried to close the subject, but his wife would not budge.

"Listen, darling." She put a gently restraining hand on his bulging biceps. "You were fortunate to have a friend at the department fill you in on the investigation. Don't deny them the right to know. It just wouldn't be right."

"All right, Pat. They'll be at the hospital in a couple of days. I'll tell them then. That'll give me time to get all the facts from my friend at the department, and maybe give me a chance to find some answers of my own." He took his wife by the elbow and steered her toward their own vehicle.

# ELEVEN

**1869**

Savannah awoke to an insistent shaking on her shoulder. She moaned and cleared the last vestiges of sleep from her mind, then slowly opened her eyes.

"You don't usually wake up with this much difficulty." Tyeshia plopped down on the bed beside Savannah.

"I think they may have given me a sleeping powder or something," Savannah murmured through the cottony feeling lining her mouth. She smacked her tongue along the roof of her mouth and frowned. Her tongue felt heavier than her eyelids. She spotted a water pitcher on the nightstand and eagerly reached for it, pouring half the contents down her throat without bothering with the porcelain cup sitting next to it.

When Savannah quenched her thirst and washed the cottony sensation away, she struggled to sit, fluffing the down pillows behind her back for comfort.

"Are you finished?" Tyeshia said sarcastically.

"Quite. And how are you today?" Savannah ignored her friend's tone.

"Look at my appearance, then ask me again how I'm doing."

Savannah took in her friend's appearance and tried hard not to giggle. Not that Tyeshia looked very bad, but compared to her usual mode of dress...well, she could very well understand her friend's distress.

"You don't look too bad, Ty," she reassured her.

"I'm wearing a dress that looks like it belongs to someone from Little House on The Prairie. My hair looks like someone combed it through with a porcupine. I don't have a spot of makeup on my blotchy face. I've just awakened and realized that we were, without a doubt, hurled back in time somehow—which, by the way, I want a serious explanation for—and you say I don't look all that bad!"

"Truly, you don't, Ty," Savannah said sincerely. "In fact, you have a natural beauty that you should flaunt more often."

"There's no such thing as natural beauty."

"Well, if it will make you feel better your skin is not blotchy at all, and I think you look lovely in your Laura Ingles dress."

"Who?"

"Little House on the Prairie?"

"Oh! Well, now that I've gotten that off my chest. Start talking!"

"Well, it would appear that something has hurled us back in time."

"Something...what did you do, take a duh pill with that water you just drank? I already figured that part out, or don't you remember? What I want to know is how and why, not where?"

"Well, I tried to explain the rest of my conversation with Black Calf in the car last night, remember? However, as I distinctly recall, someone didn't want to hear it!"

"Savannah," Tyeshia breathed heavily, "I've just discovered that I'm no longer in Kansas and Toto isn't even here to keep me company, so I don't need to hear 'I tried to warn you' speeches."

"Well, *Dorothy*, stop snapping at me and sit. It's not exactly my fault that we're in this predicament."

"That's debatable!"

"What's *that* supposed to mean!"

"Well, if you hadn't dragged me to Montana with you then we'd be enjoying the comforts of air conditioning at the local mall right about now! At least I would," Tyeshia accused, sulking.

"First, I hardly handcuffed and shackled you on the trip out here! Second," Savannah continued, ticking off points on her fingertips, "how was I supposed to know that you were the missing piece to Black Calf's dreams. Third, I didn't know that he was serious when he told me we'd be making a trip *way* out of town; therefore, I could not possibly have known we'd end up here. Lastly, what makes you think that it wouldn't have happened eventually anyway. At least Black Calf's insight gives us a reason as to the why we are here. Therefore, why don't you take a chill pill so that we can think this through rationally. Knowing why we're here gives us a slight advantage, so let's stop whining and do something about it."

"What knowledge did old Mr. Loony impart, and what do you propose we do about getting home?" Tyeshia asked, her voice calm for the first time since entering the room.

Savannah breathed in and out for a few minutes, trying to calm her racing pulse.

"You're going to hyperventilate if you keep that up," Ty said automatically.

Savannah smiled and scooted next to her friend. "It's going to be okay. I know it is."

"Did Black Calf tell you that?"

"In a way, yes."

"I guess you had better tell me what he said so I'm not left out of the loop."

"Well, you are going to need to get in close with Many Feathers and wake him up when Clark comes to kill him. Supposedly, that will end his haunting days and protect your psyche in our time."

"After I wake him up and he dies we can probably get back home?"

"So the story goes."

"Still, isn't he supposed to be extremely dangerous?"

"Yeah."

"Yuck."

"I could not have said it better myself. I'll tell you this much though, if anybody can catch Many Feathers's gaze and hold it long enough to finish this, it'll be you, Ms. Thang."

"Yeah, maybe back in my century, but looking like I do now..."

"You're still drop-dead gorgeous."

"And you're being polite."

"There isn't anybody in this time going to be able to hold a candle to you. Most women lost most of their teeth by the time they're our age, so you have a distinct advantage already—all your teeth are in place and sparkling white."

Tyeshia giggled. "We might not want to be smiling too much then. It might make people suspicious."

"Or make them demand the name of our dentist," Savannah joked. She threw the blankets back and climbed reluctantly from the warm bed.

"Savannah, if it's my psyche that's in danger and I'm the one that has to wake up Many Feathers, why exactly is it that you have to be here with me?"

Savannah knew the answer to that question, but was not about to give Tyeshia the answer. The last thing she needed was for Tyeshia to go off again, this time about her inability to fend for herself. "Maybe there wasn't any choice since I was with you on this trip."

"Man that stinks. I'm sorry I drug you into this mess."

Savannah sat back down on the bed beside Tyeshia and wrapped an arm around her shoulder. "I wouldn't have it any other way. Imagine, getting to see history firsthand. It's like a dream come true."

"It would be."

"Well, since we cannot do anything but see this thing through," Savannah stood again and moved toward her armoire, "I guess we need to decide our next course of action."

"How about allowing me to kill the Mrs. Colonel?"

# TWELVE

"What did you just say?" Savannah was so shocked to hear such scorn dripping from the serious sounding request that she had to sit back down for a minute and regroup.

"Is that what you're wearing?" Tyeshia asked looking at the dress clutched in Savannah's hand.

"Don't dodge the question, Ty. Why do you want to kill the Mrs. Colonel?"

"Well on my way upstairs, the Colonel's wife told me to let you know that she will serve brunch soon."

"Oh, that's great! I'm famished. Still, why would you want to kill her over that?"

"Well, when the Mrs. Colonel finally permitted me to come inside—through the rear entrance I might add—she told me to come upstairs and help you prepare for the day. Said to tell you that brunch would be ready in half hour's time."

Savannah blushed at the implication of Tyeshia's words. The Mrs. Colonel assumed that Tyeshia was Savannah's maid despite Savannah's protests to the contrary yesterday. Her blush heightened when she noticed Tyeshia's scowl deepen.

"If you think that I'm going to help you primp your hair, you've got another thing coming."

"Ty, you know I would never demean you in any way so please don't take the Mrs. Colonel's prejudices and put them on my shoulders, okay?"

"I'm sorry. It's just hard, finding yourself in a time where equality no longer exists."

"In reality, it doesn't for either of us. Men treated women like furnishings back then."

"Then it's a double whammy for me. I'm a woman *and* I'm black."

"I'm sorry, Ty." Savannah worked her hair into a knot onto the top of her head, trying to mimic the style she'd seen the other women wearing. "If I could turn back the clock and prevent all of this from happening again, I would."

"Then I'd have my psyche taken over by a lunatic," Tyeshia rejoined angrily. "Great choice. Have control of my mind taken over by a lunatic in my time or be transported in time to a world full of lunatics but stay in control of my mind."

"Well, just try to remember that we're here to stop that maniac from messing around with your psyche in the future." Savannah stared at the corset that the maid laid out on a nearby chair and looked at Tyeshia in wonder.

"Are you wearing a corset?"

"You must be joking! I wouldn't wear that contraption. At least not when I have a good old-fashioned brazier in perfect working condition, thank you very much."

"I thought not. I'm not going to attempt to wear that thing either. Not when you think how uncomfortable it has to be. Can you imagine wearing that thing from sunup to sundown and having your innards squished regularly?"

"Like I said, I'm not an idiot."

"I just hope the dress will fit without it." Savannah glanced down at the powder blue day dress that Mrs. Colonel found for her to wear. "Well, here goes." She stood and shimmied into it.

"Why wouldn't it fit? You're petite, at best. Tall, but skinny."

"Well, most of the dress designers then had a corset in mind. Since they designed the corset to make the waist tinier, they designed the dresses with smaller waists. Anyway, I just hope I can fit into this thing without having to wear that blasted contraption."

"I managed."

"Yes, I know. I also know that the Mrs. Colonel's housekeeper is a sight bit chunkier and shorter...hey, how come your dress fits so well? I thought the Mrs. Colonel's laundress was smaller and fatter than you?"

"She is, but her sister was not."

"Figures you'd find a way to look sexy. I bet all that whining about your appearance was just for show."

"Smart-butt."

"Look who's talking," Savannah groaned as she twisted her arms around her back trying desperately to button the dress up. Finally, she threw up her hands in frustration and plopped on the bed. "Would it be too much trouble for you to give a hand, Ty?"

"I haven't heard you ask nicely."

"Would you *please* help button my dress?"

"Well, since you asked so nicely."

"I thought that women had helpers back then to help with things like this," Savannah said wonderingly.

"They do."

"Oh, really! How do you know?"

"Remember what I said? The Mrs. Colonel told me to haul butt upstairs and help you get ready for the day—dress, and all that nonsense.

Apparently, white women didn't know how to fix hair and button clothes."

"Oh, right, well remember what I said. I'm not the Mrs. Colonel, so don't take your anger out on me. As for helping women dress—why do you think clothes manufacturers started making buttons on the front of the clothes?"

"Because we black women finally got tired of seeing you white girls half-naked?"

"Funny, Ty."

"Yeah, I'm laughing so hard my sides are about to split wide open."

"You really do need to take a chill pill or your mouth is going to get us in a lot of trouble."

"Sorry."

"It's okay. At least I understand where the anger stems from."

"Hey, Savannah? Why do you keep calling that hag downstairs Mrs. Colonel? That's not her name, is it? Take a deeper breath will you, or you may have to wear the corset," Tyeshia said, tightening the fabric so that she could put the button in the eyelet.

Savannah took a deeper breath and prayed that Tyeshia could get the dress buttoned. Then she added a quick prayer after that the buttons would not pop free if the dress were too tight. "Women didn't really go by their names back then."

"Would you quit talking as if 'back then' is still 'back then'? If it hasn't registered in that brain of yours yet, 'back then' is 'now'!"

"Sorry, I can't quite get over the fact that we're actually here—and alive and well to boot."

"So, what about the Mrs. Colonel?"

"As far as I can remember, women lost their identity when they married back...I mean, these days."

"Lost their identity?"

"Uh huh. It was prevalent in the military, but not uncommon throughout."

"What do you mean by 'lost their identity'?"

"When a woman married, it's like everyone suddenly forgot that she actually had a name, especially in public; and sometimes in their own home. Remember the movie *Gone with the Wind*?"

"Of course."

"Remember Scarlett's father kept referring to her mother as Mrs. O'Hara?"

"Right."

"Well, in the military it's the same thing, only different. Here, they refer to the wife by the husband's military title. Like, Mrs. Colonel or Mrs. Major.

It helps the women know who's more senior in rank to the other women."

"That's silly."

"Maybe so, but it's the way it is here."

"Weird."

"Yeah, I know."

"Well, if the Mrs. Colonel keeps treating me like she's treating me, I may end up having to feed her my fist, that fat witch."

"How about instead, you hold on to your fist, keep a tight rein on your temper, and I'll handle the Mrs. Colonel?"

"Sounds like a plan. Speaking of plans, where do we go from here?"

"Something tells me that the answers will come to us, Ty."

"Well, isn't that insightful."

Savannah sighed heavily, then turned and faced her friend. "How do I look? Passable?"

"Better than you looked back home. I think this century agrees with you."

Savannah turned to look at herself in the full-length mirror standing against the wall and her breath caught in her throat. Tyeshia was right. This century did suit her. There was a natural blush to her cheeks and the dress brought out her slender form, accentuating her feminine curves without making her feel cheap and exploitative. She felt truly lovely. Fortunately, the dress was not as snug as she'd feared it would be.

"I guess it does at that."

"Well, let's get ourselves down to eat before they send out the hounds." Tyeshia pulled her friend away from her embarrassing perusal of herself. "Then we'll blow this joint and see about finding a way back to our own time."

# THIRTEEN

"Would you mind slowing a bit, Ty?" Savannah whispered, trying hard not to draw attention. "At least try to consider that this is *not* my fault?"

Tyeshia came to a sudden halt and Savannah had to pull back suddenly to keep from crashing into her friend's rigid back. Tyeshia turned around and Savannah felt truly sorry for her. Tears mingled with anger in the big brown orbs looking at her, and Savannah could see her jaw clenched tightly in the rigid lines of her beautiful face. She was angry, but mostly she was hurting.

"I told you to try to remember that the Mrs. Colonel's prejudices are not mine, but you seem determined to take your anger out on me."

Tyeshia's shoulders slumped and she unclenched the fists closed tightly by her side since leaving the Colonel's house. Tears streamed slowly and silently down her high cheekbones and she hastily wiped them away.

"It's not fair, Savannah. The Mrs. Colonel humiliated me. No one has ever humiliated me like that before and me unable to retaliate."

"I didn't realize how hard coming here would be—as if I really had a choice in the matter. Still..."

"It's not your fault, and it's not my fault. It's not anyone's fault, but it still hurts like heck," Tyeshia hissed through clinched teeth. "How dare she order me out of her dining room and make me go eat in the kitchen like a common servant?"

"She doesn't see you as anything but a freed slave and to her we should treat you like a hired hand—nothing more. I know it hurts, Ty, but it's the law of the land, and it's something you're going to have to adjust to fast if we're going to survive here."

"I didn't blow up and tell that witch what she could go do with herself, did I?"

Savannah grinned, "No, you didn't, and I'm very proud of you for that, although I felt like cussing the old biddy out myself."

"Then I'd say I'm adjusting just fine, thank you very much," Tyeshia spat, then turned to start walking again, only much slower this time. "Of course, if this had happened back home I'd have flattened her."

"I have no doubt." Savannah fell into step beside her friend. "But, truly, Ty, you can't draw undue attention to yourself like you did back home."

"I don't do it intentionally," Tyeshia grinned mischievously, "it's my compelling personality, remember? Attention just seems to find me."

"Well, we really need to avoid as much attention as we can, so let's find a place to talk privately." Savannah turned a corner into an alley.

"Where exactly are we going anyway?" Tyeshia asked, as if suddenly aware that they were outside and walking the boardwalks of what should be an ancient fort.

"To see if there is a place to sit behind one of these buildings," Savannah said. She reached the end of the alleyway and looked both ways searching for somewhere they could sit other than the ground. "Over there," she said, after spotting some wooden crates. She made her way over and lowered herself onto one of them, sighing when it did not collapse beneath her weight. When she'd relaxed all her muscles, she sighed again and pulled her foot up, yanked off the ill-fitting slipper the Mrs. Colonel gave her to wear, and rubbed her toes. "It didn't dawn on me when I met the Mrs. Colonel yesterday, but I think she's *the* Colonel Baker's wife." She commented, while her fingers massaged the feeling back into her toes.

"Who?"

"*The* Colonel Baker that leads an army of men against Heavy Runner's people and massacres all those women, children, and elderly at Marias River this coming January."

"Oh, *that* Colonel Baker. Wow."

"The same."

"Dear Lord Almighty."

"You know what's strange, though?"

"What's that?"

"I didn't get the impression that he was a drunkard who would attack people needlessly," Savannah observed. "He seemed like a quiet-spoken man who took his position as head of this fort seriously, but wouldn't murder helpless people without provocation—no matter the color of their skin."

"Looks can be deceiving, Savannah," Tyeshia offered. "Perhaps he's more than he seems. Or maybe he was simply following orders that he didn't like so he drowned his discontent in a bottle of Scotch whiskey, which in turn, impaired his judgment."

"Perhaps. Or maybe there's more to this story than meets the eye."

"How so?"

"What if the attack on Heavy Runner's people was more than just retribution for killing Clark? What if it became somehow personal to the Colonel as well?"

"That's a possibility, I suppose," Tyeshia agreed, "but our purpose here isn't concern about Heavy Runner's people. Selfishly, it's about me and my psyche—which, may I remind you, is under threat from a nutcase from this time."

"True, Ty, but no matter how much we'd like to separate the two, we can't."

"I don't know about that. Say instead of allowing Clark to kill Many Feathers, we prevent it. Then the Pikuni won't seek retribution for Many Feathers' death, which in turn could prevent the massacre from occurring this coming January. That means that Many Feathers could live to a ripe old age, die normally, and not have a need to haunt my psyche in the future."

"So you think that changing the past can alter the future."

"Well isn't that what we're counting on to begin with, in a way?" Tyeshia continued. "After all, if I wake Many Feathers from his sleep so that he can fight Clark honorably, then that's supposed to prevent his ghost from coming after me a hundred years from now, right? Preventing Clark from killing Many Feathers at all would accomplish the same."

"Since I don't think Clark is going to give up until Many Feathers is dead then trying to talk Clark into letting Many Feathers live isn't going to be much in the way of an alternative. This leads us back to the fact that you're going to have to wake him up and allow Clark to kill him. Back to square one—Marias River Massacre is not preventable in that case."

"Well, we shouldn't give up the alternative of trying to talk Clark out of seeking his vengeance," Tyeshia countered again. "After all, if we can help all those people and prevent their death, then we should do it."

"We'll keep reasoning with Clark as an alternative then. I guess the only thing we need to think of now is how to go about getting you hooked up with Many Feathers. Then we need to decide how to keep you safe while you're in his company," Savannah said, lowering her foot back to the ground.

"I'm not really looking forward to that particular role."

"Well, we've come up with an alternate plan regarding Clark, so is anything popping into your head on how to stay away from Many Feathers and accomplish our goal simultaneously?"

"Not a clue."

"Well, let's just take this one day at a time and maybe the answers will come to us," Savannah explained.

"We may just have to concede that some things can't change."

"True, but one thing needs to change." Savannah pulled her other slipper off and propped the bare foot on her thigh, rubbing the life vigorously back into the numb appendage. "I need bigger slippers and you need to lower your profile."

"Lower my profile?"

"That's right, Ty." Savannah knew that what she was about to say would hurt her friend, but there was no way around it. She had to say it. "Like it or not, Tyeshia, we're in an era and a place where black people were second to whites. Just because we don't hold to the beliefs as they are now, we can't keep drawing attention to ourselves as we did this morning when you stormed out of the Mrs. Colonel's house." Savannah raised her hand to stop Tyeshia when it looked like she was about to interrupt. "I know that you were too upset to notice the stares you were causing, but I wasn't..."

"I don't give a fat rat what these narrow-minded bigots think!"

"I know, Tyeshia, but that's not the point here."

"What is the point?" Tyeshia continued to rant. "That I'm supposed to walk around with my eyes lowered and say 'yes, sir' and 'yes, ma'am' to every person around me. That I'm supposed to pretend to be your hireling instead of your equal..."

"If we're going to get through this then you may have to do just that, and keep your voice down!" Savannah tried to keep a tight rein on her own temper.

"The hell I will! If you think that I'm going to cow-tow to you or anyone else then you've got another thing coming. Martin Luther King, Jr…"

"…did not exist in this period, Ty. Don't you get it?" Savannah yelled back, forgetting her own vow to avoid attention. "We are not back home anymore. We are in the year eighteen-sixty-nine. They just abolished slavery fifteen or twenty years ago. They won't give blacks the same rights as whites for another hundred years. Dadblasted, and then some, Ty! If you don't start attempting to blend in here then we may very well end up in a nastier situation than we already are. Can't you see that?" Savannah pulled her slippers back on, stood up, and then promptly knelt down in front of Tyeshia's stiff form. "I know this is hard, Ty. Truly I do."

"You have no idea because you aren't black." Tyeshia fought back the tears that threatened to start again and refused to look at Savannah's kneeling form.

"You're right, I'm not," Savannah conceded softly, "but I am your friend, and as such I have a responsibility to see you safe. That way we can get back to the time that we belong in and you can go back to being the belle of the ball that you always are."

"Yeah, I am that, ain't I?" Tyeshia wiped a sleeve across her eyes and sniffled indelicately.

"Always." Savannah was thankful that the storm had temporarily passed. "Just a short while, Ty, and you'll be back to attending those wretched parties..."

"Wretched?" Ty screeched in mock indignity. "I'll have you know that nearly every person on college grounds attends those parties."

"Yeah. I'm the only one that doesn't care to, it would appear," Savannah teased.

"Yeah, well you're just plain weird," Tyeshia grinned. "And, yes, I'm okay now."

"Glad to hear it," Savannah sighed again and stood again. "Now if I can just find a decent pair of slippers."

"Why don't we switch?" Tyeshia offered. "My feet are smaller than yours are and the slippers that I have on are excessively big for me."

"Worth a shot." Savannah sat back down on the crate and switched slippers. "Think anyone will notice?" She said skeptically, eyeing the worn threadbare slippers that now adorned her feet with the practically brand-new satin slippers that she'd given Tyeshia.

Tyeshia grinned. "Probably," she admitted, "but you have to admit those fit your monster feet better than they did mine, and vice-versa. You know, for someone shorter than me, it's weird that your feet would be so much bigger than mine."

"It's always amazed me that your size seven feet could hold up your huge frame," Savannah said.

"Hey, hey—tall, not huge," Ty corrected, "and stop worrying so much. You really are a worrywart." Tyeshia waved a hand of dismissal and stood. "Look at how far this gown scrapes the ground. Can you see my feet under here?"

"No," Savannah admitted, "but isn't Mirabel's sister going to miss her gown eventually and want it back? Not to mention the owner of this gown that I'm wearing. We really need to figure out how to get some clothes of our own."

"Well, the owner of this gown won't miss it. She used to live here too until she died of some kind of sickness last year," Tyeshia explained. "Mirabel said that I reminded her of Marguerite so I could have her clothes. They're a little loose, but not too bad a fit."

"That was sweet of her, but somewhat sad about her sister."

"Yeah, it was and is," Tyeshia agreed. "It helped that I speak Spanish though."

"Yeah, it would."

"So, again, where do we go from here?" Tyeshia asked, settling back onto the crate. "I mean, how do we start looking for Many Feathers, and don't give me that mysterious crap about him finding us."

"Well, it may very well happen just like that."

"How do you figure?"

"Look where we are now," Savannah answered, waving her hands at their surroundings.

"In the back of some building, inside a fort," Tyeshia replied sarcastically.

"Colonel Baker's fort, smarty, so if that's the case, we may be close to Malcolm Clark and your Native American."

"He's not *my* Native American."

"Lighten up, Ty. I know that."

"Sorry. I'm under a lot of stress right now."

"With good reason, but you really have to try to relax. It will help your adjustment to this era go more smoothly."

"So what are you suggesting? That we simply wander around here until Many Feathers comes to us? If you haven't noticed, we're in the middle of a military fort. What Indian in his right mind...oh, yeah—Many Feathers supposedly isn't in his right mind."

Savannah laughed shortly then creased her brow in thought again, "I don't know what to do. I guess I'm just kind of hoping something will give us a clue about what we're looking for or...I don't know—something."

"Good detective work that would be, Sherlock."

"Well, if you have something better in mind, I'm all ears," Savannah snapped.

"Yeah, food." Tyeshia laughed at the incredulous look that crossed Savannah's features. Savannah's stomach chose that moment to growl loudly causing both girls to laugh.

"That means going back to the Mrs. Colonel's house. You okay with that?" Savannah asked, concerned for her friend's feelings.

"Yeah, I'm okay," Ty shrugged. "Ain't too much I can do about it anyway, is there? Therefore, I might as well make the best of it until I can get the heck out of Dodge. At least I get to eat in the kitchen with some decent folks. You have to deal with all the insufferable bigots."

"Makes you wonder who has the better bargain after all." Savannah stood abruptly and then sighed. "Oh, these slippers are much better."

"Yeah, these are too." Tyeshia stood, wriggling her toes. "However, my belly is the main concern right now, so let's go eat."

"Too bad there's not a Burger King around the corner."

# FOURTEEN

They made their way back down the alley, giggling, but as they drew closer to the main street Tyeshia drew back a little, moving to stand behind and just slightly to the rear of her friend. Savannah stopped walking and turned around. "Why are you slowing?" She asked quizzically.

"I'm not," Tyeshia explained. "Just trying to remember my place." If Savannah had not seen the grin that split Tyeshia's full lips and the gleam of mischief in her eyes, Ty's words would have upset her, but instead she realized that Tyeshia was doing her best to fit in, just as she had suggested. Still it hurt her heart to see her friend, normally so proud, reduced to demeaning behavior.

"Ty..." she started to object, but Tyeshia raised a hand to silence her.

"Go on, Savannah," Tyeshia said, turning Savannah at the elbow to face the other way. "I'll just pretend we're playing a scene from *Gone with the Wind* in some school play. Think I could pass for Butterfly McQueen's character?"

"Sure, right." Savannah had to giggle as a picture of Tyeshia playing Sissy flitted through her mind. At least Tyeshia was trying to make an effort, so she would too. She turned and headed back up the alley, her nose stuck way up in the air.

"Better get that nose down a bit," Tyeshia whispered behind her, "or a bird might mistake it for a nesting ground."

Savannah giggled again, but kept her nose elevated. "Just trying to blend in."

"You're doing a splendid job," Tyeshia laughed softly. "I can't tell you apart from any of the other uppity...hey, what's up? Why did you stop?"

When they stepped from the mouth of the alley, a strange feeling settled over Savannah. Something inexplicably drew her attention to the end of the boardwalk. A good distance away, she watched a pair of sentries pulling mightily on the gates of the fort. With agonizing slowness, the gates opened and a group of scantily clad natives rode proudly in.

When Savannah did not immediately respond to Tyeshia's question, Tyeshia moved beside her, temporarily setting aside the playacting. "What is it, Savannah?"

Savannah did not answer. She merely placed her fingers lightly on Tyeshia's jawbone and gently turned her to face the direction in which she herself was looking. Both stood slack-jawed, unaware of how comical they appeared to the soldiers passing by on the boardwalk. The Lieutenant they'd encountered the day before stopped beside them. His gaze found what they were gawking at, and he took pity on their obvious distress by answering their unspoken question.

"They are a delegation of Blackfoot that has come to speak with Colonel Baker," he said, causing both women to jump. "I'm sorry, I didn't mean to startle you. You just seemed shocked to see the delegation riding through the gate."

"I am," Savannah admitted, her hand pressed against her chest, her breathing rapid. "What are they doing here, anyway?"

"I know you're upset about what the renegades did to you, miss, but I can assure you that you are perfectly safe within the walls of the fort."

"But why are *they* inside the fort is what I want to know?" Savannah emphasized.

"Chances are they've come to speak to Colonel Baker about the renegades that attacked your party."

"But that's not..." Savannah started and stopped. She knew that could not possibly be the reason, but he did not.

The Lieutenant looked at her quizzically then continued his explanation. "Probably want to reassure the Colonel that the attack wasn't by any one of their people. Although it wouldn't surprise me if it had been," he said shortly, his gaze narrowing on the lead rider.

"Why's that?"

"The Indian you see leading the way." He nodded his head toward the delegation, suggesting that she glance over as well. "That's a man named Many Feathers...Hey! Are you all right?" The Lieutenant caught hold of Savannah's arm, preventing her from falling over.

Savannah shook her head, dizzy at his announcement. *Many Feathers! My Lord in Heaven*, she thought.

"Miss Savannah, is you all right?" Tyeshia's voice broke through her haze and she shook her head violently again, desperately fighting the blackness that threatened to overwhelm her.

"I'm okay, Tyeshia," she whispered. "It must be the heat."

"It is rather hot today!" The Lieutenant said, noticing the sweat that had popped up on Savannah's upper lip. "Perhaps you need to get back indoors, Miss Savannah. Most of the ladies in the fort are taking their afternoon nap. Perhaps retiring to your room would be wise for you also."

"The Lieutenant be right, Miss Vanna," Tyeshia muttered exaggeratedly, "perhaps we best be getting you on back to the Mrs. Colonel's house." When Savannah did not say anything, merely continued staring at the delegation that was slowly closing the gap, Tyeshia looked at the Lieutenant, "She jes be upset over the loss of her parents, sir. Seeing them Injuns ride in here like dat done upset her overly much, I think."

In fact, the shock wore off shortly after. It took a moment more for

Savannah to register her friend's exaggerated speech and she suddenly had the urge to laugh.

"I'm fine, Lieutenant," she whispered.

"Are you certain, miss? Would you like me to get the doctor?" The Lieutenant's worried gaze focused on the paleness of Savannah's face.

"Tyeshia's right, Lieutenant. I'm still recovering from the loss of my parents is all, and seeing those Indians ride in like that...I guess it was just too much for me."

"If you are certain..."

"Yes, Lieutenant, I'm certain," Savannah said, a little more confidence in her tone. "I appreciate you stopping to assuage my curiosity."

"No problem, miss, however, I need to be heading to my post now so if you'll excuse me?"

"Not at all. Have a pleasant day, Lieutenant."

"You, too, Miss Savannah."

"Have you ever noticed how quickly men want to help a woman when she's in distress?" Tyeshia said. "Yet, the minute she looks even the slightest bit recovered, they are all too eager to be on their way?"

"I think sick women make men nervous, no matter the era. They don't want to appear helpless and weak, when they don't know what to do to make the woman better."

"How *are* you feeling, by the way? Recovered?"

Savannah looked down the street again at the approaching delegation. Savannah suddenly grabbed Tyeshia by the arm and pulled her back into the alley.

"Hey, what gives?" Tyeshia said, trying not to trip over the hem of her dress.

"Didn't you hear what the Lieutenant said?"

"No, but whatever it was upset you pretty badly."

"Yeah, well you might want to sit before I tell you then, because it's just as likely to upset you as well."

"I'm stronger than you are, so just spit it out."

Savannah grinned thinly, watching Tyeshia's reaction carefully as she spoke the next words, "None-other-than Many Feathers is leading those Indians that are riding down the street pretty-as-you-please right now." She watched the color drain from Tyeshia's dark skin and prepared to catch her should she keel over. Surprisingly enough, she remained upright, but backed against the nearby wall for added support.

"Holy cow!" She muttered.

The sound of horse's hoofs drew nearer, luring both women back toward the main street. They peered around the corner as the delegation passed.

"Wow!" Tyeshia murmured.

"Wow, what?" Savannah asked, peering over Tyeshia's shoulder.

"He is one fine-looking specimen of a man," Ty muttered.

"Who? Many Feathers?"

"You did say he was the man leading the delegation, right?"

"That's what the Lieutenant said."

"Then that's the man I'm talking about."

"Ty, he's one fine-looking *evil* specimen of a man," Savannah reminded her friend.

"Yeah, well, how do you know that?" Ty countered "Because of the word of a kook a hundred plus years from now?" When Savannah did not respond, Tyeshia tore her gaze away from Many Feathers and looked over her shoulder at her friend. She followed Savannah's gaze and laughed, "Looks like I'm not the only one who's enthralled by the spectacle," Tyeshia murmured.

"Well, you have to admit they are a formidable sight," Savannah admitted.

"A formidable sight," Tyeshia agreed, "and dadgum gorgeous too!"

Savannah's gaze drifted to the man riding just slightly to the rear and left of Many Feathers, and felt a shudder move through her.

"Now that's gorgeous," she whispered unknowingly aloud.

Tyeshia followed Savannah's line of sight again and looked at the man riding behind Many Feathers. "The man with the scar running down the side of his face?"

Savannah had not noticed that and felt another shudder run down her spine. *Who had raised a violent hand to such a magnificent face*? She wondered, and recoiled as the answer slammed like a hammer into her subconscious—Many Feathers! She tore her gaze away from the object of her attention and refocused on the man riding in front of the others. Tyeshia was obviously awestruck, but the sight of him chilled her to the bone.

"Yes, the man with the scar," she answered automatically, no longer thinking about him. Her breath caught in her throat and she clasped tightly onto Tyeshia's sleeve as Many Feathers's head turned suddenly, catching her gaze. A slight grin touched his thick lips before moving his scrutiny away where it lingered longer than was proper on Tyeshia. Savannah felt Tyeshia shudder beneath her hand and for the first time since starting their bizarre journey, found herself seriously worrying. If Many Feathers could wield that much power over her friend through a simple smile, she wondered what would happen if he managed to take over her psyche in the future.

"Let's get out of here," she whispered loudly, and pulled a reluctant

Tyeshia back into the alleyway. When the delegation moved on, she slipped out of the alley and into the first door she approached.

# FIFTEEN

"Can I help you?" The curator of the shop, a young lady about their age, asked.

"Not today. We're just browsing," Savannah smiled, trying to keep her voice steady.

"Aren't you the two young women that had the misfortune to run across some murdering savages yesterday?" She asked, her hand flying protectively to her swollen abdomen as she spoke.

"As you can see, we're quite unharmed."

"Fortunately for you. Why, just last year," the woman continued, "my brother and his wife, God rest their souls, tried making the trek from Georgia, and lost their lives to those butchering heathens. Whom did you lose?" She asked sweetly.

"Everyone," Savannah answered honestly, for in truth she and Tyeshia had lost everything and everyone on their trek through time.

"How dreadful!" The woman shook her head sadly and her gaze drifted to where Tyeshia stood rooted, staring out the window at the retreating figures on horseback. "Your poor maid must still be in shock," she continued. "Just look at the poor dear, standing there, terrified at the sight of them heathens."

Savannah was not about to clear up any misconception the woman had that Tyeshia was far from terrified, merely enthralled. Instead, she excused herself and walked to Tyeshia, placing a gentle hand on her arm.

"We need to go somewhere and talk about this, Ty," she whispered in her friend's ear. Tyeshia nodded but refused to take her gaze off the horizon, although the riders had already vanished from sight around a corner.

"It was a pleasure meeting you..." Savannah stopped, realizing that she'd never introduced herself.

"I'm Mrs. Corporal Stevens," the young woman replied sweetly, "and the pleasure was all mine, Miss..."

"Savannah. Savannah Warren and this is my friend, Tyeshia Morgan." Savannah's emphasis on the word 'friend' brought shock to the young woman's face, but she recovered quickly and pasted the sweet smile back on her face from a moment earlier. This time, however, Savannah noticed that it looked a bit more strained.

"It's a pleasure meeting you both and I look forward to speaking to *you* again tonight at the gala." She nodded stiffly and returned to her position behind the counter, busying herself with a bolt of material.

Savannah started toward the door but stopped as the Mrs. Corporal's words sank in. She whispered something to Tyeshia and then made her way back to the counter. "What gala?"

"Hmm?" The woman muttered, barely looking up from her work.

"You said that you'd be speaking to me again at tonight's gala. What did you mean?"

"Oh, that." The Mrs. Corporal laid the material aside and collected yet another piece to fold, obviously displeased at having to continue her conversation with someone below her status. "It seems that the Mrs. Colonel is throwing a party in honor of your arrival! Hadn't you heard?"

"Not a peep, but why would the Mrs. Colonel go to all the trouble of throwing us a party?" The young lady looked over at Tyeshia and frowned.

"Could I speak with you in private for a minute?" She murmured to Savannah then headed toward the back of the store.

"I'll be back in a sec, Ty."

"Sure."

"The gala is for you, not your friend," the Mrs. Corporal explained, tripping over the word 'friend', when Savannah joined her.

"Just me."

"Of course! A beautiful young thing like you has already attracted every eligible soldier here," the Mrs. Corporal exclaimed, forgetting temporarily about being haughty. "Why, I do declare that you will probably go so far as to snag you a lieutenant, or maybe even our elusive Captain Fredericks, just arrived a month past. Why, you'll probably even snare someone up faster than I did, and I was wed to my Douglas within a week of my arrival. You being prettier than me, someone will likely snatch you right up tonight. It's exciting! Why, before your arrival, we hadn't had a reason to have a ball in several years. It will be simply spectacular, I'm sure."

"I'm speechless," Savannah muttered sarcastically, "and what of my friend?" She continued trying to keep the angry tone from her voice.

"Well," the Mrs. Corporal began, her discomfort returning. She wrinkled her nose and frowned, "there are plenty of people looking for good housekeepers, but wouldn't you want to keep her with you? I mean, good house help is hard to find, and those of us that didn't bring it with us have to rely on the community workers."

"Community workers?"

"Well, that's just what I call them."

"Call who?"

"The women of ill repute that live just outside the fort," the Mrs. Corporal said as if the answer was apparent. "Haven't you ever seen these women before where you're from?"

"No."

"Well, they take in laundry and such to help provide a living for them, since no decent God-fearing soldier would ever take them to wife."

Savannah's memory kicked in and she suddenly remembered having read of these women as well. She also knew that these women—the community workers as the Mrs. Corporal called them—provided certain favors, at a price, for those very same soldiers that did not see them as fitting wife material. *Hypocrites*, she thought but kept the smile pasted on her face.

"Well, anyway. Just thought you might reconsider about keeping your maid."

"Oh, well thank you for letting me know," Savannah said prettily. "Although it had never been my intention of letting her go. Good day to you, ma'am." Savannah walked back to where Tyeshia stood, "Let's get out of here."

They walked in silence back to the Colonel's house and noticed several horses tied to the hitching post out front signifying that the delegation was at the fort to talk to the Colonel, as the Lieutenant suggested.

"Let's go around back," Savannah suggested heading that way before Tyeshia could respond.

"Like I had a choice," Tyeshia snorted and trotted to catch up with Savannah. "So, what's gotten you all bent out of shape?"

"Have you ever felt as if your life is a runaway train that you're helpless to control?"

"Not until we got slingshot back here, I didn't. Now I feel that way every hour of the day."

"Me too, but instead of getting better the train is moving faster and faster. I feel as if I'm about to be derailed."

Tyeshia pulled open the rear door and went inside, Savannah close on her heels. "You'll have to explain that a little better, but we'd best wait until we get upstairs," she added when the kitchen staff came into view.

Savannah followed but her mind continued running amok. She knew they would encounter Many Feathers eventually, but she had not been as prepared as she'd anticipated when that encounter finally occurred, nor had she been prepared for the strange feelings his companion had stirred in her as well. She simply had to pull herself together so that she could refocus on why she was here. Of course, how she was going to manage that and deal with Mrs. Colonel Matchmaker as well, she had no idea.

# SIXTEEN

"Okay, spill it," Tyeshia said the minute the bedroom door closed.

Savannah dropped heavily onto the bed, a frustrated sigh escaping her lips. "The Mrs. Colonel is throwing a party to try to get me hitched to someone as quickly as possible."

"You're joking!" Tyeshia exclaimed, plopping on the bed beside Savannah. "If that wasn't so ludicrous, it would be downright funny."

"I feel like things are getting away from us, Ty!" Savannah cried in frustration. "First, we are thrown back in time to stop a situation and before we can form a plan to do that, the situation is being thrown at us. On top of that, I've got to find a way to deal with a meddling old biddy who thinks she has a right to arrange a marriage for me at a ball that she's giving without my knowledge or consent. It's getting absurd!"

"Maybe the Colonel can ill afford to feed two more mouths, especially with as much as you eat," Tyeshia giggled.

"Ha! Ha! Aren't you just so funny?" Savannah snapped and rolled onto her belly. "It's not uncommon, what's she trying to do," Savannah sighed. "Ladies are a rarity out here right now."

"So I've noticed."

"Anyway, some women moved out west with the sole purpose of finding a husband. Too many competitors vying for male attention back east. They figured that finding a man to take care of them here would be relatively easy and felt especially lucky if they snared a military man. I guess the Mrs. Colonel feels that I need someone to take care of me since I don't have family now."

"Well, we could always leave and find a way to fend for ourselves until which time a solution presents itself," Tyeshia offered.

"Oh, Ty!" Savannah sighed in frustration. "We're in eighteen-sixty-nine, remember? We have no food, no weapons, no money—no nothing! Exactly how are we going to fend for ourselves in a wilderness where animals rule?"

"Maybe we could get help from Many Feathers?"

"What did you just say?" Savannah asked, rolling back over.

"Just hear me out, okay?" Tyeshia said quickly. "We need to be near Many Feathers, right? We saw the way he looked at us right?" Savannah did not miss that Tyeshia spoke that last part with a wistful sigh. "So perhaps we can somehow get him to agree to take us with him and then maybe when the time comes we'll already be in place. It's a sacrifice I'm willing to make," she concluded dreamily.

"You do remember what 'when the time comes' means, don't you?"

"Huh?"

"You couldn't even say what it is you're supposed to do 'when the time comes'. Wake up and smell the coffee, Ty! This is not one of your romance novels, kiddo. This is real life, and that character we saw out there is a no-good, conniving creep with an evil heart! You do remember that, don't you?"

"How do you know that, Savannah? You haven't even met the man!" Tyeshia countered, her anger rising quickly. "All you have to go on is the word of some loony tune from the twenty-first century, and all *he* has to go on are stories that his Grandfather's grandfather passed down or something like that. Perhaps he's a great warrior," she continued without pausing for breath, "who's been given a bad rap by someone who hates him. Maybe Mr. Scar Face down there is the bad guy."

"That's not nice, Ty."

"Neither is taking the word of someone who's never met the man, either, and that's exactly what you're doing—taking Black Calf's word before getting to know Many Feathers."

"Well, you're showing bias also, aren't you? Isn't your judgment impaired by your attraction to Many Feathers? Ty," Savannah whispered worriedly, "please say that you're not losing your focus simply because you've discovered that he's gorgeous."

"My focus?" Tyeshia huffed. "If by 'focus' you mean that I'm supposed to wake up that incredibly handsome guy downstairs, at some undetermined time so that he can get himself killed—no, I haven't forgotten that. Now, ask me if I'm going to do it."

"Oh, no, Ty, no!" Savannah whispered in shocked dismay. "Tell me you're joking!"

"No, I'm not joking," Tyeshia snapped. "I'm not going to stand by and watch as someone gets butchered just because someone says I'm supposed to."

"If you don't wake him up, Ty, he's going to die anyway," Savannah reasoned. "Only his death won't be honorable and all this misery we're suffering through will be for nothing."

"He won't die if he's not where he's supposed to be when Clark comes to kill him. Then we don't have to worry about him messing with my psyche in the future."

"What are you saying, Ty?"

"Remember that conversation we had in the alley, about maybe being able to talk Clark out of killing Many Feathers?"

"Of course, but we also decided that convincing an angry man to forgo revenging his dead wife isn't likely to work."

"So we dismiss it outright? Why can't we just try? That way I don't have to stand by and watch as someone dies!"

"Let me ask you this, Ty. Could you stand by and allow a murderer to go free? Many Feathers killed Clark's pregnant wife in view of a dozen or more witnesses. What makes you think that Clark's going to back down from this fight? Would you, if it was your loved one?"

"You're assuming *that* actually happened. Besides, why does it have to be me that wakes him up, Savannah? Why can't *you* do it?"

"You saw the way he looked at you, Ty. You don't think that happened coincidentally, do you?"

"Now what are you talking about?"

"Simple logic is all." Savannah started pacing, her hands gesturing with each word she spoke. "It's your psyche he chose when I opened the door back in our time, not mine. I wasn't his type—sorry."

"Just keep talking."

"Well, it makes sense that if he connected with you in our time then he would find a connection with you here in this time. That's why he stared at you for so long. He feels a bond just as you do."

"Great! That helps a lot Savannah, knowing that I have to kill someone who's linked with me so closely."

"Well, our goal should be to keep you focused on *your* goal so that you can do just that. We can't let him get to your psyche here anymore than we want him to in our time, and by the way you were talking a few minutes ago, he may already be getting to you, and he only passed us for a minute on the street. Heaven forbid that we find ourselves in his company for a prolonged period."

"Well, if we don't go with him how else am I supposed to wake him up so that he can fight Clark? If it comes to that, which I still hesitate to do."

"Well, hopefully, when the time is right I'll be with you and help you stay grounded."

"I still think the key is keeping Clark away."

"Well, we'll definitely keep that option open like we said. Right now however, we have to decide what to do about Many Feathers without having to get any nearer to him than possible."

"I don't see how that's going to happen."

"Neither do I," Savannah conceded plopping onto her settee. "I just hope something happens to direct us in this, and soon."

"Hey!"

"What?" Savannah jerked at Tyeshia's sudden outburst. "Have you thought of something?"

"Yeah, food! Weren't we on our way to eat something before all this went down?"

Savannah laughed shortly, "Sometimes I think that your stomach rules your life. Whomever you marry better keep a well-stocked kitchen, or your marriage won't survive."

"I can't help it if I'm tall and require a lot of nourishment."

"Yeah, right. What's say we head down to the kitchen. There's bound to be food there somewhere."

"Sounds like a plan."

"Well, at least we're able to formulate some kind of plan. Too bad it's not the plan that we need."

Tyeshia laughed and headed for the doorway. "Aren't you coming?" She asked when she noticed that Savannah was still sitting on the bed.

"You go on ahead of me and see if the coast is clear, and I'll join you in a minute."

"What are you going to do?"

"I just need to think for a minute."

"Sure you don't want me to stay?"

"That's the problem. The loud racket your stomach is making it impossible for me *to* think."

"Smarty," Tyeshia snapped, pulling the door open with a yank.

"I'll be with you in a sec."

"Don't hurry on my account," Tyeshia said. When Tyeshia shut the door behind her, Savannah lowered her head into her hands and sighed. She suddenly felt very old and tired.

"You didn't warn me," she accused a faraway Black Calf, "that keeping Tyeshia safe would mean going to war with *her*. I thought I would only have to do mental battle with Many Feathers. Thanks for the heads up."

# SEVENTEEN

Savannah came down stairs in time to see the Mrs. Colonel snapping at Tyeshia for being in the main entryway of the house instead of the kitchen where she belonged. Before she could intervene, Tyeshia turned on her heel and strode haughtily into the kitchen. Savannah shot the Mrs. Colonel an evil look, but it was lost on the fat cow since she'd already turned and was strolling down the hall toward the study where her husband was completing his business with the delegates.

Tyeshia stormed out of the colonel's house—the back entrance, of course. In her mind, she ranted and railed at the Mrs. Colonel's narrow-mindedness, but she also found reason to blame Savannah, since she would not have been in the main entrance if Savannah had not sent her out of the room ahead of her in the first place. It was all Savannah's fault that the Mrs. Colonel humiliated her this time.

Her long strides carried her around the corner and straight into the delegation that had left—from the front entrance, Tyeshia noticed spitefully—and was mounting their horses. Her anger fled and her breath caught in her throat when Many Feathers turned in her direction and froze, a smile playing on his full lips. She did not need to take her pulse to know that it was racing, and by the look on Many Feathers' face, she could tell she enthralled him as well.

*Clark can't kill this gorgeous creature,* she thought, smiling shyly at the man seated on his pinto mare. *No man that looks that good could be all bad,* her thoughts continued. *Black Calf and Savannah are wrong!*

A mischievous smile lit his face and suddenly Tyeshia felt like a giddy pupil instead of the twenty-year-old college student that she was. She brought her hand up to her hair and smoothed the springy tendrils away from her face, very conscious of her appearance, and smiled shyly in return.

Savannah came around the corner in pursuit of her friend, and stopped short. She saw Tyeshia standing there coyly and it did not take long for her gaze to seek out and find the recipient of her friend's come-hither stare.

*Many Feathers!*

She moved to stand beside Tyeshia, placing her hand gently on her friend's arm. Tyeshia jerked, shooting Savannah an agitated look. Many Feathers laughed at the two women, then yanked on his horse's reins and took off toward the gates of the fort.

Savannah and Tyeshia watched him leave—one with relief, the other with frustration. It was not until he'd turned a corner that the two women realized someone was still watching them. Savannah turned her head and her gaze collided with the regard of the warrior with the scar running down the side of his jaw. Savannah realized that it did nothing to detract from his handsomeness and felt her own heartbeat quicken at his perusal.

"It looks like I'm not the only one moonstruck," Tyeshia snapped. "What was that about living in a romance novel, Savannah? This is real life—remember? Or does real life only apply to me? What if that's the bad guy and not Many Feathers? What if you're wrong and I'm right? Or is that inconceivable to you?" With that, she turned on her heel and stormed away.

Savannah blushed but could not take her gaze away from the warrior still watching her intently. She instinctively retreated when he urged his mount toward her, but then realized her foolishness and stopped. It was not likely that he would abduct her in broad daylight from a heavily guarded fort, she reminded herself. If he even considered abducting her at all. He stopped beside her and looked down into her wide green eyes.

"You care for your friend?" He asked in heavily-accented English. Savannah could only nod dumbly, for she could not have found her voice even if someone had handed it to her on a silver platter. "Then keep her from Many Feathers," he continued, eyeing her curiously. "He is not a good man."

Without waiting for a reply, the stranger turned his horse sharply, motioned to the other riders and galloped away, leaving Savannah eating his dust. Savannah snapped out of her daze and self-consciously glanced around her to see if anyone had noticed that little episode. She said a quick prayer of thanks that she did not see anyone, then quickly turned and headed in the direction that Tyeshia had gone. She was slightly out of breath when she finally caught up to Tyeshia, who was walking aimlessly around the boardwalks of the fort.

"Tyeshia, wait up!"

"Oh, so the friend turned traitor wishes my company, does she?" Tyeshia snapped spitefully, deliberately picking up her pace. She knew that her five-foot-ten, long-legged height gave her a distinct advantage over Savannah's five-foot-seven stature.

"Please, Ty, don't be this way! I have something to tell you and I can't do it if you don't stop for a moment," Savannah huffed breathlessly, and sighed when her friend finally did stop. "Thank you for stopping, Ty," Savannah breathed heavily, glancing left and then right before stepping off the boardwalk with her friend. Although right now the thought of being run down by a passing horse was more appealing than the situation she currently found herself encountering.

"I only stopped to make sure I didn't get run over by a horse or something," Tyeshia snapped petulantly, as if reading Savannah's thoughts, "but since you managed to catch up to me, you said you had something to say to me," Tyeshia continued childishly, "so say it."

"That other Indian..."

"The one that has so enchanted you?"

"That's the one," Savannah blushed. "He gave me a warning, Ty." Tyeshia stopped walking and turned to face Savannah.

"What warning was that?"

"He bade me to warn you to stay away from Many Feathers," Savannah said, and watched as the cloud of anger on her friend's face turn rapidly into darker thunderclouds. She continued talking swiftly, hoping to say what needed saying before Tyeshia stalked away again. "Don't you see, Ty, that it's not just the word of an old loony a hundred plus years in the future, but one of Many Feather's own kind that speaks out against him?"

"What I see is a selfish woman standing in front of me."

"What?"

"Here you are warning me to stay away from a strange man because he could potentially be dangerous and yet you are listening to a stranger without hesitation or doubt. Could that be because of your slight crush on him, Savannah?"

"What are you talking about, Ty?"

"The Indian with the scar and don't try to deny it. I saw the way you looked at him. You're just as fascinated with him as I am with Many Feathers."

"I'll admit that he's a handsome man, Tyeshia, if that will make you feel any better," Savannah whispered, "but I'm not willing to throw my entire future away for him. Besides which he's not the evil man that Many Feathers is."

"Exactly how would you know that?" Tyeshia said her tone full of challenge. "Because Scar Face said to stay away from Many Feathers? Maybe Scar Face has a crush on me and doesn't want Many Feathers to have me. Ever think of that?"

"No, I didn't," Savannah admitted knowing that was not the case, but not daring to say so. She'd seen the way that the man with the scar had looked at them both and his interest was definitely not in Tyeshia. "Call it intuition," she said instead, "or a feeling, if you prefer. Call it whatever you want, but there is something about Many Feathers that scares me, Ty."

"Perhaps he's just too much man for you, Savannah," Tyeshia taunted, "like Bobby Ramirez was. Maybe that's what frightens you—that you can't handle a real man."

"Do you hear yourself, Ty?" Savannah murmured sadly. "Do you even hear what you're saying?" Tyeshia just stood there stubbornly, her arms crossed over her chest. "Maybe you're right, Ty," Savannah sighed. "I don't know. I could say it was intuitiveness, but that wouldn't exactly be proof positive. Maybe it is something else—who knows? All I do know right now is that I'm losing my dearest friend over this and that's something I'm unequivocally certain that I don't want to do."

Tyeshia's dark brown eyes welled with tears and she hastily swiped them away. "I guess I'm sorry too," she announced emotionally. "I really wish I could say what's gotten into me today, but I truly don't know. I feel like I'm riding some sort of emotional roller coaster."

"Kind of like my runaway train?"

"Yeah, but worse," Ty whispered. "It's like I'm not in control of my actions somehow. One minute I'm thinking clearly and the next minute it's as if a marionette has hold of some invisible strings attached to my mouth and mind, controlling *me*."

Savannah started to mention that she could shed light on what was happening to her. Nevertheless, the chasm between them was already growing and she did not want it getting any wider, so she kept her mouth shut.

"Why don't we step back to the house and grab that bite to eat? We never did have that meal we intended to have earlier," Savannah offered, knowing that they could always find solace in food. "Maybe we can sort this out over a late lunch."

# EIGHTEEN

"I've been looking for you half the day, Savannah!" Savannah choked on her soup startled by the booming voice. The Mrs. Colonel thumped sharply on her upper back, "Cough it up, dearie. I didn't mean to frighten you so."

When Savannah regained her composure, the Mrs. Colonel stepped briskly around the side of the table casting Tyeshia a withering stare. Tyeshia, to her credit, returned her gaze evenly, but said nothing.

"What can I do for you, Mrs. Colonel?" Savannah asked.

"Why, we haven't fitted you for your dress yet," the Mrs. Colonel announced as if it were common knowledge.

"What dress?"

"The dress that isn't being fitted for the party this evening because you persist in sitting there asking me silly questions instead of standing up and following me out of this room."

"Oh, that dress," Savannah murmured sarcastically.

"You can't very well attend a soiree improperly attired, now can you?"

"I don't suppose I could, but..."

"Good, then let's be on our way upstairs. I've had someone waiting for nearly half an hour to help with your dress, and we're both a mite bit put out at having to wait." The Mrs. Colonel turned her attention to Tyeshia. "We won't be in need of your services again until tonight so you're free to roam about the fort. However, please bear in mind that you are staying within the walls of my husband's command so I expect that you will comport yourself as befitting your mistress's station?"

"Oh, yessum, Mrs. Colonel, ma'am. Most 'suredly, ma'am," Tyeshia muttered, bowing her head rapidly.

"Good. Let's be off then, Savannah."

"I'll be with you in a moment, Mrs. Colonel."

"Very well, but don't dawdle. I haven't all day, you know. I have to prepare for this evening as well. There's so much to do." The Mrs. Colonel disappeared in a whirlwind leaving the two women seated at the table feeling breathless.

"I'm sorry about that, Ty."

"Don't worry, Savannah. I'm not going to explode and tear that old witch's head off—yet. I'm also coming to the realization that you were right."

"Well that would be a first!"

"I'm serious. If I'm going to survive in this period long enough to accomplish our objective, then I'm going to have to act like your servant—at least while the Mrs. Colonel is around."

"I wish things could be different."

"They can't," Tyeshia murmured. "You best be getting on before that woman sends the hounds after you."

"What are you going to be doing while I'm being fitted?"

"I'll wander around. See if I can't find out anything about anything," Ty offered half-jokingly.

"That's not a bad idea. Maybe you can find out something more about Many Feathers and his companions. Maybe if someone else speaks out against Many Feathers you'll realize that I'm not just out to ruin your happiness."

"I never really thought that and you know it."

"I know, but you were beginning to scare me for a little bit there."

"It's strange, but when Many Feathers isn't around my mind functions just fine. I'm not screwed in the head."

"Yeah, I know, and that scares me too. Well, go poke around."

"You mean you were serious about my poking my nose in where it doesn't belong?" Tyeshia asked in mock astonishment.

"Well, you know as well I do that people like to gossip; especially those under the thumb of authority."

"Got the picture. Maybe I'll go visit some of the community workers outside these ramparts that the girl in the store told you about. They're probably privy to more information than all the folks in this entire fort."

"Most likely. Well, I best be off before the Mrs. Colonel has apoplexy. Do me a favor, Ty, and be careful when you leave. It's not very safe to be outside these walls."

"I'll let you know if I find out anything."

"Me, too." Savannah stood reluctantly. "If we don't get this situation taken care of soon, they're going to be fitting me for a straightjacket," she murmured, headed out of the kitchen, and ran headlong into the Mrs. Colonel.

"I told you not to dawdle, child. We have to get your dress fitted, your bath seen to, your hair styled...oh, so little time."

"If Tyeshia made me up," she murmured with a giggle, following the Mrs. Colonel up the staircase, "the soldiers would be swarming around like bees to honey."

"What was that, Savannah?" The Mrs. Colonel asked, looking over her shoulder.

"Just talking to myself, Mrs. Colonel."

"Well, see to it that you don't do it any longer. We don't want people thinking you're sick in the head. Understand?" She said.

"I'll try not to," Savannah muttered dutifully.

"We're here Mrs. Sergeant," the Mrs. Colonel announced, opening the door to her drawing room. "We've got a lot to do, so let's get straight to it, shall we?"

Both women descended on Savannah and before she realized what was happening, they were disrobing her.

"What in heaven's name is *that* contraption?" The Mrs. Sergeant exclaimed, staring at Savannah's brazier.

Savannah instinctively crossed her arms over her breasts, blushing deeply. "This is my bra," she said without thinking.

"What is a 'bra'?" The Mrs. Colonel asked, eyeing the piece of clothing suspiciously.

"Well, it's a...it's meant to...that is it's..." Savannah stammered, embarrassed.

"From the looks of it, Mrs. Colonel, it seems to be some form of a corset that's meant to hold your breast in place," the Mrs. Sergeant said.

"Exactly!" Savannah replied, thankful that she had not needed to explain it further.

"Where exactly did you get it?" The Mrs. Sergeant asked, curious.

"My, um, mother. She, um, bought it in France, I think," Savannah muttered. She knew that a lot of current fashion derived from the French and could only hope that explanation would suffice. It would not do her any good if they knew that they had not invented the bra until after nineteen-ten.

"Well, French or not," the Mrs. Colonel frowned, "it simply will not do with the dress that I have for you to wear. Didn't I loan you a corset, child?"

"Yes, but..."

"Well, then, where is it?" The Mrs. Colonel demanded, her patience already wearing thin.

"It's in the wardrobe in my room."

"Mrs. Sergeant, go and get the corset so that we can get on with this," the Mrs. Colonel ordered. The Mrs. Sergeant surprised Savannah when she ran from the room without first throwing a salute.

*Whatever happened to that quiet, reserved lady that I met yesterday that was holding on demurely to her husband's arm*? Savannah wondered tacitly, while the Mrs. Colonel paced the room. *This has got to be an evil twin or something.* As if reading her mind, the Mrs. Colonel stopped pacing and turned to face her. Savannah blushed and smiled slightly. *Whew! Maybe I'd better stop thinking around her.*

The Mrs. Sergeant ran back into the room a moment later, breathing heavily. "Got it!" She said proudly.

"Good! Then let's get to it. Time's wasting."

Savannah was still standing on a stool in the middle of the room with her arms outstretched and aching half hour later, her own patience wearing thin.

"Now! Let's see what else needs altering. Then I'll turn the dress over to you, Mrs. Sergeant, so that you can make the final adjustments for this evening."

"Why ever are you throwing me a big party on such short notice?" Savannah asked, trying to keep the irritation and impatience out of her voice.

"Well, why ever not?" The Mrs. Colonel replied. "Can you think of a better way to introduce you to the people of our little fort at once?"

"Door-to-door?" she muttered under her breath.

"What was that, Savannah?" The Mrs. Colonel said around a mouth full of pins.

"Nothing, Mrs. Colonel."

"Are you talking to yourself again?" The Mrs. Colonel said admonishment in her tone. "I thought I told you to stop that."

"Sorry. Bad habit."

"Well, break it," the Mrs. Colonel ordered. "I don't want our delightful Captain Fredericks to think you are some kind of nut case. Now what do you think, Mrs. Sergeant?" The Mrs. Colonel asked, stepping back to inspect her handiwork.

"I'm certain that this will suit just fine."

"Well, I'm glad you like it. Now, let's carefully slip it off." The two women gingerly tugged the gown downward until it fell in a pool at Savannah's feet. "Step down, child," the Mrs. Colonel instructed, offering her a hand in assistance. "Do you think that you can make these adjustments before the party tonight, Mrs. Sergeant?" The Mrs. Colonel asked, forgetting Savannah for the moment.

"Without a doubt, Mrs. Colonel."

"Then you best be about it."

The Mrs. Sergeant left quickly, leaving the Mrs. Colonel alone with Savannah. She helped Savannah don the day dress loaned to her from another unknown person, then motioned for Savannah to sit on the bed.

"We should talk, Savannah," the Mrs. Colonel said in a kind voice that had Savannah thinking that the nice twin had returned. The Mrs. Colonel sat beside her and picked up Savannah's hand, patting it gently. "I know that you lost your family recently, my dear, so I feel a little obligated to take care of you as if you were my own." Savannah stiffened slightly, but only smiled in response. "Thus, it is mine and my husband's place to see you safely settled. Do you understand?"

"I think so, but I really don't..."

"Let me finish, child," the Mrs. Colonel interrupted. "I don't have a daughter to talk to about these things, and I know I may sound a bit awkward and unsure, but it's necessary that you be prepared. Okay?" Savannah looked at her quizzically; unsure herself about where the Mrs. Colonel was directing this conversation, but she nodded her assent and kept her mouth shut.

"Good," the Mrs. Colonel smiled, took a deep breath, and plunged ahead. "Now, I know you're probably a little uncertain what your future holds, but I can assure you that after this evening, things will be a lot brighter. I realize that Captain Fredericks isn't the warmest of men—have you met him, by the way?"

"No," Savannah answered quietly, "but you are the second to mention him to me."

"Ah, well," the Mrs. Colonel sighed, "he's only just arrived a month past and spends most of his time in his office with his paperwork. He needs a fine wife to come home to."

"But, really I'm not..."

"Now, now, don't worry about anything," the Mrs. Colonel interrupted again. "I'm certain that once he lays eyes on you, he will be more than willing to take you as his wife, and if not—well, there's always Lieutenant Mitchell. Either way, I'm more than certain we'll have you married off by the end of the week."

Savannah thought of all the times that Tyeshia had tried to set her up and moaned in frustration. *At least she hadn't been trying to marry me to a stranger.*

"Mrs. Colonel," Savannah began hesitantly. "I appreciate all that you're doing for me, truly, I do, but I just am not interested in marrying anyone right now."

"Oh, pish-posh. Of course you are," the Mrs. Colonel countered. "You're probably just nervous about what to expect on your wedding night." The Mrs. Colonel noticed the blush in Savannah cheeks and smiled knowingly. "Just remember, dear, it may not be a pleasant task, but it's a necessary one so that you can give your husband a son. Once your task in providing a son is complete, then most times you don't have to suffer the humiliation any longer. At least you know that, as a Captain in the military, your husband will definitely be a gentleman."

Savannah sat in stunned disbelief. The woman was giving her a distorted lecture on the birds and the bees.

"Well, I'll let you rest for a bit now." The Mrs. Colonel stood and made her way to the door. "I'll send your maid up later to help you dress. If my maid can find your maid that is."

The door closed quietly, leaving Savannah to ponder a way out of yet another disastrous mess.

# NINETEEN

"Hello," Tyeshia smiled, approaching the three women hunched over an enormous bucket of steaming water, scrubbing clothes.

"Sorry, but we don't have room to hire any more help." One woman stood, arching and bending the kinks out of her back. "There's another fort to the north of here. You might try finding work there," she offered kindly, wiping a red, calloused hand against a dirty, sweaty brow.

"Oh, I already work for someone at the fort," Tyeshia offered, and immediately regretted being so forthcoming. The women glanced at one another and then shot Tyeshia an 'it's about time you left' look.

"Well, ain't you the lucky one," one of them murmured snidely.

"Isabelle, watch your tongue and mind your manners."

The woman named Isabelle rolled her eyes, and then began scrubbing at a piece of clothing more vigorously than required.

"Begging your pardon, but the women here would give their soul to find a decent job working for someone at the fort. The work would be a bit easier, and there'd be more respect given. Here...well, let's just say our existence is the best it can get. My name's Harriet McGill. This here's Isabelle Carter." She indicated to the woman with dark hair and the bad attitude. "And that's Margaret. Leastways that's what we call her since she hasn't talked since the day she arrived. What's your name?"

"I'm Tyeshia Morgan."

"Well, it's a right nice pleasure to meet you, Tyeshia, but what brings you 'round to our door. Your employer isn't about ready to kick you out on your fanny is he?" Isabelle and Margaret looked up eagerly and Tyeshia cringed. They were like vultures waiting to swoop down on a fresh kill. She was certain that they'd like nothing better than to take her place with her employer—if she really had one.

"No, no, nothing like that," she assured them quickly, and they all went back to scrubbing the clothes dejectedly. "I was just out walking and saw you working. Thought I'd stop by and pay a visit."

"Why?" The woman named Isabelle asked suspiciously. "One of those uppity do-gooders trying to find dirt on us, so as they can run us off our land. Well, you go back and tell them it ain't gonna work. We ain't on their precious land, and we got a right to be here just the same as they do."

"Isabelle, get a hold of your tongue, woman!" Harriet hissed. "You really do have to learn to control that temper of yours."

"I promise, Isabelle," Tyeshia responded, addressing the one woman who seemed most disgruntled by her presence, "that I'm not trying to gather dirt on anyone. I was simply taking a walk and thought I'd stop and say hello. If I've offended you by doing so, I'll be happy to take my leave." Tyeshia said, but Isabelle merely stared at her.

"It was right nice of you to stop by, Tyeshia," Harriet smiled sweetly, "but as you can see, we got lots to get done before the sun sets..."

"I understand," Tyeshia said and turned to leave.

"Tyeshia," Harriet called, stopping her.

"Yes?"

"You be careful traipsing around outside the security of the fort. It ain't safe."

"By unsafe, do you mean the Indians?" Tyeshia asked, moving back in Harriet's direction.

"Yeah, the Indians, and the trappers and any other evil-minded varmint that happens to be passing through—all sorts of bad element hanging about most of the time," Harriet confirmed.

"Don't they ever bother you ladies—the Indians that is?" Tyeshia stopped beside the bucket and sat on a stool. She had her foot in the door now, so to speak, if she could just keep them talking.

Harriet shrugged and bent back to her task. "Nah. They don't bother with us none."

"That's curious. You'd think to be out here all alone would make you easy pickings."

"We're too old for them to bother with," Isabelle laughed shortly. "'sides that, we give them what they want free of charge, so they got no call to mess with us."

"You mean you take in their laundry and wash it for nothing!" Tyeshia exclaimed incredulously. The three women glanced at one another for a moment and then burst into laughter. Their reaction took Tyeshia aback briefly, then realization dawned about where their laughter stemmed and she felt an embarrassment like none she'd ever felt prior. Mostly for prying into their lives like a trashy tabloid reporter.

What she could not understand, however, was how they could laugh in the face of their situation? It just did not make much sense to her.

"You can't really be that naive!" Isabelle snickered.

"No, I'm not," Tyeshia defended. "I guess I just didn't realize what you women endured out here." With that revelation, the three women grew quiet. "I mean, I'd heard rumors that you gave the men at the fort entertainment, but—well, don't you just get tired of having to bed down with whoever wants it?"

"Don't get uppity with us, girl," Harriet snapped, dropping the shirt she was working on in the bucket of rinse water. "It ain't like we got much of a choice. Leastways, we get food and a few coins out of the deal. That's better than what most women get."

"I guess I'm a bit more innocent about things out here than I thought."

"I reckon you are at that," Harriet huffed and picked up her discarded shirt.

"Have any of you ever heard of a native that goes by the name of Many Feathers?" Tyeshia asked as casually as she could, bringing the topic around to what she really wanted to know. She just could not believe that a man as gorgeous as Many Feathers could be all that bad. Her heartbeat increased and her palms began to sweat as Harriet and Isabelle began filling her in about him—and what they were saying was far from pleasant.

"He's a snake in the grass," Isabelle offered.

"T'ain't no good in that savage," Harriet muttered, and Margaret just shivered as if a cold draft had run past them all. Tyeshia felt cold herself as the women continued talking over each other.

". . . can't stand to have him touch me."

". . . wouldn't put up with his shenanigans if I wasn't so darned afraid of him."

". . . put a bruise on my arm the size of a peach."

". . . always threatening to scalp my mane."

The conversations buzzed in Tyeshia's ears until she became dizzy. She stood abruptly and started walking back toward the fort. She had to get away from here fast, something inside told her. She wanted to return to the fort quickly, but Harriet was following her, calling her name.

"Hey, wait up!" Harriet tugged on Tyeshia's arm, spinning her around to face her. "Are you all right? You look mighty pale under that dark skin of yours."

Tyeshia nodded, but could not force any words past the lump in her throat.

"You was fine 'til we started talking about that no-account Many Feathers. Have you had a run-in with him too?"

"Of sorts," Tyeshia finally choked out.

"He ain't hurt you, has he? If he has, you report him to your employer and they'll file a report or some such nonsense. It may keep that lowlife away from you in the future."

"No, it was nothing like that," Tyeshia whispered hoarsely. "It's just that what you were saying made me realize that I needed to get back to the fort before it got any later, otherwise losing my scalp may be a distinct possibility," Tyeshia laughed nervously.

"Smart idea," Harriet concurred. Harriet stood looking at Tyeshia for a few minutes more, "but there's more to it than that, ain't there?" Tyeshia didn't answer, just stood there clutching her skirt. "You know, a smart woman would hightail it in the other direction if they ever run across Many Feathers," Harriet lectured with a knowing look on her face that had shivers running down Tyeshia's arms.

*What did she know?* Tyeshia wondered. *She could not possibly have guessed my attraction to him, could she?* Her next words belied that thought.

"You look like a smart woman. Fact is, makes no difference how good looking a body finds that heathen, there ain't no heart in that man. If you got any doubt about that, take a good look in his eyes. You won't see a soul." Without waiting for a reply, Harriet spun around on her heels and went back to her small little cottage. The other two women were quickly hanging the laundry on a wire that they had already washed, trying to beat the waning sun.

Tyeshia turned wearily and made her way back to the fort. Even though she told Savannah she'd meet her in her bedroom this evening to help her get ready for the party, she suddenly felt drained and tired. She also felt depression creeping up on her. Tomorrow would be soon enough to talk to Savannah and listen to her say, 'I told you so'. Right now, all she wanted to do was lie in bed and mope.

# TWENTY

Savannah begged off the next dance. Her feet ached and she felt the beginnings of a headache. She rubbed her temples with her fingertips and wished she could take off her borrowed slippers, which were once again a size too small, and rub her aching toes.

At least when Tyeshia forced her to go to a party she could always hide in a corner, unnoticed, for the entire evening. Not so here. This was a party thrown in her honor, and they expected her to dance with every male present—married or not.

She tugged at the top of her dress, trying to conceal her breasts, which threatened to spill out with every spin around the dance floor. Then she tried to suck in a deep breath, but failed. She cursed the Mrs. Colonel under her breath for making her wear the corset. How the heck women in the nineteenth century ever breathed long enough to create offspring for the next century was beyond her. She'd only had the thing on for a few hours, but she was ready to help the Mrs. Colonel commit hara-kiri, and then do a striptease on the dance floor. To make matters worse, she'd had to sit through a Tyeshia-bashing several hours earlier and she was still smarting over that one. The Mrs. Colonel's comments regarding Tyeshia's inattention to duty were still ringing in her ears.

*"I told your maid that we wouldn't need her until this evening. Does she not understand that 'this evening' means before the party so that she can help you prepare? Now, instead, I have to loan my own maid to you and rely on a less experienced girl to help me get ready. I'm going to look like a clown!"*

*"I can use the other..."*

*"Absolutely not! You most certainly don't need to look like a clown. Sue Ann is the best there is. If anyone can find you a husband with her ministrations, it's she."*

Savannah was shocked from her musings by a sharp command.

"Why are you sitting in a corner, Savannah?"

"I'm afraid I'm a little tired, Mrs. Colonel. I'm not used to dancing so much."

"I don't understand. Didn't your mother introduce you to society properly, child? You seem old enough to have wed already. You're not...oh, Lord, say you're not! No! You couldn't be. You're too well spoken."

"What?"

"You're not from a poverty-stricken household, are you?"

"No. We did lose everything before the war was over," Savannah improvised quickly, "and it took us several years to recover fully. By then, I guess, my mother just felt I was past marriageable age and decided I would do better staying and helping her with the house."

"You, poor dear! I had no idea!" The Mrs. Colonel settled into the chair beside her, causing the small frame to creak in protest. She took Savannah's hand in her own. "Still and all, we need to find you a husband, and we can't do that with you hiding in a corner. Age doesn't matter much here; all that matters is that you find a good man to keep you safe in this savage land. I wish I knew what was keeping Captain Fredericks. He's the one I want you to get to know. I think you two would suit nicely."

Savannah was about to respond, but noticed that the Mrs. Colonel's attention was no longer focused on her. She followed her gaze and stifled a gasp. Standing at the door of the ballroom was three uninvited guests: a white man in dust-covered buckskin and two of the Indians she'd seen with the delegation from earlier that morning. One was the man with the scar. The anger emanating from the white man was nearly palpable, but his eyes revealed more than just anger, there was also pain. A great deal of pain.

When the Mrs. Colonel rose from the chair and moved toward the men, she did likewise, curious about what had brought them crashing into the Colonel's house and wondering what emergency would make them interrupt the party.

Colonel Baker intercepted his wife and tried to prevent her from making a scene, but no one was going to deter the Mrs. Colonel.

"I will know what that turncoat wants in my house, Ezra, and that's final!" She whispered sharply to her husband.

"He isn't exactly a turncoat, my dear, since he never served in the military."

"Any man that turns Indian is a traitor to his country and doesn't deserve to breathe the same air as decent folks."

"Very well, my dear, let's find out why he came here, but let me do the talking." He took her arm and continued across the expansive floor. The room full of merrymakers parted to let them through, whispering among themselves.

Savannah stuck close to their heels and stopped just behind the Mrs. Colonel. She caught the eye of the man with the scar and blushed as his gaze quickly raked over her fancy dress coming to rest briefly on her breasts, which, thanks to her corset, appeared larger than normal. She felt a flush rise in her face and lowered her gaze when she saw a small smile form on his mouth.

"Perhaps we can adjourn to my study and discuss why you felt the need to disrupt my wife's party," the Colonel said, speaking directly to the white man.

Savannah eyed the white guy curiously and then a thought struck her like the proverbial lightning bolt. Could it really have happened so soon? She lifted her gaze back to the man with the scar. However, his attention was no longer on her. She shifted from one foot to the other and tried to think of another way to attract his attention again without being too obvious.

The group of men turned and started to leave the room. Time was up. Savannah needed to get his attention quickly or it would be too late.

"Colonel Baker, sir!" Savannah stepped forward, placing herself discreetly between the man with the scar and the others. When she did not continue talking, however, the Colonel shot her a look of impatience.

"What is it, Savannah?" The Colonel asked. Savannah was so busy with the hand signals behind her back that she did not readily hear the Colonel until he fairly snapped at her. "Savannah!"

"Sir?"

"What is it that you needed, my dear?"

"Oh, well, I was just wondering if you would like me to, um," Savannah said, wracking her brain, her fingers still working furiously behind her back in an attempt to signal the man with the scar to meet with her outside, "have the kitchen send in some refreshments for your guests, sir."

"I don't think that will be necessary, my dear, but thank you for thinking of us. Now go on back into the ballroom and join the Mrs. Colonel."

"Yes, sir." Savannah turned and stopped short. The man with the scar was no longer standing behind her. She had not heard him leave and none of the other men indicated that they'd seen him depart. Could it be that he left before she'd started signaling to him? She'd feel pretty stupid if that was the case. Either way, she had to find out if she was right about why these men had come to visit Colonel Baker. If she was right, then hers and Tyeshia's time was quickly ticking away.

# TWENTY-ONE

"What were you doing, Savannah?" The Mrs. Colonel cornered her the minute she reentered the room.

"I was just seeing if the Colonel wanted any refreshments, ma'am," Savannah hedged, and continued walking toward the French doors in the rear of the ballroom. She hoped that the Mrs. Colonel would peel away and seek to entertain elsewhere, but no such luck.

"I can hardly comprehend your lack of discernment in some matters, Savannah. First, you claim to have befriended a slave woman while attending college in the east, and now you think to offer refreshments to a bunch of worthless barbaric heathens! You really must learn to think carefully before you do something my dear, or tongues are likely to start wagging."

"I'm sorry, Mrs. Colonel, but my parents were Christians, and they believed, and taught me, that every man and woman is equal in the eyes of God. Now if you'll excuse me, I need some fresh air." Savannah saw the blush creep into the Mrs. Colonel's face and knew that she'd recognized the speech as the dressing-down that Savannah intended it to be. She also knew that there would be hell to pay tomorrow for daring to address such an important person in such a belligerent tone, but she could not help herself. The Mrs. Colonel had worn her patience about as thin as it was going to get without it disappearing completely. Perhaps the corset had cut off more oxygen to her brain than she realized. Perhaps she could use that as an excuse when she found herself face-to-face with an irate Mrs. Colonel come morning. Not that it would help.

Savannah stepped into the fresh evening air and wished she could draw in a deep, cleansing breath. She knew it was not going to happen if the corset remained strapped restrictively around her waist, so she resigned herself to closing her eyes for a moment to enjoy the peace and quiet.

Wounded Eagle watched from a safe distance as Savannah stopped on the balcony right outside the ballroom. He released the breath he had not realized he'd been holding. So, those strange hand signals she'd been doing rapidly behind her back *were* meant for him. He wondered why the white woman wanted to speak to him and let his mind fantasize over her and her intentions. She was, undoubtedly, a beautiful woman. Did she see him like other white women did—as a rebellious form of entertainment? He hoped not.

She appeared more an innocent than a seductress. Still, he could fathom no other reason why she wished his company if not for the very same reason as other white women he'd encountered in his life. He always managed, in the past, to curtail the temptations provided by so many other women when his wife was alive. No longer did he have her as a reason, and this white woman was a temptation that he may not wish to resist if she should offer herself to him.

He waved in her direction when he noticed her squinting into the darkness. Her gaze settled on his location and she lifted her skirt slightly and stepped gingerly from the balcony onto the springy grass.

"Miss Savannah?" A voice called from the French doors when she was about halfway to her destination. "Are you out here?"

"Blast," Savannah muttered, looking back over her shoulder. She moved sideways into the shadow of a large pine tree, hoping to remain unnoticed, but it was not to be. The movement attracted the attention of the man standing in the doorway and he moved toward her.

"Blast," Savannah muttered again, looking over her shoulder at the place where the Indian was hiding, but her gaze could not penetrate the shadows to detect where he'd gone. Perhaps the soldier heading her way had scared him off.

"Just great!" She muttered under her breath. "There went my chance."

"What was that?" The soldier asked as he approached.

"Nothing," Savannah said shortly. "What can I do for you, sir?" She said courteously.

"You are Miss Savannah Warren, are you not?"

"Yes, but I don't recall meeting you before, sir."

"I'm Captain Michael Fredericks, at your service, miss. It's a pleasure to make your acquaintance."

"I've heard a great deal about you, Captain. It's a pleasure to meet you finally," Savannah said politely, but her stomach felt suddenly ill. "Did you just arrive at the party then, Captain?"

"Yes, and I'd like to apologize for being delayed. I had some paperwork to catch up on," he explained; however, Savannah could sense the stiffness behind the words and his demeanor was anything but relaxed. Did he know the reason for her being out of doors, or was this simply his normal manner around women? "And, please, call me Michael."

"I'm not certain that would be appropriate, Captain."

"Well, if the Mrs. Colonel has anything to do with it, we'll be husband and wife by the end of the week, so I don't think we need to stand too much on formality, do you?"

Savannah definitely caught the tenseness in his tone that time and looked into his eyes. It only took one quick glance for her to realize that the good Captain Fredericks was as put out with the Mrs. Colonel as she herself was. Well, there was only one way to find out, and that was to ask.

"If I ask you something, Cap...Michael, would you answer the question honestly?" She asked.

"I will do what I can, dear lady," he answered with a slight bow, confusion replacing the irritation in his gaze.

"Do you wish to marry me?"

Michael took a step back, his gaze widening.

"I've shocked you with my forthrightness," Savannah smiled and tried to put the Captain at ease, but his gaze remained wide and wary. "I guess my outspoken nature is one reason that I've not managed to land a husband in my twenty years of life," she explained, but instead of accepting her explanation, his frown increased.

"You say you've reached your twentieth year? How can it be that you look no more than a child?"

"Oh. I eat well, exercise, and take care of my skin." Savannah laughed lightly at his continued look of bewilderment.

"It would appear that you make a jest at my expense. May I ask why?"

"Jest?"

"You are hardly at your twentieth year in life, yet you try to convince me otherwise. Is this candidness your attempt at trying to persuade me not to marry you?"

"Actually, no, but I would like to know if you wish to marry me?"

Michael sighed at having his own question sidestepped, but humored Savannah with an answer to her own inquiry.

"I'm sure that I would be honored to take you to wife, Miss Savannah," he answered politely, "you are a very beautiful lady, and I'm more than certain you will suit my needs as a military wife nicely." Michael delivered the gallant answer in a stiffly formal manner that made Savannah laugh softly.

"Oh, without a doubt. Still, you didn't quite answer my question now did you, Captain?"

"Michael."

"I'm sorry—Michael," Savannah corrected.

"Now, how have I not answered your question, Savannah?"

"I asked if you wanted to marry me, not whether you thought I'd make a suitable wife."

"Are they not the same?" The Captain asked, truly befuddled.

"Not really," Savannah sighed. "People marry for all sorts of reasons, Michael, but many times they don't *wish* to marry, and because they don't take the time to know each other beforehand, they end up dreadfully unhappy. Is that what you want? To marry simply because I'm the only available female and you're the highest ranking unmarried military officer available, which means you get first whack at me?"

"I'm not quite certain I know what a 'first whack' is, but think I follow your meaning. I'm also beginning to realize that your presumptuous nature is genuine and not at all an attempt to put me off," Michael smiled.

"Yeah, I guess I am—presumptuous, that is. Sorry if it offends you."

"Not at all," Michael continued to smile. "Now that I know that you are not merely trying to shock me or play at games with me, it's refreshing to talk to someone that speaks their peace, even if it is a woman."

"Thanks, I think."

"Now, you are worried we won't suit?" He tilted his head in question and waited for her to confirm that he'd figured it all out. Savannah merely shook her head and sighed, lowering her gaze to look at the darkened grass swaying in the gentle breeze. Michael raised a hand and gently lifted Savannah's chin, forcing her to raise her gaze back to meet his.

"There is a way to find if we suit, Savannah." Without waiting for a response, he slowly lowered his head and kissed her softly. Politely. Savannah waited for the bolt of lightning to strike that she'd heard women speak about when the right man finally kisses you, but nothing happened. Therefore, she patiently stood and waited for the kiss to end. No tongue dancing here, she thought irreverently as his lips moved over her closed ones.

When Michael finally stepped away, his demeanor stiffened even more. "That did not please you?" He whispered, looking at Savannah's unaffected gaze.

"It's not that, Michael. I simply don't know you well enough to feel anything."

"I see," he murmured.

"I truly don't wish to offend you, but I have no desire to marry you—or anyone else for that matter," Savannah explained in a rush.

"How will you support yourself? Who will take care of your needs?" Michael asked, but Savannah could see the relief etched in his features. So, she had guessed right. The good Captain did not want to marry her. He was probably one of those married to his career. "You're not one of those Suffragists, are you?"

"Suffragist? Lord, no," Savannah exclaimed. Although she was glad that women had freedoms in her time that they probably never would have, had it not been for the Suffragists Movement, she just could not see herself as an unfeminine man-hater, as the Suffragists were purported to be. Savannah wanted a husband and children—eventually—but she also wanted to make sure that the man she married knew how to treat her like a lady in public and a woman in private. A gentleman like the good Captain Fredericks just would not fill the bill. "I'm just not ready to marry yet, and if you'll search your heart and mind, Michael, you'll realize that we really don't suit."

Michael sighed and then laughed. "You're right, Savannah. You really are a fantastically beautiful woman, and had the Mrs. Colonel forced us to wed, I would have done everything in my power to make you happy. In the end, however, I think you and I both would have been dreadfully miserable, as you suggested. I'm simply too dedicated to my work to pay enough attention to a wife."

"Well, I'm glad that's settled. Now if I can just figure out a way to prevent the Mrs. Colonel from finding me another husband until I'm ready to leave."

"You're leaving us?"

"In a few more weeks, I figure."

"Where will you go?"

"Back home," Savannah answered vaguely. "Now all I have to do is keep the Mrs. Colonel from matchmaking until it's time for my departure."

"Maybe I can help with that."

"How?"

"It just so happens that I'm due to leave on extended duty day after tomorrow and will be gone at least two weeks. What I propose is that we announce our engagement tonight and that will allow you time to complete whatever business you need to complete and leave. I'll return to find you gone and bereave suitably to where I cannot take another woman for my wife for quite some time."

"How positively ingenious," Savannah laughed, liking the Captain more by the minute. He was a very sweet man and she hoped that he did find a bride one day that would understand the demands the military made on his time.

"Why, thank you, miss." The Captain made a courtly bow and then extended his arm. "Shall we join the other guests?" He said formally.

"Do you think that the party-crashers left by now?" Savannah asked, placing her hand lightly in the crook of his arm.

"Long ago, I'm sure," Michael answered, leading her toward the patio. "I thought I saw them leaving when I came in search of you." The news made Savannah sigh loudly in frustration. "Is anything amiss, Savannah?"

Savannah smiled wearily at her companion, "I guess I'm just tired is all and am not looking forward to returning to the party."

"Perhaps we'll make our way to the servants' entrance, so that you can escape up the stairs to your room. I'll be happy to make your excuses for you."

"Would you mind?"

"Come." Michael tugged on her hand and led her further along the back of the house to the servant's entrance. He peered inside to make certain that no one was about, and then pulled Savannah behind him. "You go quickly up the stairs before someone misses you, and I will reluctantly join the party."

"Why don't you head on back to your place?" Savannah offered, stopping in the kitchen doorway. "You don't want to be at the party any more than I do. Besides, if you join the party without me, then the Mrs. Colonel is likely to drag me back down to dance with you."

"Oh, that would be dreadful," Michael said in mock horror.

"However, if you are missing as well, then she may just assume..."

"That we're off having a little tryst?" Michael finished for her.

"Something like that," Savannah said quietly, a blush tinting her cheeks.

"It would appear that I'm not the only genius hereabouts."

"Why, thank you most kindly, sir," Savannah said, taking a deep formal curtsey.

"Wait."

"What? What's wrong?"

"We have to go back in; otherwise we cannot announce our engagement."

"Can't you just let it slip to the Colonel tomorrow? It's bound to be all over the fort by noonday."

"I suppose that will work." Michael rubbed his closely shaved beard thoughtfully then took Savannah's hand in his own. Raising it, he placed a light kiss on the back of her hand and smiled slowly. "You are a delightful woman, Savannah, and now I will bid you a fond adieu. Goodnight."

"Goodnight, Michael, and thank you for your understanding—and your help."

"It is truly my pleasure. Sweet dreams." With a final bow, Michael turned on his heels and left the kitchen, leaving Savannah feeling suddenly alone. She listened to the voices drifting from the ballroom and prayed she could make it to the safety of her room before someone spotted her. She crept along beside the wall, listening intently for the sounds of approaching footsteps, groping along in the dark shadows of the foyer. She found the balustrade and sighed. With another quick glance in the direction of the ballroom, she darted up the stairs and into the safety of her room, the rendezvous with the scar-faced Indian temporarily forgotten.

# TWENTY-TWO

## **Present Day**

A soft knock at the door brought Tyrez Morgan to his feet. He walked to the door of his daughter's hospital room and opened it, surprised to see the visitors standing in the hallway.

"May we come in?" Abigail Warren whispered hesitantly. Her husband stood behind her with his arm draped in support around her shoulders, his red-rimmed eyes slightly swollen as if he'd spent the week since his daughter's funeral, crying nonstop—which indeed he had.

It had been exactly a week since the Morgan's had attended Savannah's funeral. Since then, they had heard nothing from Savannah's parents, and Tyrez began to wonder if they would come by the hospital and check on Tyeshia as they had offered the day of Savannah's funeral, or if they'd only asked to come by as a courtesy gesture.

He'd kind of hoped that they had not really meant the offer, since he did not relish the thought of talking to them about what he'd found out about their daughter's death. Still, they were here now and it was time that they knew—if the police had not already filled them in.

*Not likely*, he thought as he waved them into the room. *If I hadn't had a friend on the force, I probably wouldn't have discovered the facts either. After all, the police don't like inexplicable accidents, and they sure as heck don't like trying to explain inexplicable accidents to parents.*

"Hello," Patrice Morgan said. She came forward to embrace Abigail in a swift hug. "I'm so glad you came by to see our Tyeshia."

"I'm sorry we didn't stop by sooner," Thomas Warren spoke up, "we just...that is to say, we..."

"It's okay, man. We understand." Tyrez clasped Thomas's shoulder and gave it a reassuring squeeze. "We know it's been a difficult week for both of you, so don't bother apologizing. In all honesty, it surprises me that you came by at all," he admitted. "If I was grieving the loss of my daughter, I'm not that sure I'd have thought to stop by and check on someone else. So you're definitely a stronger man than I am."

Thomas lowered his head and sniffled slightly, fighting back yet another bout of tears. His wife wrapped her arms around his waist and gave him a tight hug.

"We wanted to stop by and talk to you both, if it's okay," Abigail said softly, releasing her husband's waist.

"Please, sit." Patrice nodded to one of two available chairs in the room. Abigail sat and clasped her hands in her lap. Her husband moved to the back of the chair and placed his hands on his wife's shoulders. Patrice took the other chair in the room, and waited for one of them to speak.

Thomas glanced at the still figure lying on the bed, tubes protruding from nearly every seeable orifice. "How's Tyeshia faring?" He whispered.

"The doctor says she's the same as she was a week ago," Tyrez answered.

"I'm sorry to hear that," Thomas murmured.

"No need to be," Tyrez said. "That's a good thing, not a bad one. It means she's not getting any worse. Our girl is a fighter, so I know that once whatever difficulty in her brain that's keeping her from getting back home to us resolves itself, she'll wake up and be right as rain."

"I wish I had your positive outlook on things," Thomas murmured.

"Well, that outlook would likely be a little different if my baby girl was...well, you know."

"Yes, I know."

"We wanted to find out if you'd heard anything from the police about the accident yet?" Abigail asked, ringing her hands excessively in her lap. "We have not found any answers."

"It's as if the police are deliberately avoiding us," Thomas finished in an angry whisper.

"Likely they are," Tyrez sighed heavily. All eyes shot in his direction, seeking answers. Tyrez sighed again and turned away from the questioning gazes. He placed his hands against the nearby wall and leaned down, letting his head relax on his shoulders. He took a few deep breaths and tried to collect his wits and his thoughts. After all, it was not an easy task to have to tell parents that their daughter should not be dead.

He remembered his own reaction when his friend in the department informed him that his daughter should not be laying in a coma. To compound the situation further there were no answers forthcoming as to the whys and wherefores, and probably never would be, so the knowing of it did not help at all.

Maybe oblivion was better than knowledge in this case. Maybe he should just keep the knowledge to himself. A quick look at his wife's face disabused him of that idea and he pushed away from the wall. "The police don't have any answers," he began, pacing the room and trying to keep the agitation out of his voice, "nor are they likely to have any."

"I don't understand," Abigail whispered, her pale face growing paler.

"What I know came from a detective on the force. A friend of mine. Otherwise, I may be as much in the dark as you are."

"I see."

"I wish I could agree, but even after I tell you what I have to tell you, you will be far from seeing." Tyrez pulled the door to the room open and flagged down a passing nurse. "Could you bring a couple of more chairs in here, please?" The nurse nodded, and Tyrez turned to face the others in the room again. "We all should be sitting for this."

The silence stretched and the tension mounted as they waited for the nurse to return with the chairs. A collective sigh of relief went up when the knock at the door finally arrived. When Tyrez placed the chairs and everyone was seated, he began to speak again.

"Like I said, I have a friend on the force. He was confused about the accident."

"What's confusing about an accident?" Thomas questioned, feeling goose bumps rise on his arms.

"Most accidents—nothing. Accidents happen and people die all the time. In this case, however, our girls, by all intent and purposes, should have survived. I know, because I've been to the accident site."

"You're right, we don't see," Abigail responded softly.

"There's no evidence the girls were hit by another driver, and there's no explainable reason why their car ended overturned in a ditch without showing the least bit of damage. It was upside down, but the accident did not dent the roof. There were no skid marks, suggesting that they'd slammed on the brakes, and the strangest thing of all, the guardrail that was on the side of the road didn't appear as if they had hit it."

"Maybe they ran off the road on the side before they reached the guardrail and then the car flipped," Thomas offered, trying to find an explanation where there did not seem to be one.

"Let me see if I can explain this just a bit better. Like I said, I've been to the accident site." He stood and moved to the wall, drawing his finger along the white, semi-gloss paint in demonstration. "Let's say that this is the highway." He drew his finger in a straight line. "These guardrails line both sides of the highway." His fingers drew another line parallel on top and bottom of the first imaginary line. "First, the police found the car on this side of the highway, flipped over the guardrail. That's the right-hand side of the highway—which meant they would have been heading west."

"But that would mean that they would have been heading toward the reservation. According to the time they left home, they should have been heading back toward Havre at that hour, which is east from their original destination," Thomas interjected, confusion written all over his haggard features. "Unless the accident happened early in the day."

"If that was the case," Patrice said, "then the police would have found the car and informed us sooner than the next day. Agreed?" Everyone nodded, agreed that the accident had to have happened on their return trip, which means they should not have been on the right-hand side of the highway.

"It gets more confusing, believe me," Tyrez continued. "Now, according to the police, the car was laying on its top, right about here." Tyrez placed his finger flat to show the guardrail again, then tapped at a point about half an inch above the imaginary guardrail, centered. "For the car to have landed here, in this position, it would have had to somehow jump the guardrail, and I mean literally jump the guardrail, which is highly improbable, but if it did manage to jump clean over the guardrail and land upside down, the top would have been crumpled, dented, squashed, something. To have been literally unscathed as it was, would mean it could *not* have jumped the guardrail, but that, in itself, could not be possible since to be in the location it was found, the only way to reach that location is *to* jump the guardrail.

"When you add the facts that there are no skid marks, near the crash site, suggesting the driver suddenly slammed on the brakes, which is how most cars end in a ditch upside down, then there is no logical explanation how this car ended this close to the guardrail, in this location, overturned, without denting either the guardrail or the car."

"You said 'the driver'. Wasn't Savannah behind the wheel?"

"We don't know. Both bodies were outside the car closer to the guardrail, which is another oddity. The car purportedly flipped over suddenly. This means that the accident should have trapped Savannah and Tyeshia inside. Of course, the accident did not dent the hood so it might not have trapped them..."

"So they managed to get out of the car and crawl toward the highway," Thomas speculated.

"They didn't have a scratch on them, just like the car, nor any indications that they'd pulled themselves across the ground. It was as if someone had simply laid their bodies out and then left them there."

"Could someone have dumped the car and left the girls there for passing traffic to find?" Abigail asked, trying to find a solution in her muddled mind.

"Okay, but how and why?" Patrice asked, trying to help them work out the puzzle. She had been just as confused as they were when she'd first heard the news, so she understood their confusion. She'd had more than a week to absorb the information and it still perplexed her. Maybe by brainstorming together, an answer might present itself, which was why she was glad they'd decided to come by the hospital and pay a visit. She'd been waiting anxiously for them to come since Savannah's funeral.

"I don't know, I just..." Abigail stopped talking, her hands gesturing in helplessness.

"The reason we're glad you came by," Tyrez said quickly as it looked like Mrs. Warren was beginning to lose her grip, "is we were hoping you could fill us in on the details of the girl's trip. What they were doing? Where they were going? Anything that might help shed light on what may have happened to them."

"They were visiting the Blackfoot reservation, I believe," Thomas Warren supplied, leaning his elbows on his knees. "Savannah was researching for her term paper and brought Tyeshia along to help her find a research topic of her own. According to where they found the car, however, they must have already been heading back to Havre, so what I can't understand is how they ended on the opposite side of the highway facing away from Havre. Are you sure they didn't find any skid marks, or any other indication that would suggest an accident?"

"They found skid marks consistent with the car's tire tread that showed the girls slammed on the brakes and did an about face," Tyrez admitted, knowing that it only added to the confusion.

"But I thought there was no indication of an accident?"

"There wasn't," Patrice said softly. "Police found tire tracks several miles from the accident sight. All they prove is that something caused the girls to turn around hastily and head back toward the reservation. It sheds absolutely no light on the accident itself."

"Maybe one of the girls forgot their purse?" Abigail offered lamely. They all knew that had not been the case since all of their possessions had been found in the unscathed vehicle, so no one responded to that particular theory.

"Is there anything else you can tell us about what they were doing? Did they plan to go anywhere else besides the reservation?" Patrice asked, leaning forward in her own seat.

"No, the reservation was their only stop. What I don't understand is why they were on their way back so soon. Savannah usually spent the night in Browning before heading home, especially since she never finished her research before dark. It just isn't like her to head out so late in the evening."

"Maybe something upset them and they turned for home sooner than usual?" Patrice offered.

"Who is it they went to see, Thomas?" Abigail asked, laying a hand gently on her husband's thigh.

"Some old Indian. Savannah never told us his name."

"Maybe I should pay a visit to the Blackfoot reservation. See if I can find out what we need to know there," Tyrez stated impulsively.

"I can stay here with Tyeshia and call you if there is any change," Patrice offered, consenting readily to her husband's suggestion as if it were already a done deal and he'd be leaving the hospital within the next few minutes.

By the discussions, it was apparent to Thomas and Abigail that he planned to do just that, and it was even more plain a minute later by Tyrez's next statement that he expected Thomas to join him.

"Okay, sweetheart. It's only an hour or so away, so it shouldn't take long to get back if you call. Thomas, would you like to join me? Maybe Abigail can stay and keep Patrice company."

"I'd like that," Abigail smiled encouragingly toward her husband. In actuality, the thought of her husband leaving her alone, and heading in the same direction as her now dead daughter left a cold feeling in the pit of her stomach. Still, she needed to know what had happened, and if that meant letting her husband go with Tyrez, then she'd just have to be strong enough to do that.

Thomas saw the nervousness in her eyes and bent down in front of her. "This may be the only way to find answers," he whispered, echoing her thoughts.

"I know, dear," Abigail smiled, fighting against the nervous flittering in her belly.

"We won't be gone but a couple of hours and I'm sure that Patrice would like the company," Thomas assured her again, and Abigail realized that he was stalling. He too hesitated in departing, knowing that he'd have to travel where his daughter traveled. Worried that he too may not return from the journey, should whatever mysterious force that killed Savannah and Tyeshia overtake them.

She patted his hands lightly and smiled again. "It's the only way to find answers," she repeated with more confidence than she felt. He nodded and stood, turning to face Tyrez.

"When would you like to leave, Tyrez?"

"Well, it's early enough in the day, why don't we eat lunch and then head out?"

"Sounds good. What would you ladies like for lunch?"

A murmur from the bed disturbed the quiet energy permeating the room.

"Tyeshia? Baby?" Tyrez ran to the side of the bed and gripped his daughter's hand. Patrice moved to the other side, and took Tyeshia's other hand in hers. The cold, clammy feeling of the hand belied the warmth of the blood still flowing slowly through Tyeshia's veins, and Patrice shuddered.

Tyeshia's eyes flew open, but everyone in the room could tell they were not seeing anything. "Daddy! Mommy!" The figure on the bed called out, her sightless gaze scanning a distant horizon. "I'll be home soon, okay? I just have to finish something. Don't worry for me. Can you hear me? Please say you can hear me. I do love you both so much."

"We can hear you sweetheart. We can!" Tyrez said loudly. "Patrice, go get the doctor."

"Thomas already has," Abigail offered, standing at the foot of the bed.

As suddenly as they opened, Tyeshia's eyes closed and all was quiet again.

The doctor burst through the door and shooed everyone back away from the bed. "What happened?" He asked abruptly, placing a stethoscope next to Tyeshia's heart.

"She opened her eyes and spoke to us," Tyrez whispered in awe. "She opened her eyes and spoke to us," he repeated, as if only just realizing what he'd said. A grin split his full lips and he grabbed his wife in a bear hug, lifting her from the floor. The couple broke into fits of uncontrollable laughter, followed quickly by huge, racking sobs as realization that their daughter was going to make it hit them with monumental force.

The Warren's were also hugging each other and crying—not from joy, but from the knowledge that their only daughter would *never* be coming back.

# TWENTY-THREE

## 1869

Tyeshia sat up suddenly, her mind in a fog and her body drenched in sweat. "Mommy, Daddy?" She whispered into the humid evening air, but of course, they were not there. She looked out the window at the rapidly sinking sun and cursed under her breath. She'd fallen asleep when she returned to the fort and now the Mrs. Colonel was going to have to find someone else to help Savannah dress for the party.

"Great!" She muttered, flopping back onto the bed. "Another reason for her to criticize me."

"¿Que sú dice?" A voice murmured from across the room, causing Tyeshia to jump. She forgot Mirabel.

"Nada, Mirabel. I didn't say anything."

"Okay, you maybe come eat now. It is getting dark and you no have eaten your dinner. Come!"

"What did you make?"

"Arroz con pollo."

"Chicken and rice?" Tyeshia rolled her eyes and sighed exaggeratedly in anticipated appreciation. She plopped heavily onto the chair, rubbing her belly. "Sounds great! Thanks for cooking for me. *Gracias para comer.*"

"Is okay. I glad you like food. Need to eat more. You are too skinny for any man will like you," Mirabel teased.

"I'll have you know that where I come from, the men were flocking around me just like a rooster to a hen," Tyeshia huffed in mock indignation.

*"¿Que?"*

"Um, let's see. *Muchos hombres quieres mi cuerpo in mi pueblo. ¿Entiendes? Mi español es muy mál.*"

"*Sí, entiendes.* Where I come from, no man have you. You *mucho* skinny. Not good for bearing *bambinos.*"

"Who said I want to have any babies? *No quieras bambinos.*"

"All *mujeres* want to have *mucho bambinos.*"

"Not this *mujer*. This woman wants anything but."

Mirabel rolled her eyes and started murmuring under her breath in rapid Mexican. Tyeshia grinned and dug into the rice and chicken dish that tasted heavenly. Tyeshia had already learned in the short time staying in the small room that Mirabel was a nag that fussed over everyone around her like a mother hen, but she was a good-natured nag, so Tyeshia let her fuss. She reminded Tyeshia of Savannah, except Mexican of course.

Tyeshia paused in mid-bite and wondered just how her friend was doing at the party. What would happen if the Mrs. Colonel succeeded in finding her a husband? Would Savannah forget the reason for their being there? Would Tyeshia be forced to act as Savannah's maid for the rest of her life? "No way!" Tyeshia muttered and shoved another bite of food in her mouth.

# TWENTY-FOUR

Savannah sighed and squeezed her eyes tightly shut, trying to force her mind to calm. She leaned against the closed door in her quiet sanctuary, savoring the silence and the temporary moment of peace. Finally, a chance to rest.

She reached behind her back and struggled to undo the buttons lining her dress then let out a string of whispered curses when she realized that she was not going to be able to undress without the help of one of the Mrs. Colonel's maids, or the currently elusive Tyeshia. "There is no way I'm calling anyone to help me right now. If I do, they will inform the Mrs. Colonel of my whereabouts and she'll drag me back down to the party." Savannah drew in a restricted breath and moaned. It was going to be very awkward trying to rest in her ball gown and corset, but she was simply going to have to do the best she could. She pulled back the covers on her bed and crawled under, struggling to straighten her skirts.

"If I miss anything from this period," she grunted, pushing at her skirts as they flew up toward her face, "it won't be hoops and corsets." Finally, after one final shove, the hoop collapsed and Savannah quickly pulled the blanket up to keep it that way. She lay stiffly on her back, drawing in shallow breaths. After what seemed an eternity, her eyelids drooped and she fell into a semi-restful slumber.

Her eyes popped open moments later, and she struggled to find a breath as a hand pressed firmly against her mouth and nose.

*Whoever this is, they are going to be on the receiving end of a well-placed fist if they don't let go soon*, she thought angrily. Especially since every breath she did manage to take was precious right now, and this character was preventing even that small measure of pleasure.

"Do not scream," A voice next to her ear murmured. "Do you understand?"

Savannah nodded the best she could and was relieved when the hand moved from her face. She took several small, insufficient gulps of air and slowly pulled herself to a sitting position, hoping that the movement would not startle her attacker into doing something foolish.

"Who are you?" She whispered, squinting in the darkness to where the intruder sat beside her on the bed.

"Light your candle and then you will know," the voice replied.

Savannah leaned over and groped for the matches kept near the candle, her gaze darting warily toward the intruder. Her hands shook furiously and she dropped the first two matches before finding the wick. Relief flooded her as the room burst into light, but it was short-lived.

"What are you doing in here?" She demanded, when she saw who was sitting on her bed.

"You wished to speak to me, and since we were interrupted earlier, I thought that now would be a good time."

"You did, did you? And just how long were you hiding in my room?"

"I waited outside until I saw your light go out. Then I came in."

Savannah saw the open window and stared skeptically at the intruder. "My room is on the second floor. How exactly did you manage to get in here?" The man simply smiled mysteriously, but did not answer.

"So, why am I here? What is it that the white woman wishes to speak with me about?" He responded in that heavily accented English that Savannah found charming.

"I'd like to ask you some questions, if I may? Can you tell me what your name is, so that I know who I'm talking to?" Savannah asked. She watched his eyebrow arch, but his full lips split in a grin.

"They call me Wounded Eagle," he said softly.

"My name's Savannah." Savannah held out a hand, but Wounded Eagle merely sat staring at it. "It's how we introduce ourselves," she explained. She reached over and picked up his hand, but he quickly jerked it away.

"Do not touch me."

"I'm sorry, but I didn't realize..."

Wounded Eagle sighed. "Do not think on it longer. I know you are not familiar with our customs and our ways. That is why I'm here. If you were an Indian maid, my being here would tell my people that I had chosen you for my woman. To touch each other declares the same."

Savannah blushed deeply, not simply because of what he said, but because the thought of him claiming her as his woman did not seem such an unpleasant thought. She cleared her throat loudly and shook her head slightly, forcing the thought from her mind, then plunged forward. If she were correct, then events were already set in motion.

"Do you remember who I am?" Savannah asked, knowing that she looked a sight bit different then she did when they first met. Formal attire had a way of changing a person's appearance drastically.

"You do not look the same, but I think it was you who I met outside the Colonel's house when I rode with the delegation. It is your hair. It is the color of wheat in sunlight and is very hard to forget."

Savannah blushed again, but determined that she would keep focused. Her friend's life depended too heavily on her to allow a cute face to distract her. "That's right. You bade me to warn my friend to stay away from Many

Feathers. Remember?"

"I remember well. Is this what you wish to speak with me about now?"

"Sort of."

"I do not know what this means."

"Well, it means that I find myself in a quandary and I'm not quite certain what to do about it."

"Your speech is strange to me, Savannah. I do not understand what it is you are trying to say." Savannah looked at Wounded Eagle trying to discern whether she could trust him. What if Tyeshia was right and he was just as bad as Many Feathers. *No*, she thought, *he has kind eyes, and he hasn't attacked me yet, still....*"Would you consider yourself a man of honor? Someone I can trust?" Savannah asked and watched as his brow knitted in confusion.

"I'm a man of my word, but why is it that you need to talk to me about me?"

"I just needed to know if you were someone that I could depend on, someone that I could trust."

"You need my help?" Savannah merely nodded, her hands wringing nervously in her lap. "Is it to do with Many Feathers?" Savannah merely nodded again. *What's happened to my voice*, she wondered? She did not have any problem talking a minute ago. Then again a minute ago she was not about to try to involve an innocent person in something that could be dangerous.

"Has he hurt you?" The hate in Wounded Eagle's tone was so strong that it stunned Savannah momentarily, and she could not respond even if she *had* found her voice. She shook her head instead. "You can no longer speak, Savannah?" Wounded Eagle smiled, his voice calm again. She looked up and her breath caught. He was looking at her with a soft understanding in his gaze that finally put her at ease.

"Yes," Savannah whispered. "It's just that I'm not certain where to begin or whether I even have a right *to* begin? To ask what I want to ask."

"Why don't you start at the beginning? It is always easier that way."

"I want to know about the man you came here with tonight." It was not exactly the beginning, but if she was right and the white man in his company had been Clark...she had to know.

"I came here with two men."

"The white man. Was he Malcolm Clark?" Savannah dreaded the answer, for she perceived that if it was Clark, then Many Feathers might have already killed White Dove. It would not surprise her if it were Clark, however—the time of year, and the fact that everything else was coming together in front of her eyes told Savannah that the visit to the Colonel's house had everything to do with White Dove's death.

"He has lived with the Pikuni many months. Long before you came to live at the white man's fort. How is it you know who he is?"

"Then it is Malcolm Clark," Savannah said thoughtfully, not answering Wounded Eagle's question. "Why did you all come to speak with the Colonel?" When he only stared at her, she added, "It's important that I know. Truly, it is, or I would never ask."

Wounded Eagle looked at her intently, trying to discern her motives, but could see no deception in the depths of her green eyes. Still, her curiosity of the white man stirred feelings inside him that reminded him of when he'd been courting his wife and had to compete with his best friend for her affections. What he could not understand is why he'd be covetous of a white woman he'd only met briefly twice, and why those possessive feelings made him want to scalp anyone who spoke with her. He swallowed hard and took a deep breath as if by doing so he could shove the insane emotions deep inside himself. His racing imaginings slowed and reason returned. Surely, it could do no harm simply to answer her questions. "One of our warriors turned against our people. He killed Clark's wife and unborn child. My chief chose to banish him from our village."

"Many Feathers."

The Indian leapt from the bed and backed toward the wall, a wariness creeping into his eyes. "How do you know this thing?"

"Call it a wild guess."

"What is this 'wild guess'?"

"Let's just say its intuition. A hunch," Savannah answered, hoping to assuage his fear. "Remember you told me that he was a bad man; well, I simply put two-and-two together."

"I do not know what this 'hunch' is, or this 'two and two', but I do know that you speak knowledge that you should not have. Do you have the sight?"

"What's that?"

"To be able to see things beyond now. Only a Shaman has the sight, or a person who is evil."

"Oh, I'm not evil, and no, I don't have the sight. Not technically, anyway. The knowledge I have is only limited to an event involving Malcolm Clark and Many Feathers. Beyond that, I'm pretty much in the dark about things."

"Then you are a Shaman? I have never met a woman or a white person who is a Shaman."

"I'm not really a Shaman, either. I'm simply a person who has information about certain events that are to take place because of something that someone told me." When Wounded Eagle continued to stare at her blankly, she shrugged her shoulders lightly and sighed heavily. "I'm sorry I can't explain better than that, but it would only confuse you more. Now can you tell me why you and Clark needed to tell the Colonel about Clark's wife?"

Wounded Eagle answered, but his posture remained tense. "Many Feathers killed Malcolm Clark's wife. We are here to let the Colonel know that Many Feathers is no longer a member of our people and cannot speak for them."

"Not to seek assistance in hunting him down?" Savannah asked confused.

"Why would we do that?"

"So that Clark can kill Many Feathers for killing his wife."

"Clark cannot kill Many Feathers."

"Because he is still Pikuni, though he is no longer a member of the tribe."

"You know much, white woman." Wounded Eagle's gaze narrowed, and he moved further away, inching toward the windowsill.

"My name is Savannah, remember?" She answered distractedly.

"If you do not have the sight then how do you know so much, Savannah?" He asked, the wariness in his gaze as prominent as the scar lining the side of his face. Savannah's glance moved to the scar and she frowned.

"Because of what Many Feathers did to your face, that is why you carry the name Wounded Eagle?" It was more a statement of fact than a question. Wounded Eagle's hand strayed to the scar, his eyes widening in disbelief.

"You must have the sight, but say you are not a Shaman?" He murmured. "I must leave."

"Don't leave, please!" Savannah sprang from her bed and hastened toward the window. She stepped in Wounded Eagle's path, cutting off his escape route. "Call it another wild guess," she offered with a smile, hoping to take the fear from his gaze. "I naturally assumed it was Many Feathers. I mean, if he's nasty enough to kill a pregnant woman, then I'm sure he wouldn't hesitate to attack another man of his tribe. Am I right?"

"You are a strange woman, Savannah, but I do not feel you are a bad person, so I will stay a bit longer."

"Thank you, and you don't have to be afraid of me."

"I fear no woman!"

"Of course. I didn't mean you are afraid of me, but afraid of what you think I know."

"What do you know, Savannah?"

Savannah hesitated. She felt compelled to confide in him for some strange reason, but if he took her explanations as the ravings of a lunatic, he could turn his back on her. Then she'd have to face the coming conflicts alone. "If I tell you what I know," Savannah began hesitantly, "I need you to promise and hear me out, not condemn me as a crazy white woman whose brain is gone."

"I do not think that Savannah has no brain, so I will listen to what she needs to tell me."

Savannah sighed and moved back toward the bed, motioning that Wounded Eagle sit on her settee. When she settled on the side of the bed, Savannah looked at Wounded Eagle, extremely hesitant to tell him what she knew. A battle raged in her mind—tell him or keep the information to herself. With Wounded Eagle by her side, she stood a better chance if things came down to a confrontation with Many Feathers, but did she really have to reveal what she knew to solicit that help? Could not she simply ask for his help and leave him in dark, in regards to full knowledge? If she did not tell him everything, though, she may be unable to explain adequately her knowledge of certain events. That may serve to make him more suspicious than he already was, which could send him climbing out the nearest windowsill at the first opportune moment.

Before beginning, she sucked in as much air into her lungs as her corset allowed, praying that Wounded Eagle would believe her words. "Clark will kill Many Feathers..." she said abruptly, but did not finish.

"He cannot!" Wounded Eagle interrupted.

"I'm sorry, but he will. Your chief will warn him not to, may already have done so, but he will not listen because his anger and grief are too strong."

"How can you...?"

"Please let me finish."

"Finish." Wounded Eagle waved a hand in her direction, confusion, and doubt written all over his strong features.

"Thank you," Savannah sighed nervously, twisting her quilt in her hand. "Again, what I'm going to tell you may seem crazy, but I'm the least crazy person you'll ever meet. The only reason I'm telling you this is that I may need your help sometime in the future."

"What help can I give Savannah?"

"I am here because of an old Pikuni named Black Calf..."

"I do not know this name," Wounded Eagle interrupted.

"That's because he does not live near here," Savannah answered mysteriously. "Anyway, he had a dream. In that dream, he sees Many Feathers kill Clark's wife and unborn child. He then sees Clark kill Many Feathers, and finally he sees the Pikuni rise up and kill Clark." Although this was not exactly accurate, she knew that most Native Americans held dreams in high esteem and needed Wounded Eagle to believe what she said. Wounded Eagle's eyes widened, but he kept silent. "Because the Pikuni kill

Clark, the army will send a detachment of soldiers to attack the Pikuni..."

"Then we will be ready for them and will kill them first!" Wounded Eagle declared bravely, jumping to his feet.

"It's not that simple," Savannah whispered. She leaned over and placed a hand on Wounded Eagle's arm, forgetting his dictate not to touch him. He looked at her hand, but she did not remove it. "Please sit. What I have to say next will not be easy for you to hear." Wounded Eagle sat reluctantly. Savannah placed her hands back in her lap, ringing them in unease. Suddenly she realized how difficult revealing to her and Tyeshia what he'd known, must have been for Black Calf. Still, he'd been brave enough to do so, and she had to be equally brave. No matter the outcome. "The army will not attack your people, but the people of a chief named Heavy Runner."

"My uncle?"

"He's your uncle?" His declaration truly astonished Savannah, for this was information she'd not known and it showed on her face. "I'm so sorry. I did not know he was your uncle. Perhaps I should not have spoken out."

"What is it that you know?" Wounded Eagle demanded, clasping Savannah by her arms, pulling her to face him. *It seems his dictate of hands off does not apply to him.* Savannah thought wryly.

"Events are not set in stone," she hedged. "Some things may be changeable. Like, right now, if you take your hands off my arms they may not break," she hissed in pain, and Wounded Eagle abruptly released her.

"I'm sorry for my anger and for hurting you, but you must finish telling me what you know."

"The army will send a detachment, but they will attack the wrong camp," Savannah whispered, rubbing her arms. "They will kill many of Heavy Runner's people, including him, in the attack." Wounded Eagle stood and paced slowly in front of her. Savannah continued speaking quietly. "I've already tried to think of a way that we can prevent this, but am not certain that we *can* prevent it."

"There must be something someone can do; perhaps we can warn Heavy Runner so that his people may be prepared to fight."

"Fighting will only create more fighting which will only cause more unnecessary deaths. Right now, Heavy Runner's people will be the only casualty to this mess—sad as the thought is. If Heavy Runner's people rise and fight, the army will see that as provocation and it will be the only reason they need to send more troops to attack more villages, until the destruction will be widespread. If there is a way to prevent it from happening without alerting Heavy Runner, then that is the route that we need to take," Savannah continued explaining.

"Again, I do not understand," Wounded Eagle interrupted in frustration.

"There's a lot to this, I know, and I'm not making it clear," Savannah sighed. "I guess there is really no two ways around this. I'm going to have to tell you everything, and hope you don't think I've completely lost my mind," Savannah started speaking, slowly explaining first her research into the Marias River massacre of Heavy Runner's people, and how this gave Many Feather's spirit a doorway to find and control someone else's spirit.

She continued about how he chose Tyeshia because she was more like him than Savannah; to Black Calf, who was also dreaming of Many Feathers and the control he was trying to seek, in death, using Tyeshia. Finally, explaining why it was imperative that Tyeshia awaken Many Feathers, so that he can fight to an honorable death with Clark and no longer need to control Tyeshia's mind in the future since he will be at rest.

"There is one way to prevent the massacre of Heavy Runners' people." Realization dawned, striking Savannah with its clarity, as if by discussing everything with Wounded Eagle it had opened a door in her mind allowing the answers to free themselves. "It's assumed, by historical writings and stories handed down, that the Army attacks Heavy Runner's tribe because of Clark's assassination by the Pikuni. If they allow Clark to kill Many Feathers without the Pikuni seeking retribution, then the army will not seek retribution for Clark's death and slaughter hundreds of Heavy Runners' people. Do you think you could convince your people to stand down and do nothing without revealing what you know?"

"So the Pikuni must stand by and watch Clark kill Many Feathers and do nothing?"

"He's not just a white man, but a member of your tribe, and it's not as if there's any love lost for Many Feathers. Or have you forgotten what the man did to you, Malcolm Clark, and no telling to how many others? He's evil, remember?"

"Yes, he is, but his blood is Pikuni. Evil or not. Banished or not. He is the brother of my chief. To say that his death must go unpunished is not something the elders of my tribe will accept easily. I do not like him, but I am not sure that even I could allow this thing."

Savannah shook her head in frustration, rubbing her hands over her face. "This is splendid! On top of dealing with a stubborn friend, I now have to deal with a stubborn Indian."

"Explain."

"Simple. Without Tyeshia's cooperation, and possibly yours, things will not change here, which means that when I finally get back to my own time, nothing will have changed there. Therefore, everything will have been for nothing."

"Your friend, she is the one with the dark skin that has attracted Many Feathers attention?"

"Yes, and he's most definitely attracted hers. So much so, that she's decided not to wake him to fight Clark."

"Then Many Feathers will die as he did before and nothing will change for you?"

"Wrong. She's going to wake him up, but only to try to convince him never to sleep beside water again. She's convinced that if she does that, Clark will not find him, and her and Many Feathers will live to a ripe old age and have tons of children."

"Hmm, she is not thinking too clearly or she is very foolish to think that a man bent on revenge will stop before he finishes what he starts. If, as you say, Clark is determined to kill Many Feathers, he will not stop until he has done so."

"Exactly, but she's too enthralled to see reason, and you are no better," she accused. "You won't convince the council of the wisdom of letting Clark be, because your pride tells you that Many Feathers' death needs avenging. Yet you know that by avenging the death of that evil s.o.b., you will only be causing the destruction of your uncle's people. So where's the sense in that?"

Wounded Eagle ran a hand tiredly over his face and sighed deeply, "You say you are not a Shaman in your time, yet you are a very wise woman. The words you speak are true, although I only understood part of what you said. I will do what I can with the council, but cannot promise to make them see reason as you have done for me."

"That's all I ask. Whew! What a week. It was bad enough getting slung back in time, but now I have to contend with the Mrs. Colonel trying to marry me off to the Captain, who doesn't even want to marry me and all the fighting I've been doing with Tyeshia...it's taking its toll on me."

Wounded Eagle stood looking at Savannah curiously. She was a strange woman that claimed to be from the future. He wanted to believe her mind was gone, but she spoke clearly and with knowledge that said she spoke true. He would risk believing her, and offer her help.

"What is this you say about the Mrs. Colonel?"

"Oh, that." Savannah sighed and plopped wearily on the edge of her bed. "It's only that the Mrs. Colonel thinks that I need a husband to look after me and has selected Captain Fredericks."

"I have met Captain Fredericks. He is a good man."

"Yes, but neither of us cares to marry the other." Savannah rubbed a hand over her face and through her hair. Her fingers caught on the bun at the top of her head and she realized that she had not removed the pins from it. Distractedly, she reached up and began pulling them out.

Wounded Eagle watched in awe as her hair, the color of wheat, fell in strands, piece by piece, down her back. His heartbeat increased and his mouth went dry. Did the foolish woman not realize that she was driving him into the arms of insanity? Next, she would be disrobing in front of him. Did not the women in her time have any care for decency?

"Why do you not wish to marry the Captain?" He forced the words past the lump in his throat, nearly choking when she pulled the last pin and shook her blond mane free from its knot.

"We don't suit. Besides, he doesn't wish to marry me any more than I want to marry him."

"He is a foolish man then."

Savannah glanced up and her breathing stilled. Wounded Eagle was staring intently at the hair cascading down her back, his dark eyes more opaque than before. His knuckles were white where they held onto the back of the one straight-backed chair in the room.

Savannah remained unmoving, uncertain how to handle the sudden tension that had arisen. She watched his gaze wander over her with a desire that astounded her. His gaze met hers and for a split second, she thought he would make his way across the room and detail with his actions what his gaze was saying. Instead, he glanced sharply away and released his breath in a whoosh.

"I should not remain here," he said softly and moved toward the window. He had one leg over the sill and stopped, as if suddenly realizing that he'd forgotten something. "The people of my village would never force you to marry someone you not did wish to marry," he said quietly and pulled the other leg through the window, sitting on the ledge, his back toward Savannah.

"I like your people already," Savannah laughed quietly.

"Then perhaps you would like to live among them." He did not turn when he spoke, so Savannah was not certain she'd actually heard the words. When he turned and faced her again, throwing his legs inside the window, she had no doubt she heard him correctly. His eyes and features spoke volumes—desire, fear, determination all warred within him. "If you accept, it will allow you to stay free, stay close to me and when the time arrives, we can set out after Many Feathers and your friend. Chances are, she will be with him by then," Wounded Eagle spoke rapidly, his heart pounding in his ears. He could not believe the words he spoke, and the look that Savannah gave him made him doubt his own sanity.

"Tyeshia suggested something similar, but I know a lot about your people from the history books and I know that they would not easily accept a white person among them."

"I would make it easy. You could even have your own lodge, if you so choose since I know how the white man likes privacy. You would be my guest." Wounded Eagle could not understand his persistence. Obviously, the white woman was not eager to accept his offer.

"Well, based on some of my research," Savannah said, warming to the idea, "I'm certain I can help in some daily chores, but they do not allow women to hunt, so how would I feed myself?"

"You will be my guest," Wounded Eagle repeated. "I will see to your needs."

"That's very kind, but won't your wife object to you seeing to the needs of another woman?" Savannah was looking at her hands, which had started to tremble in her lap. She could not believe that he had asked her to join him in his village, but crazier still was that she was entertaining the notion—and liking it.

"I have no wife." A smile that caused Savannah's heart to flop over appeared on his lips. "Even if I did, I'm sure she would not object to my helping someone."

"I'd object if you were *my* husband," Savannah said rashly, and instantly regretted her outburst. A strange light lit Wounded Eagle's gaze and she felt a blush creeping into her cheeks.

"Why would you object, Savannah?" Wounded Eagle's voice was a mere whisper, but the question pounded Savannah's ears as cannon fire and she could no longer find her voice. She kept her gaze pinned on the carpet and struggled to breathe. A pair of moccasins came into her line of sight and she groaned mentally. The bed shifted under his weight, as Wounded Eagle took a seat next to her. "Why would you object?" He asked again. His voice, tone silken, sent shivers along her spine.

"I don't know. Jealously, I suppose," her words emerged with a croak and Savannah moaned again—aloud this time.

"My people do not hold jealously, so my wife would not mind my helping you—if I had a wife. Yet you would be jealous if you were my wife? Do you not think you could trust me?"

"Trust you?"

"To take only you to my bed."

*Don't do it, Savannah*! Her mind yelled. *Don't take the bait. You're playing with fire, and skating on thin ice simultaneously*! However, her mouth had blocked its ears, ignoring the mind's warning, opening boldly to utter words that seemed foreign in nature to Savannah's normally demure character.

"*Could* I trust you?" Savannah pinned Wounded Eagle with a look that caused his own heart rate to increase yet again.

"If you were my woman, Savannah, I would not have a desire to touch another." The conviction in his voice shook Savannah to the core, but there must have been doubt etched on her features. "Shall I prove it to you?"

"No." Savannah lowered her eyes again, and tried to bring her mind, body, and mouth under single control. "I believe you," her voice was barely audible, and she was still finding it extremely difficult to breathe.

"You should," Wounded Eagled laughed suddenly and stood, moving back toward the window. His demeanor appeared confident, but she rattled his insides and he needed fresh air. "So," he said after a few moments, "will you come with me?"

"I will go with you," she said.

"You will?"

"It's a wise decision."

"It is?"

"Do you now wish you hadn't asked?" Savannah looked up into his opaque eyes, widened with astonishment over her assent.

"No!" Wounded Eagle's gaze drifted to her mouth. "Your acceptance just surprises me. I worry you may regret your decision. So be certain this is what you want, Savannah."

"I'm more certain that I'd rather go with you than stay here and be forced to marry a complete stranger."

"Am I not a stranger to you?"

"You are, but you aren't," Savannah explained. "I can't explain it. Somehow, I feel like I should ask for your help. You also have an honorable air about you that tells me I can trust you."

"Since you believe this, then I must warn you about something."

"That sounds ominous," Savannah laughed nervously.

"The people of my village may decide we should marry, since you will be in my company—alone—for the time it takes to reach my village."

"Oh, I don't think we have to worry about that, since Tyeshia will be coming with us. She can come, can't she? I wouldn't want to leave her here alone."

"She may come," Wounded Eagle agreed, less than enthusiastically.

Savannah moved to where Wounded Eagle stood and impulsively placed a light kiss on his cheek then quickly turned away, blushing furiously at the surprise that lit his gaze.

"When do you want to leave?" She asked, moving away from where he stood.

"I will wait for you downstairs. Take only what you need, and change into clothes in which you can travel. Do you have such clothing?" He eyed her evening gown with doubting admiration.

"Only what I came in," Savannah admitted reluctantly. "It's a bit unladylike, but traveling in it will be easier than what I'm wearing now."

"Then prepare, and meet me as quickly as possible."

"What about your friends?"

"Clark and Little Beaver have already begun the journey back without me. Besides, I do not wish to travel with them knowing what I know. I must have time to think," Wounded Eagle said quietly. "We will return another way to my village, so that our paths do not cross. Hurry and prepare. It will be daylight soon and we will need to be well away from this place."

Savannah nodded. She turned toward the wardrobe and pulled out her twenty-first century clothing, glad to be able to wear them again. "By the way..." Savannah turned, but found she was addressing empty space. "Man, he's good," she murmured, wondering how in heaven's name he'd managed to leave without drawing her attention.

# TWENTY-FIVE

Tyeshia refused to open her eyes at the incessant shaking on her shoulder, instead murmuring death threats to the person that dared bother her. When the death threats did not work and the shaking persisted, however, she cracked open an eyelid and sprung to a sitting position. Her eyes widened further and she slid as far back against the headboard as she could. The distance did not seem nearly great enough.

"What are you doing in here?" She hissed, glancing frantically around to make sure that her outburst had not alerted Mirabel.

"Come with me!" Many Feathers commanded, holding out a hand to her. He did not seem to care who might hear, for he spoke at a normal level, but Tyeshia cared. If he raised the alarm, then soldiers would come, and they would want to know what an Indian was doing in her room and why she, personally, had not screamed bloody murder.

"Keep your voice down! We are inside an armed fortress, you know," Tyeshia said, her words escaping between clenched teeth. "What do you mean, go with you? Go where?"

"Come with me!" He repeated. His tone was a little more insistent, either not understanding her words enough to turn down the volume on his booming voice, or not caring enough to do so. That made him either very brave or extremely stupid in her book.

"Why in heaven's name should I do that?" Tyeshia asked. Pro and Con faced off in her brain. Pro started the challenge, listing all the reasons she should crawl off the bed and straight into his arms: handsome, strong, virile, he likes you, he came for you, you're supposed to stay in his company anyway. Con responded: dangerous, evil, demented—need I go on?

Tyeshia had to admit, both sides had very good points, which did not help make her decision any easier. However, Many Feathers' response swayed her decision in his favor.

"You will be Many Feathers' woman. We will start a people of our own, since my people have turned their back on me," he explained, as if it was already obvious and she should be honored, which in fact she was.

Still, a shiver of apprehension ran up her spine. Why did he have to remind her about why they'd banished him? Of course, everyone could be wrong and his people may have simply banished him for stealing the chief's favorite horse, or something. She swayed from him again and began to get a little dizzy in the head—go, run, go, run—the internal battle raged on.

"Why would they turn their back on you Many Feathers? Aren't you a great warrior among your people?" She asked, seeking clarification—

anything to help stop the bickering between the Pro and Con inside her head.

"Many Feathers is the best warrior of the Pikuni, but my people have banished me for taking a stand against the white man that would dare to take a Pikuni maiden for his wife."

"A white man?" *Oh crud.* Dread suddenly clutched at her heart for she knew which white man, and what had finally driven his brother, Mountain Chief, to send him away. "How did you punish this white man, Many Feathers?" She asked, wondering why she really needed to know. It was plainly obvious—blast her morbid curiosity.

An evil grin split his sensual mouth and Tyeshia drew further back against the small headboard. "The traitorous woman who dared to marry him lies dead by my hand. Her mixed-blood child with her."

"You killed a child? One of your own?" Tyeshia asked incredulously.

"The child was not yet born. Both deserved to die. She was a traitor to my people, but it is me that they are sending away!"

"Won't Clark come after you?" Tyeshia asked. She was suddenly afraid of the man in front of her. Con was winning.

"How do you know this man is whom I speak of?" Many Feathers eyes narrowed into slits of suspicion, and Tyeshia's fear grew.

*Oops. That was a big boo-boo*, she thought. "The news of his wife's death," she improvised quickly, "has already reached many."

"I had not expected it to reach the fort so soon," Many Feathers said thoughtfully, but did not question her explanation further. She let out the breath she'd been holding, and repeated her previous question. "How do you know that he'll let it go, Many Feathers? What makes you think he won't come after us?"

"Then you will come with Many Feathers?"

"I don't know, I..."

"We do not have time for you to decide. It will be daylight soon and we will need to be far away by then. Now come!"

*He's strange*, Tyeshia thought. He is extremely concerned about being in a fort full of soldiers during daylight hours, but shows absolutely no concern for the fact that he's in the same fort in the middle of the night with the same bunch of soldiers, or he'd keep his voice down like she asked. What did he think? That those soldiers became deaf after midnight?

"Please, just answer that one last question and then I'll decide," Tyeshia said, borrowing a little more time to try and help her decide what to do. Dadblasted, why could Savannah not be here as she was supposed to be? She was the decision-maker in this little field trip.

"He will not know where we have gone. Anyway, he is but a white man. He is no match for my skills, and if he does come after us, I will kill him."

Tyeshia thought about what Savannah said regarding Clark's attack on Many Feathers. Neither of them had thought about whether Clark could kill Many Feathers if she did wake him. What if the opposite occurred? What if she woke Many Feathers and he succeeded in slaying Clark instead? Could she still return to the future and live in peace without this man commandeering her mind? Or would she remain behind to live as Many Feathers' woman forever.

Pro was gaining distance over Con. Perhaps fate meant for her to return to this time—not to watch a great warrior slain so that she can live in relative peace in her own time, but as the start of a great and powerful new race of Native Americans.

Whatever the outcome, she apparently had to go with Many Feathers. Destiny seemed to have use of her and she was not one to mess with destiny. Pro crossed the finish line first and Tyeshia slid across the bed, placing her hand into Many Feathers. He jerked her towards the window forcibly.

"May I get dressed first?" She asked, suddenly feeling shy.

"We must hurry. If the white man finds me here..." He didn't need to continue, for Tyeshia was very aware of what would happen if they found an Indian inside a locked fort at night. She dressed quickly and they snuck out the back window and to an unlit area along the ramparts.

"Wait!" She tugged at Many Feathers' arm, preventing him from sliding through the small opening in the fort wall.

"What is it that we must wait for, woman? Light will be upon us soon and we must be far away from here."

"I need to let Savannah know that I'm going with you."

"The white woman?"

"Yes."

"She is your friend?"

"Yes."

"I did not see this. I see a white eyes who seeks to control a woman whose skin is the same as mine. Just as the white men at the fort try to control all of my people."

"But..."

"Go, but I will not wait for you to bow down before a white eyes. I am leaving!" He quickly slid through the opening and vanished.

Tyeshia stood in indecision for a moment, then quickly knelt and pushed herself through the opening.

"Good," a voice said beside her in the darkness. "Now, come! My horse is tied nearby."

With a quick glance over her shoulder, Tyeshia turned and ran after Many Feathers, hoping her impetuousness would not be her downfall.

# TWENTY-SIX

Savannah rushed about the dimly lit room, throwing what little possessions she had onto the bed, which fortunately was not much. Collecting her meager belongings was not going to be the problem with meeting Wounded Eagle quickly, she thought, trying despairingly to reach the buttons lining the back of her dress. Getting out of her dress was. The first three buttons came open easily, as did the bottom buttons, but her shoulders ached and her cursing increased, as she tried desperately to reach the center. With a cry of despair, she tugged sharply at the material until she heard it rip.

"I'm sorry, Mrs. Colonel," she whispered to the empty room, "but I had no other way of getting undressed." She quickly pulled the rent material away from her body and repeated the struggle with the corset. She sighed when her fingers finally found the tied ends of the strings. She pulled them free and then took several deep breaths, loosening the remaining strings. With a few more inhalations and tugs, the corset released its uncomfortable grip on her abdomen and she shimmied out of it, slinging it aside with disgust.

"One thing's for certain, I'll never wear *that* contraption again." She took several more lung-stretching breaths then pulled on the clothes in which she'd arrived. She quelled the urge to kiss her brazier, and said a quick prayer of thanks to its inventor instead.

Within a few minutes, Savannah donned her modern attire and she had her hair pulled back in a comfortable, practical ponytail. She quickly yanked the case from one of her down pillows, and stuffed it with the things that the Mrs. Colonel had given her, then cracked open her bedroom door.

She'd briefly entertained the notion of heading out the way that Wounded Eagle had gone, but dismissed it just as quickly. She did not have wings, and even in blue jeans, she was lousy at descending from anything higher than a stepladder. She peered out to make certain no one was around and then snuck out into the dimly lit hallway, quietly pulling the door closed behind her. Leaning over the balustrade, she listened carefully for signs of anyone approaching then furtively made her way down the stairs. When she reached the bottom, she made a quick dash for a nearby potted plant as two men strolled out of the ballroom.

"She's a looker, all right. Too bad we won't get a shot at her," the one standing closest to her said in a disgruntled voice, and then took a long draw on a cheroot.

Savannah covered her nose and mouth as the smoke drifted over to her, nearly causing her to sneeze.

"Especially not after the good Captain Fredericks got a look at her. No, siree. We enlisted men don't stand a chance."

"Way I see it, they'll be married off before the end of the week," A man with dark thinning hair snorted unpleasantly.

*You don't know how wrong you are*, Savannah thought with amusement. She stifled a giggle as she thought about hers and the Captain's plans and was even more thankful to him now than ever for his helpfulness. After all, if he had not agreed to announce their engagement, then the Mrs. Colonel could very well stick her with one of these arrogant baboons—then again, not.

After all, she was leaving now, so the Mrs. Colonel would not have time to find another suitor, should the Captain not follow through with his and her arrangement.

*Wait a minute*! She thought suddenly. *What's going to happen tomorrow when the Captain and the Mrs. Colonel find I've gone missing? The Captain knows that I was planning to leave soon. Perhaps he'll decide that I didn't want to take any chances with the Mrs. Colonel's matchmaking skills, should she not buy the engagement announcement. He's a smart man, after all, and shouldn't have any difficulty drawing a conclusion about why I've gone. He'll probably assume I got cold feet about announcing a fictitious engagement and decided to cut my stay at the fort short.*

*Of course, the Mrs. Colonel may not approve of my decision to leave and send Michael out to find me. I hope that he'll respect my decision to leave and only make a half-assed attempt to find me. Otherwise, I'm going to have a heck of a time explaining why I'm in the company of an Indian. Would you two please go back inside the ballroom?* She pleaded silently as she felt time slipping past. She wondered just how long Wounded Eagle would wait for her before deciding she'd changed her mind and leave her.

"Wonder what Clark and those heathens wanted anyway?" The one closest to her pondered. He turned toward where Savannah hid and stuck the stub of his cheroot into the potted plant. Savannah held her breath and sucked in her stomach, trying to blend in with the shadows.

"That soldier reject has quite a nerve showing his face at this here fort. Especially after he went and turned Injun on us."

"It surprises me that the Colonel didn't just throw the turncoat out on his fanny."

"Colonel Baker is too concerned with making peace with those heathens to kick his no-good backside outta here."

"Yeah, well, one of these days those no-account varmints are going to get their just desserts—Clark included."

"There you are, gentlemen," a voice intruded. "Did you find our fair guest of honor?"

"No, sir, Colonel, sir!" Both men snapped to attention. "She must have retired to her room for the night, sir."

"We checked everywhere, sir, and there weren't no sign of the lady," the other chipped in.

"Well, we best rejoin the other guests then. I'll inform the Mrs. Colonel that it's time to draw this shindig to a close. We have more pressing business to attend to, than to humor the women, especially when the main attraction has disappeared."

"Yes, sir," the two men snapped, then followed the Colonel back into the ballroom.

Savannah released an audible sigh of relief then quickly stifled a startled gasp as a voice whispered close to her ear.

"I'm glad they are gone. Now we can leave."

Savannah spun around in the tight confines and found herself nose-to-nose with Wounded Eagle, her heart beating loudly in her ears. "How long were you standing here?" She whispered breathlessly.

"As long as you," Wounded Eagle whispered, a grin on his face. "I came to search for you. When I saw you sneaking down the stairs, I hid behind this fake tree to wait for you. Then those two men came out and you jumped behind here with me."

"I had no idea you were here," Savannah whispered in astonishment.

"I blend in with my surroundings very easily," Wounded Eagle teased.

"One benefit of having dark skin," Savannah snapped, irritated that he'd been there and she had not known it. "If they'd have found us, it wouldn't have boded well for either of us."

"You are afraid of your military men?"

"No. Just smart," Savannah corrected. "If my memory serves me correct, these men were vicious. If they'd found us together, they'd have turned that viciousness toward us."

"I would not let them harm you," Wounded Eagle announced proudly.

"That's very sweet, Wounded Eagle," Savannah replied, "but what's to stop them from hurting you. One against a hundred isn't the best odds for winning a fight."

"You are concerned for me?"

"Of course! Watching you get butchered isn't on my list of priorities, you know!"

"I do not know what you mean, but it is good that you are worried for me. Now come, we must leave." Wounded Eagle moved from behind the potted plant. "Stay close behind me so that they do not see you." Wounded Eagle bent at the waist and moved quickly and quietly in the direction of the servant's entrance, stopping again when the door to the ballroom opened. People started drifting out to collect their wraps and call it a night.

"We can't stand here, or someone will see us," Savannah whispered in

Wounded Eagle's ear.

"If we move, they may see us."

"It's a chance we'll have to take." Savannah moved around Wounded Eagle, peered again down the hallway, and made a dash for the kitchen door. Without breaking stride, she darted through the rear entrance. Only then did she slow her pace, turning to ensure Wounded Eagle followed. Not that she doubted he would but she wanted to make sure.

She bent at the waist, leaning against the wall of the house, taking deep breaths and trying to steady her erratic nerves. She was certain she'd find a few gray hairs when she next inspected herself in a mirror.

"You are okay?" Wounded Eagle placed a gentle hand on her shoulder and Savannah straightened.

"I'm fine. I've just never had to sneak around in the dead of night with a few hundred soldiers only one room away."

"We must leave now. You are sure you are okay?"

"Absolutely."

Wounded Eagle shot a quick glance in the direction of the kitchen door and then back at Savannah's attire. "Are these the clothes your women wear in your time?"

Savannah's skin turned a deep pink, and she lowered her gaze to the snug-fitting jeans and loose-fitting red-colored blouse. In her own time, she would be considered modestly dressed, but here in eighteen-sixty-nine her clothing was causing quite a scandalous reaction. Even Wounded Eagle was shocked, and he appeared to have less on than she did in his breechclout, thigh-high leggings and buckskin shirt and shoes. At least she was not showing half her thigh to every person who walked by like he was. She wished people would stop making her feel weird and out-of-place. Maybe she did not dress appropriately for the times, but at least she did not look like the local prostitute.

"Where I'm from, this is closer to what a nun would wear."

"I do not know what this 'nun' is."

"Let's just say that if I was in my time, I'd be wearing clothes befitting a virgin. Understand that?"

"You are a virgin. Yes, I understand that." Wounded Eagle crouched suddenly, his gaze darting to the side of the house. "Get down and stay in the shadows behind me!"

Savannah quickly sank to her knees, pressing herself against the framework of the house. She listened intently, but did not readily hear the voices coming around the corner as Wounded Eagle obviously did. Did he possess built-in radar like a bat or something?

She detected the men's voices a moment before Wounded Eagle pressed himself firmly up against her, effectively shielding her from sight. If not for the tenseness of his body, she'd think that he was taking advantage of the opportunity to take advantage of her. Something inside her told her that Wounded Eagle was a man of honor, not a jerk in sheep's clothing.

"People are coming, but they are still far enough away where they will not see us if we move. Can you make it to the far corner of the house before they come around this side?" Savannah nodded and Wounded Eagle shifted away from her. She stood and then took off at a dead run the minute Wounded Eagle gave her the signal. She heard him close on her heels and darted around the corner of the house just ahead of him.

Again, she found herself leaning against the side of house bent at the waist, but this time she was fighting for breath, not trying to calm her racing nerves.

"You are very fast for a woman." Wounded Eagle was kneeling beside her, his own breath coming in short gasps. "It is good that you are wearing your virgin clothes, or we would still be back there trying to explain our presence to those soldiers. Still we need to keep moving before the sun rises over the horizon. Can you tell me where your friend is staying?"

"She's staying with the Mrs. Colonel's laundress. Follow me." Savannah took off through the darkness toward the servant quarters on the far end of the fort before Wounded Eagle could object.

She used every military tactic she'd seen soldiers use in the movies, ducking stealthily behind trees, and sliding along behind the buildings lining the dirt street. Soon they were behind Mirabel's room.

"Give me a boost," Savannah whispered.

"What is this 'boost'?"

"Lift me up so that I can get in the window. I'll go in and get Tyeshia." Savannah gasped when Wounded Eagle soundlessly grasped her by the waist and hoisted her easily to the window ledge. She glared down at him, but figured it would not do any good to berate him for scaring her when he'd only done exactly what she'd asked.

She pushed open the window and with a grunt of exertion, pulled herself in, toppling unladylike onto her derriere. As quietly as possible, she moved to the nearest bed, hoping it was the one Tyeshia slept in.

"*Lo siento, Señorita, pero su amiga no es aqui*," a voice whispered across the room just when a lantern was lit, casting the room in a dim yellow glow. Savannah gasped sharply, her hand flying to her mouth to keep from screaming before realizing that Maribel had been the one speaking to her.

"*No habla Español, mucho*," Savannah whispered in reply, falling back on the small amount of Spanish she remembered from high school. "*¿Habla Ingles?*"

"*Sí. Un poco*," Mirabel murmured. "Your friend, she is no here."

"Do you know where she went?" Savannah asked slowly. "*¿Donde estas,* *mi amiga?*"

"She go with the man."

"Man?"

"*Sí.* He have hair like me." Mirabel quickly released her braid and then pointed to her hair. "Like this." Mirabel's long, black hair fell below her waist. "*¿Entiendes?* Understand?" Savannah nodded and Mirabel began deftly returning her hair to its braided state.

"Many Feathers," Savannah murmured, and Mirabel stopped in mid-braid.

"*¡Sí, Sí Señorita!*" Mirabel clapped enthusiastically. "That was his name! I remember she said this name to him."

Savannah moved over to Mirabel's bed, "Do you happen to recall where they said they were heading?"

"No, I no hear too much. I hear him say he—what is word, um, *desterrado*—es, um, I think is 'banish', *sí*, that is word—banish. He no very good man, I think."

"No, he's not, Mirabel. Thank you for your help, but I have one favor to ask, if I may?"

"*¿Que?*"

"Um, *yo necessita su ayuda con algo. Una favor.*" Savannah said, hoping that she was indeed asking for her help. For all she remembered, she could be ordering a cheese pizza.

"*Sí*, I listen."

*So, I got it right. Great!* "Could you not mention tonight to anyone—ever? Even if someone comes and asks? *Necessita su silencio. No hablar.*"

"You no wish me tell someone about tonight?"

"That's right."

"*Sí.* This thing I can do."

"Thank you, Mirabel. I have to go now."

"*¡Tengo cuidado, Señorita y el Dios bendice!*"

"*Gracias*, Mirabel. I'll be very careful." Savannah walked to the window and peered down into the darkness, "Wounded Eagle, are you down there?" She knew he was, but did not want to jump from the window unless she was one-hundred-percent certain that he would be there to catch her.

"I'm here," Wounded Eagle replied quietly.

"I'm climbing out now. Can you catch me?"

"Yes."

Savannah crawled onto the window ledge, then turned around and swung her feet out first. She lowered herself as far as she could until she was hanging on by her fingertips. She felt a strong pair of hands grip her hips and released her hold on the windowsill. Her skin tingled where he touched her, even after he removed his hands, and she had to shake herself mentally to focus on what it was he was saying.

"Where is your friend?" Wounded Eagle repeated, looking up at the window expectantly.

"She's gone already—with Many Feathers," Savannah whispered.

"He did not waste time coming to get her, did he?"

"It would appear not."

"He never could be without a woman," Wounded Eagle snapped scornfully. "I believe that he slept with every woman in our tribe, and still it was not enough."

"I don't think he intends to harm her and really think he has some sort of attraction to her. Unless, of course, he looks at every woman the way he did her that first day he saw us. Besides, she was supposed to go with him at some point and time, remember? I guess I just did not expect it all to happen so soon."

"It is time that we go also. We have much distance to go before the sun rises. You are sure this is what you want to do?"

"I already told you that it's a very wise plan. How else am I supposed to find Tyeshia in a strange wilderness and handle a warrior like Many Feathers, if not with your help? Without you, my task would be over long before it began. With you, I have a good chance of getting Tyeshia and myself back home alive."

"I will help you all I can, if only to avenge all those whose paths have ever crossed Many Feathers and suffered for it."

"Including you?"

"Are you asking if he will die by my hand?"

"You're pretty perceptive."

"No. Fate has ordained that the hand of Malcolm Clark kills him—my brother."

"It's ordained that you try to stop the Blackfoot from doing anything about it. I wonder who has the easier task."

Wounded Eagle laughed shortly, and then took her hand. "I do not think fate is being very kind to either of us. Come, the sky is changing colors and we are still standing here."

"Lead on, Kemosabe."

"Who is this?"

"Never mind. Just lead the way. I'm right behind you."

Wounded Eagle gave Savannah a quick glance and then shook his head. He was extremely happy that she had decided to join him and his heart felt light at the prospect of spending more time with her. When her friend had not appeared at the window, his heart soared like an eagle on the wind. He liked the feel of her also. She was a strange and beautiful woman, unlike any he'd ever met before. The fact that she was from another time, a foreigner to him, explained her unusual manner, but it did not matter to him. If the elders of his village forced them to marry after spending so much time alone, he would not fight the decision. He was finally ready to settle down again and raise a family, and he could think of no better woman than the one by his side.

All the women he had known paled in comparison to this one. He felt a little guilty at not reminding her about the possibility of a marriage contract, but quickly brushed the thought aside. If she did not approve of the arrangement, she could always return to her own time. He brushed that thought aside quickly as well, for that was a thought he dared not linger on.

Savannah squeezed through the small opening in the wall of the fort, staying close behind Wounded Eagle. *And a cute behind he has too,* she thought, laughing silently. She knew she was risking a great deal by traveling with a strange man in the wilderness alone, but she did not exactly have many options open to her right now.

If Tyeshia had not stolen away with Many Feathers, Savannah could snuggle up in her bed at this very moment, dreaming about the man she was following through the woods right now. She wondered what would happen if the elders of his village forced Wounded Eagle to marry her, as he said they might. Would he object at the prospect of marrying a white woman from the future? From the way he'd reacted in her room, he did not seem opposed to spending more time intimately with her.

Of course, she would not mind either. Still, that did not mean she was going to jump into bed with him just because he was a gorgeous man who'd shown an interest in her. No siree bob. The risks were too great. The chance of disease or worse—an unwanted pregnancy.

That would be an easy explanation for her to give her child when he or she was old enough to ask about their father, 'Oh, honey, your dad existed a hundred years ago; that's why he's not in the picture anymore.' Of course, that meant that if his people insisted on his marrying her, she would have to stay here forever in this time. Was that something she was willing to do if it came down to that? She watched him duck under the limbs of the trees, his muscles rippling with every move. He turned to check on her progress and smiled broadly. *At least if we did get married and have kids, they'd be beautiful babies,* she thought, then winced as a branch snapped back and smacked her in the forehead.

"I'd better start paying more attention to where I'm going and less to the man leading me, or I'm going to end up with broken body parts." Savannah rubbed her forehead and laughed, jogging to catch up to Wounded Eagle who had managed to widen the distance between them in just a few short minutes.

# TWENTY-SEVEN

**Present Day**

"What do you think we'll find out here?" Thomas held onto the armrest with a death-grip as they literally barreled down Highway 2 at over a hundred miles per hour toward the reservation. "Do you think that the Old Indian they were coming to visit will really know what happened to them? After all, they were well on their way home when the accident—inconceivable accident—occurred, so what could the Indian possibly know about it?"

"Call it a hunch, but I have a feeling that something the old guy said may have upset the girls to the point where they weren't paying attention to what they were doing or where they were going." Tyrez drove with an air of assurance that would have been relaxing to most people, but not Thomas. He looked at Tyrez's knuckles, as Tyrez spoke, and they were nearly white with the tension of gripping the steering wheel. That meant that Tyrez was not as controlled as he sounded and that could very well mean an accident could happen—and going one-hundred-plus miles per hour was not a speed that bode well for the passenger should the car stop cooperating with the driver.

"But we've already decided it wasn't an accident, or never should have been anyway, so it shouldn't matter what the old Indian said. The fact remains that the girls' accident occurred after leaving the reservation—should never have occurred at all."

"I know, Thomas, but I still can't shake this feeling that the answers we're looking for are partly at the reservation. I can't explain it any better than that."

Thomas felt the speed on the car slow and looked over at its driver. Tyrez's attention was focused out the window and he was slowing, pulling over to the side of the road. "Is this where...?"

"Yes," Tyrez said, "this is where our baby girls ended up."

Thomas sat for a moment, scanning the scene and trying to convince his legs to cooperate and step out of the vehicle. It took a few more minutes, but he finally felt confident enough that if he opened the door and stepped out, his legs would not collapse beneath him. He slid from the passenger seat and walked unsteadily around the scene of the accident, but could see nothing but bushes and trees. They had long ago removed the car and since there had been no seeable damage to the vehicle, not a trace of glass or debris remained behind to mark the site where one girl died and the other lay fighting for her life. It was as if the accident never happened at all.

Tyrez had told them all that there was no evidence to suggest that an accident occurred, but seeing it first-hand only increased his confusion. Small bushes, which the car should have flattened, were springing full of life, as if a vehicle weighing a ton had never laid to rest on top of them.

Thomas moved toward the road again and looked at the blacktop, gray now from years of elemental abuse, but could see no signs of skid marks anywhere—just like the police reported. He examined the guardrail willing there to be signs of the red paint of the convertible the girls had driven on that fateful day, but nothing stood out under his scrutiny. Not even a tiny, microscopic paint chip or dent—nothing.

"Are you sure this is the right place?" Thomas whispered as Tyrez came to stand beside him.

"Yep. Mile marker one-hundred-ten. It's engraved on my brain. I'll never forget."

"It's like a scene out of The Twilight Zone."

"You said it. I didn't."

"It's unearthly, isn't it?"

"Damned strange, yeah. Unexplainable, definitely."

"I don't like unexplainable."

"Neither do I."

"Well, let's go see if there are any answers at the reservation."

"Let me just ring up Patrice and see if Tyeshia has opened her eyes again." Tyrez reached in his coat pocket and pulled out his Motorola phone. He punched out the number to the hospital, grim faced, as he waited for the operator to answer.

"Room six-zero-one," He said to the barely audible voice on the other end.

Thomas moved around the guardrail again, looking over the scene, knowing that it was hopeless, but wanting to give Tyrez a little privacy. Still he could not block out the conversation entirely and sadness drifted over him as he listened to words filled with despondency.

Every time something or someone confronted him with his daughter's loss, his heart constricted and his breathing became shallow. He wondered whether his daughter had felt the same tightness in her chest when death came to claim her. Sometimes at night when he tried to sleep, he would dream of her. She would smile at him and mouth unheard words, as if trying to comfort him, console him, and he would awaken with a peace in his heart. Then a harsh reminder of his daughter's death would encroach on that peacefulness and he would again plunge into an abyss of gloom that he had a hard time dispelling.

A hand on his shoulder startled him from his reverie and he turned to face Tyrez. "Any change?"

Tyrez merely shook his head and turned back toward the car. They made the remainder of the drive to the reservation in silence, each man lost in thought.

# TWENTY-EIGHT

**1869**

"So where are we going?" Tyeshia was tired, filthy, and hungry, but she followed Many Feathers unerringly, more out of desperation to survive than affection. She was scared, and she now regretted leaving so hastily with a man she did not know, following him through a wilderness for which she was unprepared.

They had been traveling nearly nonstop for two days. Tyeshia had not known she had it in her to walk for that length of time and said a quick thanks to the treadmill in the dormitory. If she'd been out of shape, she never would have been able to make this trek, not that she was thrilled at doing so.

"It is not much further," Many Feathers responded without slowing or stopping.

"Can't we get another horse or something?" Tyeshia said, her tone whiny. "I'm tired of walking," *Preferably a stronger horse*, she thought. She did not want to see another one get its throat slit just for getting a sprained hoof like the last one did. She was still fuming over that one—partly angry with the horse for getting hurt and partly put out that Many Feathers would kill it so callously and then offer to cut up the meat for their evening meal. Disgusting!

"I forget that you are not too different from the white woman you call 'friend'," Many Feathers said. He finally slowed to a stop and turned to face her. "We have much distance to cover before we can rest, so you need to be stronger. Here, drink." He handed her the canteen and then lowered himself to the ground. Tyeshia dropped the gear and flopped heavily across from him, drinking deeply.

"That's another thing," she continued complaining after she drank her fill, "why am I carrying all this crap? You're the man."

"My hands must remain free to protect you," he explained in a tight voice. Tyeshia could see that she was wearing on his nerves, but her nerves were just as frayed and she was bone-tired on top of that.

"What do I look like—a pack mule? You're twice as strong as me, so why don't you carry the stuff and I'll watch for danger."

A spark lit Many Feathers' gaze, "you can use a bow and arrow? So you are a woman warrior?" There was something in his tone that Tyeshia could not quite put her finger on, but it was there. Threatening enough that Tyeshia decided to back down. She had been in enough word wars to know that it was not *what* they said, but *how*. She wondered what would have happened had she been too tired to miss that particular tone. She shuddered and lifted the canteen again, wisely holding her tongue.

When he stood and started walking again, she reluctantly hoisted the gear and followed. If she had not been so afraid of the jungle and all of its wild critters, she would have slung it all down in an angry fit and stormed off, but there was nowhere to go. That realization struck her so hard that she stumbled and nearly fell. She really was not in Kansas anymore and not only did she not have Toto for a companion, she did not have Savannah either. All she had was a surly companion who would not recognize a joke if he told it himself.

As if cued, her mind picked up the country tune, *What Was I Thinking*[3], playing it repeatedly as if to remind her that she really needed to stop acting on her impulses and start thinking first.

---

3 ***What was I Thinking*** *(2003, ASIN# B0000AM6FV)* by country artist, Dierks Bentley. Label: Capitol

## TWENTY-NINE

The maid knocked. Then knocked again, but her persistence was met with continued silence. She grew more worried with each strike against the hard oak surface. When the occupant of the room failed to respond after more than ten minutes of ceaseless pounding, the upstairs maid lifted her skirt and sprinted down the stairway. A hand shot out from the shadows as she reached the bottom stair and jerked her to a halt.

"What you be doing running in this house, Carnation. You know the Mrs. Colonel don't hold to unladylike behavior from her housekeep?" It was Rose, the Mrs. Colonel's head housekeeper.

"I be truly sorry, Missus Rose, but there be something wrong in Missus Savannah's room. She must be awful sick or something because she just ain't answering my knock and I been doing it for a while now. I need to let the Mrs. Colonel know so she can fetch the key and open the door."

"What's this about Savannah?" The Mrs. Colonel came out of the dining room carrying her napkin. Rose winced because she knew that the Mrs. Colonel hated to have her breakfast disturbed. She explained the situation to the Mrs. Colonel and shot Carnation a 'this better be serious look' before turning and heading up the stairs behind her employer.

"She's probably just sleeping soundly, is all. There certainly isn't need for all the fuss, I'm sure." The Mrs. Colonel shot her head housekeeper a disgruntled look over her shoulder and Rose turned and glared at Carnation.

Carnation was wide-eyed and worried, but not for herself. She was worried for Missus Savannah, for she had not a doubt that something bad had happened to the sweet lady, and her gut feelings were never wrong.

When the Mrs. Colonel reached the door in question, breathing labored, she had to stop for a moment to catch her breath. When at last her breathing returned to normal, she rapped on the door with an insistence that dared anyone inside not to answer. No one did. At last, her own concern growing, she unlatched the key ring hanging from her skirt's sash and inserted the master key into the lock. With a sense of foreboding, she shoved the door open and stormed inside.

"Open the curtains!" She demanded. Her eyes squinted as she tried to penetrate the dimness that enveloped the room. Carnation moved quickly across the room and with a swoosh, yanked open the heavy draperies that covered the one large window. The women standing in the room squinted against the sudden brightness.

It did not take long for their gaze to take in the chaos in the room.

Someone had thrown the bedding back as if they'd been sleeping there. The dressing table was in disarray, the contents of which someone strewn over the surface carelessly, and the gown that the Mrs. Colonel had made for Savannah lay in a heap on the floor, the corset, and other undergarments nearby. Instinctively, Carnation picked up the gown to put it away.

"Give that to me!" The Mrs. Colonel snatched the silky material and flipped it over, examining the rent material. Obviously, Savannah had removed the gown on her own or someone helped her remove it against her will. She wandered slowly around the room looking for anything that might help explain the condition of the room and the gown—then she found it. Her breathing constricted and she felt close to fainting. *How could this have happened?* Her mind railed. "Go get Colonel Baker!" Her voice was a distracted whisper. Rose saw the paleness on her mistress's face and her worry grew. The Mrs. Colonel never lost her cool.

Rose turned and snapped orders at Carnation. With a quick, unnecessary curtsey, Carnation darted from the room. Rose moved to stand next to her employer wondering what held her gaze in such fascination and stifled a gasp of her own.

"Tell me I'm not seeing what I'm seeing, Rose."

"It looks like a footprint, Mrs. Colonel, but not from a boot. It's shaped like a foot, but smooth like..."

"A moccasin. Dear Lord Almighty! Our Savannah's been abducted by Indians!"

# THIRTY

"This place is beautiful!" Savannah exclaimed, sliding off Wounded Eagle's horse straight into his arms. If the sight of the waterfall had not enthralled her, she would have noticed how his hands lingered on her waist and his gaze roamed over her facial features as if trying to memorize the beauty before him. He reluctantly released her after another moment and she moved away. She stopped by the edge of the bank and scanned the expanse of the blue-green water, amazed at the clarity. "I can see nearly to the bottom."

"You seem surprised." Wounded Eagle moved to stand beside her.

Savannah laughed, "I guess I'm just used to pollution."

"What is this 'pollution'?"

Savannah laughed. "See, only a person from an earlier era wouldn't know what pollution is. Me? I'm so used to breathing the smog from cars and seeing trash littering our lakes, rivers, and oceans, that it's a part of daily life."

"I did not understand much of what you just said. I'm sorry."

"No need to apologize. I know that I must talk funny to someone from this era. Let me try again, okay?"

"Okay."

"Where I'm from, buildings take up nearly every inch of land. The sky is dirty because the horses we drive aren't live animals and they spit out grimy smoke that fills the skies. People use so many paper products, producing so much waste that there is no longer any place for it to fit. Most of it winds up in our lakes and oceans, killing many of the fish that swim there. It makes things look really dim and ugly. Still, there are a few places similar to this, places that modern advancements have not destroyed, but they get fewer and fewer with each passing year. Even in *those* places, the water is no longer a clear blue-green as now."

"Then why do it? Why not change it?"

"There are people that are trying to change things, to make it beautiful like it once was. However, the businesses that cause most of the pollution have a lot of money and power and it's hard to fight against them. Most people have just learned to accept things the way they are. Anyway, it's nice to see things the way it used be. It's beautiful."

"Yes, it is," Wounded Eagle murmured looking over the lake, but thinking about the woman standing next to him. "Has anything else changed in this time of yours?"

"Everything and nothing."

"I don't understand."

"I know, and now it's my turn to be sorry because I can't really explain. So much has changed, but so much is still the same as well."

"What about men and women? Do they still marry and have children?"

"Oh! You don't even want to get me started on the sexes," Savannah said, moaning in mock frustration. She looked at Wounded Eagle and laughed, his face registered such shock. She placed a gentle hand on his arm, "Let's sit, and I'll see if I can explain a little to you. It's not as complex as pollution and businesses, but it's still complex." She sat on the bank of the lake, pulled her knees up to her chest, and propped her chin on her arms. Wounded Eagle sat beside her, his legs crossed and his manner expectant. "Men and women still marry, and some reasons are the same as now—money and prestige. Some even marry for love. I hope I'm one of those. Anyway, most people opt to live together instead of marrying and they seem content. I think the biggest difference is the attitude toward sex. Men and women sleep with many different people before finally settling down with one person, if they settle down at all. Some people settle down, but still have sex with other men and women other than the one they marry. Basically, we live in a free sex society that allows almost anything. Now, in this time, a man can sleep with whomever he pleases, but a woman would not dare. In my time, men and women both have the same right to sleep around. It's somewhat sad, since diseases are prevalent in my time."

"You are not one who has chosen this life though. You said you are still a virgin."

"My parents are Christians who believe a woman should save herself for her husband. I believe the same. I don't think it should be a common thing for a woman to have sex with a man just because he's sexy or cute or tells her how beautiful she is."

"Have you never felt desire for a man?"

"Yes," Savannah murmured, a blush creeping into her cheeks, "but not until I arrived here in this time."

Wounded Eagle stiffened slightly beside her, jealously surging unexpectedly through his veins. "Captain Fredericks?" He asked so softly that Savannah nearly missed it.

"Hardly." Wounded Eagle's head jerked up at this strong denial.

"Then who has caught your eye, Savannah?" The answer was so plainly visible in her pale green eyes when she finally looked at him that it momentarily took his breath away. Uncertain that he was seeing what he was seeing, he asked again, his voice barely audible and strained to his own ears, "Who?"

Without a word, Savannah moved closer and placed a light kiss on his lips. "You." She pulled her head back and looked into his startled gaze. "Yes, I know. It kind of took me by surprise, too."

Wounded Eagle's astonishment turned to wary displeasure at that statement, "Because I'm Indian," he stated with certainty, as if he understood all.

Savannah laughed and placed a hand lightly on his arm again, "Men are silly, no matter the era."

"You laugh at me."

"Yes, I'm laughing at you, because you think you've got it all figured out when you aren't even close."

"I wish I understood your words more clearly."

Savannah smiled, "I guess I should explain another thing about my time—this one is a good thing though."

"Explain," Wounded Eagle said, but his heart did not wish to hear anything more about her time. She said she wanted him, but was she pleased by this discovery? How could she be, when he is everything that society teaches a white woman to hate?

"In my time, there is very little prejudice. People from different races date and marry all the time."

"They do?"

"Yes, they do, so you being a Native American doesn't concern me one bit."

"I'm Pikuni, not this Native whatever-you-said, but that does not bother you?"

"No."

"Then why were you surprised when you discovered your desire for me?"

"Because I've never known a man for such a short time and felt what I feel for you. I don't believe in love at first sight, yet whenever you are near me I feel like I'm on top of the world. The only explanation I have is that fate brought me here so that I could meet you."

"Me?" He asked. Savannah nodded and smiled. A wide grin split Wounded Eagle's lips. "I'm glad for this because I want you too, Savannah." Without waiting for a response, Wounded Eagle placed his hand on the back of her neck and drew her closer. Slowly, he lowered his mouth to hers, "Very much," he whispered.

His mouth claimed hers in a kiss that sent sparks shooting from the roots of her hair to the tips of her toes. She melted against him and he deepened the kiss, slowly lowering her torso to the soft, springy grass.

With a will he did not know he possessed, he reined in his desire, not wanting to frighten her away. She felt him pull away and opened her eyes. He smiled softly and placed another light kiss on the tip of her nose.

"If it were up to me, I would claim you as my woman right here, right now. But I will not dishonor you. You have saved yourself for your husband and I will not claim what is not my right to claim." Savannah's cheeks again turned as pink as her shirt and she started to sit, but his hands pressed against her shoulders to prevent her from rising. "Make no mistake, however," he grinned, placing another quick kiss on her lips, "that I will claim you as my wife when the time is right. Now, however, we must rest and then leave. I only wanted to show you this place, because this is where I think Many Feathers will bring your friend."

That snapped Savannah out of her aroused state and she sat up quickly, "What makes you think that?"

"Long ago, before Many Feathers changed, he was a young warrior with big dreams, but his path never seemed to lay with that of the people. When he was a young man, and I still called him 'friend', he brought me to this place. This place seemed to touch a part of him that he'd started to close off from everyone."

"I can understand that. It even makes me feel peaceful."

"Yes, it does. Anyway, he claimed this land for his own. He told me that one day, he would bring his woman and raise his children here. Begin his own tribe to lead them in his way. That surprised me, since he had already begun isolating himself from friends and family. He started participating in ceremonies forbidden, and taking every woman he wanted to his mat, whether they wanted to or not. So I could not see him settling down with one woman and making a life of peace for himself." Wounded Eagle lifted his hand and ran a finger distractedly down the length of the scar.

"When did he do that to you?" Savannah lifted her hand and traced the same path that Wounded Eagle's finger had.

"About a year after he brought me here." The frown on Wounded Eagle's face deepened as thoughts of the past came flooding back to the present. "I was away hunting for me and my wife."

"You're married?" Savannah's heart flipped and her stomach sunk. "You said you weren't married!"

"I was." The tone of his voice stopped Savannah's thoughts in their tracks. He'd lost his wife.

"How?"

"When I came home from the hunt, I entered my teepee. Many Feathers was forcing my wife to have sex with him. He claimed that she'd invited him to her tent. Her humiliation was so great that she killed herself and our unborn child. I sought justice and challenged him to a fight—hand to hand—to the death." Wounded Eagle sighed deeply, running his hands through his course black hair. "Because Many Feathers is our chief's brother, the chief would not allow a death fight. He proposed that we fight until the first blood was drawn. If it was Many Feathers' blood, they would avenge my wife and Many Feathers would pay restitution, by giving me ten of his best horses. If it were my blood, my wife would remain dishonored and Many Feathers would go free. They gave us one knife and they tied one hand behind our back."

"Isn't that the Apache way of fighting?"

"Yes, but this was the way that Mountain Chief wanted it done."

"You lost?" Savannah said quietly, her heart breaking for the man sitting beside her.

"I won—and lost." Wounded Eagle gave her a look full of irony and smiled bitterly. "I drew first blood, slicing a thick piece of skin from his upper arm. The fight should have ended, but before the chief called a close, Many Feathers swung around and sliced my face with his own blade. It was determined to be an even fight. They restored my wife's honor and Many Feathers paid nothing."

"How horrible! How could you live for so long in the same area with him, knowing what kind of man he was becoming? Especially after what he did?"

"I didn't stay. I left the village and wandered through the mountains for seven years and only returned this past summer. The chief accepted me back into the tribe with the warning that I must let what happened stay behind me. Doing it was hard. Especially with Many Feathers grinning at me, every chance he could.

I changed my name to Wounded Eagle as a constant reminder to him of what he had done. Every time he spoke my name, it would remind him. He didn't seem to care. He had changed in those seven years as well. The evil one had taken completely over him by then and he was uncontrollable. The warriors—my friends—told of how much he'd grown to enjoying killing."

"That's what Black Calf told me. That Many Feathers could kill without provocation for the smallest thing—real or imagined."

"Yes."

"Then why did your chief allow Many Feathers to go with delegations, to meet with the army and such if they could not trust him?"

"I think the chief wanted to believe that he could change his brother. That there was still good in him. Since he was his brother, he was the rightful leader of any delegation."

"Still, why wait until Many Feathers killed White Dove to banish him? Was she related to the chief as well?"

"No, but she was Pikuni."

"So was your wife!"

"My wife died by her own hand. White Dove died by the hand of Many Feathers."

"Semantics, Wounded Eagle. He still caused her death."

"Yes, but the fight cleared him of any wrongdoing."

"That stinks."

"Yes, that stinks—if you mean what I think you mean."

Savannah smiled shortly, "Well, he cannot escape his fate this time. Clark will wake him and kill him."

"Clark may fail."

"Let's hope and pray that he doesn't. Otherwise, there could be a heck of a lot more little Many Feathers running around in a few year's time."

That thought sent shivers racing down both their spines. "I still have to talk to the council. See if I can prevent retaliation."

"You'll do it. I know you will."

"Your confidence in me is very helpful. It makes me feel as if I could move a mountain."

Savannah smiled and snuggled into the crook of his arm. "Do you think that staying here would be safe—just tonight?"

"Hmm. I suppose it would. I did not see any signs of Many Feathers nearby."

"That's good. I'm suddenly very tired."

Wounded Eagle drew her tighter against him and laid them both down again on the soft patch of grass.

"Sleep well, my woman."

# THIRTY-ONE

**Present Day**

"Excuse me. Could you help us, please?" Thomas flagged down a pedestrian. The woman stopped walking and smiled pleasantly. "We're looking for an elderly man," Thomas said vaguely, unsure of how to describe someone they had never seen or met. A quizzical expression on the young lady's face rewarded his effort.

"We don't know who it is we're looking for," Tyrez interjected and the puzzled expression on the woman's face increased.

"I don't think we're going about this the right way," Thomas muttered, rubbing a hand over his face in frustration. The young lady glanced back over their shoulder and nodded slightly, moving away from the two men. "What do we do now?" Thomas asked, looking at the people passing by who were watching them with strange expressions on their faces.

"Well, I guess we start going door-to-door and see whether any of them received a visit from two college-aged girls recently."

"That's a better idea than I had."

"Which was?"

"Nothing."

"Perhaps I can save you the time and effort," a voice sounded from behind them, making both men jump. "You must be Savannah's father," said the elderly Indian eyeing Thomas from head to foot. "She looks like her mother?"

"Almost exactly, except the hair coloring. She gets that from me."

"Her friend—I do not recall her name, since I only met her once, but she looks like you." The old man moved his gaze from Thomas to Tyrez. "Unless her mother is tall and strong-boned also."

"No. Her mother is a petite woman with soft cherub-like features. And who might you be?"

"I'm the man you seek."

"How did you know we were looking for you?"

"I know," Black Calf said mysteriously. "Please follow me. We will go to my house and talk."

The two men glanced at each other warily, and then followed Black Calf back to his home. When Black Calf seated them in his living room, he raised a wrinkled hand to prevent the barrage of questions he felt certain would start.

"Something has happened to Savannah and..."

"Tyeshia," Tyrez offered.

"Yes, yes, of course, Tyeshia, or you would not be here. What has happened?"

"There was an accident," Thomas supplied. "Tyeshia is in a coma, but Savannah…". His voice broke, and he was unable to finish. Tyrez put a reassuring hand on Thomas's shoulder and finished telling Black Calf what had happened.

"They buried Savannah over a week ago. We're here to find out if something happened while they were visiting with you that may have caused them distraction or anger. Anything that may have prevented them from driving safely."

"Mm, buried," Black Calf murmured, rubbing his hand across his smooth chin.

"You don't seem surprised or upset by this news," Tyrez commented and Thomas winced when those big black fingers dug accidentally into his shoulder blade.

"Tyeshia will return," Black Calf answered assuredly, "however, I'm truly sorry for the loss of Savannah. She was a bright young girl, but I'm sure she'll find happiness where she is now."

"I know our little girl is in heaven, but it doesn't make it any easier to bear her loss."

"Heaven? No, no you misunderstand me. She is not dead, but on a very long journey, and she will not be returning. I truly expected it to be the other way around. Savannah was supposed to protect Tyeshia; keep her from doing something foolish. I do not want to offend you, sir," Black Calf continued, his gaze settling on Tyrez, "but Tyeshia has a hot temper. When they left here, I told Savannah to keep Tyeshia safe from harm, but I did not honestly expect she could do so. I did think, however, that it would be Savannah returning to us and not Tyeshia, so this news is a bit of a shock."

"You might want to explain yourself a little better," Tyrez demanded in a calm tone that belied his angry expression.

"Let me get you something to drink and then I will explain everything that's possible." Black Calf rose and left the living room, leaving the men on the couch sitting in stunned silence.

# THIRTY-TWO

**1869**

"Is it much further?" Tyeshia's whiny tone was increasing with each passing hour. On day two of their trek, she had been ready to shoot their now dead horse again and scalp Many Feathers, but at least she'd had some spunk left in her. After two more days of nearly nonstop walking and living off beef jerky and water, she was ready to call it quits.

She knew she was reaching the breaking point because she'd been at that point more than once, and the same signals always marked it—she started sassy and slowly progressed to whiny. Even her own ears hurt when she started grouching in that exaggerated nasally tone. If it hurt her ears, she could only imagine the effect it was having on Many Feathers' ears.

To his credit, he did not scalp her and dump her body in a deep ravine. That had her wondering why his people gave him such a bad rap. After all, no one who could put up with her grousing day in and day out could be all that bad. So, if that was the case, did he really have a short fuse and would he really kill just anyone, unprovoked? Maybe not. *Still, he did admit killing that woman, White Dove, and her unborn child,* she thought. *Could be that she deserved it?*

Signal two that showed she was ready for the insane asylum—she started making very little sense and could not even argue reasonably with her own self.

*At the rate I'm going, he's likely to turn on me like a rabid dog and kill me, as well.*

"No! I won't believe that," she said, continuing her one-sided conversation aloud. "He chose me. We have some sort of connection. How can someone hurt their own soul?

*You do it to yourself all the time—remember?*

"Oh, do shut up!"

"That is a wise decision," Many Feathers said, coming to a sudden halt. "You should conserve and use your energy for more important things besides talking so much." That tone was back. Tyeshia halted and looked at her companion warily wondering just how much further she could push him before he started pushing back.

The final sign that she was close to the breaking point was that she did not give a fig about her personal well-being.

"Would it just be possible to stop for a short while and eat a decent meal?" She asked.

Many Feathers walked closer and latched onto Tyeshia's chin, lifting her face toward the sunlight filtering through the trees. "You look tired," he said and then smiled slightly when her stomach rumbled loudly, "and you are hungry."

"Very tired and very hungry," Tyeshia agreed, bobbing her head idiotically.

"Being tired and hungry will make you stronger. Have you never been without food?"

"Nope. Three squares a day."

Many Feathers looked at her quizzically, but did not respond to her unusual speech. Instead, he turned around and looked toward the distant horizon, then back at Tyeshia.

"Our destination lays another day's walk to the north. You can wait to eat for another day. If you are hungry, eat the pemmican that I gave you."

"I'm sick to death of jerky! I want real food!" Tyeshia was on the verge of tears. She tossed their gear to the ground and stomped her foot childishly. Many Feathers lashed out and struck her hard across the face. Tyeshia fell with a thud next to their gear. Her cheek ached and she tasted blood on her lips. It was the final straw. She snapped.

With a loud, angry wail, she jumped from the ground and drove her five-foot-nine stature into Many Feathers' belly, knocking him to the ground. In one fluid motion, she straddled his waist and pounded him with her fist. Many Feathers lay stupefied for a moment, raising his arms instinctively to ward off the blows that landed consistently on the center of his chest. When his mind came back on track, he reared up at the hips, tossing Tyeshia over his head like a sack of potatoes.

Tyeshia landed face down and coughed as the dirt from the ground found its way into her mouth. She spit several times, and then started to rise, but a foot stamped onto her back, knocking her flat, and leaving her breathless.

Many Feathers straddled her waist and yanked up on her braid, pulling her neck roughly back on her shoulders. She felt, rather than saw, the knife pressing against her throat.

"If you ever raise a hand to me again, I will slice your head right off your shoulders," he whispered near her ear, then slammed her head into the ground and stood up.

Tyeshia lay motionless for a few minutes until the dizziness from the impact passed. Slowly, she rose on hands and knees and finally she pushed herself onto unsteady legs.

"Pick up the gear and let's go," Many Feathers said, then turned and started walking.

Tyeshia glared at his back, but did as he bade. Not because she wanted to, but because she did not have a choice. She was trapped in Many Feathers company. She knew it and so did he. How was she supposed to stay with him long enough to wake him up to allow Clark to kill him if she could not stand to be in his presence for more than a day? What had she been thinking when she saw him?

"You weren't thinking," she said aloud, reprimanding herself. "All you saw was a cute face in a gorgeous body." That sounded familiar and she added feelings of guilt to the other feelings running around in her mind. "I'm doing the same thing I did to Savannah, only to myself. This is my Bobby Ramirez. I accused Savannah of being incapable of handling him because he was too much man for her. Now, here I am in the same position. Man, am I really this dense or just plain blind and horny. If I am this dumb, I'm going to have to start taking my education more serious, like Savannah suggested, then maybe I can use the brain God gave me a bit more productively," Tyeshia muttered, slinging the satchel over her shoulder. She hesitantly set off after Many Feathers, still muttering to herself. "The only problem I see now is what to do about this mess? If I stay with him too much longer, I won't have to wait for Clark to wake him up and kill him—I'll end up doing him in myself. Of course, I'm assuming that I'm capable of killing a man. He keeps starving me and treating me like a load of crap and I may be capable of anything in a few days. I only hope it doesn't come to that. My hope right now is that Savannah has discovered me missing and is doing something to find Clark quickly."

## THIRTY-THREE

"This can't be happening! Not in our fort!" The Mrs. Colonel was sitting in the front parlor, rocking back and forth, moaning. Repeating the phrase incessantly. That was how the Colonel found her an hour earlier, sitting on the edge of Savannah's bed, clutching the torn ball gown in her hand. It had taken a lot of prodding and tugging, but he finally managed to get her to her feet and escort her to the solarium. If she did not weigh so much, he probably would have carried her out to save precious search time. It also did not help that she refused to allow him to leave her side.

"Now, now, dear! We don't know she's been abducted by Indians." Colonel Baker patted his wife's hand reassuringly.

"This can't be happening! Not in our fort," she moaned again.

The Colonel sighed. It caused his heart to ache, seeing his normally stalwart wife reduced to a simpering invertebrate, but he simply could not sit here all day and console her. He had to take command and begin a search for Savannah.

"Rose, come here, please." He stood and turned toward the doorway, knowing without a doubt that the housekeeper would be there. She was always nearby. *A reliable woman*, he thought, but instantly regretted it. His wife was reliable too. She just could not deal with this kind of stress. It was too soon after the loss of their only child, for her mind to handle the strain. *Perhaps I shouldn't have taken this command. Maybe moving hadn't been the answer after all. Not that I could've predicted something like this happening.*

"Yes, Colonel Baker, sir."

"Stay with the Mrs. Colonel. Try to get her to eat or drink something. Talk to her. See if you can't snap her out of this."

"This can't be happening! Not in our fort."

Rose shook her head in dismay, "It's hard on her, sir. She started to think that maybe Miss Savannah could be the daughter..."

"I know, Rose. I know," the Colonel sighed and looked back to where his wife continued her rocking, her agonizing cries stabbing him in the heart. "I'm going to go upstairs and look around. We'll find Savannah, but I need you to help convince my wife of that."

"I will, sir. You know you can count on me."

*She's very reliable*, he thought again, but only smiled in response. He stood to leave the room, but his wife clutched his sleeve in a desperate move to keep him at her side. To this point, he hadn't thought she realized he was actually there. "I'm sorry, my dear, but I cannot find Savannah if I can't leave and start searching. Do you understand?"

"This can't be happening! Not in this fort," she reiterated, her voice a little stronger than before. "Don't let this happen to me again. You've got to find my little girl. You've got to bring her home to me."

"I'll do my best," the Colonel assured, then nodded at Rose and left the room. If the Mrs. Colonel lost another daughter, even if the second one was of no blood relation, her mind could very well snap for good. He could not let that happen.

# THIRTY-FOUR

Savannah snuggled against Wounded Eagle's back, her arms wrapped tightly about his waist, a smile on her face and a song in her heart. He'd said he was going to make her his wife. The smile faded and the singing stopped as realization dawned. That meant staying here forever. Did she really want to do that? "What if I don't have a choice?" Savannah had not realized she asked the last question aloud until the horse slowed to a stop and Wounded Eagle turned to look at her over his shoulder.

"A choice about what?"

"About going back."

"Did you have a choice about coming here?"

"No."

"Did you not?"

"I don't know what you mean. Of course I didn't have a choice. The light overtook us, covered us, and suddenly we were here in eighteen-sixty-nine. What choice did I have?"

"This Black Calf told you returning here to protect your friend from Many Feathers was necessary for you."

"Yes."

"Did you doubt for a minute that what he said was true?"

"Only for a fraction of a minute."

"In your heart and mind, Black Calf convinced you that you had no choice but to follow the path laid out for you. So when you saw the light coming toward you, you accepted your destiny without question and allowed it to direct you." When Savannah continued to look at him quizzically, he sighed and tried again. "Had you decided that Black Calf's truth was untrue; had you not convinced yourself that the lights were a source of time and accepted the fate laid out for you..."

"The lights may have passed directly over us and we'd be back at the college dorm right now having a good laugh. So it wasn't the light, but the influence and belief of its power of time that brought Tyeshia and me here?"

"So should the lights return to claim you, you simply have to deny its power over your will and you will stay here with me. Do you wish to stay here with me and be my wife, Savannah?"

"I do wish to stay with you, but what if all of what you say is pure conjecture? What if I have no choice but to return to my time when the lights return?"

"I stopped to hear a passing minister speak once."

Savannah's eyebrow shot up and Wounded Eagle laughed.

"We are not all sun-worshiping heathens, Savannah."

"I didn't..."

"I know you didn't, but that is what most whites think of us now."

"What were you saying about the minister?"

"I stopped to hear him speak. He was a soft-spoken man and I liked him very much. He taught, not yelled."

"And?"

"He said that God gives every man a will to choose which path he takes. Do you believe this also?"

"Yes."

"Then the path you chose to take was because you willed it, which means that if you will to stay with me, then you will."

"You're pretty smart for a sun-worshiping heathen."

Wounded Eagle placed a quick kiss on Savannah's lips and then laughed, "And you are a strange woman, but at least I know you will be *my* strange woman. Do you wish to stop for a while? We will reach my village sometime tomorrow if you want to keep going."

"Shouldn't we eat? I mean, who knows how much activity we'll face when we get to your home tomorrow and it may be some time before we eat another meal."

"We have plenty of jerky," Wounded Eagle began, then altered his comment when he saw Savannah wince, "or I can catch us something to eat. There is still plenty of light."

"Could you, please? I don't think I've had a decent meal since I got here."

"It is settled then. I know a small meadow over that rise not far from here that will be good for making camp."

"You're a doll!"

"No, I'm a man."

"Without a doubt."

"I hope you would not doubt my manhood."

"Not in a million years."

"Good." Wounded Eagle spurred his mount into a trot. Within half an hour, they reached a small clearing surrounded by a stand of trees. Wounded Eagle dismounted and tethered his horse to a nearby branch. The horse immediately took advantage of the abundance of grass. "You should be safe here, but if something should happen, take Eagle's Wing and ride," Wounded Eagle said, patting his horse's neck. "He knows the way back to the village."

"Very well, but nothing's going to happen."

"Can you start a fire?"

"No problem. I'll even see if I can't scrounge around and find some wild onions to throw on the meat. Add a little flavor." Savannah reached up and placed a kiss on Wounded Eagle's smiling mouth. "Now make sure to bring back plenty of food. Your woman is starving."

"So am I." Wounded Eagle wrapped a strong arm around Savannah's small waist and pulled her flush against his body, "but not only for meat. We will marry when we reach the village."

"Good, cause I'm starving for more than meat, too." Savannah reached a hand up and pulled Wounded Eagle's mouth down to meet her own. Wounded Eagle reluctantly pulled away.

"I want you, Savannah, but..."

"I know," Savannah smiled softly and backed away, giving them both the room they needed to cool their raging desires. "I wish that there were more men with honor like yours."

"Sometimes it can be a curse," he grinned, staring down at his erection.

"Well, I may not have one of *those*, but it isn't any easier for me. Now get gone, before I turn myself into a whore."

Wounded Eagle's laugh lingered in her ears, long after he vanished into the copse of trees.

# THIRTY-FIVE

**Present Day**

"You are full of crap, Mister!" Tyrez jumped from the couch and paced the small room. "I don't know what in hell kind of weed you've been smoking lately—and exactly what kind of crap you fed my daughter. It's no wonder they drove off the side of the road with all that mess running around in their heads."

Thomas and Black Calf watched the display go on for another five minutes, waiting patiently for Tyrez to run out of steam. When he finally slowed his pacing and ran out of insults to hurl, he returned to the couch and lowered his head between his legs. He pulled his hands over the back of his head and rocked to and fro, moaning, "This isn't real. This can't be happening."

Black Calf leaned forward and placed a hand, gnarled with age and arthritis, gently on the top of Tyrez's lowered head. "I know this is hard for you to understand and you must realize that what I told them had nothing to do with what happened. How does that saying go, 'you shouldn't shoot the messenger'? I only told them of my dreams and what they foretold. The rest was not my doing. I was not in the car with them when they left here."

"Still, how is something like this possible?" Thomas asked. "I just can't believe that some unknown force has hurled my daughter back in time. I mean, I saw the body. I buried her, for goodness sake. Yet you're telling me that what I buried was not Savannah, but an empty shell?"

"Does it not make you feel better that your daughter is still alive somewhere? Or do you find comfort in the fact that her body is laying buried in the earth."

"Since you weren't with them, you can't possibly know whether they were transported back in time. For all you know, the girl in that grave is my daughter and she's dead!"

"This is true, but I do not believe this and neither should you. The dreams I've had of Many Feathers are fading, and that to me means much. I'm sorry that Savannah is no longer with us. I will miss her visits. She was a sweet, intelligent woman who brought joy to my life whenever she came to see me. I do know that when Tyeshia awakens, and she will awaken because I feel this very strongly, that she will confirm everything that I have told you."

"When? When is my daughter going to come back to me? Tell me that, old man!" Tyrez said, his tone demanding.

"When their task is through, that is when she will return."

"What if she doesn't ever come back?"

"I cannot think this, for that would mean their task failed and Tyeshia is dead. It would also mean that Many Feathers lives and will seek another somewhere to control."

# THIRTY-SIX

**1869**

Only one hour after they'd begun their journey again, Many Feathers stopped walking abruptly. "Your skin is dark, but your heart is white," he said softly, not turning completely to look at Tyeshia. "Perhaps thinking you could be my woman was wrong of me."

Tyeshia's eyes widened with worry. What had caused this abrupt change? Surely not her whining. She'd been doing that nearly nonstop for the past four days. Okay, maybe it had been her whining. Tyeshia wondered what this confession would mean for her. Would he now desert her and make her find her way back to the fort alone? Or would he simply do away with her now that she was not what he'd hoped for? Lord, she hoped it was not the last one.

"Still, I feel there is inside you a fighting spirit, and you have courage," he continued, giving Tyeshia a spark of hope, "even if you are foolish and weak in body."

"Why are you telling me this?" Tyeshia asked cautiously.

Many Feathers turned completely and looked at her as if seeing her for the first time, "Because I want to know what I should do about you. I want a woman who is mine and will bear me many sons. I want a woman who will stand and fight by my side, not fight with me. I chose you because I felt something with you that I've never felt with any woman until now. Do you not feel it too?"

"Kind of, but to be honest, I don't think it's a romantic connection—not anymore, at least. Sure, I admit that when I left the fort with you—which I did of my own accord—that I found you attractive. I thought about what we would be like together, but I never even considered the fact that you wanted children. I mean, marriage and children didn't even enter my head."

"Then why do you think I brought you with me?"

"I don't know. I guess I wasn't thinking about that," Tyeshia said, knowing exactly why she'd come with him—not to bear his children, but to make sure he died. "Maybe it's better we call it quits and you take me back to the fort," Tyeshia said, suddenly aware of the terrible mistake she made by leaving with Many Feathers without Savannah there to act as a buffer. Of course, that still left the little problem of who would wake him up when Clark entered the picture.

"I do not think so," Many Feathers said. Tyeshia's nerves tightened with that response. That had not been what she expected. Perhaps fate determined that she be the one to wake him after all—despite what she wanted.

"But, why not? Haven't we just decided that we made a mistake and weren't meant for each other?"

"I want children and you will give them to me."

"What?"

"You will bear my children," Many Feathers repeated.

"I will not! For your information, buster, I don't happen to want any children. What makes you think I want to have your babies?"

"You are a woman."

"Oh, so that automatically makes me a baby-factory? I don't think so."

"You do not wish to have children?"

"Not particularly," Tyeshia said, folding her arms in front of her chest. She was not certain how he would take that bit of news, but she was not going to lie and pretend that she wanted to have his babies when the thought of having children with anyone never appealed to her. Many Feathers shook his head as if to clear it and then looked at her again with a strange light in his gaze.

"Why would the gods send me a woman that doesn't want to have my children, who talks too much, and is always fighting with me?"

*Maybe they're punishing you for all the bad things you've done to other people*, Tyeshia felt like saying, but decided not to. She already angered him enough, she had no doubt. Better not to provoke him any further than necessary. Instead, she decided to settle for the old guilt trip tactic. It always worked on her boyfriends back home. "Well, the fighting crap is your fault. If you'd fed me, then I would have remained perfectly sane and reasonable, but no, you had to try to starve me to improve strength that doesn't need improving. Then when I lose it, you hit me and threaten my life? What kind of bull malarkey is that?"

Many Feathers shook his head again and looked up at the sky as if searching for answers. The look he gave her the second time convinced her that no one up there was listening to him. "If I feed you, you would have my children?" He asked, clearly misunderstanding her previous point.

"Hell, no!" Tyeshia exclaimed. "You feed me and I'm likely to be more reasonable is all."

"You are a strange woman and I don't think I like you very much anymore. I do not know now why I chose you," he murmured.

"Well, you haven't exactly been a picnic either, buster. You think that you are everything I bargained for? You're not the only one who feels like they made a huge mistake, let me tell you."

Many Feathers moved closer, drawing his knife from his legging.

Tyeshia's eyes widened and she stumbled backward, tripped, and landed with a thud on her bottom end. Many Feathers leaned over her, his knife only inches away from her mouth. His gaze had an evil glint that made Tyeshia vow to plant seeds and grow smarts—soon.

"Perhaps if I cut out your tongue, you would be more pleasant company," he threatened, and Tyeshia clamped her lips more firmly together. "I will hunt and you will eat. If that doesn't work and you continue to fight with me, then I will cut out your tongue and feed it to you." He slid his knife back into his legging and walked away, leaving Tyeshia sitting there with her mouth clamped and her heart pounding.

# THIRTY-SEVEN

"Come in!"

Captain Fredericks opened the door to the commander's office and stepped inside. He allowed his eyes a moment to adjust to the dim interior and then moved forward, standing at attention in front of his commanding officer's large pine desk. "Relax and have a seat Captain."

"Thank you, sir."

"We have a situation, Captain. A grave situation, indeed." Colonel Baker said, and then stopped, rubbing his hand wearily through his gray hair.

"What would that be, Colonel?"

"You haven't heard then?"

"I'm sorry, sir, but I decided to stay in my room all morning to try to finish the requisitions that I could not complete due to the party last night."

"Never one to shirk duty, are you son?"

"No, sir!"

"You're a good man, Captain, which is why I think my wife wanted you as a mate for Savannah. The Mrs. Colonel had come to think upon the girl as a replacement for the child that she lost." The Colonel's hand made another trip through his disheveled mane and Michael began to wonder just what had his commanding officer so distracted. "Were you aware that we lost a daughter several years ago, Captain?"

"No sir, I wasn't." Michael felt a shiver of dread run along his spine. Whatever it was that had his commanding officer so distraught obviously pertained to his long, lost child and Savannah. Still, if he let the Colonel lead this conversation much longer, he'd never find out what the heck was wrong, "Is Miss Savannah ill, sir?"

"Sick? No, no. Not sick. Missing."

Michael shot forward in his chair. That got his attention. "Missing, sir?"

"The Mrs. Colonel found a footprint inside Savannah's window. Also, the gown that she had on appears forcibly removed. Things aren't looking so good, Michael."

"Savannah mentioned something about leaving and returning back east when she completed her business here. Perhaps a friend came to get her earlier than anticipated and she left during the night so as not to disturb the household. Is her maid still here?"

"No. She's missing too."

"See, there you have it. The women decided to leave the fort and return east. No big mystery." Michael did not believe for one minute that was what had happened, but he needed to find a way to get the Colonel to focus again, to start reasoning again.

"There's just one problem with that theory, Michael."

"What's that, Colonel?"

"The man that took her was wearing moccasins."

Michael stiffened further and his brow knitted in concentrated confusion. Did the same man abduct Savannah and her maid also? If so, why not take the Mrs. Colonel's housekeeper also, why stop at just the two women. Which tribe would be bold enough to sneak into a fort in the dead of night and kidnap the women—period? There was definitely something amiss here.

"Good. I'm glad to see I have your attention, because I'm putting you in charge of this investigation. I want Savannah found and returned unharmed and I want those responsible brought to justice. Understand?"

"Yes, Colonel Baker, sir."

"I don't want my wife to suffer the way that she suffered when Indians abducted and murdered my daughter. I won't see her in that kind of pain again."

"I understand, sir."

"Good. Then go find your fiancé."

# THIRTY-EIGHT

"My home is over that next hill."

"Can we stop for a minute? I think we need to discuss our next course of action."

Wounded Eagle pulled his horse to a stop and dismounted. He lifted his hand and helped Savannah down, then pulled his bedroll from the horse's rump and laid it out for them to sit on. "I do not think I understand exactly what it is you just said, but you obviously wish to talk to me before we get to the village, so I will listen."

"It's just that I think we need to have a plan. How are we going to handle this? What are we going to do after we get to your village and you talk to the council? Are we going to set out immediately after—who? Who is it we are going to try to find, Clark or Many Feathers?"

"Hmm. I have thought on this long and hard. We know where Many Feathers will be going, almost for certain."

"Right."

"Then perhaps it is up to us to let Clark know where Many Feathers will be."

"But you're just guessing at that. You don't know where he will be."

"It is a guess, yes. But it is a guess that is very good, I think. I do not doubt that Many Feathers will turn up at that lake before long."

"So the only hard part is going to be convincing the council not to take action against Clark."

"Exactly."

"Then I guess we'd better get to it."

"Would you like to marry before or after I talk to the men of the council? I say before."

Savannah blushed, but felt pleased that he still had thought about her with all the difficulties they were going to face in the future. "Before is good. The council may just decide to kick me out on my rear end when they learn that I want them to show restraint against Clark. Being your wife may make them think twice."

"Hmm, good point. We'll wed before then—not that you really had much of a choice," Wounded Eagle teased, then hoisted a blushing Savannah back onto his mount.

# THIRTY-NINE

**Present Day**

"What do you propose we do?" Thomas said, his grip tightening on the handle above his door. He understood the anger inside Tyrez that drove him to speed along the Interstate at over one hundred miles per hour, but wished he could find the courage to ask him to remove his foot from the accelerator. The tenseness in his voice mirrored the death grip on the handle, but Tyrez either did not notice or did not care.

"About what?"

"About what Black Calf told us at the reservation. Do you think we ought to tell Patrice and Abigail?"

"What do you think?"

"Tough call," Thomas admitted. "They are in this as much as we are, so we owe them the courtesy of revealing anything we've discovered, but I'm not sure it's a wise decision since we don't know how they'll handle it. I mean, look at the way we're handling this." Thomas really wanted to say 'look at the way *you're* handling this', since he was doing pretty okay. He'd already had a taste of Tyrez's temper and did not relish the idea of him turning it in his direction. "Maybe we should stop and talk this thing through before we get back to the hospital. After all, you don't want to go storming in half-cocked like you are right now."

"I'm fine."

"Sure you are, if you consider an explosion ready to happen, fine. Then you're just great."

Tyrez shot a quick look at Thomas's tense demeanor and then down at the speedometer. With a sigh, he slowly lifted his foot from the accelerator until the digital display read seventy-five. "Better?"

"Now that I know I may live to see my wife again—much better."

"Sorry about that man. I guess what that kooky old man said scared me witless."

"Kind of makes you wonder if this is how the girls felt when they left him."

"Yeah. Been thinking about that a lot."

"Still doesn't explain the unexplainable accident though, which kind of lends credence to what the old man had to say."

"Do you really think that when Tyeshia comes back to us, she'll confirm his strange story?"

"Well, we won't know until she does come back, so we might as well go back to the hospital and wait for that to happen. Tell the women?"

"Yeah. They're going to need to be prepared when Tyeshia wakes up."

"I don't think any of us are going to be prepared for anything ever again."

# FORTY

**1869**

"That was delicious." Tyeshia settled back against a rock and rubbed her full stomach. The problems she had with Many Feathers were temporarily placed aside in her mind now that food sated her. "I didn't know food could taste so divine," she murmured.

Many Feathers rubbed his mouth on his sleeve and tossed a stripped bone aside. His appetite for food was satiated, but watching Tyeshia as she moaned in pleasure over her own food, raised his lustful appetite. He had waited to take her to his bed because of his urgency to get as far away from the white soldiers as possible. That meant being without sex for a week, far longer than he'd ever waited before. Perhaps now that she'd been satisfied, she'd see to his satisfaction.

"You are agreeable again?" He asked.

Tyeshia smiled pleasantly, "I'd agree with the devil himself right now."

"Perhaps next time you can clean and cook our meal like a woman is supposed to do. Do you remember everything I showed you?"

"Yeah, I remember," Tyeshia shuddered slightly, "but I really don't know if I can skin an animal or not. Can't we just hire a cook or something?" Tyeshia was half-joking, but she could see by the way his lips compressed that he did not see the humor. Tyeshia wanted to tell him to lighten up or take a chill pill or something. However, she remembered the threat he made about cutting out her tongue and by the look in his eyes she had not a doubt he would not hesitate to try if she pissed him off again. "I'll try it," she murmured instead, suddenly feeling tense again.

"Good."

*Man*, she thought, *maybe I can buy him a sense of humor the next time I go to the store.* She rubbed the back of her neck and stretched out on the ground, yawning. Exhaustion, after the four-day hike, and the big meal added to her drowsiness.

"Why do you lie down?" Many Feathers asked.

"I'm sleepy." Tyeshia stretched again, and then squirmed around on the hard ground trying to find a comfortable sleeping position. "Do you think that maybe we could sleep in tomorrow morning? I'm really bushed."

When Many Feathers did not answer immediately, Tyeshia shot a look in his direction and her tension mounted again. She'd seen that look in plenty of men's eyes in the past and there was no mistaking its meaning. Well, she was not about to compromise on that one thing. She may not be a virgin any longer, but she still had morals and she never, ever slept with a guy before knowing him at least three months—especially if she discovered she did not even like him. It just wasn't going to happen, and the look she sent him in return told him just that. He ignored it.

"Come," he ordered. She lay there. She may have to endure his company until Clark could finish him off, but that did not mean she had to sleep with him. Yes, he may be a cute guy with a gorgeous body, but they'd already determined that it was not a match made in heaven. Surely, he didn't plan on sleeping with her after telling her just a few hours earlier that he'd made a mistake in bringing her with him and that he didn't even like her.

"Many Feathers," she said softly, trying to keep a fighting tone from creeping into her voice, "you can't really expect us to...well, you know. Not when we despise each other."

"I have been without a woman too long, so that is exactly what I expect," he said and waved his hand in a commanding gesture for her to join him. Tyeshia swallowed hard and tried to come up with another alternative that would allow her to keep her personal integrity *and* her tongue.

# FORTY-ONE

"*Buenas Dias*, Mirabel." Captain Fredericks entered Mirabel's little room shortly after noon, followed closely by a Sergeant and a Lieutenant who quickly moved to where Tyeshia slept and began searching for any clues as to her whereabouts. "*Yo tengo preguntas y mi Español es muy mal. ¿Se habla ingles*, Mirabel?"

"*Sí, Señor Capitán, pero* I don't know nothing about things."

"*Buena.*" Michael pulled up a chair and moved to sit in front of the Mrs. Colonel's laundress. He could see by the way she nervously clenched her skirt in her hands that she did know something about something, but whether that knowledge was something that would do him any good was something to be seen. "The young lady who was staying with you is missing."

"*Sí, Señor.* She is called Tyeshia."

"Very good, Mirabel. I wasn't aware of her name, so you see you do know something after all."

Mirabel smiled at the handsome Captain and felt pleased that she could help him without breaking her word to Miss Savannah.

"Now, could you tell me whether Savannah came to get Tyeshia last night."

"Oh, no *Señor.* Miss Savannah she come, but Tyeshia was already left and I don't know nothing else about nothing else. *Lo siento, pero* I cannot help you more." Mirabel's fidgeting ceased and she stood abruptly. With an agitated purpose, she filled her little kettle with water and slammed it on the coal stove, deliberately keeping her back to Michael.

Michael understood all too well and didn't push the issue. He'd discovered what it was that he came to discover, all without Mirabel realizing that she'd provided a huge chunk of the puzzle in that one little sentence she did speak.

"*Muchas Gracias*, Mirabel, *para su tiempo*. You've been a great help."

"I have!" That statement turned Mirabel quickly and she looked suddenly ill. "Then I no keep my word to Miss Savannah. I supposed to tell nobody nothing."

"Rest assured that you did not let Miss Savannah down, Mirabel. Only by not helping me find her would you be letting her down."

"Miss Savannah is gone with the Indian too?"

*Tread carefully, Michael,* he thought. If he pushed her to tell him anything more, she would feel she had broken a promise of some sort to Savannah and she would close up. *Prod her along gently otherwise you will never find out anything more.* "We think that Savannah has left to go after her friend." They did not know any such thing, but he needed to keep her talking, needed her to feel useful. "Do you remember the name of the Indian that Tyeshia left with, by any chance, so that we can help Savannah find her friend?"

"*Sí.* I know, *pero* Miss Savannah say to me not to tell nobody anything about what happen last night and I no want Miss Savannah angry and thinking I cannot keep my word."

"I don't think that Miss Savannah knew that Tyeshia was in danger when she asked you to help her, so I don't think she would mind if you helped me. She's a really good friend of mine and I don't want anything to happen to her—or Tyeshia."

"Tyeshia, she is in danger?"

"That depends on with whom she left. Do you remember his name, Mirabel?"

"*Sí.* His name is Many Feathers. I hear her say this name to him when he come into the room to get her."

Michael felt the hairs on his arms rise. People, everywhere, knew Many Feathers because of his viciousness. *What would Savannah's maid be doing with a man like him?* He wondered tacitly. "She left with him willingly?"

"She was no so happy to see him, I think, but he tell her to go with him and after much arguing she go."

"How long after that did Savannah come in here?"

"No very long. Maybe *una hora.* One hour."

Michael had the pieces of the puzzle, but that last bit of information left him clueless yet again. If Savannah knew that Many Feathers had taken Tyeshia, why wait an hour to do something about it. If she didn't know that Tyeshia was gone, why pay a midnight visit to her room looking for her?

Well, one thing was certain. He would have to send a detachment of soldiers to find Tyeshia and rescue her from the clutches of Many Feathers. Perhaps that would be where Savannah went and he'd find her also. Of course, that didn't explain the moccasin print in her room either. Where the hell had that come from?

Michael shook his head to try to force the information flying around inside to connect. It was not working. The more information he collected, the more confused he got. With jerky motions, he stood and jammed his hat back onto his head.

"Sergeant, Lieutenant! Let's go! Miss Mirabel, thank you again for your help."

"I hope you find them, *Señor y por favor*, no tell Miss Savannah I say something."

"Your secret is safe with me, Mirabel. Good day." He tipped his hat and strode out after his men, wondering what the heck he was supposed to do next.

# FORTY-TWO

"Well, what did they say?" Savannah asked when Wounded Eagle ducked into their teepee later that evening.

"Is that the way you greet your husband, woman?" Wounded Eagle reached down and pulled Savannah up and against his body. "Now kiss me, wife, before I'm forced to put you over my knee," Savannah giggled and placed a chaste kiss on Wounded Eagle's down-turned mouth. He growled and pulled her closer. "Is that the best you can do? Maybe I need to take control of this kiss."

"Maybe...hmm," Savannah moaned when Wounded Eagle's mouth came crashing down on hers. He pressed his tongue against her lips and she opened for him, her knees collapsing against his intense onslaught. With a satisfied moan, Wounded Eagle swept Savannah off her feet and laid her on the bed of skins. He continued kissing her deeply, his desire rising. With reluctance, he ended the kiss and smiled down into Savannah's bemused gaze.

"Now that's more like it," he said. Savannah blushed and pulled down on his neck to kiss him again, but Wounded Eagle pulled back. "I thought you wanted to know what the council had to say," he teased, running a hand up and down her bare leg.

"I do, but I also want you to kiss me again. There's been so much urgency surrounding our lives and since we married we haven't had a chance to be alone. So I'm sure that God will forgive me a trivial amount of selfishness if I want my husband to show me more affection before reality intrudes again." Savannah tugged at Wounded Eagle's neck again, but he tightened his neck muscles making her efforts ineffective.

"You only wish for me to show you a *little* affection?" Wounded Eagle's hand shot up under Savannah's borrowed buck-skinned dress and cupped her firmly. Her hips shot up and she sucked in a breath. "Are you sure?"

"Wounded Eagle!" Savannah gasped, but could not find enough air or words to finish what she wanted to say.

"Hmm. I think the discussion about what the council had to say can wait for a little while, don't you?" Wounded Eagle's tone was calm, but his heart was pounding and his own desire was evident.

"Wounded Eagle!" Savannah managed again, but Wounded Eagle claimed her mouth again in a thorough kiss. Without releasing her mouth, he shed his clothing. Reluctantly he came up for air and pulled Savannah to a sitting position.

"Raise your arms!" He commanded breathlessly. "Otherwise, I will rip this dress from your body."

If Savannah had a breath left in her body she would have giggled at his eager command, but she did not, so she merely raised her arms and allowed him to pull the dress free. He tossed it aside with a fierce moan, then lowered her back to their bed and kissed her again, his hands roaming eagerly over her nude flesh.

Savannah was not certain what she was supposed to do to contribute to their lovemaking so she simply imitated him, allowing her hands to run freely over his taut body. She gasped when her hand contacted the evidence of his desire.

Wounded Eagle stopped and lifted his head. He smiled down at her quizzical expression, but said nothing. Without breaking eye contact, he searched for her hand. Gently, he brought it back into contact with his staff and placed her fingers around its throbbing mass, then sucked in his own breath as his self-restraint weakened.

He closed his eyes and sought control, for he knew that she was untouched and he did not want her to suffer because of his infantile inabilities to control himself.

When he looked into her eyes again, wonder and a newfound yearning filled them. He rose up over her and nudged her knees apart with his legs. Her hand slipped free of his manhood and she sought to regain her hold, but Wounded Eagle grasped her hands and raised them over her head, trapping them in his strong grip.

"If you touch me again," he gasped, "I'll embarrass myself."

Savannah's eyes widened and her blush deepened, but she did not look away. She marveled at the power each had over the other's desires.

This is what love is, she thought. To be able to trust someone totally to hold you when all ability to reason flees, takes a powerful bond that can only be love. Sex with a stranger—lust—does not require a bond, for a stranger never relinquishes total control.

Savannah's mind quit functioning again as Wounded Eagle slid into her. She gasped and tried to wriggle her hands free of his grip, but he held her tightly, sending light kisses raining along her face and neck. With a desperate cry, she wrenched her hands free, gripped his shoulders, and lifted her hips, drawing him fully into her. He felt her barrier give way and winced. He stopped moving and looked at her, but all he could see in her eyes was an unadulterated hunger that nearly broke his control.

He grasped her hips and lifted her, sliding to his knees. With a smile of satisfaction he withdrew then entered her again, stopping when he could go no further. Savannah's eyes closed and she moaned in pleasure.

"Look at me!" Wounded Eagle croaked. "Please don't close your eyes."

Savannah's eyes flew open and she looked at her husband, poised proudly above her. Sweat glistened along his bare chest and she understood the restraint he was using to prevent hurting her. Did not he know that very restraint was driving her insane?

She smiled a sensual smile and raised her hips higher, felt the tip of his manhood press deeper and knew a moment of triumph when she saw his resolve break, then she was plunging over the edge with him in an out-of-control spiral that seemed endless.

Wounded Eagle retreated and invaded repeatedly until Savannah's vision became blurred. Still she kept her eyes open for him, watching in amatory wonder as her husband's desire and her own crashed together in a concluding symphony that left her full of awe and adoration.

# FORTY-THREE

**Present Day**

"Is there any change?" Tyrez asked his wife, after giving her a tight embrace that startled her. Her husband had always given his affection freely, but this embrace was different somehow. It felt more like a desperate need than a simple sentiment and that had her wondering just what had happened to him in the short time he was gone. A quick glance at Abigail told her that she was thinking the same thing about her husband as well.

"No change," Patrice whispered, taking her husband's hand and leading him to a nearby chair. "What did you find out?"

Abigail pulled a chair over and gently pushed her husband into it, sitting in the chair next to him, her own gaze expectant, "Anything at all?"

Tyrez bounded up and started pacing. Thomas began twisting his hands uncontrollably in his lap, and both women's anxiety levels shot up. Tyrez noticed the worried look on his wife's face and forced himself to settle back into his chair.

"It's not what you think, Sweetheart, so don't look so alarmed, okay?" Tyrez took both of his wife's hands in his and placed a light kiss on each of them, smiling at her reassuringly.

"Tyrez is right, darling." Thomas patted his wife's hand and smiled. "What we discovered is good news, in a way. Isn't that right, Tyrez?" Tyrez grimaced at having the ball of explanation tossed back in his court, but he knew he could not keep putting off the inevitable forever.

"What we're going to tell you will be hard to comprehend and you may not want to accept it. Still, we wouldn't be telling you this at all if we didn't believe with absolute certainty that what we're telling you are the facts."

Both women nodded mutely, their gaze still wide with unease. Tyrez sent Thomas a 'the ball's back your court' look and Thomas winced. Thomas squared his shoulders and stood up, moving over to the bedside where Tyeshia lay in quiet repose.

"She'll be back," he said quietly, looking with longing at the ashen features of Tyeshia who lay with tubes protruding from nearly every orifice of her body. "Black Calf said she would." Again, he selfishly wished that it were his Savannah laying on the starched white sheets of the hospital bed, but it wasn't, and all he had to hope for was that Tyeshia would bring word about his daughter's wellbeing when she finally returned to them. It was all he had now, and it was small consolation. He turned from the bed and looked at his wife.

"Savannah is alive, Abigail, but we'll not be seeing her again in this lifetime." His wife's eyes widened and he realized too late that he'd handled it poorly. Fortunately, he didn't have to say anything else, for Tyrez picked up the ball and finished the explanation for him.

"Black Calf said that the girls were alive, but unreachable..." Tyrez started, but Abigail's outburst interrupted him.

"What do you mean unreachable? If my daughter is alive, then who did we bury a week ago? What game is it you both are playing at? Do you think that Patrice and I are so fragile that you have to come in here and fill our heads with nonsensical lies?"

"Abigail, calm down, please," Thomas pleaded.

"I will not calm down!"

Patrice stood and enfolded Abigail in her arms, "Let's hear them out, Abigail. I'm sure that they don't mean to upset you or hurt us. They're our husbands, remember? They have self-interest in our daughters' well-being." Abigail nodded numbly and moved from Patrice's embrace into her husband's. "Go ahead and say what you need to say, Tyrez. We'll reserve judgments and questions until after you've finished." Patrice returned to her chair and sent her husband a 'try to choose your words more carefully' look, but otherwise held her tongue.

"The girls have been visiting an elderly man by the name of Black Calf. He told us that someone or something sent the girls back in time to help prevent an evil man from possessing our daughter in this time. When their task is through, Tyeshia will return."

"Why not Savannah?" Patrice asked for Savannah's mother, whose expression bordered on a mental breakdown.

"He didn't know why she'd been chosen to remain behind, but as he said, it's better that she be alive than..." Tyrez couldn't finish the statement, but the damage had been done. Abigail let out a piercing ululation that raised goose bumps on his arms. It ceased abruptly when she turned in her husband's embrace and collapsed.

## FORTY-FOUR

**1869**

Tyeshia paused in her chore of skinning the last two rabbits for their evening meal to watch the muscles ripple in Many Feathers' back as he hauled another log into place on the cabin he was building for her. She wondered again for the thousandth time if she would feel differently about him if he treated her with kindness instead of like a bedmate to take at his pleasure without regard for her own needs and wants. If he did, would she then willingly stay with him and bear his children as he wanted her to do?

The location he chose for them to live, beside a waterfall, was stunning, but Tyeshia barely saw the beauty. Humiliation and self-recrimination bogged her down and she was finding it harder with each passing day to pull herself out of the state of depression into which she was slowly sinking. To fight against it, she created a fantasy world where her life was perfect. Much like those in her romance books.

She let herself drift along with the daydream as she had so often over the past week. In her fantasy, Many Feathers is a great warrior. He loves her and chooses her because of her beauty and courage. The pedestal he places her on is so high it reaches the clouds; his lovemaking so gentle her heart nearly breaks with the expanded love inside.

Reality, on the other hand, had a nasty way of intruding on her daydreams, but she clung to them as much as she could throughout the long, hot days—playing scenes from her imaginative life repeatedly. Expanding them to encompass grandeur on a monumental scale.

She glanced at the sun, already setting on the horizon, and shuddered. Evening was the most dreaded time of day for her. It was then, after the evening meal, that Many Feathers noticed her again. It was then he would command her to come to him. It was then he would take her violently and painfully, fulfilling his own needs and leaving her defiled and abased.

If she had not been so opposed to sleeping with him the first week they were together, then perhaps he would be treating her with more regard now? She knew it was as unrealistic a thought as her ever loving him and bearing his children, but it was the only thing to which she had to cling.

Her mind still cringed when memories of their first time together invaded her private dream world. She had tried desperately to talk him out of bedding with her without provoking his temper, but had succeeded in neither effort. Her scalp still tingled where he'd gripped her hair viciously, twisting it until numbness set in where pain had begun. The bruises lining her face, arms, and legs were finally fading but he added fresh ones on a daily basis. She waited for oblivion to claim her so that she would not have to suffer the humiliation of their joining, but it was not to be.

The assaults were now a daily occurrence. Whether or not her body had sufficiently recovered from the last attack, did not matter to him. And her body never quite recovered. He did not even give her a chance to acquiesce and she dared not fight back. He just grabbed her by the hair after the evening meal, beat the crap out of her, and copulated with her.

Now her abdomen ached every time she stretched and bent and she wondered vaguely whether she had suffered internal damage. She also wondered how much longer her punishment would last—for she had not a doubt that his constant abuse was payback for her incessant arguing. She almost wished he'd carried out his threat to cut out her tongue. At least it would have been over.

She nicked her finger on the sharp edge of the cutting knife and watched the blood pool in a small dot, increasing in size until it spilled over the side, leaving a small stain in the dirt below. She glanced up at Many Feathers and the lowering sun, then back down at the next drop of blood that spilled over the side of her finger.

The knife was sharp enough, but could she do it? She ran the knife experimentally and lightly over her wrists, staring in fascination at the tiny indentation that followed in its wake. Did she have the courage to end her torment right now? Courage that failed her at times when she wanted to stand against Many Feathers as she had the first few days after she'd left the fort with him?

A hand appeared from out of nowhere and snatched the knife away, startling Tyeshia. She fell backwards off the log, winced at her continued sensitivity, then glared at the silhouette standing over her.

"What are you doing?" Many Feathers asked in that low menacing tone that sent shivers of fear racing up and down her arms.

"Nothing," she murmured quietly, lowering her gaze.

Many Feathers knelt, grabbed a handful of her hair, and yanked her head back. Tyeshia cried out in pain.

"If you die at all, woman, it will be by my hand. Since I have use of you, that's not going to happen."

"I want you to kill me!" Tyeshia shouted in a moment of audaciousness. "I would rather die than stay with you a moment longer!"

"You will not die." Many Feathers stroked her cheek with his free hand in such uncharacteristic tenderness that Tyeshia burst into tears. "You will remain at my side and bear my children."

"No!"

"Yes. The gods sent you to me for a reason, even if we do not care for each other. Fate has ordained it and you cannot change it."

*Fate! No! Don't listen to him, Tyeshia*! Her brain screamed through her growing haze of despair. *Fate has ordained that he dies a short time from now, so hang in there, girl! Don't let him win! He's physically stronger than you, but you have the willpower of a mule in heat. Listen to me, Tyeshia. Don't give up!*

Tyeshia yanked her hair free from his grip, but winced when she felt a chunk of it pull free. "I'm fine. You can give me back the knife now."

Many Feathers gave her a smile that even had her mind back peddling. He glanced over to where two of the rabbits he'd caught hung on a spit over the fire pit. "I think maybe you should turn the other meat before it burns. You can cook this meat later. As for the knife, I will hold it for now, in case you decide to try to cut my throat during the night."

"That's a tempting proposal." She did not see the hand that struck her, it moved so fast, but she did feel its sting. It made her eyes water and her jaw ache.

"You've grown brave again, woman. That is a trait I despise in you." He yanked Tyeshia up by the hair and pulled her across the campsite, slinging her onto the pelt that served as their bed. "Perhaps you need a reminder of what you are here for."

"No!" Tyeshia cried out when he reached for the ties to his pants.

*Maintain courage in the knowledge that he will die, Tyeshia*! Her mind yelled again. Tyeshia clung to that hope by a thread as Many Feathers assaulted her with a violence that left her consciousness teetering on the edge of an abyss.

*Courage*! She wanted to laugh. After all, that was what had turned his wrath against her, and ironically, it was the only thing that would help her survive.

# FORTY-FIVE

"What have you discovered, Captain?" Michael sat across from Colonel Baker and felt ill at ease. He'd been on the investigation nigh unto a week and he still did not know where to go next. No one seemed to know anything and no one could remember seeing anything, so he had no leads to go on except the information he'd gotten from Mirabel.

Although that gave him a clue as to Tyeshia's fate, he'd yet to discover any valuable information as to Savannah's fate—and the footprint in her room still baffled him no end.

"Not much I'm afraid, sir."

"Where do you propose to go from here, Captain?"

"That depends on what you mean, Colonel?"

"Well, you may not have discovered anything yet; however, that moccasin print has my wife convinced that savages abducted Savannah and she is becoming extremely difficult to live with right now. Do you take my meaning, Captain?"

"I believe so, sir, but the meaning that is eluding me right now is what you'd have me do—form a detachment and go after her?"

"That's exactly what I'm proposing you do."

"We're undermanned here already, Colonel. For me to take even a small detachment would leave the fort's securities severely undermined. Savannah is a sweet girl, and I'll readily admit that her disappearance worries me, but is it worth weakening our defenses over?"

"Indians have abducted a white woman, Captain..."

"We don't know that, Colonel."

"We have enough evidence at hand to make it our business to find out firsthand, Captain." The Colonel ran a hand wearily through his graying hair and sighed. "If Indians abducted Savannah, then it's just a matter of visiting the local tribes and conducting a search. If she's there, bring her back."

"If she's not?"

"That's a question I'd rather not entertain, Captain. Not while my wife still draws breath leastways. Do you have any notion of how difficult living with a determined woman with a mindset that won't alter paths is?"

"No sir, I can't say that I do."

"Well, I do, Captain, and ever since my wife found that footprint on Savannah's bedroom floor she's been crawling up and down my hide to find that girl. Now, if I have to weaken my forts securities to appease my wife then, by George, that's what I'm going to do because my life right now is a living hell."

"Very well, sir. I'll leave at first light."

"Just find her and bring her back. If for no other reason than my peace of mind."

"Understood, sir."

"Very good. You're dismissed."

Captain Fredericks jammed his hat on his head and left the Colonel's office with a determined stride that vanished shortly after exiting the building. The Colonel was placing a lot squarely on his shoulder's for no other reason than to appease his distraught wife. What was he supposed to do with that? He shook his head and frowned, then waved at a passing soldier. "Sergeant, I want five of the best sharpshooters in the fort assembled for inspection at oh-five-thirty tomorrow morning. Weapons-ready. Understood?"

"Sir, yes sir!"

"Dismissed." The Captain watched the soldier trot away and then made his way back to his office. He needed to consult with a map of the local tribes if he was going to conduct a search of all of them.

# FORTY-SIX

Savannah stretched lazily, a sated smile forming on her lips. She rolled onto her side and watched her husband who was still sleeping, his chest rising and falling steadily with each breath he took. She wanted to touch him, to feel him again, but she was loathed to waken him from such a peaceful slumber, so she satisfied herself with merely watching him. Her gaze wandered leisurely over his body, her mind still reeling over his lovemaking the night before. He'd ignited feelings in her that no other person had ever awakened and sent her soaring to heights she was certain she would never reach again—unless it was with him.

He was gentle and fierce in his lovemaking, but never did he forget to pleasure her nor did he leave her behind when he reached his climax. He always carried her along, ensuring she reached pleasures beyond mortal imaginings and then he'd join her. They'd soar together, then come crashing down and comfort each other in a warm embrace.

"I don't need one of Tyeshia's romance books after all," she mused. "There *are* perfect mates out there. Even if I did have to get slung back in time to find one."

"Perfect, am I? And what's a romance book?"

Savannah jerked back, her hand flying to her chest. "You startled me! Why didn't you tell me you were awake?"

"You were enjoying the sight of me and I didn't want to disturb you."

"Oh, you arrogant..."

"Good morning, wife. How about a kiss?" Before she could finish her tirade, Wounded Eagle pulled her down on top of him and kissed her thoroughly. "So," he grinned, looking up into her dazed expression, "what's a romance book and am I really perfect?"

"You are as perfect a mate as I could have ever hoped for, Wounded Eagle," Savannah snapped playfully. "Does that satisfy your ego well enough?"

"Hmm. It makes me proud to be a man. I am glad I please you, Savannah, for you definitely please me."

"I do?"

"You doubt it?"

"Not really."

"Good. Now what is a romance book?"

"It's just a story that takes women away from their lives for a little while. The men in it are usually unattainable hunks after which women pine. I used to think that such a man was beyond existence—until I met you."

"I have read one of these books of which you speak."

"You have?"

"Hmm. I was staying with a friend in the city for a short time. I got bored and went downstairs to find a book to read. His wife had many of these books. Do I really 'make your womanhood reach peaks that rival the tallest mountains'?

"Good heavens! You have read them, haven't you?"

"I told you I had."

"And it would appear that the text hasn't changed much in a hundred years. They still say about the same thing."

"So, do I?"

"Sweetheart, there isn't a peak high enough to compare to where you take me."

"That is good, and I will take you there again soon, but first we must discuss what the council said yesterday."

"Is it good news or bad?" Savannah stood and reached for her dress.

"What are you doing?" Wounded Eagle tugged at her leg and pulled her back down on top of him.

"I can't very well discuss such a serious topic lying naked in bed. It's a distraction. Now, let me up so I can get dressed. You get dressed too." Savannah pushed half-heartedly at Wounded Eagle's chest. "Besides, I'm so hungry I could eat a rhino."

"What's a rhino?"

"Never mind. What have we got to eat?" As if cued, someone rapped softly on the flap of their teepee.

"Come!" Wounded Eagle said. The flap lifted and a young woman entered bearing a tray filled with food. Savannah's eyes bulged and her stomach growled. She wanted nothing more than to dive into the platter mouth first, but her manners prevailed.

"Thank you," she said. The woman smiled and backed out of the flap. Savannah turned to Wounded Eagle, a question in her gaze.

"We will begin feeding ourselves in time, but for now, we are celebrating our marriage, so the people bring food to quench those appetites that we cannot quench ourselves. Go ahead and eat. I can see by the look in your eyes that you are no longer hungry for what I can give you."

Savannah laughed, "I'd argue with you about that, but I'm afraid I wouldn't be very convincing."

Wounded Eagle scooted across the pelts and grabbed a piece of meat from the large tray. "My stomach would say the same about you." He took a large bite and smiled at his wife, saying a prayer of thanks to the God of her people for sending her to him.

"Are you going to stare at me the entire time that I'm eating?" Savannah shifted uncomfortably beneath his gaze and Wounded Eagle laughed.

"My mouth feasts, but so do my eyes—on you."

"Yeah, well I want to stuff my face in a very unladylike way and I can't do that with you staring at me." Savannah nibbled at a piece of flat bread and eyed her husband in mock irritation.

"Go ahead and eat your fill, Savannah. I like a woman with a healthy appetite."

"Well, that's something you don't hear men say every day!" Savannah eyed her husband again and stuffed the remaining piece of flat bread into her mouth. Her cheeks bulged ridiculously. She could not prevent the giggle that welled at the incredulous look that crossed her husband's face. Crumbs sprayed from lips that she tried hard to keep pressed closed. With a Herculean effort, she chewed the bread and swallowed, then fell back and laughed until tears sprung to her eyes and her sides hurt.

Wounded Eagle laughed as well, "You are truly a strange woman, Savannah."

"Yeah, I know. Now, what did the council have to say about Clark?"

Wounded Eagle took another bite from his meat and chewed thoughtfully for a few minutes more. "It is not good. I told the council of my concerns that Clark may try to kill Many Feathers because of his tragic loss," Wounded Eagle started, and then took another bite from his meat. He swallowed, took a drink from a nearby par fleche, and then continued speaking. "Mountain Chief assured me that the council had warned against such action, and wanted to know why I thought that Clark would go against his orders. I lied, which I do not like to do, and told them that Clark had voiced hatred for Many Feathers and spoke of avenging his wife.

"I tried to persuade the council that to allow Clark to kill Many Feathers would not be as raising a hand against the people, but killing an evil that they should not allow to remain free. My chief was not pleased with me. He repeated to the council that no one was to seek retribution against his brother or they would face the wrath of the people. I'm afraid I failed you, Savannah."

"I'm so sorry, Wounded Eagle. It was a valiant effort that would have been wonderful had it worked out, but I did have my doubts as to its success. At least we can go forward with a clear conscious, knowing that we did what we could to prevent harm to your Uncle's people. Perhaps that is one part of history that we can't change."

"Maybe before this is through another answer will present itself."

"Perhaps." Savannah leaned over and placed a reassuring kiss on his lips. "So where do we go from here?"

"We head to Helena. If we can't make the council see reason, maybe we can make Clark."

## FORTY-SEVEN

**Present Day**

"She'll be all right, won't she?" Patrice knelt on the other side of Abigail's prostrate form, worried sick for the poor woman. "What kind of news was that to spring on a mother who just buried her only child?" She said, sending an accusatory glance at both men. She patted Abigail's face gently and was glad to hear her moan.

"I think she's coming around," she said.

Thomas squatted next to his wife and picked up her limp hand in his, "Abigail, sweetie, can you hear me?"

Abigail moaned again and her eyelids fluttered open, "What happened?"

"You fainted, dear, but otherwise you're okay," Patrice explained gently. "Here, let us help you off the floor." Patrice waved at her husband and both men lifted Abigail gently beneath the elbows and lowered her into the chair she'd occupied earlier. "Would you like some water?"

Abigail nodded and lowered her head onto her hands. "I can't believe I passed out. I've never done anything like that in my entire life."

"Well, the news you got wasn't exactly easy on the mind," Patrice reassured. "And the manner in which they delivered it left a lot to be desired." She shot another scathing look at both men who had the good sense to bow their heads in shame. "Now, let's see about going over what we know and try to reason it out, shall we? Tyrez, you said that this Black Calf was almost certain that the strange accident our daughters were in was the result of a time transport and that they are, at this very moment, alive and well, somewhere in the past. Did I get that correct so far?" Patrice was in her element. As an attorney, it was up to her to delve into mysterious circumstances and return with perfectly logical explanations.

"That's the way he explained it to us, dear."

"Well, if nothing else, it gives us the answers we were looking for about how an illogical accident could have occurred, but time travel?"

"I think I'd prefer to believe Black Calf. I'd rather accept that my daughter is alive and well somewhere in time, rather than dead and buried," Abigail whispered. "Still, the idea of never seeing her again is hard."

"Well, dearest," Thomas reassured, "we already had to come to grips with the fact that we'd never see her again. At least this way, we know she has a chance at happiness somewhere else."

"So what do we do now?" Abigail asked.

"We wait," Tyrez answered.

"For what?"

"For Tyeshia to waken. If Black Calf is right, she'll be coming back before too much longer and she can confirm or deny what Black Calf told us."

"What if she can't do that?" Thomas asked.

"Then we'll start from square one. No need to borrow trouble." Tyrez pulled his chair next to his daughter's bed. "We're waiting on you, honey. Come back home soon."

# FORTY-EIGHT

## 1869

Savannah was dusty, parched, fatigued, and sore. She and her new husband had left their village shortly after they'd eaten to begin the long trek to Helena. After three days riding through mountainous terrain, stopping only at sundown and setting out again at first light, Savannah was just about ready to call it quits. If it had not been for Wounded Eagle, she probably would have.

How Black Calf thought that she could help Tyeshia on her own in this harsh, unforgiving time was beyond her. Perhaps he sensed that there would be help waiting for her when she arrived, for without Wounded Eagle, her task would have been over before it had even begun.

They stopped near a stream just before sunset, on their third day. Savannah slid wearily from her horse and looked longingly at the water. She needed a bath—again. She knew, however, that she would have to wait until she unpacked all of their gear, saw to the horses' needs, got a fire started...the to-do list was unbelievably long.

Wounded Eagle wrapped his arms around her waist from behind and pulled her up against his hard frame. "I miss my woman in my bed," He murmured in her ear. "Perhaps tonight we can make up for lost time?" He brushed the hair away from her neck and planted feathery kisses along her neck. He chuckled when he felt the shiver run through her.

She turned in his arms, "Why wouldn't you make love to me before now? I miss you terribly."

"Tell me how you were feeling a couple of days ago."

Savannah blushed and lowered her gaze. Wounded Eagle put his fingers beneath her chin and forced her gaze to return to his. "That is why we have waited," he answered knowingly. "To take you to my bed before now would have been selfish of me. Tonight, however, it should be okay. You feel better?"

"Yes."

Wounded Eagle smiled with pleasure and kissed her lightly. "I will go hunt for our dinner, but tonight we'll feast on more than just game."

Savannah watched him leave and set about her chores, humming a tune. With a grunt, she pulled the saddle and gear from the horses' backs and set them aside, then quickly brushed them down. After that, she tossed the reins over a low limb near a patch of thick, lush grass.

She quickly gathered wood for the fire as the last of the daylight dwindled. With a strike of a match, the surrounding duskiness burst into imitation daylight. She rolled out their bedding, collected a clean set of clothes, and set out for the nearby stream. Wounded Eagle would be back shortly with the food for her to clean and cook and she wanted to bathe as quickly as possible before he got back.

A noise in the bushes stopped her progress. She peered into the growing darkness, but could not see anything. As slowly as possible, she edged back toward the camp. She read once that wild animals tend to avoid fires. She only hoped that applied to animals from the nineteenth century.

She stepped on a twig and froze as a low growling hiss came from the bushes again. Then she saw them—a pair of yellow eyes peering at her from a bush near the bank of the river. Savannah was not an expert, but she was almost certain that the eyes peering at her belonged to a very large cat. The cry it emitted a moment later sounded familiar and then it registered. She'd heard that sound on a National Geographic special about cougars. The horses must have heard the sound and recognized it too, for suddenly they reared, pulled free from the tree and galloped away, leaving Savannah alone and shaking uncontrollably.

*Don't move*! She shouted to herself when her feet threatened to follow the horses. If she didn't move, then perhaps the big cat would simply go away. If she didn't move, it was possible the enormous kitty wouldn't see her as prey. If she didn't move, maybe she'd live to make love to her husband tonight.

She didn't move. The cougar did!

Before Savannah could turn and run, the cougar jumped from its hiding place and pounced, knocking her to the ground. Savannah screamed and instinctively latched onto the fur lining the side of the cat's face, locked her elbows, and pulled at its head with all the strength she could muster. She started screaming repeatedly, praying that Wounded Eagle would hear, and come running.

If he did not, then she'd become Kitten Chow, Tyeshia would be in danger of losing her psyche to a madman, and Wounded Eagle would be widowed only days after marrying her.

"Wounded Eagle, help!" She screamed again, when the razor-sharp teeth moved a millimeter closer to her face. She felt sharp claws pierce her sides and flinched. Still, she stubbornly refused to unlock her elbows and release her grip on the cougar's head.

# FORTY-NINE

Wounded Eagle knelt and eyed the doe, his breathing almost nonexistent. Normally he would not kill an animal larger than a rabbit to feed only two without the luxury of time to cure the remaining meat, but the doe was a small one and after an hour of tracking in near darkness, with only the moonlight to see by, it was also the only animal he'd located.

With barely perceptible motion, he lifted his arm and pulled his bow from across his back, slid an arrow from the sheath and positioned it on the bowstring, then took aim. His arm muscles strained with the effort of pulling back on the string, but never quivered. The doe lifted her head. Wounded Eagle sighted down the arrow.

All hell broke loose.

The deer heard the noise first and bolted. The sound of pounding hooves startled Wounded Eagle and he released his arrow, killing a nearby tree trunk. He dove for cover as the two horses shot past mere inches from where he'd been sitting. He had not seen any identifying marks on the horses, but instinct told him that they belonged to him. He stood and brushed himself off, wondering what Savannah had done to startle them, and then he heard her screams.

"Savannah," he whispered, hoping his mind was playing tricks on him. Another terrified scream rent the air. "Savannah!" Like the deer a moment ago, Wounded Eagle bolted, bounding over the uneven ground at an astonishing rate of speed. He burst into the campsite a few minutes later and slid to a halt, quickly taking in the horrifying scene.

The first thing he noticed was that Savannah was trying to ward off a very large, very mean-looking Cougar. It was nearly twice her size. The second thing he noticed by the light of the fire, was the blood seeping from her sides. It made the dirt beneath her the color of rust, and turned his stomach upside down.

Wounded Eagle pulled an arrow from its sheath, but unlike when he sighted on the doe, his arm was definitely quivering and pulling back on the string with any amount of success was hard. With a cry of frustration, he yanked on the string, sighted along the arrow, and released his grip. He watched in satisfaction as the arrow embedded itself in the huge cat's skull. The cat screamed in pain, fell on its side, and then was silent. So was Savannah.

He tossed his bow and arrows to the ground and raced across the short distance, leaping over the campfire in his haste to reach her quickly. She was still seeping blood, but it was not a great amount and her breathing was steady. He lifted her carefully and sighed when she moaned. He lowered her to the bedding and then sprinted over to where the supplies were at the edge of camp. With jerky motions, he tore through the saddlebags and pulled out the first aid kit that Savannah had fortunately insisted on assembling before leaving the tribe. *Her forethought very well could save her life*, he thought, as he knelt beside her again.

He unbuttoned her blouse gingerly, not out of fear of rending her blouse, but because he feared jarring her and causing her more unnecessary pain. He pulled the material aside and recoiled. Four pea-sized puncture wounds lined her side near the back and one larger one had pierced her near the front. Still, he thought, she was fortunate that the cat hadn't torn at her skin, shredding it and exposing her insides. He leaned down and peered closely at the wounds and shuddered. Pieces of her blouse had torn off when the cat tore through it, and those pieces were now lodged like little dots inside each puncture. He was going to have to get them out before binding them or risk the wounds festering.

He shifted the bed closer to the fire, added more sticks to increase the light, and then knelt beside Savannah again. With a confidence he far from felt, he set to work.

He reached for his canteen, twisted the cap free, and poured a small amount of water on each wound, hoping that it would dislodge the material clinging stubbornly to her skin. When that did not work, he sat back on his haunches and sighed. There was no getting around it—he would have to dig the material out.

He pulled his knife from its sheath and held it over the open flame for a moment, then allowed it to cool while he examined the wounds again. He'd seen people die of loss of blood and said another prayer to her God to help him and her in their time of need. Crouching near the ground, nearly prone, he gently flicked at the first piece of material. Savannah jerked and he stopped. She moaned again and her eyes fluttered open.

"What...?" She fell silent as she noticed Wounded Eagle lying beside her.

"Glad to see you are still among the living," he grinned encouragingly, "but I've got to clean these wounds out and it's going to hurt like hell. Think you can hang in there a few minutes more, my brave wife?"

Savannah nodded, but could not force the words past the painful lump in her throat. She clenched her fists and squeezed her eyes tightly, as Wounded Eagle quickly and efficiently cleaned the wounds. It took a huge effort not to flinch, but she understood that if she did she'd cause more damage than need be.

Satisfied that he'd done all that he could, Wounded Eagle poured some more water over the wounds, and then tore a large piece of his shirt to wrap around her waist.

"Wait! Don't bandage it yet! Do you have any whiskey?" She croaked.

"To help with the pain?"

"No. To pour over the wounds. It will help ward off infection."

"Ah! I have heard of this." He rummaged through the satchel and found the cayenne. "This will do." He heated some water and mixed the cayenne into a paste, then carefully applied it to each puncture. When done, he lifted Savannah to a sitting position and secured the makeshift bandage.

"Did we pack some Goldenseal?"

Wounded Eagle rummaged through the satchel again and found the plant. "Tea?"

"Tea."

"Are you sure you are not a Shaman in your time?" He asked while he stirred the Goldenseal into the heating water over the fire.

"Why do you ask?"

"Because of the things you know about medicines?"

"Oh! No, I'm not a Shaman. In my time, herbs are a form of alternative medicine that originated with the Indians. Some people prefer to take herbs than deal with drugs. I just happen to be one of them."

"Drugs?"

"Like opiate or laudanum. I think those are drugs in this time?"

"Yes. I have heard of these and you are right. People who take these things grow to depend on them too much and lose control of their minds."

"Well, the drugs we have aren't bad, but can cause problems that I'd rather not deal with. So I studied up on herbs and started taking them instead. Of course, herbs can kill too if not taken properly."

"Anything can kill, Savannah. That's why the Shaman is the one who does the medicine. If people take herbs without knowing what it is for, it can hurt them or kill them."

"So, how do you know what to do? Are you a Shaman?"

"No! My father was."

"Really? Cool!"

"Do you need a blanket?"

"What?"

"You said you were cool."

"Sorry. That's just an expression we use in my time. It means that what you said was really interesting."

"Hmm. Your speech is strange sometimes. Sometimes I do not even know what it is you are saying."

"Yes, I know, but all you have to do is ask and I'll be happy to explain."

"Your wounds. They are not bothering you?"

"Hurts quite a bit, but I'm so happy to be alive that I barely notice."

"You will still need to rest several days before moving. How long do we have before Clark sets out after Many Feathers?"

"I don't know exactly, but I do know that it will be soon," Savannah replied.

"If we don't reach him, then we may not find him at his ranch."

"What are you thinking, Wounded Eagle?"

"We are only one day outside Helena. Perhaps I can make a travois so that we can continue our journey. That way we can reach Clark before it is too late. I only worry that it will be too much for you to handle."

"Actually, I think it's an excellent idea."

"You do?"

"It's better than the alternatives."

"What are those?"

"Waiting here until I'm better, or leaving me here alone."

"I would never leave you here alone."

"And we can't wait until I'm better, so start building. That way we can leave at first light."

"You are a remarkable woman, wife."

"Yes, I am, aren't I?"

Wounded Eagle laughed, placed a light kiss on Savannah's lips, and headed into the woods to collect the supplies he needed, and to retrieve the horses that had bolted.

Savannah waited until he was out of sight and then grimaced as yet another sharp pain shot up her side and slammed into her head. She had not wanted to alarm Wounded Eagle or do anything that would prevent reaching their destination, but now she wondered at her own foolishness. Each puncture wound felt as if someone inserted a red-hot poker into it. She wondered whether that was the wound, or the cayenne. Fortunately, she had the cayenne and the Goldenseal to help ward off any infection, but she wished like hell that she had something to help with the pain.

*Tylenol with Codeine would work*, she thought longingly. Still, she did not feel too weak, which meant she'd most likely survive this ordeal with nothing but some scars as a reminder. She just wasn't thrilled about the suffering. If she asked Wounded Eagle to find something for her pain, he may decide to forgo their leaving tomorrow morning and Savannah could not risk that.

If they missed Clark, they may very well miss their last opportunity to talk him out of his quest for vengeance. Anything that prevented her from taking care of business was a hindrance she could not afford. Tyeshia's life could very well depend on it.

She sucked in another breath as the shooting pain continued, then closed her eyes, focused on breathing steadily and tried hard to concentrate on something pleasant—*Tylenol with Codeine.*

# FIFTY

Wounded Eagle looked down for the hundredth time from his perch in the saddle and wondered if they should stop or push on. Savannah's eyes were closed. Whether it was because she was tired or because the pain finally knocked her out, he could not be sure.

He was angry with himself for pushing her this hard after suffering such an attack, but she'd insisted and they really needed to keep going. Too many lives depended on them.

Still, he could see the pain in her gaze when they *were* open and wished he could do something to help alleviate that pain. To stop and let her rest properly was a temptation for him, but something in his mind told him that Savannah would protest greatly. The danger to her friend, Tyeshia, was more important to her, and she would move heaven and earth to prevent any harm from coming to her. Savannah's loyalty was admirable, but it was also driving him insane.

He looked down again and winced when he saw the crease between her brows intensify, and more beads of sweat pop along an already crowded forehead.

Perspiration, which could not have come from the afternoon heat, drenched her shirt. It was barely sixty degrees. She'd obviously developed a fever during the night, but he had nothing to help with that anymore than with her pain. She'd just have to sweat it out. She was a strong woman and he could only hope that her strength would see her through this ordeal.

Helena came into view.

Here was another problem. How to find Clark without going into the city. If he took Savannah into Helena, she could see a doctor about her wounds, but they would probably blame him for her injuries and lock him away in a jail simply for being Indian. If he rode in alone, they'd probably lock him up for being Indian and asking questions about one of the local white citizens. Either way, it was lose-lose situation.

Without benefit of knowing exactly where Clark's ranch was, they could wander the outskirts of Helena for days without finding him. If there were not so many homesteads on the outskirts, it would be a possibility to consider. Those homesteaders would undoubtedly report to the local lawman however, who would hunt them down and throw him in jail for being Indian and in the company of a white woman. He hated cities. A visit to his friend in Chicago a few years ago ingrained in him that whites and Indians were too different in their ways to coexist peaceably. He'd been a novelty in Chicago; here he was a savage that the white man would willingly kill.

Yet, Savannah told him that those differences did not matter in her time, that his people and hers coexisted harmoniously, even married each other. Now however, those differences were too great, and made him hesitant to enter Helena.

Maybe coming after Clark had not been the best idea after all.

"What's the scowl on your face for?" A voice below him interrupted his thoughts, startling him. His horse felt the change in his demeanor and reared slightly. He whispered a calming word in his horse's ear and rubbed its neck, then smiled down at his wife. His smile faded when he noticed the pallor of her skin.

"Still trying to be brave, wife?" He asked, leaping from his saddle and kneeling beside her.

"No, actually I'm feeling much better."

"You do not look as if you feel better."

"I know," Savannah smiled. "I probably look like I'm knocking on death's door, but I can only assure you that I'm not." When her assurances failed to erase the look of worry on his face, Savannah continued. "Would you feel better if I said that I hurt like hell and wanted you to find something to annihilate this pain for me—please, please, please?"

Wounded Eagle laughed with relief more than at her attempt at humor. He was glad to see that the pain was not so bad she could not attempt levity. "We have reached Helena. I'm sure the doctor in town will have something that will help ease your pain."

"I'd rather you just buy some whiskey and I'll drink half the bottle. That should do it."

"You do not wish to see the doctor?"

"I don't think that would be safe, and by the scowl I saw on your face a moment ago, you don't think it would be such a great idea either."

"Hmm. You are right. If I am honest with you, wife, I do not see how we are going to go on. We have no way to find Clark and to go into town and ask for him would not be smart. I should have thought about this more before leaving the people, but I was too blinded by you."

"Are you calling me a distraction?"

"If you mean what I think you mean, then yes."

"That's nice."

"It is?"

"Of course, but it doesn't solve our current situation. Did you figure out what we should do while you were sitting on your horse scowling?"

"No."

"Well, then. I do have a solution, but I don't think you're going to like it much. Truth be told, I don't particularly care for it, but it may be our only option."

"I will listen." Wounded Eagle lowered himself to his knees from his crouching position and ran a hand over his wife's brow. Cool. That was good.

"I told you I was doing much better. Now are you really ready to hear what I have to say?" Savannah took Wounded Eagle's hand and kissed the back lightly.

"Yes. I only wanted to make sure you were really good."

"Like I said, other than the pain in my side, I feel perfectly all right, which is important because what I propose is going to test that to the limit."

"I do not like the sound of this already," Wounded Eagle said, his brow knitting in renewed concern.

"Then you really are going to hate it when you hear it. What I propose to do is to ride into town, buy some whiskey, ask around for Clark, and ride out again."

Wounded Eagle sat watching Savannah for a long while, trying to decide if she was serious or simply suffering from craziness due to her pain. The determination in her gaze never wavered under his intense scrutiny and he decided she was serious. He also decided she was crazy. "You will not go," he said finally, shaking his head firmly.

"Why? It's the only option left open to us."

"You cannot walk or sit a horse. How are you going to ride into town and walk around without collapsing?"

"Determination can do a lot for a body," Savannah argued.

"What?"

"We need to find Clark to help Tyeshia. If I have to suffer a little discomfort to accomplish that, then I will have to find the resolve to do it."

"It is madness!" Wounded Eagle stood and paced back and forth beside her.

"You're making the horse nervous, honey. Come sit back down."

"No! I will not let you talk me into this, Savannah. It is madness!" He repeated.

"Yes, I know."

"It won't work!" He argued.

"Yes, it will," Savannah countered.

"You could do yourself more harm."

"You will be here to patch me back up."

"You are still too weak."

"I have a few holes in my hide, and admittedly they hurt when I move, but I'm not weak." Savannah reached up and latched onto her husband's hand. He stopped and looked down at her determined countenance, feeling the battle swinging in her favor.

"You need whiskey," he conceded reluctantly.

"Yes, I do," she whispered softly.

"You won't get thrown in jail for being an Indian," he added inanely.

"No, I won't," she agreed, understanding that his concern was making his logic senseless.

"Can you stand?"

"With your help," Savannah smiled and placed her hand onto his arm.

"No, not that way." Wounded Eagle removed her hand from his arm. "Relax your body and I will lift you up. If you pull yourself up, you may damage yourself needlessly. Go limp."

Savannah sucked in her breath when Wounded Eagle lifted her under her arms. Sweat popped out on her upper lip, but she kept her mouth closed, determined not to show any sign of weakness that would cause Wounded Eagle to change his mind about letting her do what needed to be done. She shook off the dizziness that struck her, and sat up straighter.

"See. I'm fine."

"Liar."

"Okay, I'm not great, but I can make it the short distance into town and back. I'm sure I can."

"Let me check your wounds. If they have opened from this slight exertion, then you will go nowhere." Without waiting for consent, Wounded Eagle pulled up the tail of Savannah's blouse. Carefully, he lifted the edge of the bandage and checked the puncture holes lining her sides. The cayenne had done a good job. There was no bleeding.

Reluctantly he lowered the shirt back down and looked into her eyes, still clouded with pain. It was madness, but Savannah was right. They were out of options and they did not have enough time to explore others.

Savannah watched the struggle play across her husband's face and sighed. She too wished there was another way, but realized without a doubt that this was it. It was up to her to find Clark.

"Help me onto the horse, sweetheart," she whispered. When he did not readily move, she placed a hand lightly on his bronzed cheek. "I know that you are worried, but I need to do this."

Wounded Eagle gently clasped Savannah's face in his hands and placed a light kiss on her lips. He looked at her for a moment more, and then turned toward the horse. "Come, it will be dark in a few hours and you need to be back before then." When he reached the horse's side, he eyed the height skeptically. "I cannot lift you up or I will hurt you."

"Thread your fingers together. I'll step on them and you can hoist me up that way. It's probably better if your remove the saddle and I can ride sideways."

"You cannot sit astride?"

"It may put too much pressure on my sides to stretch my legs that far. It's better if I just sit sideways and then I can lower myself without any assistance when I get to town. Since this is not a sidesaddle, it's probably better if you keep it here." Neither one of them stated the obvious. How she was supposed to get back *on* the horse once she'd finished her business. It was a hurdle she would simply have to cross when the time came.

Wounded Eagle removed the saddle, then knelt and threaded his fingers tightly together. "Do this carefully, wife."

Savannah stepped into his hands and gingerly pulled herself onto the horse's back, latching onto the mane to help haul herself up. She adjusted herself on the back of the horse and then smiled down at Wounded Eagle. His scowl was back.

"What's wrong now?"

"How will you explain your clothes?"

Savannah looked down at her modern attire and sighed. It would seem she was destined to encounter one problem after another. She racked her brain for a solution just as her gaze settled on Wounded Eagle's clothes.

"Give me your shirt and hat!"

Wounded Eagle looked at his wife questioningly, but complied. Savannah quickly braided her hair and piled it on top of her head, then jammed the hat down low over her brow. "It's a good thing you decided to go cowboy, or I could not pull this off." She shrugged into her husband's flannel shirt and quickly buttoned it to her chin. "Voila! I'm now a man."

"Anybody who could think you are a man is blind in one eye and missing the other."

"Well," Savannah smiled, "let's hope that incorporates every person living in Helena."

Wounded Eagle popped the horse on the rear and sent Savannah on her way, the smile on his lips belying the worry in his heart.

# FIFTY-ONE

It was late afternoon when Savannah rode into town. She looked around and sighed in relief. There were many people milling about or walking from place to place, so one person on a horse should not attract too much attention. At least she hoped she would not. Unfortunately, a man riding bareback sideways was obviously a rare enough occurrence that every head in town turned as she made her way toward the local saloon. *So much for being inconspicuous*, she cringed mentally.

She slid from her horse and winced as the movement jarred her sides. Gingerly, she wrapped the reins around the post and moved prudently toward the swinging doors. She stopped just inside to allow her eyes to adjust to the dim interior and then moved toward the bar. Off the horse, she attracted a lot less attention, and once the occupants of the saloon had given her a cursory glance, they went back to their drinks and games of chance.

"What can I get for ya, kid?" The bartender leaned on the bar and looked at Savannah curiously. "A glass of milk?"

Snickers erupted nearby and Savannah straightened her shoulders. She had not counted on looking like a young boy, but with her soft features and diminutive stature, that's obviously what she passed for. Would the bartender refuse to sell her whiskey if he perceived her to be too young to drink? Did they even have a legal age limit like they did in her time?

"I want to buy a couple of bottles of whiskey," she said in the deepest voice she could muster.

"Don't you think you're a mite bit young to drink whiskey? How about a sherry instead?"

Savannah knew that they were teasing and testing her. Sherry was a woman's drink and the bartender was telling her she was too feminine to be partaking of something as strong as whiskey. A funny thing was, he did not realize just how close to the mark he was, but if she was going to get her whiskey, she was going to have to think of something fast.

She could not exactly call the man out and prove she was manly enough by challenging him to a showdown. For one, she did not know how to shoot a gun and even if she did, she did not have one to shoot. She could challenge him to a fight, but he might accept. With no other options available, she did the only thing she could—she started to cry. Then she removed her hat.

"I ain't no boy, but my pa didn't think you'd sell whiskey to a girl and he's going to be real mad if'n I don't bring some back. He's going to beat me something awful. Especially after he done dressed me like a boy and sent me into town for him." Savannah wiped her sleeve across her nose and looked wide-eyed at the bartender to see if her little charade worked. It did.

"Good gravy and taters! You just take it easy, little lady. I'll give you the whiskey. Just stop sniveling and put your hat back on. You're disturbing the other customers and I don't need no trouble." Savannah did as he suggested while he reached down and pulled two bottles of Jack Daniels from beneath the counter. "Here you go little lady, now you vamoose on outta here, okay?" Savannah smiled and reached into her pocket for the coins needed to pay for the whiskey, but the bartender just waved a hand at her. "No need. Call it a gift. Just leave."

Savannah lowered herself carefully from the stool and made her way to the exit, all eyes pinned on her snug-fitting jeans. She would have to get out of town soon or word would be all over as to her true gender. She shoved the two bottles of whiskey into her saddle bags, resisting the urge to uncap one and take a swig, then headed down the boardwalk in search of the sheriff's office. If anyone knew where she could find Clark, it would be the Sheriff.

She was halfway down the boardwalk when luck finally decided to shine its light upon her. Coming out of the mercantile, spitting distance away, was none-other-than Clark himself. Seeing Clark would have surprised her had fate not been handling her time travel exactly like this since she arrived. Of course, while fate provided access to the players in this little drama, it did not provide a script, and she was at a loss about how to get Clark to follow her out of town so that she and Wounded Eagle could talk to him.

If she followed him on her own, she may very well find his home, but finding her way back to Wounded Eagle would be a strain on her directional abilities. She could plead for his assistance in some nonexistent dilemma, but he might gather a posse together before agreeing to leave town with her.

*Lord, why can't things be a little easier*! She wondered, as she watched him load his purchases on the back of his packhorse. Fortunately, he had many purchases or Savannah may have found herself still standing there deciding the next course of action long after he'd mounted and ridden away. After racking her brain for a solution, Savannah finally decided there wasn't one. She was just going to have to wing it.

Savannah closed the short distance between her and Clark and waited for him to acknowledge her. When he ignored her and continued loading supplies, she moved between him and his horse. That got his attention, but Savannah wished it hadn't. He looked angry enough to spit nails and her interruption only added fuel to his blazing gaze.

"What do you want, boy?"

"I've come with Wounded Eagle," she said in a loud whisper. "We need to talk to you. You are Malcolm Clark, aren't you?"

That got his attention. The anger in his gaze changed to one of wary surprise. "I don't recall ever seeing you with the people before. Who are you and why should I believe you are here with my friend?"

"You don't remember me, I know, but I was at Colonel Baker's house the night that you and Wounded Eagle came to talk to the Colonel. That's how I recognized you. My name is Savannah Warren and Wounded Eagle is my husband."

If it was possible, Clark's eyes grew wider and the look of surprise changed to outright shocked astonishment. Well, maybe the direct tact was the best route after all, Savannah thought smugly.

"Wounded Eagle is married to a boy?" That was not exactly the response that Savannah expected to her announcement. Obviously, he had not been paying close enough attention, or he would have heard her name. Unless Savannah was a boy's name in this time—not!

"Silly goose! I'm a woman," she admonished quietly.

"A woman that dresses like a man? What has Wounded Eagle gotten himself attached to?"

"Would you please stop dwelling on my state of dress and listen to me? I'm only dressed like this because we had to travel quickly to find you. I don't dress like this all the time! Now would you please come with me and talk to Wounded Eagle? He's just outside town!"

Without waiting for him to agree, Savannah turned and stormed toward her horse the best she could without causing herself more damage. She brought it back a few moments later and parked it beside his great steed.

Clark looked at the stallion and smiled slightly. He walked up to the pinto and rubbed his hand up and down its muzzle. "How are you, old fella? I hear you brought your master here to see me. Is that true?" The horse whinnied as if in understanding, its head bobbing rapidly. "Well, let's go find out what he wants, shall we?" Clark turned from the horse to face Savannah. "It would appear you speak the truth since you ride my friend's horse."

"I'm glad you agree. Now, could you help me mount the horse so we can leave?"

"Yep. You're a woman all right."

"It's not that. I'm hurt and can't mount on my own."

Clark looked at Savannah carefully for the first time and noticed the sweat dripping into the collar of the shirt, the paleness of her face, and the lips drawn into a thin line. "Wounded Eagle sent an injured woman into town? What's wrong with that Indian?"

"You said it. Indian." Savannah leaned against the side of the horse and closed her eyes for a moment, trying to gather what little resolve she had left. "We really need to get back now," she whispered. "Could you please clasp your hands together for me to stand on so you can give me a lift up?"

Clark moved quickly to comply. His demeanor changed so drastically from gruff to gentlemanly concern that Savannah wanted to cry. After Clark aided Savannah with mounting, she turned the reins and led the horse down the main street heading out of town, thankful to be heading back to her husband. The whole trip had taken her less than an hour, but the pain she suffered from the short journey made it feel more like days.

# FIFTY-TWO

Mountain Chief stood side by side with his warriors watching the approaching soldiers warily. The first thing that entered his head was that Many Feathers had created more mischief for him to answer to. Although he'd finally agreed to banish Many Feathers from the tribe, he still kept up with his whereabouts and his antics. The latest news to arrive was that people had seen Many Feathers in the company of a dark-skinned female. A female that had last resided at the fort. Add to that the strange request from Wounded Eagle not a week past to let Clark kill his brother without facing any consequences...he definitely felt the stirring of trouble.

Michael sat mounted on his horse on the hillside watching as the Indians filed from their tents and moved to stand, shoulder-to-shoulder, against a perceived threat—him. He looked around at his men and motioned them to stay where they were while he went forward to ask the questions that he hoped would shed some light on Savannah's disappearance.

He'd decided to start with this tribe since he had seen a few of the members of this tribe at the fort—the very day of the disappearances, in fact. And it was pretty much determined that one of the women had left with Many Feathers, a previous member of this tribe.

Michael took a deep breath and spurred his horse forward. He rode straight up to the man standing in the front of the rest of the men and women, judging him to be the chief. Michael had encountered Many Feathers but twice since his arrival at the fort, but his features, like those of every person he'd ever met, was etched on his mind and filled his memory filing cabinet. He had a thing for faces, and except for a few hundred extra wrinkles lining the face of the man in front of him, he was the spitting image of Many Feathers.

When he'd closed the distance to within ten feet, Mountain Chief raised a hand for Michael to stop. "Why does the army ride into my village?"

"We're searching for a couple of women," Michael said, still seated on his mount.

"We do not take your women."

"I know," Michael appeased. "I've come here because one of the women was last seen leaving the fort with your brother. The other...can we go somewhere and talk, please?"

Mountain Chief scrutinized the soldier seated on his mount, trying to discern his intent and honorableness. He did not know this man, but his gaze held within them a peaceful light that many men lacked in this age of mistrust between the People and the white man.

He nodded for the white soldier to follow and then turned toward his shelter. When both men were seated inside, Mountain Chief immediately launched into defense of his people—old habits died hard. "My people are not responsible for the actions of my brother. He is no longer a member of this tribe. And since his whereabouts is unknown to us, I'm not sure how it is I can help you."

Michael was also a good judge of character and of reading people's honor—the chief was not telling the whole truth, but he could understand the whys behind the deception. Although the Army and other tribes knew that Many Feathers was trouble, he was still this man's brother and therefore entitled to the protection that Mountain Chief provided as leader of these people. He gave the chief a look that said as much and then explained his reasons for being there, "Although we are concerned with the whereabouts of the dark-skinned female, we at least know who she is with and are certain that we can find her in time. It is the other woman with whom we need your assistance."

"What other woman?" Mountain Chief stiffened slightly, always afraid of being accused by the army of some wrongdoing.

"She's a white woman with long golden hair that went missing the same night as her friend with the dark skin."

"A woman with long golden hair?"

"That's right," Michael continued. "We know that they didn't leave with Many Feathers together because Savannah—that's her name, by the way—came searching for her dark-skinned friend later. Tyeshia is her name. Then Savannah up and disappeared in the company of another Indian who is unknown to us. It is this that has us concerned because we do not know whether Savannah left freely with this Indian, like Tyeshia did with Many Feathers, or if he took her."

"Why do you come seeking answers here?" Mountain Chief hedged. He did not like the fact that not only was one woman missing from the fort, but two—and both were in the company of a tribal member.

*He knows something,* Michael thought and immediately his brain went into gentle prod mode. As with the seamstress, Mirabel, he could lose valuable information if he pushed the wrong buttons, so he compiled his thoughts carefully, searching for the best path to take. He chose the direct approach.

"I'm going to be honest with you because I feel you are a man of honor and would not want me to lie," Michael said, "but I also need you to hear what I'm saying and not feel as if I'm accusing you of anything because I'm not. Is that a fair proposal?"

"It is." Mountain Chief sat back and relaxed a little. He liked this man, even if he did not like the uniform he wore.

"The day before the women disappeared was the day that Many Feathers and two other delegates from your tribe visited the Colonel at the fort," Michael began, trying to stay within the boundaries of fact and avoid accusatory speculation. "That very next evening, a witness has Many Feathers in Tyeshia's room convincing her to leave the fort with him.

"Later that evening, the same witness says that Savannah came looking for Tyeshia and she told Savannah with whom Tyeshia left."

"Maybe Savannah left alone to go in search of her friend," Mountain Chief offered.

"That's always possible. However, that would not explain the moccasin print that was found inside her bedroom window or the fact that someone had forcibly removed her clothing," Michael finished and watched with satisfaction as the chief's eyes widened and sweat popped out on his lower lip. *He knows something*, Michael thought again and had to control his own reaction when the Chief unwittingly spilled the beans.

"If this man abducted her, why did she come here willingly and marry him?" The Chief blurted before he could control himself.

"She is here?" Michael sat forward, wanting to throttle the man sitting in front of him, for making him go through all the rigmarole of explanations and games.

"No!" Mountain Chief said quickly. "She left with her husband in search of her friend nearly a week ago."

"They are married, you say?" Michael felt a moment of anger at Savannah, for she'd told him that she had no desire to marry. Did she deliberately deceive him so that she could run off and marry an Indian? And why would her clothing be rent, if the man she left with did not do it? There were still too many unanswered questions. "Do you know where they've gone? Please be as honest with me as I've been with you."

"Very well, I don't know if I should help you," Mountain Chief said with a concerned knit in his brow. "Is that honest enough for you?"

Again, Michael understood all too well Mountain Chief's hesitation and voiced them, "You don't want to help because you feel that the army may make the women leave their men and return to live at the fort or perhaps that the army will seek to incarcerate your brother and this other fellow—what's his name, by the way?"

"Wounded Eagle."

"Is that why you don't wish to help me?"

"That," Mountain Chief conceded, "but also something else."

"Whatever it is, I'm certain that I can work with it to everyone's beneficial end."

"You have to keep my brother alive."

# FIFTY-THREE

Wounded Eagle saw them coming from a distance and ran out to meet them. It astonished him to see his friend riding up the embankment with his wife, but his concern for her far outweighed the happiness at seeing Clark and knowing that their search had come to a quick and fruitful end.

Savannah did not look well. Her skin was even more pale than normal and her lips were pressed tightly together. She was also leaning on the horse's neck and riding close beside Clark's horse, as if he was helping her to stay mounted. Not good.

Wounded Eagle gave Clark a short nod of acknowledgment and then turned to help his wife dismount. Her legs bore her weight, but barely, so Wounded Eagle lifted her and carried her to lie on her bedroll near the fire.

"Hello, Sweetheart," she said softly, placed a kiss on her fingertips and transferred it to his lips. "I missed you."

"How are you feeling?" He asked, quickly removing his shirt and lifting her blouse to inspect the wounds beneath. A couple of the small punctures had reopened, staining the bandage with Savannah's blood.

"Is there anything I can do to help?" Clark asked, peering over Wounded Eagle's head.

"There is cayenne in our saddlebag. Boil some water and make me a paste," Wounded Eagle said, grateful to have someone to aid in his wife's care, so that he would not have to leave her side.

"Guess what," Savannah whispered, smiling.

"What do I need to guess, wife?"

"I found him."

It took Wounded Eagle a moment to realize she was teasing with him. He'd learned that it was her way of letting him know to relax a little and that she was going to be just fine.

"I see that," he said, placing a light kiss on her mouth. "You never cease to amaze me, woman."

"I do what I can." Savannah's eyes were drifting shut and within a few minutes, she fell into a restful sleep.

Clark appeared a few minutes later with the poultice and a clean shirt from his own saddlebag and watched his friend apply the concoction and wrap the wounds with a gentleness he had not seen since before his previous wife's death.

Clark knew Wounded Eagle to be a fun-loving, giving man, and it filled his heart with pleasure to know that his friend had ceased grieving after nearly eight years and had finally settled down again with a woman who obviously loved him a great deal. Why else would she risk her own health but to ensure Wounded Eagle's safety? Amazing.

He'd found the same in White Dove, but Many Feathers' evil had cut his happiness short. Now, it was time to make the bastard pay for all the hurt he'd caused and he did not give a damn for the consequences. His only hope was that one day he'd find someone to mend his wounds the way this strange white woman with her strange speech and strange dress had done for his dear friend. He settled by the fire and started a pot of coffee while he waited for Wounded Eagle to finish tending his wife.

"Want a cup?" He asked when Wounded Eagle joined him a few minutes later.

"Never developed a taste for it. I only brought it because Savannah likes it." Wounded Eagle wiped the sweat from his face and looked at his friend for the first time since he arrived in camp. "You look old and haggard, my friend," he said bluntly.

"I *am* old and haggard. What happened to your wife?"

"A cougar attacked her."

"And she lived to tell about it?"

Wounded Eagle smiled proudly, "She is a rare woman."

"So it seems," Clark agreed. "Now tell me why you two have come in search of me so urgently, and if you tell me that Mountain Chief sent you to try to stop me from killing that no-account heartless vermin he calls a brother..."

"He doesn't know we are here, but we do want to talk to you about killing Many Feathers," Wounded Eagle interrupted.

"You're here to help me then?"

"There is much I'm not sure that I can tell you. However, I was hoping that we could find another way to make Many Feathers pay for what he has done without you having to shed his blood," Wounded Eagle said and then quickly held up a hand to silence his friend when it looked like he was about to interrupt. "I have talked to the council of elders in your stead to try to make them see reason."

"What reason? What are you talking about?"

"I tried to convince them that Many Feathers should die. That they should allow you to kill him because he is evil and does not deserve to live a moment longer."

"I take it you failed?"

"Mountain Chief has warned the entire tribe again that any man who raises a hand against his brother will face the whole of the Pikuni nation."

"It is a risk I'm willing to take."

"And I'm trying to make you understand, Brother, that if you do this thing, there will be nowhere that you can hide. The Pikuni will search you out and kill you."

"And what I'm trying to tell you, Brother, is that I have nothing to live for anymore, so I don't care whether the Pikuni finds me."

"What about caring for the lives of hundreds of other people? Would you care then?" Both men fell silent as the soft voice drifted across the short expanse.

"You are awake so soon, wife?"

"How can I sleep with you two making such a huge racket?" She said, a twinkle in her eye. "But Malcolm didn't answer my question."

"Perhaps it is best that he not, Savannah," Wounded Eagle interjected. "He doesn't know, and it's probably best that he doesn't."

"Know what?" Clark asked.

"Can I talk to my wife in private for a minute, Malcolm?"

"Yeah, sure." Clark tossed the remains of his coffee into the fire and strolled to where his horse was munching on a green patch of grass. He plopped nearby and laid down on his back, his arm flopped over his face to shield his eyes from the light of the setting sun.

"If we don't tell him," Savannah jumped in the minute Clark was out of hearing range, "then there will be no justifiable reason for him to stand down. Then we probably could not prevent your Uncle and his people from being butchered like cattle."

"I know."

"Then let's tell him and let him decide what to do. If he decides to go forward with his quest for vengeance, then we've done everything we can do."

"Many Feathers needs to die, Savannah. We cannot allow him to live any longer and destroy other people with his hatred and violence."

"So, you are saying that Many Feathers' death will justify the loss of your Uncle's people."

"No." Wounded Eagle ran a hand through his hair and sighed deeply. "I'm saying that we cannot be certain that the massacre of my Uncle's people will happen if the Pikuni allows Clark to kill Many Feathers, and if my people then go after Clark and kill him. Did you say there was no recorded reason given for the massacre of my Uncle and his people? Only speculation?"

"True."

"Then perhaps it doesn't have anything to do with Clark killing Many Feathers or the Pikuni killing Clark. Maybe something different brought it on."

"Tyeshia suggested the same thing."

"Then I think we should take Clark to Many Feathers and allow him to seek vengeance for his wife's death. Maybe it will heal his soul to take a man out of this world that has caused so much pain to so many people. I came here ready to offer suggestions for retaliation against Many Feathers—anything but death by Clark's hand, but my heart is not in it. Many Feathers needs to die."

"And what about your Uncle?"

"Well, I think we should see one thing finished before we take on another thing, don't you?"

"It's probably for the best."

"I'm glad we agree, now how are you feeling?"

"I feel like talking to Clark and then striking out after Tyeshia as soon as possible. What about you?"

"Perhaps I should turn you over my knee and spank you for suggesting such a thing."

"You wouldn't strike a wounded woman, would you?" Savannah teased. She knew that her wounds warranted her husband's concern and that she should be reasonable and take time to heal completely before setting out, but friendship and responsibility for that friendship wouldn't allow her.

"I wouldn't count on that—especially if you keep being stubborn."

Savannah sighed and lowered her gaze. When she returned her gaze to meet her husbands, her worry for her friend was so evident that it nearly broke Wounded Eagle's heart.

"Every day that I allow Tyeshia to stay in the clutches of that mad man puts me a day closer to losing my dearest friend. I know that the travois cannot move quickly, but at least it will get us closer. Please say you understand."

"I understand that your heart is beautiful and I'm happy that I found you. So maybe we should inform Malcolm that we know where Many Feathers is, pack up, and get ready to move out."

"I love you," Savannah said.

"I love you too, my heart. Just don't make me regret agreeing to your stubborn demands."

"Me? Stubborn? Where did you get a silly notion like that?"

Wounded Eagle rolled his eyes, gave his wife a quick kiss, then went to fill Clark in on their plan. If all went well and no more problems arose, he was certain they could be at the waterfall—and their confrontation with Many Feathers—inside three days.

# FIFTY-FOUR

Michael reviewed the conversation he'd had with Mountain Chief over in his brain a thousand times over the last couple of hours. What had he been thinking? He mentally kicked himself—again—and rewound the conversation back to the beginning:

*"Whatever it is, I'm certain that I can work with it to everyone's beneficial end."*

*"You have to keep my brother alive."*

*"Are you under the impression that his life is in danger?" Michael asked. "The army isn't in the habit of killing men needlessly, simply for a charge of kidnapping."*

*Mountain Chief merely snorted.*

*"Perhaps I should say that I'm not one that would kill needlessly. All you have to do is ask yourself whether you think you can trust me."*

*Mountain Chief stared intently into Michael's eyes, but Michael's gaze never wavered.*

*"I believe you are a man of your word," Mountain Chief replied after the brief scrutiny. "One of the few white men I've met that are, but the army is not my concern—Malcolm Clark is.*

*I thought your concern was this Wounded Eagle, now it's Malcolm Clark? Who is Clark anyway?"*

*Clark is the man who would kill my brother. Wounded Eagle is the man that may help him do this thing or do it himself since Many Feathers is responsible for both men's' wives deaths. You are the man that must stop them and keep my brother alive."*

*"No offense, Mountain Chief, but from what I've heard in my short time out here, your brother may just deserve to die."*

*"True, but not at the hands of a white man."*

*"Well, now that we've cleared that up, what exactly are you asking me to do? I won't kill Clark to stop him from killing your brother, if that's what you want. My only concern is the women."*

*"I do not wish either man dead and your women concern me also."*

*"Then what do you want?"*

*"I want you to keep my brother alive and bring him back here to me—so that I may kill him."*

*"Surely, I didn't hear you right!"*

*"My brother is a dangerous man, but he still deserves to die by the hand of his family."*

*You're asking me to escort a man to his death deliberately. You realize that?"*

*"You have never arrested a man before that stood to die for his crimes?"*

*"Of course, but this is different."*

*"How? Simply because no one has accused him of a crime against the army?"*

*"What if I refuse to do what you ask?"*

*"Then you will receive no help from me or my warriors."*

*"And I need that help, don't I?"*

*"If you do not agree, then you and your men could wander around for weeks and never locate my brother. By then, he could kill the women you seek."*

*"Wounded Eagle knows where to look for him also?"*

*"Yes, most likely. He and Clark, along with the white woman you are looking for, are probably already on their way now—even as we speak."*

*"How likely is it that Many Feathers can kill two men and will kill the two women also?"*

*"Very likely on both."*

*"How many men are you sending with me, and when can they be ready to leave?"*

*"Two, but there is another thing."*

*"What's that?" Michael asked warily.*

*"You will go alone. The rest of your men will wait for your return."*

*"This is where I want to refuse such a ludicrous demand, but you are going to tell me why I shouldn't?"*

*Mountain Chief smiled. He liked this man. He was patient and funny, "If your men stay here, then you are more likely to bring my brother back to me..."*

*"Are you threatening harm to my men?" It was the first time since entering the tepee that Michael felt his control slipping. Mountain Chief simply smiled reassuringly, which was far from reassuring.*

*"If Many Feathers sees a detachment from the army, he will kill the woman and go on a killing rampage that may cause the death of the white woman you seek."*

*Michael relaxed a little, but only a little, "A detachment of soldiers can take him out before he could harm anyone."*

*"I would not be so concerned if I thought that was possible, but maybe with you and my warriors help, you can capture him before he knows anything is happening and then you can bring him back to me."*

*"Very well. Have your men ready to ride out immediately," Michael said, then stood and left the tepee.*

Now, as he rode behind the two selected warriors, his nerves were taut and his mind on full alert. He trusted Mountain Chief as far as he could, but that little nagging doubt would not leave him alone. First, he could not believe he agreed to capture a man and lead him to his execution for unproven crimes against humanity. Still, if the rumors were true, no man deserved it more. If it meant getting the women back unharmed, then he'd make a deal with the notorious Sitting Bull himself.

He was not keen on riding without backup however, and that little voice in the back of his head kept teasing him that they were playing him. That they were leading him to his own execution, and that those Indians were, at that very moment, carving his men up, and feeding the parts to the pack of dogs that he'd seen outside the village.

He fingered his Colt 45 and kept his gaze pinned on his two companions. If something did happen, he'd go down fighting.

# FIFTY-FIVE

Tyeshia sat up a little straighter, her eyes squinting into the setting sun.

*There!* Her mind shouted so loudly that Tyeshia instinctively winced and glanced over to where Many Feathers stood waist-deep in the lake, fishing. She looked back toward the tree line again to make certain her eyes weren't deceiving her. They weren't. There was definitely someone creeping around out there, but were they friend or foe? How could she find out?

She glanced back at Many Feathers, but his attention was on the fish, his back turned. Good. Friend or foe, she didn't care. Anything was better than staying with Many Feathers for another second. She'd just have to tell someone where he was and let them come and kill him. She'd had enough.

Of course, she'd have to be certain that the killer knew to wake him up first and give him a chance to defend himself. After all, she didn't want this sadistic bully controlling her in the future. She stood up and glanced back at Many Feathers. Still turned. She judged the distance to the tree line. If she ran at her fastest speed, she could make it before he noticed her missing. Just maybe.

*Can you?* She asked tacitly. *You are not exactly in tip-top shape right now. And what if the person you send after Many Feathers forgets the dictate to wake him, or worse—he can't kill him. What then? Do you really want to take that chance?*

"I know I can't make it. But what else am I to do? They obviously know I'm here, but should I do nothing and hope they come to me? What other choice do I have? I have to believe they've come for me. I guess I don't have much of a choice at the moment, do I? I only hope that whoever it is can hear my plea in their head, or otherwise this situation is really going to have me screwed."

# FIFTY-SIX

"What do you see?" Savannah whispered loudly, irritated at her promise not to move from the pallet.

"I see Tyeshia," Wounded Eagle said. "It looks like she spotted me and is trying to decide what to do about it. Good, she sat back down."

"Where's Many Feathers?"

"Clark's gone further ahead to see if he can spot him. Tyeshia keeps looking toward the lake, so that's probably where he is."

"What do we do now?"

"We wait until dark."

"Why?"

"If we go now, Many Feathers will spot us and most likely kill Tyeshia and make a run at us before we reach him. I won't risk hers or your life."

"Do you think he'd really kill Ty? But why would he do that?"

"I'm not saying he will, but if I know Many Feathers—and I do—he may just kill her out of simple meanness."

"He's right, Savannah," Clark said, crawling back toward him. "There isn't any good in that man."

"That's what Black Calf said," Savannah muttered and looked at her husband. "You'll keep her safe, won't you?"

"I will do everything I can for her," Wounded Eagle assured her.

# FIFTY-SEVEN

Michael slid across the ground on his belly, mimicking his escorts. They'd abandoned their horses earlier and continued on foot, now they were crawling, and Michael was clueless. He had not seen or heard anything that would lead him to believe they'd found their prey, yet these two warriors were behaving as if Many Feathers was right in front of them. Well, Mountain Chief had said that they kept tabs on his brother, so maybe he *was* just ahead of them. That's what he'd been telling himself for the last fifteen minutes anyway, but still no sign of the man.

Without warning, his guides stopped and Michael shuffled up to lay beside them. The one nearest to him pointed off to the left and Michael followed the silent communication. His eyes adjusted to the low light of the setting sun and then he spotted it—a campsite.

"Can't we get closer?" He asked, not bothering whispering. Obviously that was a mistake by the look he received.

"You must be quiet. Noise carries a long way."

"Well," Michael repeated in a whisper, "can't we get closer?"

"No. We will be seen."

"What do we do then? Just sit here and watch them forever?"

"We wait."

"For what?"

"For darkness."

# FIFTY-EIGHT

He could not perform when she agitated him. He groused and refused to eat the pemmican, and kept his distance from her until he fell into a restless slumber. Tyeshia breathed a sigh of relief. She had not known her suggestion of a fishing foray would work so well, but it had and now she would be spared the humiliating assault on her body that normally followed their evening meal. Only one other time had she been spared his abusive advances, and that was when he'd become extremely flustered—as he was this evening. The last time, he'd been working on the roof of the house. The roof collapsed repeatedly under his weight while he was trying to complete it. His response had been the same as tonight—complain, ignore, and sleep.

That was last week and it had been such a blissful evening that Tyeshia set her brain on the task of finding another way to send him into a state of agitated stress so that she could rest again. Bathing one evening in the lake, an idea hit her—or rather nibbled her big toe. She'd heard somewhere that some Indians did not fish for one reason or another—probably from Savannah, during one of her endless lectures.

Wherever she'd gotten the information from, it had been accurate enough, at least regarding Many Feathers. When she'd gently broached the subject of fish for supper that afternoon, he'd looked at her as if she was an alien from another world. Fishing is a time-consuming, tedious sport for those who enjoy it and have the equipment with which to catch something. For someone for whom fishing is a foreign concept, hates the idea, and has nothing but bare hands for catching the fish—it's downright aggravating. Just what Tyeshia needed to set Many Feathers on the course for leaving her alone.

He had not been easy to convince, but she'd turned on every womanly charm at her disposal and even promised a pleasurable evening afterward—knowing that it would not actually take place made the offer all the easier. After half-hour, he'd reluctantly conceded and set about attempting to catch their meal.

Now, watching him toss and turn on his mat, Tyeshia scanned the horizon again, but could no longer see beyond the light produced by the flames of their cook fire. She closed her eyes and said a quick prayer that whoever had been out there earlier was still there and would ride in on his mighty steed and sweep her away from her tyrant captor. She allowed the fantasy to sweep her away, but never took her gaze off the horizon.

# FIFTY-NINE

"It's time," Clark whispered as he watched Many Feathers lay down on his mat and roll over on his side.

"We have to move in carefully," Wounded Eagle whispered. "If Many Feathers should hear our approach..."

"Don't even say it!" Savannah interrupted. "We have to believe that we'll be successful, or we could jinx the whole thing."

"What did she say?" Clark asked, trying to understand Savannah's strange speech. Wounded Eagle merely smiled however, and pulled Savannah carefully into his embrace. He still did not understand all of her strange words, but although the meaning was lost to him, he understood the emotion behind them. She was concerned for her friend, and fear heightened that concern, although they were so close to a resolution.

"Do not fear, Savannah. I will keep my word and keep your friend from harm."

"She has to wake him up," Savannah whispered against his shoulder. "Remember. You can't let Clark kill him until Tyeshia wakes him up."

"If she forgets her task, I will see it done myself," Wounded Eagle promised.

"I don't know what I would have done without you."

"You were not meant to do without me."

Savannah pulled back and smiled up at her husband, "Can you pull me through the trees, so I can see what's happening. I'll go insane if I don't know what's going on."

"Very well, but you must promise me that no matter what happens, you'll stay on your travois."

"I promise."

"Clark," Wounded Eagle turned to his friend and whispered loudly, "can you help me move Savannah?"

"Hey! I don't weigh that much!"

Wounded Eagle snorted playfully and Savannah reached out and punched him on the arm. Clark gripped one pole and Wounded Eagle grasped the other. Together they moved along carefully on their knees toward an opening in the tree line. Savannah grinned. At least she knew it wasn't because of her weight, but merely a precaution at being seen, that it required the two of them to move her. When they broke free of the tree line, Savannah pushed herself to her elbows and then sucked in a painful breath as she pushed herself to a sitting position.

She peered through the darkness until her gaze found the fading firelight from the campsite in the distance. Her gaze found her friend, sitting stiffly beside the fire, and it was obvious by the tilt of her head that she was scanning the horizon where they were, but could not see them.

"Hang in there, Ty," Savannah whispered, "help is on the way."

"Remember, Savannah," Wounded Eagle admonished, "no matter what you see, you must promise to stay here."

"I promise."

"Very good. Let's go, Malcolm," Wounded Eagle whispered, after placing a light kiss on his wife's lips.

"Be careful, love," Savannah whispered.

"I will," Wounded Eagle promised, and then set off in a crouch after Clark.

# SIXTY

"It is time," the warrior lying next to Michael murmured so quietly that Michael almost missed it. Michael nodded, but knew that they missed his confirmation in the darkness, especially since his escorts had already started moving rapidly toward the campsite, bodies crouched at the knee. Michael took a second to check his Colt and then moved off after them, hoping that his footing held him on this dark, foreign land. The last thing he needed was to step in a prairie dog hole or something.

He squinted into the darkness and saw one of his escorts a few feet ahead of him. Without a second thought, he stood erect and sprinted after him, until he was trailing directly behind the sure-footed warrior. He bent back into a crouched position and continued, feeling smug that if anyone fell into a prairie dog hole and broke a bone, it would not be him.

As he neared the campsite, a movement off to his right caught his attention. He stopped and peered into the darkness, but could not distinguish anything out of the ordinary. He only hoped it was not a wolf or some other night predator that might mistake him for prey. He returned his attention to the objective and for the first time noticed the black woman sitting next to the fire—her gaze straining to see into the darkness in the opposite direction of his approach. Perhaps she saw the movement too, he thought, a little relieved that his mind simply was not playing tricks on him.

He was also more than a little relieved that he'd found one of the women for whom he was searching. One down, one to go. He wondered if, even now, Savannah was somewhere close by. Watching the campsite as he was. Her husband—boy that galled him—was purported to be hot on Many Feathers' trail as well. Maybe the movement he'd seen was them. Well, first things first. He needed to rescue Tyeshia and take Many Feathers into custody. Then he'd see to Savannah.

# SIXTY-ONE

Tyeshia's eyes widened when the two men moved into the light. She recognized Scar Face immediately and relaxed a little. If he was here, then chances were that Savannah was close by. She was not certain why she thought that, but something in the way that Wounded Eagle looked at her, reassured her somehow. She glanced from Wounded Eagle to Clark. Here was the man that was supposed to kill Many Feathers. She was not certain how she knew this either, but the look in his gaze told her that Many Feathers was a dead man. She sighed and stood, but Wounded Eagle lifted a hand and motioned for her to remain where she was.

Her eyes widened and she tried to express silently her role in waking Many Feathers, but Wounded Eagle tapped his chest in reply, and Tyeshia sank back down on the rock she occupied a moment earlier. At least she'd be spared that task. Even if she were relieved that the man was not going to survive, it would not be her hand that woke him.

She glanced over to where Many Feathers lay, his breathing even, unaware that they were about to cut his life short—and deservedly so. When she glanced back up at Clark and Wounded Eagle, however, doubt filled her brain. Why were they simply crouched there, not moving? And then she realized that they were staring intently behind her. She glanced over her shoulder and could not prevent the gasp that escaped.

There on the other side of camp a soldier and two more Indians stood. What were they doing there? And what did they want? She shot a glance back toward Clark and Wounded Eagle and then back toward the strangers. It did not take a psychic to know there was a silent challenge being issued across the short expanse. It appeared that both groups were after the same thing and neither one wanted to relinquish position and authority.

Well, if something did not happen soon, then these two groups would simply stand there gawking at each other so long that Many Feathers would simply awaken on his own, and then...what, she wondered? Would both groups open fire and take him down? Or would they be so intent on their own battle that he could sneak off into the night?

Well, someone needed to take action. After waiting interminably, Tyeshia sighed heavily, stood up, and headed over to where Many Feathers lay. That did it. Both groups spurred into action. They ran toward her with no regard for stealth. Wounded Eagle reached her first. He jumped her and knocked her to the ground.

"What are you doing?" He whispered harshly in her ear.

"Well, you guys didn't seem to want to do anything, so I decided to do something," she hissed back, trying to push him from his position on top of her.

Many Feathers stirred, and the remaining four men moved toward him—three with the intention on apprehending him, one intent on killing him. Clark pulled his knife from its sheath and ran, closing the short distance rapidly, but his quest for revenge was stopped short by the hand of one of the warriors, who intercepted the upraised arm with an iron grip.

Many Feathers awoke, but his momentary disbelief at seeing so many invaders in his campsite cost him precious reaction time. Michael dove on top of him and flipped him onto his stomach in one fluid motion, securing his arms behind his back.

"Get me some rope," he yelled to the warrior who was otherwise unoccupied. The warrior ran toward the lake and yanked at a root that was protruding from the ground. With a mighty tug, the root came free and he sprinted back toward Michael who was struggling to maintain his grip on Many Feathers. "That'll do," Michael said, and motioned for the warrior to keep Many Feathers securely pinned to the ground. He grabbed the long root, and then pressed his knees into Many Feathers' back. The warrior took control of Many Feathers' arms and held them steady, while Michael secured the root around Many Feathers' wrists. When done, Michael rolled from Many Feathers back and sat observing the struggle between Clark and the others. It was not a pretty sight. What had started as a preventive measure had turned into a full-fledged heated fisticuff.

Wounded Eagle had joined the fray and was attempting to circle behind Clark so that he could pinion his arms, but Clark was having none of it. He turned with a growl and threw a punch at his friend's head. Wounded Eagle ducked and moved back, awaiting another opportunity. The warrior that had aided Michael leapt to his feet and ran toward Clark attempting to knock him down at the knees, but Clark sidestepped and avoided the attack.

"You bastards!" Clark screamed. "I want that man's head on a platter and you are not going to stop me!"

"Calm, my friend," said Little Beaver, "they have tied up Many Feathers and his brother will deal with him soon."

"I want his blood," Clark yelled, trying to leap through an opening between two of the warriors, his gaze pinned on Many Feathers who lay struggling against the bonds that held him.

"He will die," assured Tall Bear, bumping Clark as he leapt between him and Little Beaver. Clark fell to his knees, winded. He looked at Many Feathers and then at the friends he'd known for many years.

"What do you mean, he'll die?" He asked, their words registering through the haze of anger. Tall Bear and Little Beaver looked at Michael. Michael wished they had not.

"What's the army doing here?" Wounded Eagle asked, moving to stand beside Clark. Michael stood up and dusted his pants, looking at each man in turn.

"Mountain Chief has charged me with the apprehension of his brother, so that he can face justice for all that he's done," Michael explained.

"What do you mean—justice?" Clark asked, suspicious of any deal made with Mountain Chief.

"Mountain Chief has asked that Many Feathers die by his hand and no other," Michael explained. A sharp cry rent the air and all eyes turned toward Many Feathers.

"No!" Many Feathers cried, "my brother couldn't kill me! He is my brother! You lie!"

Everyone ignored the outburst.

"Why the army?" Wounded Eagle asked.

"You're Wounded Eagle, aren't you?" Michael responded with a question of his own. Wounded Eagle's guard immediately went up and he merely stared at the man in the dusty Captain's uniform. "You are the reason I'm here," Michael said, trying to keep his anger in check. He still found it hard to believe that Savannah deceived him, or that she turned down marriage to him simply to marry a savage heathen. Little Beaver, Tall Bear, and even Clark, instinctively closed ranks around Wounded Eagle, suspicion written all over their faces.

"What do you want from me?" Wounded Eagle asked.

"I've come for Savannah. Where is she?" Michael asked.

"I thought you came for Many Feathers?" Clark asked.

"Many Feathers is simply part of the agreement I made with Mountain Chief," Michael said simply, "which would allow me the use of two of his warriors to find the women if I would escort Many Feathers back to him."

"Savannah is my wife. She will not go with you," Wounded Eagle stated.

"I need to hear that from her, if you don't mind."

"If you hear her say the words, then you will take Many Feathers back to Mountain Chief and leave us in peace?"

"You have my word."

"Clark and I will go get her. She is nearby," Wounded Eagle said. "You stay here and make sure that Many Feathers does not escape."

Tyeshia remained where Wounded Eagle had tackled her, an incredulous expression on her face. Savannah was married!

# SIXTY-TWO

"Is everything okay?" Savannah asked the minute Wounded Eagle came into view. "Was that Michael I saw in camp? What's he doing here? How's Tyeshia? Did Many Feathers die? Who killed him?" The questions flowed so fast that Wounded Eagle merely smiled at his wife without bothering to answer.

"Clark and I are going to take you into camp," he said, gripping the poles on front of the travois while Clark grasped the rear. "The Captain wishes to speak to you about our marriage. He wants to take you back to the fort with him."

"I won't go!"

Wounded Eagle smiled, pleased that his woman had no desire to leave him. "You need to tell him that."

"I will. What about Tyeshia? Is she okay?"

"She's fine."

"And Many Feathers? Is he dead?"

'No," Clark answered.

"Why not?" Savannah asked. "He has to die or Tyeshia won't be safe."

"He will die," Clark answered again. "I will make sure of it."

"How? How's he going to die?"

"His brother is going to kill him," Wounded Eagle responded softly. Savannah sat in stunned disbelief. That was not the answer she expected. They entered camp a few moments later and Savannah found herself crushed in Tyeshia's embrace.

"Savannah! Oh, thank God!" Tyeshia cried, running to meet the travois. She threw her arms around Savannah's neck, unconscious of Savannah's injuries. "I thought I'd never see you again. I'm sooooo sorry. Running off with Many Feathers was stupid. I should have listened to you. I don't know what came over me."

Savannah sat as still as possible, wincing as the pain struck her anew. She moaned. Tyeshia was so distraught and relieved simultaneously, that she did not hear her, but Wounded Eagle and Michael did. Gently, Wounded Eagle pried Tyeshia's fingers from around Savannah's neck and Michael pulled her away.

"What happened to her?" Michael asked. Tyeshia only then noticed that Savannah's face was pale, her lips were drawn, and her shirt was bloody.

"Oh, dear Lord," Tyeshia moaned again, crawling to sit next to her friend again. "I'm soooo sorry, Savannah. I didn't know you were hurt."

Tyeshia grasped Savannah's hand and glared at Wounded Eagle. "What the hell happened?"

"A cougar attacked her," Wounded Eagle explained.

"Where in hell were you when this happened?" Tyeshia accused, but grew quiet when Savannah tightened her grip.

"He didn't do anything wrong," Savannah answered in a tight voice.

"Is it true that you are married to this man, Savannah?" Michael asked quietly, trying to keep the hurt from his voice.

"Yes."

"Willingly?"

"Yes."

"You go, girl!" Tyeshia smiled, but then the smile faded. "What happens when it's time to go home?"

"I'm not going back with you, Ty," Savannah answered and tightened her grip when Tyeshia attempted to pull free. "My home is here now."

"Just what exactly am I supposed to do?"

"Go home when the time comes."

"And just leave you here?"

"Yes, Ty. I'm happy here."

"What makes you think you have a choice about staying?"

"I have a choice. I always have," Savannah answered. "Just let my Mom and Dad know that I'm safe, okay?"

"You think they know about this little field trip?"

"If I know Black Calf—and I do—then, yes, they know about this little field trip."

Michael looked at the two women quizzically, a strange feeling settling deep in the pit of his stomach. There was something wrong. These two women with their strange speech and their unusual friendship. They said they'd come from the east, but he didn't know very many Easterners who held close relations with slaves.

And what was this strange conversation about going home and choices? Didn't the Colonel say that Indians massacred Savannah's parents on the trip out here? If that was the case, then how could Tyeshia reassure them of their daughter's safety? He'd always found a mystery entertaining to solve, but this one was leaving more questions than answers and that was causing him to feel frustrated.

"Where exactly is home, again, Savannah?" He asked innocently, "Perhaps I can wire one of the forts ahead of Tyeshia's return and have them inform your parents of your whereabouts."

"That won't be possible, Michael," Savannah answered honestly, her gaze steady on his.

"Because Indians killed them?"

"No. As far as I know, they are alive and well."

"Then, you simply don't wish my help?"

"No, because wires can't travel through time," Savannah said, and everyone nearby gasped.

# SIXTY-THREE

"Do you think that saying anything was wise, Savannah?" Wounded Eagle asked, walking beside his wife's travois.

"Yeah, Savannah," Tyeshia said, "now Michael, and everybody else thinks you're a few apples short of a bushel."

Savannah smiled, reached up, and clasped Tyeshia's hand in her own. "I'm so glad you're okay."

"Me, too."

"As for Michael," Savannah continued, "he already knew—sort of."

"He did?" Wounded Eagle and Tyeshia said in unison.

"Well, he at least suspected something. Did you notice how he fell silent after my pronouncement—didn't argue or debate or ask any further prying questions?"

"Yeah," Tyeshia agreed, "it was like he accepted it as fact."

"Exactly. He knew we stuck out like a sore thumb here, and my declaration simply confirmed his suspicions that we were not from this area. Of course, he didn't realize that we were from further away than even he suspected."

"So, why did you do it? Why tell them if you plan to stay here anyway?"

"We're heading back to Many Feathers' village right now to make certain that Many Feathers will get what's coming to him—especially since we don't want him messing around with your psyche when you get home."

"What's that got to do with the price of rice in Hong Kong?"

"Once Many Feathers is dead, our task here will be over."

"Girlfriend, you had better stop making this explanation as long as the Brooklyn Bridge, or I'm going to make what that cougar did to you seem mild in comparison."

Savannah grinned, happy to be able to bait her friend again. She was going to miss that when she was gone. "All I'm saying is, we probably won't have control over when the lights return to take us—I mean, take *you* back. Once Many Feathers is dead, the lights could instantaneously appear with everyone watching. So I thought it best that everyone knows in advance, is all. Less of a shock that way."

"Ah," Wounded Eagle said. "Knowledge lessens fear."

"Yeah, something like that."

"And when I vanish," Tyeshia concluded, "they will know where I've gone."

"Right-o."

"Man, Savannah, I wish I had your smarts."

"You do, Ty," Savannah murmured. "You just never cared to apply them."

"Well, that's going to change when I get home. I'm telling you that right now," Tyeshia stated firmly, "When I get home, the only book I'm going to pick up is an encyclopedia."

"Don't forget to carry a dictionary in the other hand..."

"and a Thesaurus in my mouth," Tyeshia finished with a laugh. "I'll basically be turning into a black Savannah Warren."

"No, Ty," Savannah said seriously, "you'll be revealing the true Tyeshia Morgan."

"Right-on, girlfriend. Right-on."

# SIXTY-FOUR

Savannah and Tyeshia sat on the grassy knoll overlooking the village. They would witness the execution from here—which the men had suggested they do. That way they would not be subjected to too much of the atrocity, but still could see Many Feathers die.

"So, what do you think Mountain Chief is going to do to Many Feathers?" Tyeshia asked, peering curiously toward the crowd that had gathered in the distance.

"Well, according to Wounded Eagle," Savannah replied, "Mountain Chief will most likely burn Many Feathers at the stake."

"Alive?"

"Yeah, alive."

"Yuck."

"Without a doubt," Savannah agreed. "Which is why we're sitting here, not standing down there."

"Well, whatever he gets, he will have certainly earned it—every tortured second of it," Tyeshia said. Her voice was full of so much hate and anguish that Savannah wondered just what had happened to her at the hands of that evil s.o.b.. She'd pried Tyeshia gently with questions, but Ty merely shrugged and murmured, 'I'm just glad it's over', never revealing anything.

Savannah could see the fading bruises covering every part of exposed skin, so she knew that Many Feathers had not been kind to Tyeshia, but her friend had closed up tighter than a clam and refused to reveal to anyone what had transpired during her voluntary captivity.

"Ty, you'll be leaving soon, so are you sure you don't want to talk about it before you go?" Savannah asked again, futilely hoping that her friend would find a way to confide in her.

"There isn't anything to talk about, Savannah," Ty murmured, "I'm just glad it's over."

"If you won't talk to me," Savannah persisted, "then will you at least seek professional help when you get home?" Savannah had read in a magazine once that keeping emotions bottled up was unhealthy and Tyeshia had suffered enough without adding a stress-induced malady to the list.

"See a shrink, you mean?"

"Or a preacher, or something."

"You are like my sister, Savannah, so if I can't open up to you about the crap I endured, then how the hell am I supposed to talk to a complete stranger about it."

"I don't know," Savannah sighed. "Sometimes it's easier to reveal personal things to a stranger than it is to open up to those closest to you. Will you at least consider it?"

"Yeah, sure," Tyeshia conceded. "Man, Savannah, I'm sure as hell gonna miss you when I go."

"Me, too, Ty," Savannah said softly, "I mean, who is going to rag on me about my attire, if not you?"

"Yeah, and who's going to keep me on the straight and narrow now that I've determined to walk the straight and narrow, if not you?"

"There will be someone to help you," Savannah assured her, "I mean, look at what happened here in this time," she continued. "Fate gave me Wounded Eagle as a helpmate, so don't you think that perhaps..."

"Don't say it, Savannah," Ty interrupted. "The last thing I need is a helpmate or a new friend. I'm pretty emotionally screwed up right now, so the best thing for me to do is to focus on my academics and try to figure out—on my own and in my own way and time—exactly what happened here."

"I understand."

"Can I say something, Savannah?"

"You know you can."

"While I was with...well, you know," Tyeshia stumbled, looking at Savannah to make certain that she did know. Savannah nodded faintly and smiled a small smile of encouragement. "Yeah, okay. Anyway, I had time to do a lot of thinking."

"What about?"

"It's really ironic, kind of."

"You know, Ty," Savannah reprimanded playfully, "you are always telling me not to build a clock to tell you the time and now you're doing it. Is this some sort of payback?"

"Nah, but the idea does hold merit," Tyeshia smiled, but then her smile faded. "I guess I'm just finding it difficult to say I'm wrong about something."

Savannah didn't say anything to that. If Tyeshia was trying to apologize for something then Savannah knew her internal struggle must be a mighty one. Tyeshia was never wrong—by Tyeshia's standards.

"I want to set the record straight about a couple of things before I leave, so if you could let me talk I'd appreciate it, especially since we don't know exactly how much time we have left together."

"Sure. No problem."

"Remember Bobby Ramirez?" Savannah nodded, but kept her promise not to say anything—not that he was worth talking about. "I want to apologize again for that. Especially now since I realize that a man's looks don't make him a man. A lesson learned firsthand, the hard way."

"Thanks, Ty," Savannah said softly and then waited for Tyeshia to continue.

"Next, I want to say how wrong I was about you," Tyeshia said softly. "I always used to think you were nuts for making your academics your priority and not flaunting the beauty that God obviously gave you, but now I know that you were doing what should be done. I always envied your ability to put aside the fun in exchange for your future, but never thought I had it in me to do the same. I thought that to get a husband, I had to dress to the hilt and put myself out there. For some reason, something screwed up my priorities. But, you were wrong about me too—if our past conversations are any indication. Yes, I did party a lot, but believe it or not, I'm a romantic at heart. I was looking for that Mr. Right. Someone with whom I could share my life. Now I know that when the time is right, Mr. Right will find me. I don't have to go searching for him. Of course, until I find him, I always have my romance books for company." Tyeshia smiled sadly. "All this really has me screwed in the head right now, but I don't want you to worry about me. One day, I'll be able to put all of this behind me and move on. All okay?"

Before Savannah could comment, a loud wail rent the air. Both women looked down the hill just as Many Feathers was strapped to a cross that was then raised into a roaring blaze. They covered their ears as the painful mourn increased in pitch, fading moments later as the flames leapt higher, consuming Many Feathers and wrapping his charred body in a blanket of death.

"I guess it's over," Savannah whispered, lowering her hands from her ears.

"Yes, it is," Tyeshia said softly, but her gaze was focused on the horizon, not on Many Feathers' dead body.

"Oh, dear Lord in heaven," Savannah murmured as her gaze fell on the twinkling lights in the distance. "Wounded Eagle," she whispered, seeking his face among the crowd, "I need you."

# SIXTY-FIVE

Wounded Eagle felt no satisfaction witnessing Many Feathers' death, but peace settled in his heart at the knowledge that he would no longer be around to cause pain to anyone—now or in the future.

*"Wounded Eagle, I need you."* Savannah's voice sounded in his mind and he turned sharply, expecting to see his wife standing behind him, but there wasn't anyone there except Michael and Malcolm Clark.

"What is it?" Michael asked, noticing the distressed look that crossed Wounded Eagle's face.

"I thought I heard Savannah," Wounded Eagle answered automatically and instinctively began pushing through the crowd. "She needs my help."

They required no further explanation. All three men elbowed through the throng and ran hell bent for the hilltop where they had left the women, not even bothering to find and mount their horses. As they topped the ridge, all three froze.

"Oh, thank the Lord above," Savannah whispered, clinging desperately to Wounded Eagle's hand.

"What in tarnation is that heading this way?" Clark exclaimed, plopping down beside his friend.

"It coming to take us home," Tyeshia whispered, looking worriedly at her friend. "Are you sure you can withstand the power of the lights, Savannah?"

"I have to, Tyeshia," Savannah cried, "I can't leave Wounded Eagle. I just can't."

"Remember what I said, Savannah," Wounded Eagle said, wrapping a secure arm around his wife's shoulder. "Your God gives each person a will to decide which path he will follow. You simply have to choose me."

"I already have, Wounded Eagle," Savannah asserted, "let's just hope those lights agree with my decision."

"Will someone please tell me what the hell is going on here?" Michael said, worry etched on his face.

"It's time for Tyeshia to return home, Michael," Savannah answered, giving his own hand a reassuring squeeze. "The lights, you see, transported us from our time and, now that our job here is done, it's returned to take us home. The only thing is, I don't want to go back."

"Well, I'll be damned," Clark exclaimed softly, "you ain't a few wax dips short of a candlestick after all, are you?"

"No," Savannah laughed.

Conversation ceased as the lights drew nearer. Tyeshia looked at Savannah and spontaneously reached up to touch her cheek as the lights began to twinkle on her pale face.

"I can see them on your skin, now," Tyeshia murmured.

"Me, too," Savannah whispered, and tightened her grip on her husband's hand.

"I love you, Sister," Tyeshia whispered, fear creeping into her voice, "I'll always love you."

"I'll never forget you, Tyeshia," Savannah squeezed her friend's hand reassuringly, "Please don't forget to tell my mother and father that I'm okay."

"I won't. I promise."

It was the last words spoken, for the light soon covered the small, terrified group with its iridescence and when it finally passed by, four of the original five people remained.

# SIXTY-SIX

## Present Day

"Mom, Dad?" Tyeshia's dry throat felt parched and the words emerged on a whispered croak. It was enough. The four people in the room shot upright from their chairs and dashed to the bedside.

"Tyeshia, baby, was that you?" Tyrez asked, almost afraid that she would not give an answer; that his daughter's eyes would remain closed, and the words they'd all heard would simply be another fluke, like the ones before. No one wanted to leave the room, so Tyrez picked up the red nurse-call button attached to the starched-white sheets and pushed it frantically, repeatedly. His finger stopped in mid-punch as more words reached his ears from the still figure on the bed.

"Daddy, Mommy, are you there? I can't see you?"

"Follow our voice, baby girl," Patrice cried, squeezing her daughter's hand tightly. "Follow our voice and find your way back, Sweetheart. We're here. Can you hear me, baby? Can you hear me?"

"Mommy, is that you?"

"Oh, God," Patrice cried, her tears streaming down her cheeks. "It's me, baby. It's me. Can you hear me?"

"I hear you, Mommy," Tyeshia croaked, "I'm coming home."

Tyrez fell to his knees beside the bed and wept, huge tears wracking his large frame. He gripped his daughter's hand, unable and unashamed at his inability to control his emotions. Tyeshia's eyes flew open, just as the doctor burst into the room.

# SIXTY-SEVEN

## 1869

Michael stood at attention before his commanding officer's desk, his mind uncomfortable with the idea of telling his commanding officer a bald-faced lie. It had taken them three days to get back to the fort and he'd been struggling to come up with a believable explanation the entire way, and since it went against his nature to be deceptive, it was an extremely difficult task, to say the least. He'd finally arrived at the only plausible explanation that the Colonel and the Colonel's wife would accept, but he was not certain if he could rely on his men to back him up.

His men had seen him arrive at the Indian village with the women in tow. His men knew that one of those women had vanished right from underneath their noses, but they didn't know what had happened—then again, neither did he. Not really.

They also knew that the other woman—the white woman they'd spent near onto two weeks tracking down—now refused to return to the fort with them. To make matters worse, they all looked to him for reason where there didn't appear to be reason. In the end, it had come down to him doing the talking and them acting dumb if questioned. They readily agreed, but would they be able to keep their mouths shut?

"Well, Captain, you have something to report?" The Colonel could see that something was bothering his officer and that the Captain was having a difficult time deciding where to begin. However, he'd waited for nearly two weeks to hear about Savannah—his wife nagging him day in and day out for updates that he didn't have—so he'd be damned if he was going to let the Captain stand there all day deciding to speak. "And would you 'at ease' already," the Colonel barked.

"Sir, yes sir!" Michael snapped and moved to parade-rest. Although he relaxed his stance, his mind was anything but.

"Explain yourself now, Captain!"

He had an explanation, but he wondered whether using it was wise. He'd racked his brain and it was the only thing that he could say that would prevent further searches for the women. If he told the Colonel that they'd boarded a train for the east, the Colonel might try to communicate with them to see how they were faring, especially since his wife had taken such a liking to Savannah. If he told the Colonel the truth—that one woman returned home through a time portal and the other stayed behind to live with her Indian husband—they'd send him to an insane asylum to have his brain analyzed and his career would be over. If he told the Colonel that he had not found the women, the Colonel would send him out again until the end of time until he found them. No, he had no choice. He would have to use the explanation he gave to his men and hope the Colonel didn't have apoplexy.

"The women are dead, sir," Michael whispered.

"What?" The Colonel yelled, jumping up from his chair.

"I'm sorry, sir," Michael continued quietly, "but we could do nothing." *Well, that wasn't a lie*, he thought, *since there really hadn't been anything he could've done*. Maybe he'd survive this deception after all. All he needed to do was provide just enough accurate facts to clarify his story and satisfy the Colonel.

"How?"

"I can't say sir," Michael said. "I was unable to determine the cause of death. Probably exposure to the elements. They were women, sir. They simply weren't suited for this terrain."

"They were together then?"

"Yes, sir."

"Then how do you explain the moccasin print inside Savannah's bedroom window?" The Colonel asked, rubbing a hand wearily through his graying mane.

"I'm sorry, sir, but I can't," Michael said, realizing that ignorance was bliss, "perhaps the intruder came in *after* Savannah and Tyeshia vanished."

"Tyeshia?"

"Her maid, sir."

"Right, her maid," the Colonel replied absentmindedly. "I don't know," he sighed, settling himself back down into his chair, "there's just something that's not adding up somewhere. I mean, why did they just up and leave in the middle of the night, and how in blue blazes am I supposed to explain the unexplainable to my wife?"

"I wish I had more answers, sir, but I don't."

"Where are the bodies now, Captain?" The Colonel asked, but his mind was obviously still lingering on the displeasure his wife would display once he delivered the news to her.

"We gave them a decent Christian burial, sir," Michael said softly.

"Why didn't you bring them back here, Captain? I'm sure my wife would have liked to give them a decent burial here at the fort." It was apparent by the slight raising of the pitch in the Colonel's voice that he'd hoped to appease his wife somewhat by allowing her to bury the woman she'd considered a daughter, something they could not do when they lost their first, and only, daughter. Now that he could not offer that small measure of comfort, his wife was going to chew him up and spit him out.

"No ice, sir," Michael said, hoping further explanation wouldn't be necessary. It wasn't to be.

"Ice?"

"To keep the, uh, bodies fresh, sir," Michael stammered. He saw the Colonel's face pale and regretted having to include that lie. Picturing a decomposing body wasn't pleasant.

"I, uh, see," the Colonel muttered, placing his head in the tent formed from his hands, the Captain momentarily forgotten.

"Will you be needing me for anything else, sir?" Michael asked, but received no reply. "Sir?" He tried again, but could tell that the Colonel had retreated into his own agonized world, so he quietly turned and slipped from the office.

He stopped outside the door and placed his hat habitually on the top of his head, squinting into the evening sun. He wondered how Tyeshia and Savannah were faring at this moment—one slung through time and the other traversing rugged terrain with an Indian for a husband. He also wondered if he would ever see either of them again. What would he do if he did? He certainly could not acknowledge them.

He snorted and headed down the boardwalk to the mountain of paperwork that awaited him, knowing, without a doubt, that just as time had brought the two women into his realm, time would eventually erase all knowledge of their existence. He raised his hand and tipped his hat to the image of Savannah that flitted briefly through his mind, "Farewell, lovely lady. Peace and happiness go with you, always."

# SIXTY-EIGHT

**Present Day**

Tyeshia looked at the faces hovering above her bed and blinked rapidly, repeatedly. Was she really here? Or was this part of another dream, like she'd had when she first got slung back in time? It looked real. Her parents' faces weren't fuzzy like before. And before there hadn't been other people surrounding her. Nor had she been in a hospital room with monitoring equipment. Very modern monitoring equipment.

"I'm home?" She croaked, and saw fresh tears spring from all of the faces surrounding her—except the doctors. He was busy shining a light in her newly opened eyes, checking her pulse, listening to her heartbeat, poking and prodding her everywhere. She wanted to yell at him to get away from her, but, not only would that be impolite, she didn't think she could force all the words required out of her dehydrated throat. "Water?" She managed and tried to swallow nonexistent saliva to lubricate her throat.

A glass appeared in front of her and she tried to reach up and grab it, but her hands refused to move. In fact, her whole body felt as if someone mired it in cement. Her father placed a hand gently behind her head and lifted the rubbery mass from the bed. Most of the water managed to slide, blessedly, down her throat, but some of it ended up soaking the front of her paisley-printed dressing gown.

"Why...?" She whispered, but the doctor raised a hand for her to be quiet for a moment. He was listening to her heart again through his stethoscope.

"Strong heartbeat," he said. "Strong pulse. Strong vital signs. It looks like you are going to be just fine, young lady." Tyeshia heard quiet cheers from those around her, and heard her mother whispering prayers of thanks.

"Why can't I move?" She asked, wishing her voice would regain some sort of normalcy, and soon.

"Your muscles have entered the early stages of degeneration—from non-use," the doctor explained. "Although the nurses have exercised them for you rigorously, they can only accomplish so much. Now, you'll need to start working them yourself to build the muscles back up. It's slow and oft times painful, but I don't see why you shouldn't make a full recovery in the next few months," the doctor said. Tyeshia could only nod her head. "Excellent! I will leave you now to your reunion and check on you periodically throughout your stay in our lovely establishment." The doctor turned to leave, nodding to her parents as he passed.

"You're going to be all right, baby girl," Patrice said, holding her daughter's hand again. Tears welled in Tyeshia's eyes and she began to weep silently.

"What's wrong, Sweetheart?" Tyrez asked, stroking his daughter's forehead. "Are you hurting somewhere?"

"Only in my heart," Tyeshia sobbed. "I miss Savannah so much, but I'm also happy to be home."

"We know, baby girl. We know," Patrice murmured, knowing there was no other comfort she could give. After a few minutes, Tyeshia's tears stopped flowing and her mother gently wiped her eyes for her. The other couple in the room came into Tyeshia's line of vision again and her heart lurched.

"Mr. and Mrs. Warren?" Tyeshia croaked, knowing that it was Savannah's mom and dad that stood at the head of her bed. Although she'd only met them once, there was no way to mistake who they were, for Savannah was there in every line of their faces.

"Are you doing okay, now, Tyeshia?" Abigail whispered, moving a little closer to the bedside.

"Yes, Ma'am," Tyeshia murmured. "I'm glad you're here."

"You were our daughter's best friend," Thomas said. "We wouldn't be anywhere else."

Tyeshia felt tears spring to her eyes again, but bravely swallowed the lump that had formed in her throat.

"I have a message for you from Savannah," she said, and promptly burst into tears again.

# SIXTY-NINE

## 1869

"What do we do now?" Savannah asked, leaning against her husband's chest. It had been three days since that fateful day when the lights passed over them all, taking Tyeshia home.

"What do you mean?" Wounded Eagle asked, rubbing his hands up and down her arms. He still had a hard time believing that she was still with him, so while he rubbed her arms to help ward off the morning chill, it also served to confirm that she was still there. He could not stop touching her since the light passed over them and he had found her clinging to him, her eyes squeezed shut and a soft chant, 'I won't leave him', escaping her lips.

Moments after the light disappeared, her eyes flew open, and her arms latched around his neck. She burst into tears that lasted nearly ten full minutes. Later, she confessed that the tears had been a mixture of joy at being able to stay with him and pain at the knowledge that she'd never see her family or Tyeshia again.

"Well," she said, her hand caressing his leg, "where do we go from here? I mean, we've been kind of wandering about, sleeping under the stars, living off the land...don't get me wrong, it's been lovely, but, what do we do now? Are we going to find a place to settle down, or are we going to live like Nomads for the rest of our lives?"

"We are going somewhere. I'm just going slowly so that you have time to heal completely," Wounded Eagle said. "How are you feeling, by the way?"

"I'm not a doctor, but I'd say a full recovery is right around the corner. I feel fine. Now what do you mean that we're going somewhere already? Where are we going?"

"We're going to live with Heavy Runner's people for the winter."

"We are?"

"Yes," Wounded Eagle said. "That way, if trouble still plans to show up on—what date did you say?"

"January twenty-third."

"Yes, January twenty-third," Wounded Eagle murmured. "Then we'll be there to stop it."

"Well, since Mountain Chief killed his own brother—Pikuni against Pikuni—we know that the army won't seek retaliation for Clark's death, because Clark's not dead."

"True, but I want to be there in case Clark's death wasn't the reason behind the army's attack on my Uncle's people."

"I think it's a good idea," Savannah said. "I only hope your Uncle doesn't mind the intrusion."

"Why would he mind? He is my Uncle."

"Yeah, well, in my time..." Savannah started and then stopped. "I guess it's not my time any longer."

"Are you okay, Wife?"

"I'm fine," Savannah said, taking a deep breath. "I just have to get used to the fact that this is my time now."

"What were you saying about your old time?"

"That's a good way to put it," Savannah smiled, trying to think of the time change as if it was a simple move across country. "Anyway, in my *old* time, people don't barge in and stay with relatives for more than a week, or they might be considered moochers."

"What's a moocher?"

"It's what we call a person that lives off someone else, but doesn't contribute to the support of the household—like buying food, or helping to pay the bills. Understand?"

"I understand, but we would hunt for our own food and build our own house."

"Ah, so there is a difference. We're just borrowing a tract of land, not actually living with him."

"You do not make much sense sometimes, Savannah."

"I know," Savannah giggled. "So, what's Clark planning on doing? Did he get some closure with Many Feathers' death?"

"Closure?"

"Peace."

"Peace, yes."

"What's he going to do now?"

"He will return to his home in Helena," Wounded Eagle said. "One day, maybe he will find a good woman to heal his heart—like I did."

"I hope so. I hope Tyeshia will too—someday," Savannah sighed; "Many Feathers really did a number on her self-esteem."

"What?"

"He hurt her with his fists and with his words," Savannah explained. "It may be some time before she gets over the trauma she suffered here."

"I agree, but she is a strong woman," Wounded Eagle said. "She will heal quickly."

"From your mouth to God's ears."

## SEVENTY

**Present Day**

After nearly eight months of grueling physical therapy to condition her muscles to aid themselves, Tyeshia savored each day with a passion that surpassed extraordinary. In those eight months, her parents brought in a tutor from the University, at her behest, to aid in her studies; and to update her subjects, all so she would be able to graduate with her class.

Even though they were willing to help her, they worried that she might be pushing herself too hard, on occasion, but Tyeshia refused to slow. She tackled her therapy, lessons, everything, with a zeal that bordered on fanatical. What her parents could not understand was why, but as with Savannah, Ty could not let them know that she was running from the demon that haunted her nights—Many Feathers.

She'd seen him die, but he wouldn't release her, and still had a powerful hold on her. The physical abuse she suffered at his hands haunted her dreams, so she buried herself in her studies and her therapy, hoping that by the end of the day, exhaustion would lay claim to her mind and she'd find peace in her dreams. To no avail.

When the therapy ended, and she was nearing the end of her studies—only her final term paper was due—she sought help from a psychiatrist, but found little satisfaction, since she was unable to reveal everything that she'd been through without disclosing details that no one could ever know. Physically she was recovering quickly. Mentally—she was at an impasse.

Then, she received an urgent request to come back to Montana. Black Calf was dying and he needed to see her before he went to meet the Great Spirit. She wasn't certain what he wanted with her, or that she even wanted to see the weird old coot, but out of respect for Savannah, she decided to make the trip.

Now, as she sped down Highway 2 at well over ninety miles per hour toward the Reservation, top down on the rented Ford Thunderbird convertible, she savored the feel of the wind blowing through her unbound hair. Just knowing she had the freedom to get behind the wheel of a car again, gave a feeling of exhilaration. She cranked up the radio and belted out the tunes, trying to drown out the fearful voice in her head that kept telling her that visiting Black Calf again was a mistake.

Three hours into her journey, Tyeshia pulled off the Interstate and followed the signs to the Blackfoot Indian Reservation. Even though it had been over a year since her last visit to this place, she remembered it well and had no difficulty locating Black Calf's home. She wished she'd gotten lost.

She walked hesitantly toward the front door and lifted a hand to knock, but before her fist struck the aging wood, a young man—that Tyeshia had never seen before—opened the door. Still, something about him gave her the strangest sensation of déjà vu.

"You must be Tyeshia," he said softly. "Please. Do come in. Black Calf is expecting you."

"Thank you." Tyeshia passed the stranger and entered the small foyer. When her gaze had adjusted to the dimness, she glanced around noting that nothing had changed—except her.

"Is that Tyeshia?" A weak voice called from the living room.

Tyeshia moved slowly forward, ignoring the urge to turn and run. After all, the last time she'd been in this living room he'd told her she had a scary psyche and then created a situation where fate slung her and her dearest friend—whom she would never see again—back in time. Had they accomplished anything in 1869? Not in Tyeshia's book. Sure, Many Feathers was dead and wasn't controlling her mind, but he still had control over her dreams.

When she entered the living room, she paused and stifled a gasp. The man sitting in front of her wasn't the man she'd known a year earlier, but a sunken shell that appeared to be withering away before her eyes. *What had happened to him that his health had deteriorated in such a short time?* She wondered.

"I am glad to see you, my child," he rasped, "but by your face, I'd say you are not so happy to see me." Tyeshia started to protest, but he raised a hand, grinning mischievously. "Do not concern yourself, my dear," he grinned, "for I would not be happy to see me either. Do sit."

Tyeshia complied, but did not speak.

"I wished to see you before I died."

"What about?" Tyeshia whispered, hoping that he hadn't had any more dreams. Black Calf grinned knowingly, as if reading her thoughts.

"Not about what you think. Do not worry, Tyeshia. My dreaming days are done."

"I'd be lying if I said I wasn't relieved."

"I know."

Tyeshia relaxed a little and waited for the old man to speak again, but he merely sat watching her. When he finally did open his mouth, she wanted to find some tape and shut it again.

"You suffered much at the hands of Many Feathers, did you not, my dear?" Tyeshia groaned inwardly. Did he have to bring *that* up? And in front of a stranger, for the young man who'd answered the door had remained and was sitting in a corner. The only other occupant in the room.

"It's not something I care to talk about, Black Calf," she answered tightly. "If you don't mind."

"We need to talk about it, but will talk about it later," Black Calf said.

"But first, tell me—was Savannah happy when you left?"

Tyeshia grasped her skirt, fighting against the tears that threatened. Of course, he wouldn't know how Savannah fared, for she had selfishly failed to tell him. For the past year, all he knew was that Savannah had not returned, but knew nothing of her welfare. If that didn't make her feel bad, nothing else in the world ever would.

"I'm sorry, Black Calf," she whispered, intently studying the pattern of her skirt, "I should have come when I could, or sent word so that you would know about Savannah."

"You were hardly in a position, my child," Black Calf consoled. "You were trying to get better, remember?"

Tyeshia looked up into the dark brown orbs and smiled—bless his old soul. He didn't bring Savannah up in conversation to make her feel bad. He simply wanted to die knowing that his dear friend was safe from harm; perhaps hear a little about their adventures.

Tyeshia began talking; filling him in on their little 'field trip', from the day they entered the lights of time. Occasionally, Black Calf interrupted with a question or would laugh so hard that she had to pause while someone brought him a glass of water, but he'd always wave a hand in her direction when he was ready again, eager to hear the rest. When she came to the part about Many Feathers and the daily abuse, she opened up and the pain and heartache came flooding back. She recounted the horror, tears of anger and humiliation stinging her eyes.

"If I hadn't left with him like some star-struck air-headed bimbo, then I never would have found myself in that situation," she berated herself for the millionth time.

"May I say something?" Black Calf whispered softly, struggling to lean forward in his patched leather armchair. Tyeshia merely nodded, wiping a hand angrily across her tear-stained eyelids. "You suffered a great deal, but it had to happen. What you need to remember when you feel like yelling at yourself, is this—you survived, but he did not. You were the stronger one. He was not. You have the control now. He does not. He is dead. You are alive, and that which does not kill us only serves to make us stronger. Have you ever heard that before?"

Tyeshia didn't answer. She slid from her seat and scooted across the stained wood-planked floor and straight into Black Calf's embrace. A year of pent-up sorrow and bitterness released itself in her tears and when the well finally dried up, she felt lighter in spirit than she had since returning from her journey.

"Thank you, Black Calf," she whispered a short time later.

"You are welcome, my child."

A handkerchief appeared in front of her face and she looked up into the gaze of the young man who'd stayed throughout her narration. Did he think she was crazy—talking about time travel? Or had Black Calf already told him what to expect. His gaze revealed nothing but compassion.

"Can you finish telling me your story now?" Black Calf asked gently. Tyeshia stood and settled back onto the worn sofa, nodding. "That is good."

Tyeshia blew her nose, composed her emotions, and then launched into the finale of the remarkable experience. When she finished, Black Calf settled back against his chair and sighed.

"I'm glad she found happiness with Wounded Eagle." Still, something in his tone suggested that her revelation did not surprise him.

"So am I, but what is even more remarkable—I can find absolutely no reference to a Marias River massacre, and believe-you-me I've searched."

"You would not find any reference, for the massacre never took place," Black Calf winked conspiratorially at the young man and motioned for him to take a seat beside Tyeshia. "It would appear that we were right—the massacre would have been a direct result of the retribution killing of Clark, but since they never killed Clark, the army had no reason for retaliation." Black Calf leaned over and picked up a dusty binder, at least three inches thick, that she had not realized had been sitting on the table beside him.

"Here is one reason I wanted to see you today, my child," Black Calf smiled and passed the worn notebook across to Tyeshia. She could tell it was simply used to hold the aging pages inside and not the original container of the documents. She opened the notebook and slowly began reading the first page of the yellowed parchment, her eyes widening in astonishment:

*For those who would come after me, I keep this record of my life. My reason is twofold. First, that my children and my children's children will have a record of their life. I hope that my son, Little Wolf, will continue the tradition of writing in it once he is old enough and I am too aged to continue forming words and committing them to paper.*

*The second, and more important reason, is that it is my fervent hope that this binder survives a hundred plus years and finds its way to my dear friend, Black Calf, who will one day pass it on to the sister of my heart, Tyeshia Morgan, and my parents, Thomas and Abigail Warren, so that they will always remember me and know the life I lived was a blessed one. This is my fondest wish.*

*Signed this eighteenth day of July, Eighteen-hundred-seventy. Savannah Warren, proud wife of Wounded Eagle and mother to Little Wolf.*

Tyeshia looked up. Her mouth opened, but no words issued forth. She tried again, working her jaw, but she simply couldn't speak.

"There are five more binders," Black Calf answered her unasked question. "Each kept by a member of the family as Savannah requested. Each lovingly kept so that one day I could show them to you."

"Yet that would mean that one of Savannah's relatives is still alive?" Tyeshia whispered, still unable to grasp the enormity of what Black Calf was telling her.

"Yes," Black Calf smiled that conspiratorial smile again. "Tyeshia, I'd like to introduce you to Gray Eagle." Tyeshia turned slowly and faced the man sitting silently beside her, a smile on his face. That smile looked so familiar.

"You're...?"

"Savannah and Wounded Eagle's five-times great-grand son, and I've looked forward to meeting you for a very long time."

# EPILOGUE

"What are you doing, darling?" The voice sounded tired, and Tyeshia smiled. When she lost sleep, Gray Eagle lost sleep, and since she had lost sleep every night since the twins were born, he was constantly yawning. "Where's Savannah and Little Eagle?" He asked, and placed a gentle kiss on her neck.

"Hmm," Tyeshia moaned, tilting her head to give him better access. "I've already put them back to bed."

"Then why are you still sitting here? You need your rest."

"I'll be along in a moment. This won't take long."

Gray Eagle glanced down at the writing desk and smiled, "I see. Well, I love you. Try not to take too long."

"I love you, too."

Gray Eagle kissed her lightly, then turned and left the room.

Tyeshia picked up her pen and started writing:

*For those who would come after me, I keep this record of my life...*

# ABOUT THE AUTHOR

Barbara Woster is an educator, editor, and an author. She resides in Oregon with her husband, Tim. Her children inspired her to write, and it is to them that all of her books are dedicated -- with much love.

www.ingramcontent.com/pod-product-compliance
Lightning Source LLC
Chambersburg PA
CBHW071512110726
47908CB00003B/816

* 9 7 8 1 7 3 3 6 6 0 2 3 5 *